Praise for *A Grave Mistake*

'A cosy masterpiece of warm vibes, hot vampires, and chilly murders investigated by a loveable, kooky, kickass book coven. You'll fall in love between the covers!'
Eileen Mueller, *USA Today* bestselling author of Dragon Shifters' Hoard

'This glorious, heart-wrenching and hilarious vampire love story had me in an absolute chokehold. Exceptionally well crafted, richly descriptive, cosy and charming – and so very hard to put down. More please!'
Lauretta Hignett, author of *Immortal*

'Steffanie has created a vibrant and fantastical world full of powerful women, humour and addictive storytelling. Vampires, puns and a hysssterical cast of characters make this book a must read.'
Catherine Banks, *USA Today* bestselling author of Royally Entangled

'Fans of Steffanie Holmes have come to expect her kooky, spooky storylines, and characters that suck you in with their depth and humour. *A Grave Mistake* delivers on every point, and then some. If you're looking for a unique story that successfully blends humour, swoony romance, cosy modern fantasy and top-shelf spice, *A Grave Mistake* is it. One of my top reads of 2025, hands down.'
Samantha Lovelock, author of *Fragile Things*

'Delightfully wicked, witty, and oh-so-sexy – because vampires! – *A Grave Mistake* is damn good fun. No one blends cosy fantasy with gothic kookiness and delectable spice quite so perfectly as Steffanie Holmes!'
Amy Rose Bennett, author of *The Nanny's Handbook to Magic and Managing Difficult Dukes*

'Stephanie Holmes' *A Grave Mistake* is populated with intriguing characters, each bursting with distinct personality. The quirky one-liners and sharp wit linger long after the final page, cementing another amazing read from a master of the genre.'
Sue Carpenter, author of *Farewell Fairies*

'Vampires are already high on my heat-o-meter, but add in a 147-year relationship enemies-to-lovers gap twice over, a jewel heist and a stalker who just won't quit . . . *A Grave Mistake* is a one-night steamy paranormal read and no mistake at all.'
Sofia Shelley, author of *Dead Poets Sorority*

'Wow, that was a fun, fast, mysterious and exciting read! I loved the meddling nature of the Nevermore Murder Club and Smutty Book Coven, through to the staunch and fierce Arabella, and the cocky yet loyal Gideon. I highly recommend!'
Cat Sirota, author of *Forgiving Darkness*

'*A Grave Mistake* rewrites the history books through a feminine lens. This second-chance, enemies-to-lovers tale will have readers wishing they were as skilled, determined and resilient as the heroine.'
Zoe Jae, author of *The Realm*

STEFFANIE HOLMES

ATRIA BOOKS

New York   Amsterdam/Antwerp   London   Toronto   Sydney/Melbourne   New Delhi

A GRAVE MISTAKE
First published in Australia in 2026 by
Atria Books Australia, an imprint of Simon & Schuster (Australia) Pty Limited
Level 4, 32 York St, Sydney NSW 2000

10 9 8 7 6 5 4 3 2 1

New York Amsterdam/Antwerp London Toronto Sydney/Melbourne New Delhi
Visit our website at www.simonandschuster.com.au

For more than 100 years, Simon & Schuster has championed authors and the stories they create. By respecting the copyright of an author's intellectual property, you enable Simon & Schuster and the author to continue publishing exceptional books for years to come. We thank you for supporting the author's copyright by purchasing an authorised edition of this book.

No amount of this book may be reproduced or stored in any format, nor may it be uploaded to any website, database, language-learning model, or other repository, retrieval, or artificial intelligence system without express permission. All rights reserved. Inquiries may be directed to Simon & Schuster, 1230 Avenue of the Americas, New York, NY 10020 or permissions@simonandschuster.com.

© Steffanie Holmes 2026

All rights reserved. No part of this publication may be reproduced, stored in a retrieval system, or transmitted in any form or by any means, electronic, mechanical, photocopying, recording or otherwise, without prior permission of the publisher.

ATRIA B O O K S and colophon are trademarks of Simon & Schuster, LLC.

This book is a work of fiction. Any references to historical events, real people, or real places are used fictitiously. Other names, characters, places, and events are products of the author's imagination, and any resemblance to actual events or places or persons, living or dead, is entirely coincidental.

A catalogue record for this book is available from the National Library of Australia

ISBN: 9781761633935

Map © Fred Kroner 2025
Cover design: Covers by Aura
Cover images: rose/macrovector, blood/vectortatu (all via Depositphotos)
Sprayed edge image: Inna Marchenko/Shutterstock
Interior design: Midland Typesetters, Australia
Printed and bound in China through Asia Pacific Offset Group Limited

*To you, the woman who swears unbreakable oaths, has an
outfit for every occasion (including committing crime),
and will turn the blood of those who wrong you into
delicious cocktails with tiny umbrellas made from their skin.*

May you be seen and admired for the goddess you are.

Join the Nevermore Murder Club and Smutty Book Coven!

Love smutty books? Don't mind a spot of blood? The Nevermore Murder Club and Smutty Book Coven (affectionately known as the Nevermore Coven) wants YOU.

We've created this guide to help you decide if our book club is right for you or if you'd rather join a boring, normal book club that doesn't get embroiled in supernatural crimes. (Yawn.)

We're always looking for new members – pop into Nevermore Bookshop anytime for a cup of tea, some village gossip, and a little light vampire-slaying on the side.

Meet the Nevermore Murder Club and Smutty Book Coven

Mina Wilde
Mina hosts the book club meetings at Nevermore Bookshop – a rambling, slightly magical bookshop she runs with her three husbands (yes, three), who are all infamous fictional villains from classic literature brought to life. (It's a long story.) Mina is blind, but that doesn't stop her from having impeccable taste in music and being the village's foremost nosy amateur detective.

Winnie Preston
The newest member of the Nevermore Coven, Winnie is a bright, bubbly professional organiser who came to the village to help the grumpy, reclusive vampire Lord Alaric Valerian declutter his castle. Against all odds, she and Alaric fell in love and now Winnie runs a professional organising business for vampires by day and spends her nights being ravished by an ancient vampire warrior lord. #goals

Isis Meriwether
Isis is the village clairvoyant and foremost expert on magical goings-on in Argleton. Unfortunately, Isis doesn't have a single magical bone in her body, but she doesn't let that little detail stop her from casting spells that backfire. She runs the local New Age store, Spell The Tea, with her sister Dora.

Dora Meriwether
The quiet sister, Dora prefers being in her garden with a cup of tea over solving magical shenanigans, but she's used to Isis dragging her into trouble. Dora has powerful visions of the future, and is known for being a voice of reason when the Nevermore Coven needs it most.

Arabella Lestrange
The Nevermore Coven's resident vampire, Arabella has been avoiding sunlight, sleeping all day, and biting people who annoy her for 150 years – and all she's got to show for it is perfect skin and immortality. Once a Parisian courtesan, Arabella now makes her living helping vampires turn their hoarded treasure into cold, hard cash. Her hobbies include reading dark romance, always being right, and taking her pet snake Cleo VII for walks around Sanctus Estate.

Celeste Lucas
Celeste owns everyone's favourite bakery, Glazed and Confused, and supplies the Nevermore Coven with delicious treats. She's a fiercely loyal friend who goes absolutely feral if a member of the coven is

in trouble. Don't let Celeste's sensitive nature fool you – she's hiding a few secrets of her own.

Beth Duncan
Owner of the Zen and Tonic health shop and pole studio, Beth is a bright, bubbly soul who wants to help you live your best life, *or else*. Whatever you do, don't eat her brownies, as Beth has a penchant for putting mushrooms in things that mushrooms should never touch.

Maisie Collins
As reporter for the *Argleton Gazette*, Maisie has a (super cute) nose for a story and loves digging around in the archives or chasing down a murder suspect. When she's not getting into trouble over her articles, Maisie can be found collecting vintage plates or playing with her pampered pet duck, James Pond.

Komal Ahuja
Head of the village tourism board and a helicopter tour operator, Komal is adventurous and passionate about making Argleton the best village in England, vampires and supernatural shenanigans included. This puts her at odds with those who want to keep the paranormal hidden – including councillor Augustin Durant, who is as aggravating as he is handsome.

Nevermore Murder Club and Smutty Book Coven Rules

1. What is said in book club stays in book club.
2. Vampires are welcome, provided they bring their own snacks.
3. In every book club meeting, there is someone who takes the theme of the book too seriously, someone who doesn't take it seriously enough, and someone whose life the book directly relates to but won't ever know because that's the week they decided to skip. Be very certain you know which one you are.

4. Don't eat Beth's brownies.
5. When someone in your book club is inevitably accused of committing a heinous murder, the only appropriate thing to do is to undermine the police, secretly solve the case and put yourselves in mortal peril to catch the killer.
6. Listening to the audiobook counts as reading.
7. Maybe everything in life can't be solved by an evening of talking books and hexing bad men with your friends while you devour fancy cheese, but … who are we kidding? Cheese makes everything better.

NEW DEVELOPMENT CAUSING UPROAR IN VILLAGE

Maisie Collins

Argleton Gazette

Sanctus Estate is welcoming its first new residents. But not everyone in the village is happy about the development.

"It's a bloody eyesore," moans Diane Debham of Scarborough Street. "What about the ancient trees they cut down to make way for those ghastly modern buildings? I don't know how it got past planning consent."

Diane's not alone in her concerns. Over a pint at the Rose & Wimple, villagers express their concerns about the potential environmental damage and the modern architecture that isn't in keeping with Argleton's rustic village aesthetic.

"Who would build a development in the middle of the woods?" asks Merry Atkinson of Crooks Close. "None of those houses will get any sunshine. I thought rich people loved the sun."

Even our parish council is divided on the matter. Tourism Board chair Komal Ahuja is concerned about the drop in tourism revenue if the woodlands are spoiled, while Augustin Durant – the leading mayoral candidate – has been outspoken in his support for the project.

"We haven't even seen any of the new residents at the pub," Richard, our beloved pub landlord, points out. "Those types won't even attempt to include themselves in village life!"

However, Gideon Blake, the visionary developer behind the new estate, is optimistic about his members integrating with the community. "We have many long-time Argleton residents working here at the estate, and we'll be hosting events that interested villagers can attend, like our upcoming sculpture park opening. I think you'll find my members are a friendly bunch, as long as you're not packing a pocketful of garlic. Ha ha."

Personally, this reporter thinks it's lovely that so many people want to join our community. I hope to meet some of our new residents at this month's must-be-at village event – the opening of the Zen and Tonic Pole Studio!

Message from the Conclave on the Sepulchrr App

Dearest subjects of the Midnight, Nightshade, and Dusk Courts,

You may have heard of Sanctus Estate – the revolutionary new vampire estate being built near the small English village of Argleton. Some of you may even have invested your hard-earned money in this risky venture. If so, we hope this message finds you before it's too late to get your investment back.

It has come to our attention that all is not well at Sanctus Estate. The company director, Gideon Blake, is known to us from decades of criminal activity, and he's been struck from the Midnight Court for his support of human–vampire relations. He refuses to allow Conclave officials onto the estate to ensure it meets our strict guidelines for the safety and privacy of our subjects. Investors are pulling out, leaving Sanctus finances in a questionable state. If our subjects choose to buy Sanctus property, we cannot guarantee they will realise their investment.

It has also come to our attention that a husker has been at work in Argleton. The Lady of Agony administered the Mora, but she got the wrong man. Although huskers only target humans – for not even these abominations dare commit the sin of drinking the blood of an Upyr – they are a threat to the secrecy of our people. The only times humans have learned of the existence of Upyr have been when huskers were allowed to roam free. Finding this husker, before they strike again and risk the exposure of vampires, is of utmost importance.

As both victims of the husker worked for Gideon Blake and at least one of them was under a Thrall's contract, it raises questions about Blake's involvement in these heinous crimes.

For your safety and security, we urge all vampires to avoid doing business with Gideon Blake or Sanctus Industries.

The Conclave
    4670 Dig This   231 Resurrections

1

Arabella

Sinead: Arabella, welcome to Sanctus Estate – the world's first premier, non-court-affiliated luxury gated community for vampires! The keys to your new home are available to pick up from the office, and our director is excited to take you on a tour of the facilities. Welcome to the first day of your vampire dreams!

"How come you never told anyone that you're a vampire?" Winnie asks as she shoves a trolley down the junk food aisle of the Argleton market. I study the brightly coloured packages of sweets and chocolates, and a familiar resentment bubbles up inside me.

In the nineteenth century, when I was last able to properly taste food, I took treats for granted. As a courtesan, men considered sweets and pastries a cheap way of pleasing me (because most of them certainly couldn't do it between the sheets). Now I can afford to buy all the sweets I like. Hell, I can buy the company that makes the sweets and force them to write "Arabella is a majestic goddess" on every tiny, chalky sugar heart. (Not a terrible idea. I've made a mental note.) But that wouldn't change the fact that all I get when I place one on my tongue is a slight hint of sweetness and a mild stomach-ache.

Most of the time, I enjoy the direction my life has taken since I became a vampire. I like seizing the night, witnessing the sweeping changes of history, and never getting wrinkles. I enjoy being rich and wearing beautiful clothes. I (mostly) appreciate the small circle of human women, like my friend Winnie, who I've got to know through the Nevermore Murder Club and Smutty Book Coven, which I joined under duress five years ago and enjoy more than I'll ever admit. Winnie is engaged to a vampire, so she's been taking the recent news that I'm not human better than the rest of my friends, although they're more upset that I kept it a secret than that I have fangs.

(The less said about some humans, the better.)

But sometimes, I envy humans like Winnie, who is staring at a package of Wagon Wheels as if it holds all the answers to the universe, which it probably does. Chocolate is powerful like that, and I never even got to taste it.

"Why didn't I tell my friends I was a vampire? They never asked." I want to get this shopping trip out of the way. I need to get back to making arrangements for my move to Sanctus Estate. "I wanted to avoid an interrogation from one Isis Meriwether."

"Fair," Winnie smiles. Our friend, Isis, is another member of the Nevermore Murder Club and Smutty Book Coven. Isis is the local clairvoyant and purveyor of witchy supplies, and she fancies herself a font of all magical and supernatural knowledge, even though she hasn't got a magical clue. A week ago, after the Nevermore Coven's investigation into two vampiric killings led us to Sanctus Estate, I decided to reveal my nocturnal habits to my friends and offer myself up as a mole. I've been regretting it ever since, as Isis has been peppering me with annoying questions like, "Do vampires floss their fangs?", "Have you ever seen your diary or a pair of your old shoes in a museum?", and "Have you ever worn a crown of femurs made from the bones of your vanquished foes?"

(Fang hygiene is very important. My shoes have never appeared in a museum, although several sketches by Édouard Manet of my rather majestic derrière appeared in an impressionist exhibit at the National Gallery – but Isis doesn't need to know about *that* period of my life.

And a woman should wear whatever makes her feel confident. But you'll need thin, strong twine to hold the femurs together. You don't want your crown falling apart at an inopportune moment. Take it from a vampire who knows.)

I hold up two packets of Walkers crisps. "Do humans prefer salt-and-vinegar or bacon-flavoured crisps?"

"If we're going to be making fools of ourselves swinging around poles, we'd better grab both." Winnie drops the crisps into our trolley alongside some Jaffa Cakes and several frozen packages of sausage rolls. Modern humans are particularly enamoured with the little tubes of mystery meat wrapped in cheap pastry. My, how civilisation has fallen. "Reginald is bringing along a vat of hot chocolate, and Lilac says she'll provide a couple of bottles of blood for those who need it. Do you think anyone from Sanctus Estate will come along?"

I make a face. "I sincerely hope not. I don't want to see my clients writhing around in stripper heels."

"If you're writhing alongside them, maybe it will be like a team-building exercise."

"Please. The only writhing I'll be doing is—"

The words die in my throat as I catch sight of a figure across the shop.

My hand freezes over a display of strawberries.

It can't be him. It's impossible.

I'm dimly aware of Winnie calling my name, but I can't acknowledge her. My world has shrunk to the man in front of me. The man with the peacock-blue eyes, a halo of golden curls that could never quite behave, and the mischievous grin that promises exactly the kind of trouble I like. The man juggling apples and flirting with a simpering mother while her snotty brat peers out from behind her legs.

The man who *absolutely shouldn't exist.*

Him.

His fingers graze the woman's shoulder as he drops apples into her basket. Those same fingers that once lovingly undid my gold corset as he promised such filthy things …

No. I cannot think of that night.

I refuse.

I am Arabella Lestrange. I am the world's leading vampire investment consultant, and I will *not* fall apart in the village market over a man. I will put on my best fuck-off-and-die face, and I will pretend that seeing him hasn't wrecked me like Stephenie Meyer wrecked the gothic vampire milieu.

And *then* I will go home and rage.

"It can't be. It can't be him," I hear myself muttering.

Or maybe I won't make it home.

"Who? What's wrong?" Winnie shakes my arm, dragging me back from the edge of memory.

Across the aisle, the Scourge of the Seine whispers something to the little girl that makes her giggle. He smiles too, all teeth and villainy.

Why does my head feel as though it's floating away from my shoulders?

"Arabella?" Winnie nudges me.

"A hundred and fifty years ago, I fell in love," I hiss through gritted teeth. My fingers grip the trolley so hard that the plastic handle cracks. "And after he trampled my heart to dust, set fire to my dreams, and disappeared before I could torture him for the fun of it, I consoled myself with the thought that at least he was mortal and his bones would soon fertilise the earth while I lived forever. And now *that same human* is standing across the fruit aisle without a care in the world."

"Well then let's say hello."

Winnie grabs my arm, dragging me past a display of potatoes. Until now, I've found Winnie the least annoying of all my friends, as she's taken the whole "vampires live among us and I'm engaged to one" revelation with a cool head and open heart. Now, she's rapidly becoming my second-least-favourite person, after the bastard-son-of-a-Paris-sewer-rat over by the apples.

When she sees who I'm glaring at, Winnie gasps. "Arabella, that's *Gideon Blake*. Alaric's friend. He's the director of Sanctus Estate who you've agreed to spy on, remember? It's going to be very difficult to get information about Patrick and Danny's murders if you refuse to talk to him."

"I'm resourceful. I'll find a way."

"*Arabella.*" Winnie gives me a shove in Gideon's direction.

This can't be happening.

In addition to reading books about generously-schlonged book boyfriends, my friends like to meddle in local supernatural affairs. After a local serial annoyance named Danny O'Hare and Winnie's cheating ex Patrick Stock were both murdered and drained of blood by a vampire, of course they had to stick their noses in. We thought we caught the killer – the sadistic vampire Baylor Godsven of the Blood Ptolemy – and brought him to justice at Alaric's vampire ball, but some new evidence came to light suggesting there might be more to the story. My friends are concerned that Gideon Blake, the director of Sanctus Estate, might have something to do with their murders.

Now that I know who Gideon Blake is, I'm certain of it.

Even more reason to stay away from him.

I duck under Winnie's arm and make a beeline for the door. But I forget that I'm still gripping the trolley. It goes flying into a pyramid of watermelons, which topples faster than the Egyptian Empire after Cleopatra decided to hug a poisonous snake.

Watermelons bounce across the floor in all directions. One takes out the mother's legs and sends her flying, before cracking open over Gideon's shiny Armani loafers.

He stares down at his ruined shoes with a woeful frown. "Well, that's unfortunate."

That voice.

That damned *voice*.

He's smoothed over his French accent with clipped British vowels, but it's still honey oozing through my bones, dislodging memories from the darkest corners. Haunted, sacrilegious acts committed in an old church where we explored our desires, warm Parisian nights where I tasted freedom for the first time, a velvet curtain with gold pulls, a hot air balloon bobbing over the city. Golden hair on my gold-threaded sheets …

I allowed that sumptuous voice to pull me in once before. But I will not do so again.

"*Gideon*," I hiss.

He looks up, and I'm pleased that he's even more startled than I am to meet again.

"I …" He swallows. "You."

"Yes. Me." I fold my arms. "Interesting us meeting like this, a hundred and forty-seven years after you *robbed* me."

And because I'm a vicious bitch, I pluck the bright crimson apple from his fingers and raise it to my lips.

His scent hits me then. Honey and red cherries, soaked in poppy, with the copper tang of blood. Sin and sweetness. Unmistakably vampiric. Alluring. *Intoxicating.*

Utterly vile.

I take a huge bite of the apple, allowing my lipstick to smear across the skin. I trained under the best courtesans in Paris. I know exactly what I'm doing with that apple.

Gideon knows, too. He swallows, his Adam's apple bobbing. Bright-blue eyes fix on my neck, travelling down to the hollow of my collarbone.

That's right, Gideon. My neck is bare now, thanks to you.

My pulse quickens, rushing in my ears. He dares to be here, where I've made my home, where I've worked so hard to be invisible.

I take another bite. I won't allow him to see how he's shaken me.

"Arabella Macquart," he breathes.

I want to slap my name off his lips.

Winnie's eyes fly between us, lighting up at the sound of my previous name. I hate Gideon even more for giving her that – a piece of my past, revealed without my permission.

"I see you've had a little change since last we met," I smirk, piercing a piece of apple with the tip of my nail and feeding it to myself. "Immortality suits you."

"As it does you." His sparkling eyes bore into mine, blooming all sorts of depraved memories in my body. "I should have guessed you were a vampire. You never ate the treats I brought you, and you were always so cool to the touch. Cool, but never cold, especially not that night in the garden—"

"And as wise and beautiful as I am, I should have guessed you were a double-crossing thieving *bastard* out for his own gain," I cut him off before he brings up the night I refuse to think of.

"I'm …" His voice falters. Gideon steps towards me, a hand raised as if in surrender. "I can't believe it's you. I would have looked for you, but I thought you died in the fire."

"It takes more than flames or betrayal to get rid of me."

He winces. "You tried to have me killed."

I don't bother to correct him. I never tried to have him killed. If Arabella Macquart wants revenge, she gets it done herself. My revenge on Gideon was *supposed* to be outliving him, remaking myself into a ravishing, successful creature while he became ashes and dust. But now that I know he's still breathing *my* air, the murder idea is worth considering. "I see you haven't changed a bit. Still selling lies for profit in a cheap suit."

"This suit wasn't cheap." His eyes fizz with unexpected fire. "And nothing about Sanctus Estate is a lie."

Intriguing.

I think of the text from Sinead, the member services manager at Sanctus who seems oddly familiar to me, inviting me to collect my keys and view my new home. I think of the Conclave's disapproval of Sanctus, and the funds I've handed over for my property – a property I didn't know until now was masterminded by my greatest enemy.

It's too late to back out of the deal.

I don't *want* to back out of the deal.

Which means I'm stuck living in Gideon's vanity project.

What I wouldn't give for a magical collar imbued with the powers of an ancient queen to grant me my desire for revenge. Oh, wait a second—

"Arabella, maybe we should leave— Ewwww!" Winnie winces as her foot goes through a watermelon. Red goo splashes up the front of her lilac jumpsuit and across her pretty features. She wipes fruity ooze from her cheek. "We should probably leave before the supermarket becomes a war zone."

"Arabella's motto was always 'make love, not war'." Gideon's grin makes my blood boil – no mean feat for a vampire. "Isn't that right?"

"Love *is* war." I pluck a cracked watermelon from the floor and smash it down on Gideon's head.

Red gloop splatters everywhere, dribbling down Gideon's definitely-not-cheap suit. He blinks, watermelon seeds stuck to his long, dark eyelashes.

He looks like he's covered in blood.

Do not think of Gideon covered in blood. Do not think of what it would be like to drink blood with Gideon, the two of you swapping coppery sweet nectar as you kiss—

I step back, careful not to get a single drop on my Zimmermann yoke dress.

"Ma'am, you're going to have to pay for that apple." The store manager appears behind Gideon, frowning at the scene. "And those watermelons."

"Gideon will take care of it." I toss the half-eaten apple at his head. It bounces off his cheek and smashes at his feet. "He's used to leaving a mess behind him."

2

Gideon

Callista: Gideon, I'm sending this to you since my son will not pick up his phone. Baylor Godsven is innocent of the crime of killing and husking those two men.

I've just received word from the Conclave representatives that they found a human man tied up in the basement of his manor. The human has provided a complete and graphic timeline of Baylor's depraved activities over the past two months, and we can conclude that Baylor was otherwise occupied during the times of both murders. He is guilty of numerous other crimes, including hurting your friend Isis, so his conviction by the Mora holds, but you should know there is still a killer and husker loose in Argleton.

The Conclave are going to use this against you. You are drawing their ire, which could reflect upon my son and his human betrothed.

Bring this beastly creature to justice, lest I'm forced to return and see to it myself. And if any harm comes to my son or his new fiancée, I will personally peel your testicles and serve them up with a Sunday roast.

Her.

I pick up the apple from where it landed at my feet, staring down at the perfect imprint of Arabella's fangs. Those same fangs once grazed the skin along my neck and brought me to heights of pleasure no human or vampire has since been able to match.

Arabella Lestrange.

When I knew her – when I broke her heart and she tried to have my neck broken in return – she was Arabella Macquart, courtesan and proprietress of the most infamous horror burlesque theatre in Paris. Like the innocent fly, I wandered into her web and she sank her poison into me.

I lied to her earlier. I looked for her many times after our parting in Paris. I spent my considerable criminal resources trying to hunt her down, just in case she'd survived the fire. But I found nothing. I'd given her up for dead.

There were so many times when I thought I heard her laugh on the breeze or saw her gold-rimmed eyes in the darkest depths of midnight.

She's good at covering her tracks. Vampires usually are. They're used to living in the shadows.

I've never been particularly good at that, for my sins.

Lestrange suits her.

My phone beeps. It will be Sinead. There are a million things to do on Sanctus Estate as we get our first residents settled into their new homes, and with the vampire courts railing against us, I'm poised for trouble.

A few members have pulled out of their contracts, which isn't ideal. But the Conclave's public condemnation of Sanctus Estate doesn't seem to have had the effect they wanted. We've been flooded with inquiries from uncourted vampires and those willing to renounce their court affiliations. My major investor, Lord Hamish Aeternus of the Blood Aeternus – one of the richest and most influential vampire property magnates in the world – is still supporting us. I need to move fast if I'm to fund the next stage of the development and add even more amenities. And now I'm to hunt a killer for Callista …

I do not have time for a ghost from my past. Not even a delectable ghost like Arabella.

Especially not one with homicidal intentions regarding my plums.

I pay for the apple and watermelon damage. As I wander onto the street in a daze, I wipe red splatters from the apple and take a bite – as if somehow I might be able to taste her. Of course, I can't taste a thing. It's like chewing on a chunk of sawdust.

I spit the mouthful into a rubbish bin and drop the apple in too.

Being a vampire is mostly brilliant, but I do miss food. And sunlight. And opium.

The neck of a fresh young woman or a decent blood mocktail *almost* makes up for it.

But there's one taste that has haunted me since before my Kiss.

Arabella.

For nearly a hundred and fifty years, I've longed to forget her. I tried to bury my feelings for her long ago, when I buried the last of our mortal acquaintances – the painter Claude Monet, by then a dear friend who pretended not to notice that I did not age. It was for the best that I forgot Arabella, because she was human, because she too lay in the cold earth, her stillness the last great, sad beauty in a wretched world.

But I could never forget her.

And she isn't human.

If only I'd known.

One whiff of her ginger and myrrh scent and I'm back in her Parisian theatre during *La Belle Époque*, Arabella sweeping around her pole, her flawless skin shimmering beneath the lanterns as she wove magic with her body.

She was a vampire then.

I've been in love with a vampire since 1879, and I didn't even know it.

How did I not know?

With trembling fingers, I pick up my phone and dial my closest friend. He picks up on the twenty-seventh ring.

"This better be important," Alaric snarls into the phone. "I'm in the middle of finishing this pox-ridden sculpture."

Alaric is a much older, grumpier, and more terrifying vampire than me. He was once a fierce warrior – well, he's still a fierce warrior, which is why I try not to piss him off – but he's spent the past five hundred years mastering every artistic pursuit that humans have invented. Recently, he's taken up sculpting, which means his fiancée, Winnie, is constantly yelling at him to stop dragging giant hunks of marble over the newly waxed floors. Inspired by my old friend Auguste Rodin, I've commissioned Alaric to create a series of sculptures for the small community garden I'm creating within Sanctus Estate. But of course, none of them are finished yet because Alaric is an annoying perfectionist.

Being around him frequently makes me feel like a naughty younger brother, which only makes me miss *my* younger brother. It also makes me remember my Parisian artist friends, and it makes me remember *her*.

"Arabella Lestrange," I grind out into the phone.

"What of her?" Alaric sounds impatient. "She's one of Winnie's friends from that infernal book club."

"How come I've never seen her before?" I growl. "I didn't know there were any vampires in the Nevermore Coven. You'd think Winnie might have mentioned that."

"Winnie only found out recently," Alaric explains. "Humans cannot spot our kin as we can."

They certainly cannot.

"Why do you care about Arabella Lestrange?" Alaric's voice darkens.

I do not want to give him the full sordid story right now. "I'll tell you once you finish your sculptures. But you'd better explain to Winnie that if any more of her friends turn out to be ghosts from my past, it's going to cause problems."

Alaric sighs as if my distress is the greatest inconvenience. "What did you do to Arabella?"

"Why do you assume it's something *I* did? *She's* the one who tried to have me killed."

"Did you deserve it?"

She certainly thinks so. "We could have solved our problem with a heartfelt talk over a bottle of vintage blood. Instead, she went straight for the vampicide. Yes, I deserved it, but now she's here in Argleton, and she hates me, and with the Conclave on my beautiful arse, I can ill afford to entertain her revenge. This is a disaster."

"And what do you expect me to do about this?" Alaric sounds tired.

"Just … if Arabella comes knocking, asking to borrow your testicle-severing sword, could you tell her that you lent it out to someone else?"

"I have many fine testicle-severing swords," Alaric says with utmost seriousness. "She may take her pick."

"Some friend you are." My phone beeps. Sinead again. It must be urgent. "I have to go. Sanctus business."

"Yes. I hear the doorbell," Alaric says. "Perhaps it's Arabella, come to discuss torture methods with Winnie. I have many woodcuts that will assist them."

"Die on a stake, Allie."

"Don't call me Allie—"

I hang up before he can think of a devilishly sadistic means of punishing me, and find my way back to the car – a Lamborghini Huracán Sterrato in a stunning shade of crimson, since you asked. The Huracán may look a little conspicuous zipping around the countryside, but I like being conspicuous. If you're going to live forever, you might as well have no shame. I don't have anything to hide. (Well, only the precarious state of the Sanctus finances, but I'll find a way to fix that. I always do.)

As I sink into the luxurious leather, my head spinning, my phone rings. Sighing, I answer.

"Did you get the beer and snacks?"

"Huh?" I'm a million miles away, happily ensconced between a pair of exquisite thighs laid out on French silk bedsheets.

"The booze and snacks? The whole reason I sent you to the market." Sinead sighs. "You promised the human workers a party because they got that little sewage issue sorted out. If all I have to serve them are bloody biscuits, they're going to get pissed. And suspicious."

I groan. All I have to show for my trip is a soaring heart rate and a lifetime ban from the Argleton village market. "I got distracted."

Sinead sighs. "I'll send someone else out for them. Honestly, Sir. This is the only labouring crew in the village willing to work for Sanctus, and we can't risk losing them, unless you're willing to get out there with a plunger and clean up vampire shit. What is the matter with you?"

What's the matter with me is that the woman I betrayed in 1879 has shown up in my life again, and I'm still in love with her but she hates my beautiful, elegant guts.

3

The Killer

I watch from the shadow of the church steeple as Arabella and her friend leave the market. Arabella licks red juices from her fingers. She is as sleek as the night itself in a black dress that hugs every curve of her body. She's shaved off her long curly hair since I last laid eyes upon her, giving me an exquisite view of her shapely skull.

Her eyes sparkle like twin emeralds, almost as bright as the jewels she stole from me.

Blood flows through my ancient veins, warming my body from the top of my head to my cock, which grows harder than it's been in *centuries*. So hard that it's painful.

I stroke it lovingly, astounded that even with everything broken between us, she can still stir such feelings within me. My dick throbs, the pain exquisite as it pulses through my broken body. After all I've endured to arrive at this very moment, I've had to learn to love agony. It's either that or be driven insane by it.

Perhaps I am not entirely sane. After all, I'm standing in a prickly bush beneath the symbol of a fallen god, getting off on the mere *glimpse* of a woman I once had at my mercy, while *Arabella Macquart* strolls around the village as if she owns it. As if she isn't a liar and a thief.

But my luck is about to change, and so is hers.

Her long neck is bare, the surface of her dark skin shimmering as if dusted with gold. But I can sense the shadow of it on her – the thing she took from me.

The magic is here in Argleton. Even now, it calls to me, humming in my veins.

For decades I believed the collar was lost, but that was a lie spread by her tongue. Without the collar, she wouldn't be here now, rich and flawless and the owner of a brand-new home in the controversial Sanctus Estate.

You've escaped me for centuries, but you can't hide forever.

You're mine now.

My bottom lip curls as my dick pulses. Arabella has what belongs to me. She has left me in misery for over one hundred and fifty years. Before I take back what's rightfully mine, I will enjoy ruining everything she holds dear.

Mine.

The Nevermore Murder Club and Smutty Book Coven Group Chat

Winnie: It's official. Alaric's mother just texted me. Baylor has a list of other crimes a mile long, but he has an alibi for Danny and Patrick's murders.

Mina: Damn, we were right.

Komal: I love being right.

Mina: Usually I do too, but not about this. This means there's still a vampiric murderer loose in the village.

Beth: Or murderers?

Arabella: I think we can go back to the assumption that both murders were committed by the same person.

Beth: You know what they say about assuming.

Arabella: I do not.

Dora: Something about arses.

Arabella: I DO have a remarkable arse, thank you for noticing.

Maisie: We probably shouldn't have convicted Baylor in vampire court before we knew this information.

Mina: Probably not, but we must respect the traditions of vampire culture – violent torture and eternal damnation first, ask questions later.

Komal: And he did try to husk Isis. For that, I will dance on his grave.

Maisie: So what should we do now?

Mina: We have one lead – Danny and Patrick's connection to Sanctus Estate. Arabella's on the case.

Arabella: Unfortunately, new information has come to light that means I am unable to be your spy.

Isis: You promised!

Arabella: Sorry, you'll have to find some other way to pump Gideon Blake for information. Because I will not be pumping anything from that man. Ever.

The Nevermore Murder Club and Smutty Book Coven Group Side Chat (without Arabella)

Winnie: Ladies, I've made this little side chat without Arabella because there's something we should discuss.

Maisie: What is it? I'm about to head into an important meeting with my boss. The Argleton Gazette is in trouble.

Komal: And bloody Augustin Durant doesn't want to devote any more village funds because he overspent on those ugly retractable sunshades around the village green. I swear, that man!

Winnie: Before we devolve into sunshade-bashing, I'll keep this quick. I know why Arabella doesn't want to be our undercover agent at Sanctus anymore.

Komal: Because she's worried about getting her Louboutins dirty?

Maisie: Because she's too busy ironing her giant pile of money?

Winnie: I was with Arabella at the market yesterday evening, and we ran into Gideon. Did you realise that all this time we've been hanging out with Gideon, the two of them have never been in the same room together? It turns out they know each other.

Isis: So?

Winnie: Know as in … the biblical sense. Gideon broke Arabella's heart when he was human, and then he got turned into a vampire, so neither of them knew the other was still alive until yesterday. That's why she doesn't want to do the job. I think she's still in love with him, and Gideon is DEFINITELY still in love with her. They just don't realise it. Arabella was SO ANGRY with him, and in their entire conversation Gideon didn't make a single flirty comment about her arse.

Maisie: That IS unusual …

Isis: Was the vein above her right eye throbbing? That's how you can tell if she's truly irked. I know from experience.

Winnie: There was definitely a little vein thing happening, but I'm telling you, this is the beginning of an enemies-to-lovers tale, and we have a chance to make it happen. I say we encourage the two of them together. One of two things will happen.
a) They will fall madly in love, and I might get to see Arabella smile once in my mortal life.

Isis: Or b) She'll behead him with her nails.

Maisie: How will she do that?

Isis: Slowly, with lots of screaming.

Winnie: I don't think we need to worry about Arabella's safety. Alaric says Gideon can't be the husker, or he wouldn't have been able to resist drinking Isis's blood the night of the ball.

Maisie: But there's definitely something fishy about Sanctus Estate. I think it's worth investigating.

Mina: I agree. So are we going to play matchmaker and get Gideon and Arabella together?

Komal: Hell yes!

Celeste: I want to see Arabella happy.

Dora: Me, too.

Isis: Count me in! I have love spells we can use!

Maisie: And we can try good old-fashioned arm twisting!

Mina: And bribery!

Beth: And, if all else fails, we can tie them up in Alaric's dungeon and refuse to let them out until they shag away all their animosity.

Isis: Arabella has never told us anything about her life before Argleton. She's so secretive. It would help if we knew what broke them up in the first place …

4

Arabella
Then

The Antirhodos Collar was discovered in the late seventeenth century off the eastern harbour of Alexandria, near the ancient island of Antirhodos, where the Pharaohs of the Ptolemy Dynasty built a magnificent palace. According to legend, the Antirhodos Collar is cursed. While it is worn, it brings the wearer good fortune, but those fortunes are undone threefold once the collar is removed. The legend goes that during the Battle of Actium in 31 BC, the clasp broke and the collar fell from Cleopatra's neck. Cleopatra and Marc Antony withdrew to Alexandria with the broken necklace, believing their cause lost unless they could rededicate it at the temple to restore its magic. Octavian took the city before they could reach the temple, forcing the lovers to commit suicide. Reports suggest Cleopatra threw the necklace into the ocean so that it wouldn't fall into Octavian's hands. Plutarch reports that Octavian had divers search the waters for the necklace, but it was never found.

– Percival Flannery, *Archaeological Discoveries of Cleopatra's Egypt*

"Rumour has it that Lucien Vega is in the city," Catherina puffs smoke from her cigarette with one hand as she fluffs the peacock feathers in her headpiece with the other. Her olive complexion shimmers beneath the oil lamps that light the cramped dressing-room in what was once a priest's sacristy. Our guests often muse about what the ghosts of the priests think of what goes on in this once-sacred building, but I couldn't care less. Ghosts are annoying and they never tip the dancers. "He may grace us with his presence tonight."

"As long as he spends big at the bar and takes a couple of you back to a private confessional for dessert, I don't care if he's the Archbishop of Paris." I kick her shin. "You're about to miss your cue."

Catherina makes a face at me. That was perhaps a tasteless joke. Paris is still reeling from the Prussian defeat and the horrors of the *semaine sanglante* – that bloody week when the national army suppressed the Paris Commune two months after they seized power, leaving my beautiful city a smoking ruin.

But Paris is nothing if not resilient. If the City of Light has one feature to recommend it, it is survival. Paris will endure. Paris will still be a bright beacon of pleasure long after the world turns to ash.

It's no wonder I ended up here, enduring, thriving like a weed among a bed of broken flowers, dancing while the world burns around me.

Catherina checks her corset before rising from her stool and shimmying through the red velvet curtains into the wings. I hear the roar of the audience as she emerges on stage for her signature number – a lively cancan that's as provocative as it is masterful. Catherina could be making her fortune in one of the more reputable theatres in Montmartre, but as a creature of the night – an Upyr *fille soumise* hoping to rise in the ranks to become a courtesan – she prefers the company of our kind. Here, we can truly be ourselves and give in to our more provocative fantasies.

I check on the other dancers, making sure they have everything they need for the night ahead and their Prefecture registration cards within easy reach – I wish no trouble from the *brigade des mœurs*, who are tasked with policing establishments like ours. Then I check my reflection – perfect as always, every strand of my thick, curly hair in place beneath the glittering pins, and my neck dripping with jewels – and take the narrow rear stairs up to the VIP level.

The job of a courtesan is never done.

I lean over the ornate iron railings I stole from a burning *grand magasin* and survey the scene below. It's early yet – the sun only set two hours ago, so my theatre is nowhere near full. Guests circle the tables set in front of the stage, some transfixed by Catherina's titillating dance, others perusing our menu of fresh and vintage blood. In the second row, near the bar, a group of my favoured writers and artists loudly insult the tastes of the Salon. I gather Monsieur Monet has been rejected again. They are all friends of the vampire painter Édouard Manet, and the only humans allowed unaccompanied into my den. Their presence brings me joy, and without them all paying extortionate sums to have me sit for them as their model, I never would have had the money to make this place a reality.

Behind me stretch the VIP booths. Already, two of the velvet curtains are pulled closed. This former church was once connected to a nunnery. The booths were for the nuns to attend services while remaining apart from the congregation. Statues of winged angels and a writhing Christ watch over the stage. Every night during our *grande finale* we pour fake blood over the Christ to dribble over our cast below – a big fuck you to the church that has burned, tortured and hunted our kin for centuries.

In another life, I might've enjoyed being a nun. Solitude. Decent food. Only one man demanding things of you, and although the biblical God is undeniably kinky (all that fire and brimstone, yum), without a corporeal body he'd be a pretty easy customer to please.

If only the clothes weren't so *hideous*.

My fingers circle the railing, squeezing tight, wringing out a tiny, secret shiver of joy at the beauty of what I've created.

La Petite Mort. My theatre.

All mine.

Everything here is built off my own back, bought with freedom I tore from the throat of my captor. Five years ago, I came to Paris with nothing but my first name and a collar of jewels, and I've used every trick and skill I have to rise to the rank of courtesan, and now my theatre is thriving.

We're not the Moulin Rouge or the Comédie-Française. We cater to a very specific clientele. While humans with dark proclivities (like the artists now consoling their friend with another round of absinthe) occasionally wander into our den, La Petite Mort is where vampires conduct their business within the safety of our stone walls, and woo willing Thralls to sate their illicit hunger. And I can employ women like me – immortals who wish for an alternative to an eternity waiting on a husband – and enable them to claim their future.

I pioneered a vampire burlesque show the likes of which Paris has never seen – the perfect mix of blood, sex and power. I conceived my signature act when I was dancing at parties hosted by the famed architect and libertine Gustave Eiffel. The man is *nuts* about steel and towering erections, so I came up with the idea of dancing around and hanging off a vertical steel pole while I performed a bloody burlesque striptease.

Even now, while the night is still young, I see my kind leaning over in their booths, spreading their Thralls across the tables, lapping at their necks as though sampling a delicious *garbure*.

I'm pulled from my thoughts by a commotion at the door. *He* enters. Lucien Vega, the most notorious Upyr villain this side of the Seine. Any illegal goods coming through the city bear Lucien's mark. A triangle of men flank him – two Upyr and a human, judging by the smell.

Séraphine moves through the crowd to greet them, her waifish eyes heavy-lidded, her tray laden with goblets of blood as well as sweet cocktails and sugared candies for the Thralls, to keep them bright and alert. She escorts them towards the stairs. They will have one of our VIP rooms, of course.

On stage, Catherina's routine reaches its climax as she luxuriates in a bathtub filled with blood, her hands roaming over her naked curves. The Countess Bathory routine – one of our showstoppers. Later, she will mingle with our guests, her body strung with jewels and still drenched in crimson gold. Lucien Vega will throw money at her for the honour of kneeling and licking blood from her gold-sandalled feet.

She is an enchantress.

I taught her everything she knows.

I smooth the front of my silk dress and check that my jewelled collar is sitting straight as they ascend the stairs. My mouth curls up into a smile. With Lucien's money pouring into my club tonight, I'll have no trouble paying my bills.

"Welcome to La Petite Mort, Monsieur Vega." I smile down at Lucien's party, extending my hand. "Tonight, your every wanton desire and devilish dream is ours to fulfil."

And your overstuffed purse is mine to empty.

"Arabella Macquart, your beauty precedes you." Lucien's gaze falls quickly from my eyes to my chest. But unlike other men, he's not fixated on the breasts spilling out of the top of my gown, but on the jewels encircling my throat. My hand flies instinctively to the collar, covering the central scarab as if that might avert his attention. I keep my gaze lowered, demure, safe. I want him to feel as though he can have anything he wants. "My friends have told me I must seek you out for a good time while I'm in Paris, but I see that their descriptions do not do you justice. You are *ravishing*."

"You flatter me, Monsieur Vega." I raise my eyes, fixing him with the full force of my will. "Our humble *théâtre*—"

But I don't get to finish the sentence.

I'm *transfixed*.

And it's not Lucien Vega who has me forgetting my carefully rehearsed words.

To his left stands his human plaything. Unlike many of the other Thralls I encounter, this one is bright-eyed and alert, his neck smooth and unblemished. Those vibrant cobalt eyes of his are fixed on me with an intensity that stuns the words from my throat.

Lucien introduces his men, his eyes never leaving my throat. I only hear the blond one's name. *Gideon Rougon.*

Gideon Rougon clasps my hand. He brings my fingers to his lips and brushes a kiss across them that sends a shiver down my undead spine. Lust that I haven't felt since I first laid eyes on the collar in my sire's boudoir pulses through me.

I want him.

I stamp down the fluttering in my chest as I lead them to a private room. I feel Gideon's eyes on me as I light the candles and tie back the curtains to give them a prime view of the stage. If Lucien Vega throws enough money around La Petite Mort tonight, I may be able to afford to outfit the theatre with electricity, and then we could do away with the gas lamps and candles. Vampires, as a rule, are not too fond of fire. Too many of us have been burned at the stake.

"I'll have a round of drinks sent up for you and your guests." I look pointedly at the human, but Lucien offers me no explanation. "We offer a variety of services to satisfy any of your proclivities and Séra—That is, *I* will be your hostess for the evening, should you require anything more … specific."

I speak to Lucien in the code of glances that Upyr are so familiar with. I cannot assume that his human companion is familiar with our world. Many of our clients enjoy bringing un-Thralled humans to La Petite Mort to shock them, and then ply them with absinthe and whisper such scintillating promises that the human is drawn into our world. When they wake, they have a small wound on their neck and a head full of erotic memories, and they believe the whole evening to have been a dream.

Absinthe is the backbone of my business. I practically owe the green fairy a commission.

I pull the cord to summon Séraphine and order a round of drinks for us all – bloodsinthe for me and the Upyr men, plain absinthe for the human. Lucien and the other two men bend their heads together. Normally, I'd be eavesdropping on their conversation, searching for useful tidbits I might share with other customers for a price. Men always assume a pretty face in the room is deaf, mute and blind.

But Gideon's eyes make it clear that he knows *exactly* what I'm up to. Dangerous and clever, as well as beautiful – a nasty combination.

He pats the pouffe beside him. I gather my skirts and lower myself down. Our knees are so close that I can feel the warmth of his human skin through the layers of fabric. The air buzzes with the tang of his human blood, rich and alluring, like the exotic chocolate drink that's appearing in the trendiest cafes around Paris.

His eyes flick briefly to the stage, where Catherina is writhing around, sponging herself with blood while another of my girls hangs from the ceiling by hidden wires in a diaphanous angel costume, her throat slit open. Gideon's mouth quirks in amusement.

"You have quite a show here, Mademoiselle." His accent is southern, as rich and warm as the rest of him, syllables lengthening and R's rolling across his tongue. "I've never even heard of this *théâtre* before. This is more invigorating than the stuffy Palais Garnier."

"Opera isn't stuffy." I wouldn't normally question the opinions of a customer, but this human has me quite turned about. "The skill of the performers, the way they pull you into the story, it's an enchantment …"

His mouth turns down, but his eyes dance in the candlelight when he sees that I'm more than just a vision of terrifying beauty. "It's impossible to be enchanted when it's all in poxy Italian. Every time they open their mouths, I think they're singing love songs to spaghetti. It makes me hungry."

"Does the monsieur not speak Italian?" I lift an eyebrow. "How, then, does one order such a finely cut suit or request one's favourite toppings at the Montmartre *pizzeria*?"

"Alas, but I have not yet tried one of the Italian pizzas." Gideon makes a quick glance across the table at Lucien Vega. "My employer does not care for the taste of it. Or food in general. More's the pity."

"Then, you, Sir, have not truly lived." A memory rises in my mind, raw and unbidden. "When I lived in Egypt, I had a patron who used to treat me to the most exquisite pizza, dripping with mozzarella and basil and fragrant tomato. I am pleased this Italian taste has made its way to Paris, although the French do view the pizza as the gastronomic equivalent of finger painting."

I snap my mouth shut, unable to believe I've revealed so much of myself to this stranger, this *human*.

Gideon smiles with his whole face – his eyes crinkling at the edges, his mouth turning up, the vein in his neck thumping with enthusiasm. He shifts closer, the air between us stirring as I scent his attraction to me. "Aside from being a woman with strong opinions on opera and pizza, you are not from France. I thought I detected the trace of an accent."

"At La Petite Mort, we leave our past at the door. We are here, tonight, drinking wine and absinthe in the greatest city in the world. That is all that matters." I lean back, as far away from him as I can get without leaving, and bring my drink to my lips. He studies me, his smile growing wider and more flirtatious. I fix my face into an expression of aloofness – a wall of invisible courtesy between me and this tempting human. But that only spurs him on.

He leans forward, his knee brushing wantonly against mine. The sensation through the fabric of my dress stirs something in me that has been silent since the day I became a vampire.

"Then we shall toast. To the present." He raises his glass.

"To the present."

We clink. He does not drink but regards me over the rim of the Pontarlier glass, his lips too red and plump to be legal. The sparkle in his eyes is a promise, a dare.

"Do you not need to join the others?" I indicate Lucien and his men, still deep in serious talks.

"Not when I have much more scintillating company right here." His words are silk against my skin, but he makes no move to touch me, the way most customers do. Entering these walls permits men to act out their most secret urges, and too many men reveal their true natures when they see what pleasures their money can buy. But this man seems content for us to trade heated glances while we converse, which is refreshing, if odd. I touch my hand to my jewelled collar, wondering if I'm losing my magic. "Truthfully, I don't know why we've come here tonight. Lucien doesn't tell me much. I've not been working for him long. I'm only here because my brother—" A shadow passes over his face, but it's gone in a moment, replaced by that easy smile. "He will tell me when he requires my skills. Most of the time, my purpose is mainly decorative."

I'm too aware of my body, of my skin tightening, of a heat growing inside me. I'm aware, too, that I will be performing shortly, and this man will see me and my infamous pole. I can't decide if the shiver in my skin is excitement or dread. "What business is your master in, that he requires such decoration?"

His mouth twitches. "Lucien is not my *master*."

Spoken like a man. Even when he has thrown in his lot with a creature as dangerous as Lucien Vega, he believes himself to be free. But of course he does. He's never had to build something like this from the rubble up. The world is already laid bare for him.

I sigh. "What business is your boss in, then?"

"You ask a question you already know the answer to, Mademoiselle Macquart. Lucien Vega's reputation precedes him." Gideon smiles at me as he sets his untouched drink on the table, and I have a sense the smile is supposed to be threatening, but to me, it's ridiculous. "You won't charm any of his secrets from me, but we can both pretend that our paths haven't crossed on the morally grey footpath leading to the palace of cardinal sins."

"Monsieur Rougon, I *own* the palace of cardinal sins."

"Then a word of advice – if you want to part Lucien from his money, you should offer him a bath." His eyes briefly shift to Catherina wallowing in the metal tub on stage before returning to me with vivid intensity. "He and his men have … peculiar tastes."

"Then he is in luck, because that is precisely what we cater for." I draw my finger along his knee. His skin is so warm, so pliant. "What about you, Gideon Rougon? What of your peculiar tastes?"

He lets out a tiny shudder, his eyes fluttering closed, golden lashes tangling together.

"I would love to see you dance," he says. "I think you'd be magnificent."

"Very peculiar, indeed. You don't even know me."

"That's true." He rubs his chin. "Tell me, then, where were you born? Was your mother a beauty? Did your father stop people in the street and force them to admire you? Which scent is your favourite? Do you read? Where is the most beautiful place you've ever lived? When is your birthday?"

Fuming, I stand. The spell shatters. "Enjoy your evening, Monsieur Rougon."

From the way the blue of his eyes darkens at the edges, I know he catches my true meaning.

Choke on a baguette, Monsieur Rougon.

As if I would give him any of my secrets. Vampires don't even remember our birthdays, as a rule. The only milestone normally celebrated is our Bloodeve, the night of our siring, and mine is *nothing* I wish to celebrate.

"Please, don't leave." His voice grows urgent, freezing me in place. I look into his eyes and see something I wish I could unsee. Behind that flirtatious, curious nature of his, there is a wall as thick as the Bastille. We all wear masks, but never have I seen one that is a perfect mirror of my own. I could break him like a glass trinket, but I'm transfixed by the flecks of gold at the edges of his peacock irises. "I don't want our conversation to end. I mean, it would be great if you were telling me how brilliant I am, but a man takes what he can get. That's a beautiful necklace you're wearing, and you wear it with such grace."

His eyes drop to my neck for a moment, then rise to meet my gaze again. His fingers trail over my wrist. The touch is fiery hot, presumptuous, and *desperate*.

"Flattery will get you nowhere with me."

He grins wickedly. "See, I don't believe that's true. Shall we place a bet?"

"What kind of bet?"

Gideon cracks his knuckles. "You spend the evening in my company. I will employ my considerable skills of flattery and charm, and if, by the time my not-master demands we leave, I cannot make you admit that you had an enjoyable evening, then he shall pay double your price."

"And if you win, what is the prize you wish to claim?"

"I thought I was clear. You will admit that you enjoyed my company. That's the only prize I'm interested in." Gideon leans forward. "Why don't we return to our drinks and you can tell me about more operas I'll hate?"

"I hardly saw you all evening," Catherina complains as I add up the night's takings, counting off her cut and depositing the coins into her open palm. As predicted, Lucien Vega drank the bar dry of blood and booked a private room with two of my younger ladies, so I am one step closer to electricity and a new dress.

Especially since I made Gideon Rougon's master pay me double.

"I was entertaining Lucien Vega and his guests."

Catherina unclips her jewels and drops them carelessly onto her vanity. I touch my fingers to my collar, seeking the familiar coolness of the stones. Gideon's questioning from earlier unnerved me.

I'm not normally a superstitious person, but the legend of the necklace weighs on my mind. Ever since I started wearing it, my luck has changed. I escaped to Paris. I found this old church for a bargain price. I created La Petite Mort from the ether, and pioneered a dance style that I hope, one day, might make me as famous as my idol, Sarah Bernhardt.

And a delightful young human has just fallen at my feet.

He can be only a temporary amusement, but I do love being amused.

"Séraphine was the one polishing his brass while he feasted on Gisele's neck. The only time I saw you tonight, you were speaking with Lucien's human. What's his story? He doesn't appear to be Thralled. And he didn't even touch his absinthe!"

"I believe Lucien has employed Gideon Rougon's services, not his veins," I murmur. I don't want Catherina to know just how much my thoughts have lingered on the pretty Gideon. "He was an engaging conversationalist, for a human—"

A creak sounds from out in the hall, past the closed door.

"Who's there?" I ask. The theatre should be empty now; the only people backstage are the performers removing their costumes and makeup. And none of my ladies skulk around silently in the shadows.

Another creak, closer this time. A footstep in the narrow corridor.

I sniff. Beneath the scents of backstage – gas from the lamps, stage glue, sweat-soaked costumes, Catherina's cloying perfume – is another scent. Musky and masculine and foreign, but also familiar.

"You'll have to leave, Sir," I call out. "Patrons aren't allowed backstage. If you don't want to be garrotted by a silk stocking, I suggest you make your way outside now. And if you wish for the garrotting, that will be two francs. Please pass your coins beneath the door now."

Nothing.

As quick as lightning, I sweep the remaining coin into my purse and hide it in my skirts. My fingers clasp around the silver dagger I keep there. Catherina draws her blade. Ladies in our business are always prepared for penetration of one form or another.

Catherina moves to one side of the door, I to the other. I count down under my breath. We both raise our daggers.

I kick the door open and leap into the gloom, Catherina screaming like a banshee behind me. My foot lands on the creaking board. I stare into the darkness of the wings, but between the props and stacked curtains, I can see no phantom hiding.

"There's no one here." I whirl around to Catherina, who is busy searching behind her large bathtub. "Perhaps we imagined the sound."

"We're *cocottes*. We know instinctively when a man is nearby and means us danger. It is our speciality, like that move you showed me with the eggplant—"

Catherina raises her finger to her lips, and in the heartbeat of silence, I hear the floorboards creaking from somewhere behind me.

He's still here.

Skirts flying, we race in the direction of the noise, our shoes clattering up the short steps to the stage. It's gloomy and shadow-laden without the harsh stage lights, the religious statues above our heads grotesque.

I bunch up the curtains, searching for someone hiding in the thick folds of fabric. Catherina moves towards the tables in the audience when—

Glass shatters.

A high scream echoes from backstage.

Séraphine.

We fly back down the stairs. Séraphine stands in the doorway of our dressing-room, a bundle of costumes for the laundry bunched at her feet. Her hand is pressed to her mouth, her eyes wide with terror.

We rush to her side, daggers raised. She points a trembling finger into the room we'd vacated only moments before.

Only now it is a mess – the jars of makeup on the vanities have been swept off and broken on the floor. Glittering powders mix with sparkling shards of glass. That makeup is expensive and will have to be replaced before tomorrow night's performance.

In the centre of the destruction is a small songbird, the head torn off, its wings speckled with blood.

I'm so distracted by my dream of electric lamps disappearing in a puff of vandalism that I don't even notice the message until Catherina grabs my arm.

On the mirror, a single word has been dashed in blood.

MINE.

5

Arabella

Alyra: When are you moving into your new home? I'm looking forward to introducing you to my friends. They're all excited to avail themselves of your services. We'll make certain you fall in with the *right* vampires at Sanctus. I don't want any ex-Dusk Court weirdos to sink their fangs into you!

Isis: Hey, Arabella, I'm dying to know, have you ever been tempted to give a long-winded tell-all interview to a flattering biographer who begs you to grant him the Kiss?

And also, do vampires have special vampire dentists? Or are you immune from gum disease?

"I REFUSE TO DO IT." I BARK INTO MY PHONE AS I SURVEY THE CHAOS of my room. Cleo VII, my pet Egyptian cobra, uncoils herself from beneath a stack of cashmere and regards me with reproach.

I should hire Winnie to help me sort and pack my things – she is literally creating a business as a professional organiser for Upyr – but that would mean breaking the rules I made for myself over a century ago.

Rules I've broken only once.

Arabella Lestrange does not need help.

Arabella Lestrange does not owe anything to anyone.

And Arabella Lestrange does *not* risk her pretty vampire neck by stepping out of the shadows.

My rules have served me well. I dragged myself from the darkness of poverty *twice*, changed my name, and found my way to this small village where no one would ever connect me to the life I had before. I purchased my immaculate townhouse on the outskirts of Argleton in cash some five years ago from an old client who'd held on to it since Queen Victoria started moping about like the original MySpace goth.

From the outside, the building is nothing much. This is deliberate. I cannot draw attention to myself. But inside, I've spent my money wisely – on luxurious furnishings, bamboo bedding imported from Japan and fine Venetian stemware. Everything in this house has been carefully chosen for me and me alone (with the exception of the zoo-quality enclosure and rockery – that is for Cleo VII's enjoyment). In all the time I've owned it, not a single other soul, human or Upyr, has walked through the front door.

I prefer it that way.

I like to surround myself with the finest things in life. They say money doesn't buy happiness, and they're wrong. What's the point of eternity if you don't enjoy it?

Far too many vampires don't figure out this simple truth, which is why I'll never run out of clients.

And one of the finest things in life is solitude. Peace. Safety. Not having to rely on anyone but yourself.

"You can't refuse. You're our only hope." Isis wails from my phone speaker.

Ah, yes. Solitude.

I roll my eyes at the painting on the wall above my bed. It was the very first thing I purchased when I rebuilt my fortune, and although the eye-watering price tag almost sent me back to the poorhouse, it was worth every penny. A naked woman draped over a faux Greek temple stares down at me with daring eyes – so dark they're almost black, except for the golden halo ringing the edges. The figure had been painted with blotches of colour like dabs of light. The collar of jewels around her neck is rendered in brilliant shades of cobalt and crimson, the scarab at its centre invisible unless you know what you're looking at.

I whip my head away from her daring stare. Sometimes, that woman encourages me to say yes to things that could threaten everything I've built here, like joining a ridiculous book club determined to meddle in local supernatural mysteries, or accidentally buying a house in the estate owned by the man I hate most in the world.

The Sanctus Estate catalogue lies open on the table next to my phone, my latest folly on display, mocking me. The sleek renders and professional photographs suckered me in, and when I saw my new client Alyra Maythorn's home on the estate, I did something most un-Arabella-like – I succumbed to a whim.

I came home from that meeting with Alyra, Sanctus catalogue tucked under my arm. I unfolded the artful origami packaging and took in the modern design. Every house on Sanctus Estate oozes opulence and luxury, with a timeless style that will outlast the centuries. Every house is set among the trees to hide us from the world and protect us from the great circular deathtrap in the sky. All the amenities I could ever need. Security to prevent nosy humans from discovering our secrets. Even better is the company ethos – a community run by Upyr, for Upyr, without affiliation or oversight by the courts.

A promise of something more.

Permanence. Longevity. A home.

I saw myself there. I saw myself happy.

So I did something I've done only once before – I allowed my heart to rule my mind. I made the call. I signed the contract and transferred the money. A place at Sanctus was mine.

A home that I earned, a place no one could take away from me.

Now, Gideon Blake threatens to ruin it with his mere presence.

And the Nevermore Coven want me to stick to him like dried blood on a cashmere scarf.

"What's changed?" Celeste's concerned voice murmurs down the phone line.

"Arabella is afraid our little murder investigation will embarrass her in front of all her posh vampire friends," Isis humphs.

My secrets dance on the end of my tongue, but I need to hold them closer than ever now.

I called Celeste because she's more likely to take my side if I pull out of spying on Gideon and Sanctus. Celeste – who owns the Glazed and Confused bakery – is the Coven member I'm closest to, perhaps because she's almost as secretive about her past as I am about mine. I feel safe in her company. Plus, she always smells like cinnamon and lemon curd, which is what matters in a friendship.

Cinnamon and lemon curd and *something else*. Something odd and earthy and wild that I can never put my finger on, but my vampire senses tell me is not *entirely* human. But Celeste doesn't ask about me, so I don't ask about her. That's our unspoken rule, and it's worked well for us.

Unfortunately, I didn't know the Meriwether sisters were visiting the shop when I called, and Celeste put me on speakerphone, a betrayal I'll not soon forget.

"What's changed is that I don't want to do it. It's dangerous." I run my hand over my head. When I lived in Paris, I used to trap my curly hair in jewelled combs, pins and tiaras. Now I wear it in a buzzed short style that accentuates my long neck. "There is a murderer on the loose. We should leave this to the authorities. Tell Alaric's mother our suspicions. Let the Conclave handle it."

Cleo VII slithers to safety as I toss the catalogue onto the bed.

"Except that's not true, is it?" Dora says firmly. "You don't want to bring the Conclave into anything to do with Sanctus. That will bring court scrutiny down on this little vampire community, which is the last thing you want when you're moving there."

Even without my secrets, Dora makes me uncomfortable because she knows me *too* well. Humans should not have the power to see the future – even for Upyr, the magic of Dust Court vampires makes us nervous. Humans with magic are like stilettos on a trampoline – impressive in theory, catastrophic in practice.

For nearly as long as there have been vampires, the Upyr of Europe have been ruled by a series of vampire courts. The number and nature of those courts have changed over the centuries, but now there are three. The Nightshade Court, who excel in warfare. The Midnight Court, which is the court of entertainments and frivolities, and the Dusk Court – a secretive cult of magicians. Vampires are not required to be affiliated with a court, but those of us who are uncourted are still expected to obey their laws without enjoying any of the benefits.

Affiliating with a court breaks my rules. I've gotten along just fine for nearly a hundred and fifty years without relying on the courts for a handout, and I'm not about to start now.

I can't risk a court finding out that I broke one of the cardinal vampiric sins.

Isis senses my hesitation and pounces. "Winnie told us that you know Gideon from years ago. She also told us that Callista tasked Gideon with finding this murderer, and Gideon cares about Sanctus so much that he'll do anything to get the Conclave off his back. He's our best lead *and* the reason you're suddenly a vampire chicken. Did he break your heart?"

I wish I could reach through the phone and pluck out her eyes.

"I'm not a chicken, and Gideon Blake did *not* break my heart."

"That's impossible." The shop bell sounds in the background and a new voice joins the conversation. Komal. *Wonderful*. "Arabella would have to *have* a heart for Gideon Blake to break. No offense, Arabella. Don't mind me, ladies, I just came in to get a box of cream fruit buns. I've got a village council meeting tonight and I'll need copious amounts of sugar to deal with Councillor Durant. Ever since he announced his mayoral campaign he's been even more insufferable than usual—"

"Komal's right," I snap.

"I know I'm right. That man is determined to ruin all my ideas for making Argleton the best tourist destination in Loamshire, and he's the reason there isn't funding for the *Gazette*, either—"

"No, I mean, you're right that Gideon didn't do anything as dramatic as break my heart. He stole from me and destroyed the life I built for myself after my Kiss. It took me decades to remake myself into the ravishing creature you know and love." I pick up the phone and train the video camera on my face. "I simply don't relish the thought of spending time with him while he's strutting about as king of his private kingdom."

"Then do what you do best," Isis says in that annoying singsong voice of hers. "Make him understand *exactly* what he's missing out on."

"We know Gideon can't be the murderer, but we do need eyes on what's going on at Sanctus," Dora says. "Gideon has information we could use."

"Then ask him yourself."

"Arabella, you *promised*—"

I hang up the phone. The woman in the painting stares down at me, her expression filled with disapproval. I step over Cleo VII and turn to my closet. I've started packing some of my older gowns between layers of tissue.

I run my fingers along the beautiful fabrics, my mind whirring over what Iris said, before selecting a crimson suit with immaculate black patent leather piping along the seams.

Because even though I told the girls I was quitting, Isis's idea appeals to the vampire in me that hungers for revenge.

Gideon Blake deserves to suffer.

He cares about Sanctus so much he'll do anything to save it.

I know exactly how to break a vampire like him.

It will mean doing disgusting things. Smiling at Gideon Blake. Flirting. Giving him just enough to believe he has a chance with me. Debasing myself by pretending to enjoy his company. But if I can get close enough to learn Gideon's secrets, I can use them to take the one thing he cares about – Sanctus Estate.

I hold the suit up to the mirror. *Perfect.*

Cleo VII flicks her tongue in agreement.

If I must spend my precious time on this earth in the company of Gideon Blake, then I will make sure he spends *every moment* regretting his betrayal. And that begins by taking his precious development from him, the way he took everything from me.

Gideon Blake should never have crossed me. It may take one hundred and fifty years, but Arabella Lestrange always wins in the end.

SAVE THE ARGLETON GAZETTE AND AUDITION FOR THE ZEN AND TONIC VARIETY SHOW!

Maisie Collins

Argleton Gazette

Your beloved village newspaper is in trouble. Thanks to rising paper costs, dwindling advertising budgets, and a recent decision from the village council to pull our funding, the *Argleton Gazette* is short of the budget needed to keep printing our beloved newspaper beyond our 1 November issue.

If the *Gazette* is forced to shut down, it will be a huge loss for the community. Where else can you get world-class reporting on the Great Cider Mill Explosion of 2024, the inside scoop on heated village beautification committee meetings, sightings of the famed Terror of Argleton, and the latest reviews of the new cake menu at Glazed and Confused, as well as our community notices and weekly horoscopes from our very own village psychic, Isis Meriwether?

This paper has been in circulation since WWI. We're not going to let a little cost-of-living crisis, non-existent budget, or worldwide paper shortage get the better of us!

To raise funds to keep the presses pressing, we're hosting the first ever village variety show at Zen and Tonic Pole Studio!

It will be a fun night out for the whole family, but fair warning, some of the acts may be a little risqué!

Sign-ups are on the door outside the *Gazette* offices. We'll be holding auditions early next week at the Zen and Tonic studio. Come along to sing, dance, perform magic, juggle, and save our paper!

6

Gideon

Alaric: Arabella has not called about the scrotum-filleting knife. I'm sorry that you're distressed.

There was a hairline fracture on the latest sculpture. It was invisible to the human eye but to a vampire, disgustingly obvious. I have thrown it away and begun again.

Winnie says to tell you that yes, you HAVE been secretly pining for Arabella.

Callista: The Conclave is displeased about your little real estate project. They think you're creating a stronghold of dissenters so that you can establish your own court. I informed them that your ambition stems from a desire to have blood cocktails at all hours of the day and night-time spa treatments, but I'm afraid they remain unconvinced.

You would be wise to respond publicly to their claims.

And find that killer!

I STARE IN HORROR AT THE MESSAGE FLASHING ON THE SEPULCHRR app, dredging up my past and warning Upyr not to invest in Sanctus Estate.

It's up to over 10,000 Digs.

My fingers tremble with rage as I navigate to the Sanctus profile to type a response, only to discover that my profile has been blocked from posting.

I guess we're officially on the Conclave's bad side.

I did have an inkling this could happen. At first, Sanctus had broad court support, especially from the Midnight Court – my "official" affiliation – whose highest-ranking officials were attracted to our modern amenities and the social aspects of vampires living together, and bought early shares. But they couldn't stay out of my business. Each court demanded its corner of the estate, with home designs and court-controlled amenities specifically for their members. They wanted inspections and to impose all kinds of restrictions. They levied taxes and fees and taxes on top of the fees and fees for paying the taxes. They looked at everything I created here from my blood, sweat and tears, and saw only dollar signs.

(The blood, sweat and tears are purely a poetic device – vampires don't sweat, I cry only during Pixar movies, and my blood is too precious to waste on manual labour.)

The final straw came when Alaric and Winnie announced their engagement. Even though the vampire–human copulation ban is woefully out of date, and the Lady of Agony and many others stand with Alaric, the three courts refuse to officially recognise their union or to grant my oldest friend an audience with the Conclave to discuss giving Winnie the Kiss.

So I decided to cut them all off.

Sanctus Estate is officially for solitary, uncourted vampires only. No court rules, no Conclave oversight. We are exercising our blood-given rights to live free. Judging by the interest I've had since making the announcement, many vampires are fed up with the court system and demand another way to live.

Clearly, the courts are determined not to let Sanctus out of their control … even if it means tanking the entire project.

Every vampire in Europe uses the Sepulchrr app as a social network and marketplace. It's supposed to be a private company, but prominent

Conclave members sit on its board. My entire potential investor base has seen this message.

Worse, most of it is *technically* true.

This is ... less than ideal.

We just broke ground on the next building stage. We need to sell those houses quickly, or we'll run out of cash.

The phone on my desk rings. I drop my mobile and grab the receiver. "Gideon Blake."

"You finally read the post, Sir." Sinead's voice rises with concern.

"I read it," I mutter.

"I'm afraid things are worse than they appear. Wainwright just pulled his funding."

I swallow down the urge to throw the phone across the room. Wainwright was our second biggest investor. If he's gone, we'll have to stop construction within days ... unless I can come up with another source of funding.

"Sir?"

"It's okay. It's fine. Everything is going exactly to plan."

"But Sir, we can't afford to—"

"I'm aware of our financial situation, thank you, Sinead. I said I have it all under control."

"Oh, good." Her voice calms. "I'm pleased that you have a plan. Arabella Lestrange is here to see you."

My heart clatters against my ribs. I think of the message from Alaric, unanswered on my phone.

I have not *been pining for her.*

Okay, there may have been some pining. A lot of pining.

But that doesn't mean I still want her.

I knew there was no hope for us the day she sent her sire to kill me.

And then I found a golden chemise smouldering in the fire.

I'm going to prove that one hundred and fifty years of seeing her face in my dreams is no big deal by being completely civil to her on this tour and not checking out her legs *once*.

Because I am nothing if not a gentleman.

A gentleman with a desire for legs, especially long, dark, silky legs that go all the way …

Ahem.

I straighten the lapels on my favourite suit, trying to ignore the pounding in my chest. "Send her in."

Sinead appears a moment later, shoving my door all the way open. "Arabella Lestrange, I'm pleased to introduce Gideon Blake, CEO of Sanctus Industries. Gideon, this is Arabella Lestrange, our newest resident. She's here for her grand tour."

Sinead could be reciting the ingredients of Reginald's closely-guarded hot chocolate recipe and I wouldn't even notice. From the moment she strides into the room, Arabella has my full attention.

Every inch of this woman is pure sin. Her hair is shaved close to her skull, revealing the shapely curve of her neck and the place where her clavicle dips. She wears a crimson suit with tailoring so sharp it could circumcise a man. Her shirt jacket has only one button, revealing a plunging neckline and … nothing else. She's wearing nothing underneath but a mesh bra covered in a design of coiled snakes.

This … this is a trap. It has to be.

My enemies at court have sent her to undo me.

"We're already acquainted." Arabella bites off each syllable like the testicles of all the men who've wronged her. Thankfully, there doesn't look like there's space in that suit of hers to hide one of Alaric's blades. "Gideon. It's *fascinating* to see you again."

Her lips curl back into a dangerous half-smile as she stretches out her hand to me. Her nails are painted in a glossy crimson to match her suit, and each of them is sharpened to a point.

I'd prepared myself for every eventuality, but not *this*. Not this beguiling creature. Not the courtesan with the seductive smile tugging on the corner of her lip.

I might almost believe this is the Arabella from 1879, the Arabella she became when we wandered the streets of Paris, anonymous in the crowd, or when the lamps were put out and it was just the two of us arguing over a game of backgammon. The Arabella she was when no one else was watching.

But that's impossible, because I know the *real* Arabella, and now that she knows she didn't get rid of me, she'll be keen to finish the job.

So what is this?

And why do I want it so, so much?

"You haven't changed a bit." I take her hand. Instead of shaking it, I bring it to my lips, brushing them lightly across her knuckles, giving her skin the tiniest of scrapes with my fangs. She doesn't react at all. "You're just as ravishing as ever."

"I think you'll find I've changed," she says.

"Is that so? Then I look forward to learning about the new, more *forgiving* you."

I am trying very hard to keep my eyes on her face. It's quite difficult with the plunging neckline of her suit jacket and the way she folds her impossible legs into that perfect triangle as she sits opposite me, but I'm managing.

Mostly.

"I'll leave you to your tour." Sinead's voice drips with boredom as she closes the door behind her.

I'm alone.

Alone in a room with the woman I've grieved every day since the night I left her.

Alone with a woman who would be well within her rights to castrate me.

I am so dead.

"So …" I flatten my hands against the table. "Drink?"

She lifts one of those sharp eyebrows. "Do you make a habit of drinking on the job, Gideon Blake? You certainly have changed."

"I'm offering the finest blood on the market. I still don't drink alcohol. My clients are here to enjoy the finer things in life, and that includes sharing a glass of blood in public without worrying what humans might say. Would you like fresh or will a vintage suffice?"

"Vintage, please. I find fresh so … messy."

I pour two glasses from the bottle on my desk. This is a drop Alaric gave me to celebrate his engagement to Winnie – a fine nineteenth-century railroad worker, all peaty and full-bodied. I lean across the wide expanse of my oak desk, which today feels not nearly wide enough, and hold out the glass to Arabella.

As she reaches across like a scandal in motion and takes the stem in her delicate fingers, her skin brushes mine.

A frisson of *something* descends my spine. Hatred or fear or wanting … I can't decide which. Perhaps all three at once.

Only Arabella can make me feel so unsure of myself.

She tilts the glass to her lips and her head falls back, exposing that long, graceful neck of hers. I suck in a breath.

My memories of that neck are of it clad in heavy, glittering jewels, resplendent as an Egyptian queen. I've only seen her neck naked once before, and that was the night I betrayed her.

She licks a speck of blood off the corner of her lips. "Out of curiosity, what would happen if I asked for fresh?"

"Many humans on our staff – like Sinead – are Thralls employed by Sanctus Industries. As long as the vampire obtains their consent, these humans are happy to offer blood to any of our members."

"Mmmm." Arabella's eyes dart in the direction of my office door. She purses her lips, and I think she's about to say something else, but she sips her blood in silence.

I raise mine to my lips but don't drink. I'm too wound up.

"I'm surprised to see you here." I set down my glass. "I didn't think there was much money in courtesan-ing or horror burlesque in Argleton, although I did hear something about a pole-dancing studio opening …"

"I've been out of that business for some time."

"What do you do now?"

Her eyes narrow. "Am I required to reveal this to get my keys?"

"I'm making conversation, Arabella. An activity you once relished."

"Only because it gave me easy access to a man's purse." She sips her drink. "I have my fortune, so I don't need to indulge men like you any longer."

That one stings.

Why do you care? I chide myself. *You left Arabella in the past, remember? After she tried to have you killed. Or are you done lying to yourself?*

"I am in finance," she volunteers, looking as though the information leaves a rancid taste in her mouth.

I raise an eyebrow. "Finance? You never struck me as a numbers woman."

"I am a *money* woman. I sell off those useless trinkets Upyr have hoarded over the years and provide them with the funds in usable currency to maintain their lavish lifestyles. Few others do what I do, and I am the best because I understand the art of discretion. Some of your members are clients of mine. I thought you should know this since I'm to be …" Her lip curls back as if she's tasted something foul. "Residing here."

I lean forward, interested. "Our members will be grateful for your services. Accessing modern cash is a real issue, and the courts have never been much help. Even the estate itself has issues …"

I think of the Sanctus safe, stuffed to the brim with bags of gold, Merovingian coins, Sumerian tablets, family swords, and my private safe that contains something even more precious. All that treasure on hand that I've no clue how to convert into the cash I need. Perhaps Arabella could—

"I'm not here to be of service to anyone," she snaps. "I choose my clients. I applied to live at Sanctus because I value privacy, security and discretion. I want to live outside of the courts, unbeholden to anyone. Is that clear?"

And I might believe her sharp tone, if not for the tug in her eyebrow that gives away her interest. *Still the same Arabella.*

If I want her to help me, I have to make her believe it's her idea. So I change the subject. Unfortunately, there's only one other subject to discuss with her.

I clear my throat. "If you're going to be living here, we should talk about Paris—"

"I don't see why. Unless you're planning to return my property."

"The collar is gone. It's at the bottom of the Seine."

I watch her carefully for a reaction, but she gives me nothing. She fingers the stem of her glass. "You seem uncomfortable, Gideon.

You needn't be. What passed between you and me was over a century ago. A mere fling."

It was never a fling to me.

She adds, "I'm certain you've had dalliances since Paris."

"A few," I admit. "A few hundred."

"A few hundred?" A slow smile slips across her lips. "How lax you've been. I'm pleased that once again, I come out on top."

Raw, cold jealousy snakes its way through my veins, a sensation that takes me back to those warm Parisian nights, watching every eye in the audience entranced by her as she moved around the pole like a panther stalking its prey, knowing that more than a few of them would pay handsomely for the privilege of a night in her bed.

I may be a modern man who believes in a woman's right to do whatever she chooses with her body, including sex work, but I'm also a beast. I like to *possess*. And Arabella has always been elusive. You sense that she's playing a game with you, toying with you like a cat with a mouse before the cat slits the mouse's throat.

That's what makes her so enticing.

I glance down at my tablet, where Sinead has sent me Arabella's documentation and a map to her new home. She's purchased one of our newest executive treehouses – these residences are right in the heart of the estate, surrounded by centuries-old woodland and overlooking the soon-to-be-opened-once-Alaric-stops-being-a-bloody-perfectionist-and-finishes-a-sculpture Midnight Garden. Her home is completely private and sheltered from the sun. Unlike the others, she didn't pay in treasure but in cold, hard cash.

Arabella must be doing well to have amassed enough wealth to buy into Sanctus and receive the approval of at least one of our residents. Alyra Maythorn has vouched for her on her application, and Alyra is of the Blood Kincaid, a prominent Midnight Court family.

I want to know everything about Arabella's life, every detail from the moment I left her curled up in her golden silk sheets to meeting her by the watermelons, but she's giving me nothing.

I stand, straightening my lapels. Arabella's house key jangles in my hand. She eyes it hungrily. She wants this. I remember that same hunger in her eyes when she stood on the VIP balcony at her theatre, watching the artists, bohemians, courtesans, and criminals beneath her, transfixed by the enchantments she created.

A wicked streak sizzles down my spine. The trickster in me wants to see her suffer, to unnerve her the way she's unnerved me. I am going to drag this tour out *so* long, Taylor Swift will be playing at nursing homes.

"Follow me, Ms Lestrange." I gesture to the door.

Arabella rises from her chair with the grace of a ballerina and shimmies out of my office ahead of me. I try so hard to be a gentleman, but my gaze drops to her glorious, perfectly sculpted legs in her tailored suit trousers as she shoves past me.

Worse, when I raise my eyes again, she meets them with a mocking glare.

"A lot of things change in a hundred and fifty years, Gideon," she purrs. "But not the fact that you're a scoundrel and I'm a motherfucking *goddess.*"

I let her have that one because really, I can't argue.

First, I show her around Sanctus House, which is our amenities building – a towering structure of Norwegian larch and Patrick Stock's specialist glazing. Arabella does not indicate that she's impressed by our covered tennis courts, state-of-the-art gymnasium, luxurious spa, or onsite coffin-repair shop. She pauses at the shelves in the temperature-controlled cellar, where members are welcome to imbibe from our curated blood selection as part of their membership fee. Her red-painted nails caress the bottle of a seventeenth-century Friar as a slow smile plays across her lips.

"I never imagined you as a vintage drinker," she purrs. "I thought you'd prefer direct from the source."

"You imagined me as a vampire?"

"Sometimes." Her gaze flicks to me. She lets slip a little fang as she smiles. "Mostly I imagined you as my prey."

This woman will be the death of me.

What game is Arabella playing?

Why am I so excited to be played?

I lead her across the hall into the donation room with its private soundproof booths arranged with luxe furnishings and well-stocked medical kits. "Members may book these rooms for use with their personal Thralls if they prefer not to drink in their own homes," I explain. "You are also welcome to use our Thralls if you don't have your own."

Arabella studies the Yves Saint Laurent amenity kits. "What kind of selection is available?"

"My secretary, Sinead, has a woody, smoky flavour. Giovanni the tennis instructor has a summery peach bouquet. I prefer Floyd, the masseuse. He has a slight vanilla aftertaste."

"Every member of staff is a Thrall?"

"Every permanent member, yes. It's a requirement of the role. We have several un-Thralled temporary workers through our site, most of them human by necessity."

"The Conclave would say that's far too risky."

"The Conclave has never tried to build something like this." I lead her through another door. "Welcome to Brimstone."

Arabella's eyes flicker with interest as she takes in our largest bar and entertainment area. The decor is 1920s Hollywood glamour – mirrored surfaces, luxe fabrics, gold everywhere. It's early in the evening, so there are very few members using the facilities – a couple share a blood cocktail beside one of the windows, and three male vamps converse at the bar. Lilac, our bartender, waves at me before returning to wiping down glasses.

"Our bartender mixes more than blood cocktails," I say. "As well as mocktails for those of us who prefer our blood without the tang of alcohol. Lilac is ex-Dusk Court and far too good at her craft to be pulling pints at the Rose & Wimple. If a human is not interested in working for us after they discover our true nature, she'll create a draught that can make them forget everything they've seen here. Of course, it sends a few of them a little doolally, but it's better than the alternative." I make a slicing motion across my throat.

She narrows her eyes. "If the Conclave finds out you've been giving humans a *potion* instead of following the rules—"

"Don't tell me that you care about following rules?" I grin.

"I don't. I want to know what kind of drama I'm buying into."

I swim in her gold-rimmed eyes. "I'm not going to blindly follow rules I think are stupid, and I'm not the only one. That's why Sanctus has been so popular. We shouldn't go around killing humans just because they see something they shouldn't, especially when humans are so useful. Upyr have been lucky so far to avoid notice, but that won't hold forever, especially not with everything caught on camera and posted on social media. The Conclave rules are cruel and outdated, and the vampire community is open to change. They simply need someone to show them a new way. Alaric and Winnie have proven that."

Her eyes soften at the mention of her friends. "You almost sound serious, Gideon Blake."

"Deadly serious. Especially when it comes to my friends."

Arabella turns away without comment.

So Arabella Lestrange *does* have a heart.

Interesting.

"What about Danny O'Hare?" Arabella whips back to me. "Was he a Thrall? And Patrick Stock?"

I tilt my head to the side. "Is this a tour, or is it a Nevermore Coven investigation? I thought we'd cleared up their deaths. Nine pieces of Baylor Godsven have been delivered to castles around Europe."

I'm testing her. I know that we still have a husker in our midst, but I don't know what Arabella and the Nevermore Coven know yet. Hopefully nothing. I love Winnie and her friends, but I don't want them snooping around in vampire business, especially not when the future of Sanctus hangs in the balance.

Arabella isn't giving anything away. "I'm merely curious. At the ball, Baylor said, 'I'm not the only one among you brave enough to embrace my true nature.' Which implies that he had an accomplice."

"I presume the others told you about that, since you weren't at the ball. And why was that?" I round on her. I'm not the only one with secrets, and this is a good chance to direct her away from dangerous vampire murderers. "The Arabella I used to know would never give up the chance to be the most beautiful woman in a room."

Why didn't I see you at the ball? If I'd seen you ...

"I was in the kitchens, as per the Nevermore Coven plan." She smooths a hand over her buzzed hair. "And even with tomato sauce stains on my chin, I was still the most beautiful woman at that ball. Can we continue this infernal tour so I can get my keys?"

"As you wish." I lead her back through Brimstone, which has started to fill up with residents as they begin their evenings, and into the administrative wing of Sanctus House. My mouth moves a mile a minute as I elaborate on every lavish detail.

"We have the mail room and staff offices. The security suite is through here. My apartment is on the top floor of this building, so I'm onsite in case anything happens. And I'll—"

"What's in there?" Arabella's talons scrape across the red surface of an elevator door.

"Oh, that." I wave my hand as though it's not a big deal. My heart thuds against my ribs. "That leads up to the top two floors of the building. It's protected by the same high-tech security system we use on all the houses. You can't go up there without being on the system."

"And why would I want to get into that elevator?"

I brighten. "As I said, the top floor is my private apartment, so if you'd like, we can retire—"

"So forward, Gideon. You're supposed to woo a woman first."

"I thought we'd been through the foreplay. I stole from you. You tried to have me killed. Ours is a romance written in the stars."

A flicker of something like frustration passes over her face, but it's gone before I can figure out what it means. "And what of the third floor?"

I swallow. "That's the Sanctus Club – a private club for certain select members. I have sole control over the guest list."

"I see. So I should expect an invite."

I long to take her behind that door, but I know I can't do it now, while she has me off guard. I need her to understand first. I need her to not hate me, because once she sees what's in there …

My testicles will never be safe.

I place my body between her and the elevator doors, flashing her my most devilish grin. "Perhaps. If you behave."

That smile again. "I never behave."

She's flirting with me. Why is she flirting with me?

I waggle my finger at her. "Then no private club for you."

"Oh dear, how ever will I cope?"

"You'll find a way." I press my palm into her back, trying to ignore the way my hand against her cool skin is like a fire engine blaring and racing straight to my cock. "Let me show you your new home."

I watch Arabella's face as I walk her along the wide path through the manicured gardens. Her house is built on stilts, allowing space underneath for a shaded garden and outdoor seating area while nestling the main living areas within the ancient trees. The floor-to-ceiling windows reflect the woods back to us, so the house blends into the landscape. I half expect Kevin McCloud to pop out from behind the artisan, wrought iron fence and shout, "By Jove, they've done it!"

Damn, I love that show. *Grand Designs* is singlehandedly responsible for giving me the idea for Sanctus. If anything could turn me from my life of vampiric crime to eco property development, it's watching a delighted British man spouting poetry about concrete while the posh couple he's following move into a caravan "for a few weeks", attempt to build a wall out of horse dung, and stress about the Latvian window company going bankrupt.

My new goal in life is to be the vampiric Kevin McCloud, only without the architecture poetry or illegitimate children. The vampires who've moved into their Sanctus homes are awed by this place, unable to believe that they can live in a house with such huge windows after so many centuries being consigned to draughty castles by the courts.

Patrick Stock may have treated Winnie badly, but he was a genius with glass. I am only sad that he couldn't find it in his heart to take up my generous offer and went and got himself husked.

As we descend the steps to her front door, Arabella regards her new home with the same cool detachment that she'd greeted me with. Not even this majestic piece of architecture could break her facade. I notice a glass and steel enclosure filled with rocks and strange plants built alongside the kitchen and suppress a shudder. It looks like Arabella is still keeping her preferred pets.

I show Arabella how to program her security system. "Input a four-digit passcode into this screen. You can change it any time."

"Very well." Arabella steps up to the console. "Turn around."

"I'm not going to spy on your keycode."

"Yes, you've proven yourself to be trustworthy beyond reproach. Turn around, Gideon. Or I shall rotate your head for you, permanently."

I turn away as she punches in her new keycode. I don't bother to tell her that as CEO of Sanctus, I have access to override the security system on any of the houses as a safety precaution. I don't want to think about what that might tempt me to do, knowing that Arabella is only a few minutes' walk from my apartment.

A movement flickers in the corner of my eye. It almost looks like a person moving between the trees …

I sniff the air, but Sanctus is too alive with the scents of vampires, the fragrant flowers we use for the gardens, construction materials, and the woodland, for me to pick out a new scent.

It's just an animal coming closer for a look. Our fences are impenetrable, and there's no way the security team would allow a stranger to skulk around in the woods inside our boundary.

The door clicks open. I turn back to her. Arabella peers through the front door into the open-plan living, dining, and kitchen area. Her lips form a thin line that anyone who doesn't know her would take for disdain. But I notice the way her right eye twitches, her brow arching.

There it is. The crack in her facade.

She is *moved*. The way she was once moved by exquisite music or the stroke of an artist's brush.

The way she was once moved by *me*.

I sweep past her, throwing my arms wide. "Here you are, our first finished home in the executive range, and it's all yours. All the floors are Norwegian birch, the countertops are the finest Brazilian Preto Agata granite. The walls have been finished and are ready for you to hang artwork. You have artwork, I presume?"

That twitch in her eye again. "A few pieces."

And with the sultry pull of her voice, I'm back in a moonlit garden in Paris, the only sound the lap of water, the rasp of a painter's brush, and the soft whispers escaping her lips as I—

I clear my throat. "The inbuilt sound system caters to our sensitive hearing, able to play every nuance of any piece of music, and the windows can be controlled by the panel over there. During the day, you can choose a blackout shade …"

I tap a button, and the windows flick to black, plunging the room into darkness. LED lighting fades in instantly, bathing us in a warm glow.

"Or, my personal favourite, a projection of the world outside with the harmful sunlight filtered away." I click another button and the trees appear again. "What do you think?"

"It's sufficient."

"Sufficient? This is a masterpiece of home building. Kevin McCloud should be writing a sonnet to me right now."

"Who is that? You know I detest poets more than you detest opera."

Arabella's heels clack on the floor as she steps deeper into the space. Her hand grazes the metal balustrade of the stunning spiral staircase leading up to the second level. Her brow arches again as she points to the stylised crosses in the metal. "This design is familiar."

My heart hammers against my chest. *Of course she would notice that.*

"Er … the design team has borrowed inspiration from many periods in history."

She frowns. "*Which* periods of history, Gideon?"

"Oh, you know, all the highlights. The Black Death, the Sack of Rome, that time when early humans were painting blobby antelope on cave walls with their fingers." I throw up my hands. "The Belle Époque."

Arabella folds her arms.

"Fine. If you must know, I designed this particular piece." The words rush out of me. "It's the same design from the railings at La Petite Mort. From the VIP floor, overlooking the stage."

Arabella's shoulders tighten. Something that might've been grief flickers in her eyes, but it's gone before I can claim it.

"You have an excellent memory." She wraps her fingers slowly around the balustrade, one at a time, until my tongue has stuck to the roof of my mouth.

I wait for her to berate me or brandish a testicle-chopping knife, but she merely nods her head at me and moves deeper into the house. I follow her as if she's the one giving the tour.

As we continue through the house, I point out more features that have my clients so enraptured with Sanctus – the wet bar with special storage for blood. The comfortable feeding room with built-in sound system and views over a picturesque stream. The dressing-room with the custom inbuilt cabinets she requested. The bathroom with its clawfoot golden bathtub.

Arabella studies it all with detached indifference. If I didn't know her, I'd think she found it all boring.

But I *do* know her. I know that inside that perfect skull of hers, she is plotting, *scheming*.

And when she accidentally-on-purpose brushes against me as we exit the closet, I know that some part of her scheme has to do with me.

Why is she torturing me?

I know why. Her acerbic teasing, her touching me, and that incredible outfit … This is all about revenge.

Maybe she's simply trying to show me what I missed out on, what I can never have. Given how tight my balls are and how I have to keep adjusting myself to hide my erection, it's working.

But Arabella won't be content with that. If she blames me for her theatre burning, she won't stop until she burns *my* dream to ashes. And Sanctus is too important for her to ruin it over a vendetta, especially when the Conclave have me in their sights.

So where does that leave me?

It leaves me utterly at the mercy of the woman I once loved.

7

Gideon
Then

Little Prince, I have work for you. A furniture store owner named Jean-Luc hasn't paid his debts. You know what must be done. You are to go to him during the day and leave your message on his sleeping form. He may have sold his bed, so he sleeps in some unconventional way.

Do not fear him, but do not visit him after sundown.

Lucien

I hurry along the banks of the Seine. I'm late. Already the sun dips below the horizon. But I slept too long and when I wasn't sleeping, I lay in my bed, conjuring the sultry eyes of one Arabella Macquart.

My boss, Lucien, is still sleeping off his night in our luxury *pied-à-terre*, along with his other two bodyguards. This isn't unusual – I've never seen him up before sundown. He conducts his business at night, meeting his clients in private clubs or entertaining them at the opera, while I do his more unsavoury work during the day. Usually, I sleep while they party, but last night, Lucien had wanted to "treat" me for my good work.

There's only one treat I want from Lucien – to have my brother back.

I rub the scars crisscrossing my forearms. My body has changed since I came to Paris in search of Jacob. The muscles I built on labouring jobs have been sharpened by my grisly work. My skin is now a map of Paris drawn in blood.

I'm a mess, not just in my body, but in my soul.

And I can't leave. I belong to Lucien Vega until Jacob's debt is paid.

I reach my destination – a small, nondescript shop overlooking a boggy section of river. The sign outside is bright and clean, but there are indications of hard times – rubbish beneath the window, vacant shops on either side with their windows boarded up and lewd graffiti splashed about.

I step inside. The place reeks of dampness. The water must have got in, judging by the ruined furniture stacked beside the door with sales prices affixed – a pittance compared to what such exquisite pieces are worth. A stooped old man hunches over a barrel serving as his counter. There are no customers inside.

"Whaddya want?" The old man doesn't look up from his ledger as I approach.

"Bonjour." I draw my dagger from my coat. It's a special one given to me by Lucien, the blade inlaid in silver. Truthfully, it's an impractical blade, too flimsy and prone to breakage, but Lucien insists I use it. "I'm here on behalf of Lucien Vega to collect what's owed."

I spit a piece of tooth as I wander back along the Seine.

Not my tooth, thankfully. It's strangely curved and sharp.

The job went south quickly. The old man couldn't pay, of course. They never can. But he was surprisingly sprightly and tough for his advanced years. His left hook sent me hurtling into his tower of rotting commodes. His right had me seeing constellations.

It was only after I cut him with Lucien's blade that he became weak enough for me to overpower, and now I have several new scars to add to my collection.

My head thuds.

I reach the *pied-à-terre* and let myself inside. All is silent. Lucien and his bodyguards are out for the evening. I clean the knife in the kitchen and help myself to some of the bread, ham and cheese I'd purchased at the market yesterday. I left a plate of food for Lucien before I went out, but he hasn't touched it. I lick cheese crumbs off my fingers and take the plate downstairs.

The temperature drops as I descend the steps to the wine cellar. I grab a bottle from the shelf without looking at the label and make my way to the shackled figure hunched beneath the one small, barred window.

"I brought you some food." I hold out the plate. A hand reaches out from beneath the filthy blankets and snatches the plate from my hands. One aquamarine eye regards me as Jacob shoves a wedge of cheese into his mouth.

We eat in strained silence until both our plates are clean. Jacob leans against the stone wall. His chains clank together as he raises the bottle to his lips and draws out the cork with his teeth. His Adam's apple bobs, and I see the strange scars dotting his neck. There are fresh bruises and puncture marks.

Jacob offers the bottle to me with a trembling hand.

"Not for me, brother."

When you grow up with a man like my father, a man who becomes a monster after a drink, you have but two choices – you either run away so you never have to see the monster ever again, or you become an even bigger monster so that he can't have power over you. My brother and I each chose our path, and now we are both paying the price.

The hand retracts. Jacob takes a long swig. Even in the pale square of moonlight from the window above, I can see that his forehead shines with sweat.

"The wine here tastes like vinegar." Jacob makes a face, but he doesn't stop gulping down mouthfuls of the dark claret. "What I wouldn't give for a drop of the Pauillac red we used to have at home."

I hate the way he says "home" fondly, as if there was ever something to love about that place. I know that if I open my mouth to speak, I will say something I'll regret, so I remain silent.

"Have you ever tried that stuff Lucien drinks, in the dusty old bottles?" Jacob wags his finger at me. "He gave me a glass once. I nearly spat it out in his face. That's no merlot."

"I won't accept anything from Lucien, apart from his money."

And a night of debauchery in the company of a beautiful, beguiling woman.

I didn't touch the absinthe Arabella poured, but ever since I laid eyes on her, my head's been filled with fog.

"That's right." Jacob's lip curls back. "I forgot. You're here to save my poor, corrupted soul."

"Not your soul, Jacob. Just your skin."

Jacob rubs his hand over his injured neck. "And how goes it, Gideon? How many pounds of my flesh have you worked off my debt? Does Lucien get to keep my pancreas?"

"Your debt is nearly cleared."

Another lie. Every time I ask Lucien about the size of Jacob's debt, he remembers an additional payment my brother owes or shows me the interest accruing in eye-watering amounts. But what choice do I have? I can't leave Jacob like this.

"You should run, Gideon. Get out of Paris. Don't you see?" Jacob's eyes widen with fear. He scratches a sore on his neck. "Now that he knows how good you are, Lucien will never let you go. And he has his uses for me too, tied up like this."

"I'm not abandoning you again."

I hate myself for leaving him. I escaped our small village as soon as I was old enough to work. Labouring is hard, but honest. I may not have had the elegant attire or fine lodgings of Lucien's gang, but I had money for food and board and no longer feared my drunken father returning home to drag me out of bed for a beating. I thought that Jacob would be safe – our father never touched him, as he was the favourite. Instead, Jacob followed Dad into the darkness.

He drank too much, gambled too much, and owed too many bad debts to Lucien Vega. Even then, I might not have come to Paris to help him, but when I received Jacob's letter begging for help, he hinted that the things Lucien made him do frightened him. The envelope was stained with blood. So I came with my meagre savings, thinking I could clear Jacob's debts, but it wasn't enough for Lucien, especially not once he got a taste of how good I was at his line of work.

"It's the least I deserve." Jacob's body sags. He lets out a series of wet, hacking coughs. "Pass me another bottle, brother."

I don't want to give him more wine, but whatever Lucien is doing to Jacob, he needs to be drunk to endure it. I never could deny my baby brother anything. I hand him a pinot noir from the shelf just as a scraping noise and voices upstairs reach my ears.

"That will be the Devil and his minions now." Jacob waves a hand at me. "You'd best run upstairs, so he doesn't think we're conspiring to escape him."

"We wouldn't dare." I pat my brother on the head and turn away, unable to look at him any longer. He looks so much like our father after one of his beatings, all broken and sorrowful, filled with self-loathing. His chains clank and the wine in the bottle splashes as I drag myself up the narrow stone steps.

Lucien sits at the kitchen table, his eyes two bright lamps in the gloom.

"Hello, Lucien. I didn't expect you back for some time." He doesn't usually return during the night. His lips are swollen, stained with red from the wine he's been drinking. He shifts in his seat, putting me instantly on edge. "I was just giving Jacob some food."

"I came home to check on my Little Prince." Lucien's smile is all teeth and menace. "You are back late. And what has happened to your face? A quarrel with your dear brother?"

"The old man attacked me."

Lucien's eyes flash. "He should not have been awake. I told you to go during the daytime!"

"It's fine. I got the job done. Payment received." I drop the old man's purse on the table, next to one of his fingers. The leather of the purse bears my bloody handprint.

Lucien looks me over, his gaze lingering on my throat. I swallow. His smile grows wider, and the dark is playing tricks on me because it appears as though two of his teeth have grown into sharp, curved fangs.

"Excellent work, as always." Lucien sips his drink, his expression turning thoughtful as he studies me. "I have a new job for you. I know I can trust you to get this done. Last night's excursion was not simply for enjoyment. I was conducting an investigation. Do you recall the courtesan you spoke to?"

"Arabella Macquart." *How could I possibly forget her?*

Something of my feelings must show in my face because Lucien's lips curl back with disdain. "Do not allow her pretty looks or elegant manner to fool you. She is dangerous."

I lean forward, intrigued.

"You saw the necklace she wears around her neck, no?"

"The paste?"

"No, not paste. That woman wears the Antirhodos Collar – jewels that once adorned the neck of the last queen of Egypt. The scarab in the centre of the necklace is made from lapis lazuli, the snake set with emeralds and rubies. It's said that it is worth more than all the money in the world because of its magic. Legend says that the person who possesses the jewels will be blessed with long life and good luck."

If that's true, how did the collar end up around Arabella's neck? She might have been the finest woman I've ever laid eyes on, but she's a madam and owner of a theatre of ill-repute in Montmartre – a far cry from an Egyptian queen.

Everything Lucien has said makes me more intrigued by Arabella Macquart.

"I *must* have the collar," Lucien continues. "I have been seeking it for some time. But your usual techniques will not work on Arabella Macquart." He regards my bloody handprint with amusement. "She is already intrigued by you. Use that to your advantage. I will provide money so you can gain her trust with trinkets or flowers. But whatever you do, don't allow her to bite you."

"To *bite* me?" I laugh. "I don't play those games with women, Sir."

"I am serious, Little Prince. If she sinks her fangs into you, she will have you under her spell. I don't like it when people take what's mine." He reaches for the bottle and pours himself another glass. The stench of his wine itches my nostrils – a metallic tang that turns my stomach. "You've worked hard for me, Gideon. You are one of the best I've ever had, and I have taken advantage of you. I don't want you to think that your hard work is without its rewards. If you do this for me, then I will set Jacob free."

"You will?" I'm wary now, wondering if Lucien overheard my conversation with Jacob. But that would be impossible – he would have had to come down the staircase to listen in, and I would have heard him, seen him.

"I will wipe his debt clean. He will be free to leave the city, with my blessing. It's the least I can do." Lucien holds out his hand. "One final job for me, Monsieur Rougon. Do you agree to my terms?"

I stare at his hand, at those long, perfectly manicured fingers.

He's not asking me to hurt her. Arabella has no need for the collar. She has a thriving business and many other beautiful, precious jewels. And all this talk about it being good luck is just a story. If I take it from her, then I can save Jacob and break free of Lucien's hold over me.

I clasp his cold fingers in mine. "We have a deal."

The hostess at the door of La Petite Mort recognises me as one of Lucien's men. She waves me through the velvet curtains without a word, and Arabella Macquart's enchanted world embraces me like a long-lost child.

I scan the room but don't see Arabella anywhere. It's still early in the evening, so there is hardly anyone about. A man with a jagged scar across his face hunches in the shadowed booth in the corner, his pain-soaked gaze fixed on the stage. One of Arabella's girls sits at the piano, singing in a soft, sombre voice while her fingers dance over the keys. More women rush around, lighting the oil lamps and buffing the tables, ready for the night's festivities to begin in earnest. I hear laughter from backstage, a cork popping. Excitement and trepidation fizz down my spine.

I'm here to do a job, to finally free my brother and myself of this wretched, evil man. That has to be more important than a woman I barely know.

As I walk past the velvet-lined booths, I'm aware of eyes on me. I feel as though I'm the fly trapped in the web, and the spiders are about to fight to the death over who gets to tear off my wings. I approach the bar and order an absinthe, not to drink, but simply to hold, to make myself fit in. Most of the tables are still being cleaned and set, so I approach a velvet-lined booth near the stage where a group of men and a woman are involved in a rowdy discussion, their table invisible beneath a thick layer of sketches and charcoal studies.

"I was sitting beside the Seine, happily painting away, when several passing Communards took issue with the 'mysterious signs' on my canvas," one of the men is saying, waving a paintbrush around his head for emphasis. "According to them, no one who calls themselves an artist paints like I do, with such free strokes or imprecise lines! They conclude I must be a spy detailing the quays of the Seine to aid in the landing of troops, so they drag me away to be shot. If the Commune's police chief hadn't recognised me, I would have more holes in me than a wedge of Emmental cheese. I was lucky to leave the city soon after."

"I cannot believe you fled to the countryside when the cause needed you!" An older gentleman slams a beefy fist on the table as he glares at his younger companions. The lapels of his jacket are splattered with splotches of red paint.

"As well I did," the younger man shoots back. "For if I stayed, I would have been like you and Victor here, eating my favourite horse to survive."

"You must not knock horse until you have tried it." A man with an impeccably curled moustache refills his absinthe glass with a double measure, places the sugar cube on the silver slotted spoon, and pushes the glass beneath the elaborate fountain standing at the centre of the table. "It is delicious in a shallot sauce."

"Is it only me who wonders what they did when the horses ran out?" pipes up the woman, her attention not wavering from her hurried sketch of the pianist.

"My dinner guests were always well-fed, Berthe, courtesy of the zoo in the Jardin des Plantes. We dined on bear, antelope and elephant trunks in sauce *chasseur*. And when the zoo animals ran out, we served a rat pâté." The man swirls his absinthe. "It was surprisingly delicious."

"After spending three days on the latrine following the elephant trunk, I decided to skip the rat course. It was one of my wiser decisions." The older man slumps in his seat, losing interest in the discussion. He catches me out of the corner of his eye. "Ah, you there, who are you?"

"Gideon Rougon, Monsieurs, Mademoiselle." I give a deep bow. "I wondered if I might join your lively table, although if the prerequisite is sampling the rat pâté, I may have to pass."

"Greetings, Monsieur Rougon. I am Édouard Manet. You may have perhaps heard of me?" He says this in the way of a man who is certain you have heard of him.

Even I, a philistine when it comes to art, know of Monsieur Édouard Manet, the upstart artist upsetting the establishment with *Olympia* – a portrait of a naked and self-assured courtesan reclining like Titian's *Venus* that caused a fistfight to break out at the Paris Salon. I've often heard the dockworkers and shopkeepers of the city joking that they must check behind every barrel in case Manet is crouched there, painting their foibles.

"It's an honour, Monsieur Manet." I shake his hand.

"I'm certain it is. Here you have my esteemed colleagues, the painters Claude Monet, Berthe Morisot, and Pierre-Auguste Renoir, the sculptor Auguste Rodin, and the writers Émile Zola and Victor Hugo. Do you still wish to join our merry group of misfits?"

"Certainly, although I must warn you, I make no art of my own, unless you count the poetry I speak between a woman's thighs."

Berthe snorts, not looking up from her sketch. The others laugh.

"What is your business in Paris, Monsieur Rougon?" Victor (the rat chef) twirls the end of his moustache as he sizes me up. "I hear a trace of the South in your accent."

"I've come to the city from the countryside to seek my fortune." I came for a fortune, that much is true, but only because my brother was foolish enough to gamble away a fortune of Lucien Vega's money.

"Then you shouldn't be hanging about with the likes of us. When it comes to finances, we're a sorry lot. My father threatens to cut me off if I don't commit myself to a studio." Claude Monet bows his head unhappily. "But I have tried that, and it is anathema to me. I don't want to be inside, copying the works of older masters. I want to be outdoors, painting light and colour and movement and *life*, but my father finds the very idea of it undignified. He says that's not how art is done."

"Then why don't you change the way art is done?" I say boldly, swept up in the man's passion. "Declare that you are an early pioneer of the technique of *en plain air*. Give it an official title, such as, hmmm …" I glance down at the rough sketches and pastels Monet has spread across the table, taking note of the way he uses dabs of colour to suggest a scene, rather than painting every detail. "Call it 'impressionism', and instead of being an artistic failure, you will be the founder of a movement."

Claude's eyes light up. "That is a brilliant idea. What say you, Pierre-Auguste? Berthe? Édouard? Would you join me in my new movement of impressionism?"

The artists grow animated, sifting through their sketchbooks. Victor lights his cigar and tells tales of writers' quarrels. Auguste Rodin's eyes sweep hungrily over me as he sketches me in fast, furious strokes. Édouard buys another round of absinthe for the table (and something red and foul-smelling for himself).

I'm enjoying myself so much that I almost forget the true purpose of my visit to La Petite Mort, until, without warning, several of the gas lamps are snuffed out at once, plunging the theatre into near darkness. The music shifts into something slow and sultry – flute and a deep, booming drum that matches my heart beating against my ribs. One of the dancers, a slight white girl with feathery golden hair, places incense burners on either side of the stage, causing smoke to curl around the room like snakes rousing themselves from sleep. A lone oil lamp is trained on the centre of the stage, where a round steel pole extends through the centre of the floorboards into the heavens.

The drum beats faster. The flute dips and swells. From the smoke emerges a lone figure, hands raised like a goddess demanding worship.

Arabella.

She's a ghost in the mist, a lithe shadow swaying her hips gently, moving with the music. As she steps into the light and clasps the pole, I gasp.

She wears a floor-length, figure-hugging gown, made from some kind of linen so fine that it's see-through. My throat is one hard lump and my dick is even harder.

Arabella stretches out one impossibly long leg, her foot bare, and kicks, letting the momentum spin her around the pole. The see-through linen pleats of her dress whisper against her skin as her body whips through the air. The sound is the most erotic thing I've ever heard.

She's mesmerising.

As she moves through the flickering lamplight, the smoke from the incense kisses her shadowed skin, and the gems at her throat glitter like fireflies. I don't know how I ever believed the jewellery was paste.

Voices break through the spell of her performance. My new friends whisper about her.

"She's the one who used to sit for me," Auguste says, his voice tight with lust. "She has such beauty, it's unsettling. She's not unlike our new friend Gideon here. I'd like to sculpt him, but I'm almost afraid I would sully his perfection."

"If you wish to keep your manly virtue, Gideon, I suggest you steer clear of Monsieur Rodin's studio," laughs Pierre-Auguste. "Marble dust between one's cheeks is not a pleasant experience."

"Arabella sat for me, too," Édouard says in a bored voice. "She is certainly beautiful, but she is too arrogant. I prefer a woman not to be aware of the power she has over men."

"More like you prefer a stupid woman who succumbs to your charms," Berthe shoots at him. "Arabella Macquart does nothing unless it benefits her. I admire her greatly."

"But how much of that confidence is God-given, and how much is gifted by the jewels at her throat?" Édouard quips. "We've all heard the legend – good fortune until the collar is removed and the wearer is cursed forever."

"Even cursed, I'd pay a queen's fortune for a night between those legs," Pierre-Auguste sighs, furiously sketching Arabella's sweeping form. "But I've heard Arabella no longer takes private clients to her boudoir. The best we can hope for is to enjoy her dance."

The drums beat faster as Arabella darts across the stage like a panther, extending one ebony leg from the slit in her linen shift. She grips her ankle and pulls her leg behind her head in a standing split that steals the breath from my lungs.

She undulates around her pole, tearing off the linen shift to reveal nothing but shimmering midnight skin and golden pasties covering her nipples. The dark triangle between her legs beckons me, and it takes everything not to throw myself upon the stage and kneel at her feet.

As Arabella exits the stage, I rise to my feet like a man possessed. My new friends call out to me, but I barely register them. I duck through the curtain separating the backstage from the audience, pushing past women in various stages of undress as they hurry to set the stage for the next scene. I come to a narrow corridor with doors flung open and costumes flying through the air. I approach the first door, but a large man bars my way.

"You're not supposed to be back here." He frowns down at me.

"I merely wish to see Mademoiselle Arabella Macquart—"

He folds his arms across his chest. "No admirers."

My hand flies to my purse. "Perhaps a shiny coin or two might help you lead me to her chamber?"

"Perhaps, *human*, you would like to be Catherina's guest on stage during her Countess Bathory act?" His face contorts with malicious glee. "It's been a time since she filled her bathtub with fresh blood."

"Fine, fine." I hold up my hands and back away. *Why did he call me "human"? What else could I be?* "I am leaving. Please tell Mademoiselle Macquart that—"

"No."

He shoves me. Hard.

I fly through the air like a leaf tossed in an autumn breeze. I crash back through the curtain and hit the nearest table. Women scream and men shout as I crash to the floor, bringing glasses and an absinthe fountain down on top of me. I clutch my chest, gasping for air, certain the man has staved in my ribs.

How did he push me that hard?

"No luck, old chum?" An object is thrust in front of my eyes. It takes a moment for my addled brain to recognise that it's a hand attached to my new friend, Édouard Manet. I accept it and allow him to pull me painfully to my feet.

"You must be a man who enjoys having his heart torn out and eaten in front of him, because that's what Arabella Macquart will do to you. That woman is more elusive than a place in the Salon," Claude says with a grin as I collapse into an empty chair between Édouard and Victor.

"But if you intend to come back and try again, we are here most evenings, in this same booth. You may join us whenever you like." Édouard glances around the table. His friends nod their assent. "Good, then we shall have Gideon in our merry group. Now, what do we all think of this tower Gustave Eiffel is proposing to build? I for one believe *ardently* that what the Paris skyline truly needs is a giant steel triangular phallus …"

The Nevermore Murder Club and Smutty Book Coven Group Chat

Maisie: Did you learn anything useful on your Sanctus tour, Arabella?

Isis: Yes, Arabella. Did you get any "information"?

Arabella: Is that supposed to be innuendo?

Isis: Of course it is. You can tell by the "quotes".

Maisie: Not everything in quotes is innuendo, Isis. Quotation marks could indicate someone "talking" to a friend.

Komal: Hahahaha.

Winnie: Don't mind Arabella. She's feeling a little out of sorts because she had a "thing" with Gideon.

Maisie: A "thing"? Oooh, Arabella, do tell.

Arabella: I did not have a "thing".

Winnie: That's not what it looked like when the two of you met in the market.

Winnie: The fruit section was a war zone after their "not-thing".

Arabella: If you're all going to harp on about it, perhaps I won't tell you what I've learned.

Beth: We're your friends, Arabella. If you did have a "thing" with the hot vampire billionaire property developer, we're happy for you. You hold a lot of tension in your shoulders. I've been concerned about you for months, but since you refuse to let me use one of my healing modalities, perhaps a little shag will help?

Arabella: I hate you all.

Arabella: And I'm not sleeping with Gideon Blake. Not ever. Especially not now he's our prime suspect.

Winnie: What? I thought we were certain he was innocent.

Arabella: We are NOT.

Maisie: Ooooh, do tell.

Arabella: According to Gideon, if his human workers discover who they're working for, he either has Lilac drug them so they forget (highly immoral and probably illegal in both human and vampire worlds) or hires them as Thralls for the estate for any member to drink from. Do those sound like the actions of an innocent man with nothing to hide?

Winnie: But he does have things to hide. Like the fact that he – and everyone at Sanctus, including you – is a vampire.

Arabella: Pah, details.

Winnie: I don't think Patrick would have agreed to become a Thrall. So how come he ended up dead instead of getting Lilac's potion?

Mina: Arabella is just going to have to dig deeper.

Komal: Oh, she's going to go DEEP.

Arabella: I will curse you all. I hope the chocolate chips in your favourite muffins always turn out to be raisins.

Celeste: Raisins! That's a particularly cruel curse to wish upon your friends.

Beth: Ladies! We need a day off from all these murders and vampires and raisins. Good thing the Zen and Tonic Pole Studio grand opening is tomorrow night! I hope you're all ready to dance up a storm. We need to entice lots of people to join and sign up for the variety show!

Arabella: I hate you.

8

Arabella

Komal: Don't you *dare* try and skive off opening night like Celeste did! I don't care if all your clients at Sanctus see you. If I'm embarrassing myself in front of the entire village, then you are, too!

"So you couldn't find a way out of this, either?" Mina groans as I swing by Nevermore Bookshop to pick her up. Mina is blind, although she can see light and some basic shapes. She's the best amateur sleuth in the Nevermore Coven, but she's a little worried about how she'll fare in a pole dancing class. She has her guide dog Oscar's lead in her hand and a large gym bag slung over her shoulder. I'm surprised to see her three husbands scrambling out the door behind her.

"Beth had all sorts of creative threats." I glare at her husband, Moriarty. "I think she's learning from *you*. She told me that she'd change all the door locks on my new property with the sensors in the village market."

"Oooh, that's a good one. I've made a mental note." Morrie slings an Hermès satchel over his shoulder. I eye the bag with envy. Such immaculate stitching. If he ever *thinks* about crossing me, I shall bury him alive and steal it. He will learn a valuable lesson and I will look fabulous.

"Why the entourage?" I ask Mina as our group wanders in the direction of Beth's studio. "I thought we agreed that the fewer witnesses to our humiliation, the better."

"When they found out what Beth's event was about, I couldn't convince them to stay home." Mina rolls her eyes.

"We're not missing an opportunity to watch Mina swing around a pole." Heathcliff – another of Mina's husbands – pats the binoculars slung around his neck. "We intend to be a thoroughly engaged audience."

"I tried to bribe them with snacks to stay home." Mina groans. "I even tried to lock Heathcliff in the bathroom. But we're stuck with them."

"We wouldn't dream of missing this," Quoth – also Mina's husband – beams. "We're here to support you in your scantily-clad dancing dreams."

"This is more like a nightmare." Mina rolls her eyes again. "How did I let Beth talk me into this? I couldn't dance even when I had vision. What do you think, Arabella? Are you any good at dancing?"

"I am sufficient." I have no intention of telling my friends what I used to do. Until Beth started showing us videos of pole dancers and going to classes in Grimdale, I didn't even know my evocative dance style had caught on and become a staple of modern erotic entertainment. Women who don't even *need* men to shower them with money learn pole dancing for fitness and *self-expression*. It's fascinating. If I'd realised I could dance for myself instead of for the male gaze, I might have stuck with it.

I doubt dancing could have earned me a house at Sanctus or my closet full of designer clothes. But who knows? I am *quite* good.

Although tonight I may consider pretending to be not so good, so I'm not forced to reveal my secrets. But that shouldn't be too difficult. I'll just copy Mina.

As a group, we wander across the green and behind the Rose & Wimple to the old wattle-and-daub stable that Beth has transformed into her new yoga and pole dance studio. As we round the corner, I see a shadow dart around the building – probably a teenage boy hoping for a peek at something salacious. A sparkly paper banner above the renovated stable doors reads "Grand Opening" and garish pop music blasts from within.

Why am I doing this again?

"You made it!" Beth runs out and throws her arms around Mina, nearly knocking Oscar's harness from her hand. Beth smells like a hyacinth bush got into a fight with a bowl of mushroom soup. She goes in to hug me, but I step back and shake my head. This outfit is *Gucci*. You don't ruin a Gucci exercise outfit by hugging bouncy, sweaty, fungi-obsessed yoga instructors. "You have to see what I've done with the place. I'm so happy with how everything's turned out."

She grabs Mina's hand and leads her inside. People mill around a small waiting area, visibly disturbed by the candy-pink walls adorned with garbled inspirational sayings, like a unicorn threw up on a Mark Manson book. In the corner, a trestle table groans beneath the weight of all the food people brought along. Reginald has a little stand in the corner where he ladles out his famous hot chocolate. In another corner, Lilac is shaking cocktails for a growing line of vampires and humans. I smell the familiar tang of blood cocktails. Just the thing to add to a heady mix of seductive dancing, vampires and humans. This will be a *fascinating* night.

I add the crisps and sweets Winnie and I bought to the pile.

"I told everyone they didn't need to bring food. I have that sorted." Beth gestures to a pitcher of foul-smelling green juice and a platter of mushroom brownies – no doubt the source of her interesting perfume. "I wanted to introduce everyone to my vitality drink sachets! But I'm blessed to have so many people here supporting this new venture. It seems like everyone in Argleton wants to get fit, have fun, and nurture their souls all at the same time."

"I prefer my soul unnurtured, like a garden left to ruin," I mutter.

Beth is too busy to hear. "I was a little worried that the pole dancing would be too risqué for the village, but I think it's just what we all need to get our minds off the murders and—Oh look, Arabella, there are some of your friends from the estate. Maybe you can find out more about those Thralled workers."

Beth nudges me towards the doorway, where—

"Alyra?" I gasp as my new client struts through the door, followed by a vampiric entourage – two older vampires and three newly minted Upyr by the looks of them, still retaining the human colour in their cheeks and revelling in their newfound immortality.

"We found this flyer in our mailboxes." Alyra holds up a square of pink paper. "We had to see what it was all about."

"What's this?" I grab the flyer from her hand and scan the text.

> *Does your blood run cold at the thought of exercising?*
> *Do you want to stay young and vital for millennia?*
> *Does your afterlife need a little spiritual alignment?*
> *Come along to Zen and Tonic for our Upyr specials:*
> *Upyr-only pole class, Tuesday evenings at 8 pm*
> *(blood energy drinks to follow)*
> *10% off immortality elixirs*
> *15% off vampire facials*
> *Endorsed by Arabella Lestrange*

Beneath it is a blurry photograph of me, taken during one of our book club meetings. The hem of my dress is rumpled and I'm making a face (no doubt at something Isis said).

My heart stutters against my ribs.

She sent out flyers with my photograph. *When did she print these? How many vampires have seen this? What if one of them recognises me …*

"Excuse me for a moment." I grit my teeth as I crumple the flyer in my fist.

I find Beth back at the food table, pouring generous lugs of green smoothie into paper cups and thrusting them beneath the noses of unsuspecting guests.

"Beth, what is this?" I shove the flyer under her nose.

She beams at me. "I thought it was obvious. I'm drumming up business for Zen and Tonic."

"Not by mooching onto people at Sanctus with *my* likeness, you're not."

"Why not? What's the big deal?"

The big deal is that vampires have long memories, and if anyone at Sanctus used to frequent a certain Parisian horror cabaret… "I chose Sanctus because of its *privacy*. I have to live there and conduct my business. I'm trying to make a good impression and stay under the radar. You tossing my name around is going to have the opposite effect. I don't even *use* your beauty elixirs."

"You *should*. I have a special formula for vampires that will give you a healthy glow—"

"I'm immortal, Beth." I touch my cheek, which looks perfectly lovely, thank you very much. "My skin will look like this forever."

"Yes, and the death mask look was hot twenty years ago, but if you used my elixirs, you could look more like Alyra. She's one of my best clients. Don't you want that?"

I follow Beth's gaze to Alyra. Now that Beth mentions it, she *does* have a certain aliveness about her that belies her years. Her cheeks have real colour in them, her lips are rosy, and her skin looks soft, without the kind of waxy look older vampires get.

She *does* look good. Damn good.

Maybe I've been underestimating Beth's talent.

But I won't admit that to Beth.

"If Alyra loves your elixirs so much, put her name on the flyer. Take mine off."

"Fine, fine." Beth's face falls. "I don't want to fight. I'll change the flyers. Forgive me?"

"That entirely depends on what torture you have planned for us tonight," I grumble.

"You'll love it. You're so graceful – I bet you're a natural dancer." Beth grabs my hand and drags me towards the main studio. "Could I get everyone inside? Our evening activities are about to begin!"

The guests crowd the studio doors. The book club ladies crowd around Beth, pulling off layers to reveal their workout gear. We traipse in last and huddle in the corner, half-heartedly doing warm-ups while the audience gawps. I notice Winnie's fiancé, Alaric, standing with Mina's husbands, his usual grumpy expression softened with curiosity.

The studio is nothing like my beloved theatre. The lighting is all pink and purple neon. There are mirrors along one wall, and a water fountain and cubbies for students to store their clothing. Ten poles are spaced evenly around the high-ceilinged room. Dora stares at them as though they're medieval torture implements, her face growing pale as she catches sight of the audience spreading around the walls.

I follow her gaze into the crowd. Behind a hooting gaggle of older women led by Mrs Ellis of Naughty Knitting Club fame, I'm surprised to see Dora's husband, Mike. He stands with his arms folded and a sour expression – not at all the face I'd expect a man to wear when he's about to see his beautiful wife swing around a pole.

Mike is one of only a handful of men in the crowd. Komal makes a face at her arch-rival, Augustin Durant, who stands in the doorway, shaking hands with everyone as they enter and reminding them that they can vote for him in the upcoming mayoral race. He spends a particularly long time chatting with Alyra and her friends.

Komal seethes. "What's he doing here? He doesn't get to ogle us while he schmoozes for votes!" she hisses at me. "He's not even dancing. I'm going to give him a piece of my mind!"

Before I can stop her, she stomps over to Augustin and tries to kneecap him with her yoga mat.

Augustin leaps out of the way, upsetting the table holding Beth's green smoothies and making everyone in the room sigh with relief. Komal continues to berate him in a rapid-fire string of half-English, half-Hindi insults while he wipes green goo off his tie and tries valiantly not to stare at her breasts bouncing in her tiny workout bra.

I have lived long enough and read enough romance novels to recognise a future rivals-to-lovers storyline when I see it.

"Welcome, everyone!" Beth claps her hands, cutting Komal off mid-insult. "I'm so happy that you came to see what the new Zen and Tonic studio is all about. As well as our fabulous range of organic, natural skincare treatments, infused with secret ingredients to increase longevity and improve skin condition, we have a full schedule of wellness classes, including yoga, tantric yoga, and our brand-new beginner pole dancing classes."

Beth does a little back hook spin and body roll, and her captive audience hoots with delight.

"Why pole dancing? Well, it's good for core strength, flexibility, tone, and cardio fitness. It works the whole body and nourishes the soul, too. Everyone should get the chance to feel beautiful and sexy in their skin, and that's what pole dancing is all about." Beth points to a poster on the wall. "Did you know that pole dancing originated with this unnamed erotic dancer in Paris? She danced for Gustave Eiffel at one of his infamous parties, using a steel pole, and that gave him the idea for the luscious angles and elegant proportions of the Eiffel Tower. She brought the pole idea back to her erotic theatre in Paris, and it's been a staple of striptease ever since."

My eyes bug out of my head. How did she get *that?*

It's a Toulouse-Lautrec poster advertising La Petite Mort, although Beth has whited over my theatre's name with her studio. It wasn't the first time I ever sat for Henri – I've graced many of his works, but this was one of the most popular. I'm holding my pole and facing away from the audience, my legs draped artistically while the other arm holds out a mirror. You cannot see my face in the mirror, but you can see the details of the scarab beetle clasped at my throat, and above it, two tiny dots that might've been mistaken for blemishes in the paint. Fang marks – a signal to the bohemian Upyr of Paris that they were safe in my theatre.

I thought all copies of that poster had been destroyed after my theatre burned. How did one survive?

The back of my neck prickles.

Staring at this image of my past reminds me that as much as I've tried to lie low, someone, *anyone,* could find me and take it all away again.

My nails dig into the flyer I'm still holding, crumpling the edge.

Celeste watches me, her eyes asking questions I have no way of answering.

Beth is still yammering on about the history of pole, but I don't hear her, too mesmerised by that vision from my past. "We honour the origins of pole and the strippers and sex workers who perform it. Pole is expanding out of the club and into studios like this. To demonstrate the fun you can have in this invigorating, sensual and body-positive space, I'll be leading some volunteers in a short pole class. Let's cheer them on! Ladies, to your poles!"

Komal bounces on her feet with excitement. Behind her, Augustin's cheeks redden, but he doesn't look away.

Maisie groans. Isis struts across the floor wearing a purple tie-dyed bodysuit. Dora has gone white as a sheet.

I grit my teeth as I shrug off my bomber jacket, revealing the matching lilac workout set underneath. My Louboutin heels click against the floorboards. If I'm going to make a fool of myself for Beth's business, I'm at least going to look incredible doing it.

Beth leads us through a quick warm-up, shows us some basic spins and how to climb the pole, and then demonstrates the routine she wants us to learn. "You do a forward spin, back hook, and then twirl to the floor, body roll, point your yoni to the sky – give it a little sexy attitude, ladies, we're celebrating our divine feminine!"

"This is not the divine feminine," Dora mutters. "This is the divine comedy."

Everything Beth demonstrates is pretty simple and not that different from the moves I performed at La Petite Mort. Sexy dancing hasn't changed much throughout the ages. Beth puts on some floaty music, and as my fingers wrap around the pole, my body *remembers*.

I remember dancing. I remember losing myself in the music. I remember the warm thrill skittering down my spine when I gazed out at the crowd to rapturous applause. I remember flowers thrown at my feet and men prostrating themselves before me, mesmerised by what I could do with movement and music.

I remember the power in my body – a body that was mine to use and control, even when very little else in the world was mine.

I remember telling stories, speaking truth without saying a word, condemning everyone in the audience for their sins while making them worship me.

The music courses through me. I step. I spin. I hook my leg. I point my toes. I toss my head and run my hands over my body. My limbs wake up. My muscles groan with the weight of memories. My fangs drop and my lips curl into a smile. I grip the pole behind my knee and lean back, hanging upside down while blood rushes to my head.

I feel *alive*.

"What are you doing?" Beth cries out. "That's not in the routine. You could hurt yourself."

"Wow, Arabella, you're really good." Dora thuds to the floor.

"How do you make that look so graceful?" Maisie groans, her legs akimbo and her hand gripping the pole so hard her knuckles are white.

"Beth, help! I've trapped my hand!" Komal calls out as she hangs upside down, her hands gripping the pole in terror.

I ignore them all, focusing on moving with the music, memories releasing as my muscles loosen up. As I spin around the pole, my gaze catches someone in the corner of the room, standing beside Alaric, a rapt expression on his stupid, handsome face.

What is *Gideon* doing here?

And why is he staring at me like that?

If he's staring, says the vengeful voice inside my head, *give him something to bite down on*.

Isis is right. My plot to destroy Gideon using the tools at my disposal *is* fun. By the end of tonight, he will be at my mercy.

Then I can start figuring out how to take Sanctus from him.

I begin the choreography again, this time adding even more of my flair. The music hums in my veins. I roll my body and pretend to lick the pole. Gideon shifts uncomfortably. Triumph surges through me.

Even after one hundred and fifty years, I can still bring him to his knees.

I climb, gripping with my knees. I arch my back. I hang and twirl and flip to the floor.

I look around. Isis has fallen over. Mina has managed to climb halfway up her pole and is now stuck. Maisie's legs go in opposite directions, and she yelps in pain as she accidentally does a perfect middle split. Winnie isn't dancing. She slumps against the base of her pole, watching me through a curtain of golden hair.

While Beth is distracted by their nonsense, I sashay over to Gideon. My skin prickles, aware that I'm dressed in skin-tight workout clothes and spiked heels while he's in a full suit. But I'm the one who has the power.

"Gideon, what a surprise to see you here." I toss my head. If I still had hair, I'd have flipped it.

"I'm supporting this local fitness initiative," he says with a perfectly straight face. His eyes never leave mine, but I can tell it's taking every ounce of self-control he has not to look down at my body.

I want to strangle him. I want to dunk his head into Beth's mushroom juice until he stops wriggling. I want him to suffer. I want him to *beg*.

He will beg. I have to be patient. I have to stop being distracted by those peacock-blue eyes.

"How very community-spirited of you." I brush an invisible bit of dust from my top, trying to get his gaze to drop. "Be careful. You don't want to strain something."

His eyes follow my fingers. He lets out a low groan.

Got you.

I turn on my heel, accidentally-on-purpose rubbing my derrière against his crotch before sashaying back to help Dora untangle herself from her pole.

"Alright, dancers." Beth claps her hands. "You've had time to practise. Let's come together for a group performance."

Komal groans as she picks herself off the floor. Dora looks utterly terrified as she lines up behind her pole. I cast my eyes out to the small audience. Everyone is clapping and cheering, except for Mike, whose face has become a black storm cloud.

My eyes meet Gideon's, and suddenly, I'm not in the studio any longer. I'm back in Paris, the oil lamps burning low as sultry music wafts overhead, and although we have a full house, I'm dancing for one person only …

Beth starts the track. The bass line pounds in my chest.

"Three, two, one …" Beth counts us in, and I throw my head back and spin.

My eyes flick away, then meet his again as I complete the spin. I throw myself around the pole. The music hums through me, waking up long-slumbering bones.

A body roll. I break from Beth's choreography to freestyle, spinning and flipping, climbing and twisting my body. My skin burns where it grips the pole, but it's a good kind of burn. I drop to the floor in the splits, eliciting a gasp from the audience. Gideon's eyes never leave my face as I crawl across the floor, raising my fingers to beg for him. He bites his lip.

I run my hands over my body, arching my back, telling a story with my movements – a story that Gideon will recognise. Cool nights walking the streets of Paris with him, a secret garden, a salacious painting, a night that I told him meant nothing but that is etched permanently on my bones.

A betrayal.

A *burning*.

The music finishes. The whole room falls silent. I can feel every eye in the place on me, but there's only one pair I can see.

I'm dancing for him.

What am I *doing?*

9

Gideon

ARABELLA.

I thought I'd moved on.

I thought the thrill of seeing her again was just the two of us playing our favourite game.

But I can't …

When she dances like *that* … When she weaves magic with her body and fixes me with those gold-rimmed eyes like she is throwing daggers through my heart …

I've been fooling myself.

I'm still completely, hopelessly, obsessively in love with her.

I am so *fucked*.

10

Arabella
Then

Immorality in our city's theatres!

Our City of Light is beset with the scourge of new theatres and cabarets opening on every corner. With this new entertainment comes nudity, lewd behaviour and unseemly acts of all kinds! (So we've heard. We haven't set foot inside such houses of ill repute to confirm for ourselves. We wouldn't wish to sully our souls.)

And the most devilish of all is La Petite Mort. Rumours of dark and depraved acts swirl about this house of ardour, owned by one of our city's most notorious courtesans – absinthe and Satan worship, nudity and blood-drinking, and the proprietress swinging around a pole in defiance of gravity and good taste. Stay away!

– Catholic pamphlet nailed to doorways and streetlamps across Montmartre.

*M*INE.

The word on the mirror haunts me as I prepare backstage for the night's performance. I've already cleaned it off but I cannot shake the sense that I'm being watched, that something foul lurks in the shadows, waiting for me to let my guard down.

But we haven't had any incidents that point to danger, unless you count the golden-haired god, Gideon Rougon, appearing in the audience for a third time. As subtly as I can, I peek through the curtain and glance around, looking for Lucien Vega, but the baron of criminals is not here. One of my staff would have told me if he'd arrived. So the henchman is here by himself, sitting with Monsieur Manet and his friends, a glass of absinthe in front of him that he still does not drink.

Intriguing.

Humans *do* occasionally sneak into La Petite Mort without vampires accompanying them. I allow Manet's friends to enjoy the theatre without him because they're too involved in their work to notice all the blood-drinking going on, and because they paint and sculpt me in flattering ways. But generally, I don't allow humans here alone. They smell too tempting.

I can smell Gideon from my dressing-room – that saccharine honey and red cherry scent stirring something dark and reckless inside me. What is he doing here? Why has he returned? A man in the employ of Lucien Vega should not be here without his master. I know all too well where disobeying a powerful Upyr can lead.

And he should be wary of Manet. The famed artist and Upyr loves to add to his circle of bright, clever, artistic humans. But the problem with powerful Upyr is that they love to break their toys.

I finish painting my lips, chalk my hands, and check that the clasp on my collar is secured tightly. The beads and crystals in my headdress clink together pleasingly as I squeeze past the other dancers to wait in the wings for my cue. Gideon's scent swirls beneath my nostrils. I can't decide if he's distracting because I want to fuck him or feed on him. I'd settle for both. At the same time.

But that would be far too dangerous. I don't know why he's here or what he does for Lucien Vega. But I do know that I won't break my rules for a pretty face.

My mother taught me that if you give a man a fish, he'll have a full belly for a day. But if you push that same man into a volcano, the gods will ensure a bountiful harvest for the whole season.

That's what I do every night on stage – I make them want me so badly that they'll willingly sacrifice themselves … and their purses. La Petite Mort won't flourish if I give them the fish for free.

Gideon Rougon can't afford me. All he gets of me is this moment, right now.

He'd better enjoy it.

I hope he enjoys it.

I have no time to consider where that thought came from. My stomach flutters with anticipation as I step out onto the stage to the rising applause of the crowd. I soak myself in their adulation. The music begins – a harp and drum this time, a song I learned in Egypt two decades ago. The beat matches the slow thrum of my blood in my veins. A vampire's pulse.

I raise my head, bathing my skin in the warm stage lanterns, allowing the audience to drink their fill of me in my finery. Although the room is dark, my eyes immediately land on Gideon. He reclines at Manet's side, looking every bit the arrogant prince. His aquamarine eyes glint like chips of precious stone. His lips curl back into a knowing smirk, and all I want in the world is to sharpen his arrogance into a blade I can use to cut out those pretty eyes.

The drum thuds. I'm so fixated on him that I almost miss my cue, which makes me even more determined to break him. I raise my arms above my head and slowly stroke them down my body, circling my hips as I caress myself in the way men imagine they touch women but rarely do – with reverence and a tiny bit of fear, the proper honours due a goddess.

I slide my leg from the sparkling folds of my gown, pointing my toes as I show off just enough skin that Gideon's eyes widen. This outfit is one of my favourites – designed especially for me by the House of Worth, the fabric is bejewelled in diamond patterns to resemble a snake's skin. I can't help the smile tugging at the corners of my mouth as I reach behind my back to unlace the skirt.

The crowd gasps as I drop the fabric at my feet, revealing my scaled corset and the tiny triangle of bejewelled fabric at the apex of my thighs.

I have to use glue made of gum acacia, sugar and corn starch to hold it in place, but the hours of picking dried gum acacia from my nethers are worth it for the effect it has on Gideon Rougon.

His eyes are as wide as two moons, his lips pursed together, his hand clasped to his chest as if his heart has stopped.

I love it.

I spin on my heel and step up to my pole. We've rigged a system into the base that allows the pole to spin freely so that when I twirl around, it twirls with me, creating a dizzying effect that leaves my audience reeling. I spin, hooking my leg, losing myself in the music and the whirling, flickering lights. Every time my gaze falls on the audience, it lands right back on Gideon.

I hang upside down, my curly hair fanning out beneath my jewelled headdress as I unclasp my corset and tease them with what's beneath. Gideon squeezes his eyes shut, appearing to be physically in pain as I toss away my corset, leaving me spinning in only my jewelled pasties and the glittering collar around my neck.

My bedazzled armour protects me from men like Gideon, reminding me always where I came from and what I need to do to keep this life I've made for myself.

I flip from the pole onto the stage, landing in the splits. The audience gasps and applauds as the curtain rolls down. The last thing I see before the stage is plunged into darkness is Gideon's twin cobalt eyes, wide with awe and longing.

"You were sublime, as usual." Catherina puffs her cigarette in my face as I hurry backstage to change. "You should be on a bigger stage, dancing beside Sarah Bernhardt, not slumming it here with us in Montmartre with the moralists out for our heads."

"I'm exactly where I'm meant to be." I wince as I remove the pasties, taking the gum acacia and a chunk of skin with them. Secretly, I think she's right. I'd give anything to have a career like Sarah, to have her easy freedom without the constant need to ensure I have a man enthralled. I finger the jewelled collar still affixed around my neck. "And I'd like to see the church come for my head. Good luck getting through this armour of gold and stone."

"Do you think the person who broke in was one of them?" Catherina asks as she expertly glues on false eyelashes. "They may be trying to scare us out of business. Or maybe it was that creepy Upyr with the scar who sits in the corner all night nursing a single glass of blood—"

"Mademoiselle Macquart," Jacques, our muscle, pokes his head into the dressing-room. "There is a fella out here wants to speak to you. The same one from the other night. I've threatened to weave his intestines into a summer *chapeau*, but he's insisting."

With his towering stature and ropes of muscles, Jacques cuts an imposing figure even without his fangs, but he's an absolute teddy bear who has no wish to weave anyone's innards into a delightful hat.

I groan. "Can't you put his head through a wall? I'm not allowing admirers backstage, especially not after last night."

"He says he knows you. He told me to give you this."

Jacques holds up a pretty porcelain plate, the scalloped edges resplendent with blue flowers that perfectly match the lapis lazuli scarab clasped at my throat. Upon the plate is a cold slice of pizza covered in foie gras and oysters, and a note. The crooked handwriting reads:

The gastronomic equivalent of finger painting.

Gideon.

"Yes, fine. I'll speak to him." I rise to my feet, wrapping a silk dressing gown around myself and belting it low to give a tantalising slash of my dark skin and glittering collar. Catherina raises an eyebrow, but she's too afraid of me to say a thing. I glare back at her, making it clear she's not to follow me, and walk with Jacques to the curtain that separates backstage from the theatre patrons.

Gideon waits at the curtain, his grin no longer smug but lopsided, hopeful. "Mademoiselle Macquart."

His voice is blood and chocolate, sliding hot and rich down my throat. He bows deeply, those golden curls glimmering beneath the oil lamps.

"Monsieur Rougon." I hold out the plate to him. "If you're attempting to impress me, you have failed. This pizza is cold."

"If it were warm, would it impress you?"

I wrinkle my nose in disgust, and Gideon laughs. "It's from Monsieur Hugo's favourite *pizzeria*."

I drop the plate into Jacques' beefy hands. "The man ate rat pâté. I don't trust his tastes."

"Then you are a woman of far more intelligence than I." He holds his stomach and makes a face. "I had three slices."

"My condolences to the person who cleans your privy."

Gideon holds out his hand. "Do you have more enchantments to weave on stage tonight, or may I buy you a drink?"

In my mind, I tell him that I'm working, that if he wants my company he must pay for more than a drink, and that he is an infernal annoyance who is no longer welcome at my theatre, but what happens is that my mouth opens and one word slips out: "Yes."

I blame the scent of his blood, hot and sweet and eager.

I lead Gideon to one of the unoccupied VIP booths and order cocktails from Séraphine. He settles himself onto the plush Louis XV chair opposite me, looking every bit like he deserves to be here. Our drinks arrive – a cocktail of blood and tomato juice, because I've deduced that Gideon doesn't drink alcohol, and I have a theory I want to test. We sip. Gideon makes a face and sets down his glass.

"I don't know why Lucien loves the bartenders here so much." Gideon coughs into his hand. "This drink tastes like an abattoir."

Interesting. He still doesn't know we're drinking blood.

I swipe his drink from the table and gulp it down. Gideon makes me feel untethered. I need the blood to bring me back to myself. "More for me. Your master isn't with you."

"I'm by myself tonight." He inclines his head towards me in a mock gentlemanly manner. I study the smooth skin of his neck. "And Lucien's not my *master*. He's a client. I'm my own man."

He's delusional.

This can only end badly.

I stand. "I'll need you to return to Monsieur Manet's table."

"Pardon? We haven't finished our drinks."

I wave two empty glasses in his face.

"Fine, *you* finished our drinks. But that's only because they were disgusting."

"Taste is subjective." I wave my hand at the door. "Except for my taste, which is immaculate and above reproach. As were these cocktails. Now go. We reserve these rooms for our more distinguished, *paying* guests. If Lucien is not joining you—"

"*Please.*" Gideon grabs my wrist midair. My skin sizzles where his fingers touch. I haven't felt the warmth of a human body for a long, long time. "Indulge me. I can pay you."

I twist my arm, breaking his grip and grabbing his wrist. I slam his hand down on the table, hard enough that I may break fragile human bones.

"There are many pleasures for sale at La Petite Mort, Monsieur Rougon." I fix him with one of my withering glares. "I am *not* one of them."

"Understood." His eyes bug out as he tries to free his hand, but a human man cannot compete with my strength. "I didn't mean that you were for sale. I merely meant that I know a lady's time is her own, and I would not presume to take up yours without adequate compensation."

"I have work to do." I feel myself wavering. It's those eyes like jewels, that voice of blood and honey.

I could *devour* him.

I *want* to devour him.

"You are a courtesan. I find it difficult to believe that you are backstage sweeping the floors. Come." He gestures to the seat, then winces at his hand. "Sit with me. Smile at me again and I might let you break more of my fingers."

There are a million reasons why I should deny him, or snap his wrist, or drive the silver-inlaid knife I keep in my corset through his palm. And yet …

"Fine." I tilt my chin as I release his hand. "But any part of you that touches me again, I'll cut off."

"That seems reasonable."

We settle into our chairs, facing the stage. Séraphine arrives with another round of drinks, setting down first an elaborate glass and a gold fountain filled with ice water, and then a fresh apple juice for him and a bloodsinthe for me. Gideon eyes my drink with interest but does not comment.

Good boy.

I set my glass beneath the fountain and turn on the faucet, allowing the ice water to slowly drip onto a sugar cube, melting it into my drink and turning the absinthe a milky colour – *la louche*. Once the glass is three quarters full, I pour in the shot of blood.

We clink glasses. I watch the stage as our cancan chorus enters. This high-energy, raunchy dance style is taking over the Paris theatres, but as always, La Petite Mort adds our twist to the spectacle. Our dancers' bodies are painted with white bones. Their peacock feathers are adorned with white paint, and instead of being lively and upbeat, the music is haunting and surreal. They are the *danse macabre.*

I glance over at Gideon, expecting him to be enthralled by the mostly naked women prancing across the stage. Instead, I have to suppress a delighted shudder when I see that his eyes remain fixed on me.

"An interesting theme for a cancan," he says, that obnoxious left eyebrow arching like a gothic cathedral roof. "The *danse macabre.* Is this your choreography?"

"It is." I lift my chin.

"You have quite the fascination with death."

"Death is the last great equaliser," I answer. "Poet or politician, fisherman or king, we will all meet death in the end. It is up to you whether you run screaming from your fate or greet Death with a smile and a curtsey."

Or, in the case of some of us, cheat Death of his prize.

I touch my finger to my collar, a symbol of the life I carved for myself with bloody, broken hands, the life that I stole from another who didn't deserve it.

Gideon regards me as he sips his drink. I ask him about his work. Men come to places like La Petite Mort to talk about themselves, to feel for a few precious moments as though they are so powerful and clever that they can be adored by us. One of the first lessons my mother taught me was that behind the walls of our boudoir, women hold the power.

But Gideon brushes off my questions. "I want to know more about you, about this place."

I tell him the usual story that suffices for humans in polite company – that I followed a lover to Paris, was entranced by the stage, and left the lover but not the city.

It does not satisfy Gideon. He picks at each detail, turning them over in his mind and asking ever more deep and probing questions. It concerns me that I might reveal a hole in my story, a chink in my armour through which this human man might undo me.

Thankfully, Zola and Renoir get into a fistfight over Zola's opinion of Renoir's new work, which Zola is declaring looks like an elephant threw up onto a gooseberry bush.

He's not wrong, but I'd never say such a thing to Renoir. Artists can be so temperamental.

Still, at least they're not as bad as *poets*.

Gideon leans over the balcony and calls down encouragement as Renoir and Monet get Zola into a headlock and threaten to dunk his head in the privy until he admits that Renoir is the greatest artist of all time. By the time they're done with their shenanigans, the room is in uproar, and Jacques has to circle in an intimidating manner to restore calm.

"My brother would love it here." Gideon waves at his friends. His eyes flutter closed briefly, long eyelashes tangling together. "He had dreams of being an artist. He is good, very good. He could submit work to the Salon or find a wealthy patron, but he spends far too little time with brush in hand and far too much time with his head in a bottle or between some *grisette*'s legs. He takes after my father like that."

Ah, so that is why Gideon doesn't touch alcohol.

I understand all too well how vice turns men into monsters.

"You should send him here. We have plenty of amusements for men with bottomless purses and little ambition."

Gideon looks away, his mood suddenly sombre. I find myself wishing to pull him back into my aura, longing for that cheeky human who looks ready to fall to his knees for me.

"I am no artist," I say. "I prefer to be a muse."

"I don't believe that for a second. I saw you dance."

I scoff. "Dancing is a *profession*. It's a mask you wear to entertain, to tell a story. It's not art the way Monsieur Manet and his friends do it."

"I watched you, Arabella." Gideon leans forward, his eyes dancing. "You had this expression on your face I've only seen before on my brother when he's in the middle of a painting. You went somewhere else. You transcended. You may have conceived that dance for the audience, but you perform it for *you*."

Never before has someone stripped my desires so bare, nor cared enough to correct me on a lie.

"I'm visiting the Louvre tomorrow," he says, not waiting for me to answer. "Would you like to join me?"

"The museum is only open during the daylight hours," I say.

"And?"

"During the day, I sleep." I gesture to myself. "All of *this* happens while I sleep."

"You cannot make an exception?"

"I cannot."

No matter how much I might wish to.

"As you wish." Gideon leans back in his chair, that carefree grin back in place. This time, it looks a little uncertain, as if he's realised for the first time that he's playing a game and he's unlikely to win. "Perhaps another time."

I don't reply. There will never be another time for me and the daylight.

Gideon moves on, his mind whirring over a series of topics so fast that I can barely keep up. He talks about arriving in Paris from his family's country home, about his brother's financial woes, about what he was doing during the brutal suppression of the Commune (cowering in a cowshed outside of the city, probably eating rats), about Sarah

Bernhardt and how she should be our queen, and about me, peppering me with questions that leave me breathless.

I thought I'd left behind such petty, human emotions, but Gideon's candour makes me long for my youth, when I believed in things like love everlasting, family loyalty, and men who were kind and good.

Too soon, Séraphine pokes her head into our private room and informs me that the curtain has come down and did I wish her to put out the oil lamps?

I rise from my chair. I hadn't even noticed the musicians stopped playing. "No, you go on home. I will see to it. Please escort Monsieur Rougon to the entrance."

"I would like to walk you home," Gideon says. "It's dangerous out on the streets for a lady."

I crack my knuckles. "I am more concerned for the safety of anyone who crosses me."

"I believe that." Gideon takes my hand in his and brings it to his lips, brushing a kiss over my knuckles. "You are a formidable, evil temptress, Arabella. You may be the queen of sin, but I wish fervently to be your favourite."

I bow my head, not giving him an answer. I don't trust myself to speak.

It's always better to keep a man guessing, hoping for another scrap of your attention. I've already broken too many of my own rules tonight.

Gideon's hand slips from mine, and I have to fight the urge to grab it again and press it to my cheek.

He heads downstairs with Séraphine. She tosses her head back and laughs at something he says. A bolt of jealousy pierces my chest. Séraphine will happily lie on her back for a bit of extra cash, and I doubt Gideon Rougon can resist her charms.

It's for the best, I tell myself as I listen to Séraphine's grating laugh. *I will break him. This unnatural hunger gnawing at my stomach will drain him dry.*

And if I took him to bed, there's a tiny chance ... a faint possibility ... that he could break me.

I won't allow that.

The door closes behind them. I'm alone.

I brush my fingers over my collar. My eyes flutter closed, and I remember the queen who last wore these jewels.

Cleopatra fell in love, gave up her power to a man, and her story ended in tragedy. I cannot allow that to be me. I won't lose my empire over pretty aquamarine eyes.

A great weariness overcomes me. I dart downstairs and step backstage, heading for the dressing-room. I'm eager to return to my lodgings and bathe. Maybe I can wash the scent of Gideon from my skin—

What is that?

I'm drawn to a bouquet of lilies sitting on my dressing table. Jacques must have placed them there for me, from one of my admirers. My head swims as a cloying sweet scent touches my nostrils.

I must truly be going mad. How can I smell Gideon when he's no longer here?

I take a step closer to the bouquet. A note hangs from the ribbon, and it says only one word.

MINE.

My heart thuds.

The flowers look *wrong*. My hand flies to my mouth as I see—

They are drenched in blood.

11

Arabella

Damien: Dearest sweet Arabella, I need some funds, *fast*. How quickly can you convert sixteen pounds of Knights Templar treasure into cash? It's mostly jewel-encrusted crucifixes, etc, but there are some saints' bones and old hunks of wood that might be from the ark. Call me, darling!

"Arabella, you were amazing. How did you DO that?" Beth squeals. The Nevermore Coven crowd around me, excitement and awe on their faces.

"You're like a human pretzel." Komal jiggles my arm. "You defied gravity! I can't believe you never told us you could dance."

"Of course she didn't tell us. Arabella has to maintain her status as a woman of mystery and intrigue," Isis declares. "Unfortunately for her, I saw a vision of her performance. I knew months ago. That's the advantage of being a powerful clairvoyant. But I didn't say anything because it's Arabella's secret to tell."

"How very magnanimous of you." Dora shoots her sister a look, then rubs my shoulder affectionately. "I wish I had your grace. Or your bravery."

Her smile is warm, but her eyes are wide with fear, her gaze locked on the crowd behind me. I don't have to turn around to know she's watching Mike. He has been worse lately, his behaviour going from disagreeable to controlling. It might be time he received a visit from the unfriendly neighbourhood vampire. But first, I have to extricate myself from a revenge plan that's working only too well.

Winnie throws her arm around me. "You are incredible. I'm so honoured to have you as a friend."

My cheeks burn. Winnie is a new friend, and although I'm wary of new people, especially humans who've recently become aware of the supernatural world, she's quickly become an important part of my life. My whole body hums with warmth, a strange sensation for a vampire.

I haven't danced since the day I left Paris. After Gideon took everything from me, I lost the ability to feel the music. So why did it come back tonight, of all nights, while he was watching?

Maybe this giddy sensation has nothing to do with the dance. Maybe it has more to do with the anonymous message I just sent to a high-ranking client reporting Gideon's attendance at Beth's pole studio, to make his position with the Conclave even more precarious?

"Seriously, Arabella, you've done this before." Beth plants her hands on her hips. "I've been having lessons for six months and I can't do half those moves."

"I used to be a dancer," I murmur. "In a previous life."

A life that Gideon Blake stole from me.

"I know it's hard to believe, but Arabella is being modest."

I stiffen at the sound of Gideon's smooth voice. He stands behind Beth, disgusting mushroom drink spiked with blood in hand, impeccably tailored suit hugging his body, his mouth quirked in that cheeky half-smile of his. The old, polished Gideon is back, his mask firmly in place. Does he know what I saw while I was dancing?

Did he *intend* for me to witness the pain in his eyes or the raw wound of his lips?

We're both playing games with each other, and I *abhor* losing.

"Arabella? Modest?" Komal's eyebrows shoot waaaay up. "Those things go together like … like two things that don't go together."

Gideon's gaze flicks to each of my friends, drawing their attention while avoiding meeting my eyes. "Arabella wasn't simply a dancer. This majestic creature once graced the stage at La Petite Mort, the most secretive and notorious cabaret theatre in Paris."

"I didn't grace the stage. I *owned* it." I glare at Gideon, but he's not looking at me. And he won't *shut up.*

"In fact, Beth, I'm pretty sure the woman on your poster is a certain grumpy vampire temptress we all know and love." Gideon holds out his hand. Wordlessly, Beth peels one of the old Toulouse-Lautrec posters from the wall and hands it to him. The girls crowd around it, peering at my portrait while I silently plot all the ways I might separate Gideon's head from his body.

"You can't see the model's face, but it sure looks like Arabella." Komal's eyes are two round saucers.

"Arabella, did you *invent* pole dancing?" Beth's voice rises an octave. "Vampires are so fabulous, it's annoying."

"Why don't you all talk louder?" I hiss. "I don't think *every* person in Argleton has heard my secrets."

I glance around the crowd, that creeping sensation of being watched prickling at my neck again.

"Look at your corset!" Dora whispers, hugging her oversized sweater against her chest. "And those jewels around your neck. You're so glamorous. I wish—"

Whatever Dora is about to say next is cut off with a whimper when her husband grabs her arm and yanks her out of our circle.

"Mike, you're hurting me," Dora cries.

"We're leaving. *Now.*" Mike glares at Beth, the vein above his eye pulsing in a way that would make me hungry if only his blood weren't so unappetising. Rage can make humans smell like brussels sprouts. "I can't believe you made my wife take her clothes off and grind her arse in front of the whole village."

"It's just a bit of fun." Beth coos in her calming yoga voice. "We're all adults here. Why don't we go out to the lobby, have a mushroom shake, and I'll explain to you—"

"You think a bunch of leering men ogling my wife is *fun*?" Mike glares at Gideon. "He's the worst of them, with his jaw on the ground and his tongue out like a panting dog."

Gideon *is* the worst, but Mike is a close second with this nonsense. I will not stand for anyone hurting my friends.

"Better a panting dog laying at my goddess' feet than a jealous arsehole who doesn't even know he *has* a goddess," Gideon says breezily. "And I wasn't looking at your wife. No offence, Dora."

"None taken," she says glumly.

"*You* should have been watching your wife, instead of watching me, because you missed the most beautiful thing in the world – raw female sexuality." Gideon pats Mike's shoulder affectionately, like a father advising a son. "Remember that for next time."

"There will be no next time." Mike's face is as red as arterial spray. People in the crowd behind him stare at their shoes, doing the typical British thing of pretending they're not profoundly uncomfortable. No one intervenes. "I'm getting this place shut down."

No matter what century we're in, there are always men afraid of the power of women.

My fangs slide down, itching to sink into Mike's neck, despite the foul scent, and give him something to really be upset about. But one terrified look from Dora and I stop myself. She doesn't want us to interfere, especially not in front of everyone.

As much as I yearn to introduce Mike's testicles to the knife I keep in my boot, I don't want to do anything that will cause Dora more hurt. But Mike should watch his back.

No one – *no one* – gets away with hurting my friends.

Dora tugs on his arm. "Mike, please don't—"

"Get in the car." Mike yanks Dora towards the door. "You're not going to make a fool of me in front of the whole village. I don't want you to set foot in this place or talk to *those women* ever again."

"That's Dora's decision, don't you think?" Beth says sweetly.

"Please, Beth," Dora begs. "It's fine. I just want to go home."

"That's my sister you're manhandling." Isis steps forward, her hands clenched into fists. "If you hurt her, I will curse you so that every two-factor authentication you try to complete will be unnecessarily complicated—"

"I'm the man in my relationship, Isis, not you. It's my job to handle this." Mike laughs woodenly. "And unlike Gideon here, I'm a *real* man. Real men don't need to look at strippers or hurt their wives. But they also don't tolerate being humiliated. We're going home, and I don't want to see or hear from any of you. And no filling our letterbox with hex bags again, either."

"You can't keep me from my sister!" Isis yells.

"Watch me!" he shouts back.

Before Isis can reply, Mike drags Dora out of the studio, slamming the door behind him so hard the wall shakes.

"He's a pleasant fellow." Gideon's eyes narrow at the door as the room returns to a normal level of conversation.

"One of these days, I swear I really will curse that bastard." Isis is shaking all over.

"To do that, you'd need actual magical powers," I remind her, although more gently than usual, because for once she and I are in agreement.

Isis cradles her head in her hands. "Thanks for bringing that up, Arabella, and reminding me that the Meriwether sister who has real magic refuses to use it to put her mean husband in his place."

"Will he really stop us from seeing Dora?" Winnie's lip wobbles. She hasn't seen one of Mike's outbursts, which are getting more frequent.

"He'll calm down in a few days and forget about what he said. But he doesn't like us very much." Beth sighs. "I guess that's only going to get worse now that I run the studio and we know Arabella used to be an erotic dancer."

"He never used to be like this," Isis sniffs. "He was always a grump and a killjoy, but I've never seen him grab Dora like that. I don't know what's changed him, and Dora doesn't want us to interfere."

Dora doesn't need to know.

A silence settles over our group.

Gideon meets my eye and the rage I see there mirrors my own. He nods once, flashing me a slow smile with a sliver of fang.

"You ladies should have seen Arabella's theatre." Gideon waves his arms dramatically, smoothly changing the subject. "It had this wild gold-and-crystal chandelier, velvet-lined booths, dancers dressed as Egyptian goddesses, Greek monsters, and Countess Bathory, and these creepy religious statues over the stage that would sometimes drip fake blood on the audience."

"Excuse me, that was *real* blood," I correct him. "I had to keep the vampire patrons coming back. And in the middle of all of this was poor innocent human Gideon, with no idea that every Upyr in the place wanted to suck his neck."

"You were a human when you two met?" Winnie squints at Gideon in surprise.

"I was. Innocent and mortal and naive, although after a few visits to Arabella's theatre, I could no longer claim any of those things." Gideon's wicked smile makes my fingers itch to slap him. "I wish you all could have seen it. La Petite Mort was exquisite. It makes my little enterprise at Sanctus look like a cheap student pub."

"Oh yes, when are we going to get to visit your famous private Sanctus Club?" I allow my voice to drip with sarcasm as if I couldn't care less what was inside.

Secretly, I want to know. There might be something in that club I can use against him. But I'm not going to ask. I want Gideon to invite me. I don't understand why he hasn't.

Arabella Lestrange believes that a door closed to her is a door that should be burned down.

"Yeah, we want to go to your secret club!" Komal bounces up and down.

"We promise we'll behave. I'll bring along my tarot cards and do readings for your guests," adds Isis.

"I'll make Alaric come along. He can complain about the noise, bore people's ears off with long, in-depth discussions of sculpting techniques, and make us leave before ten pm so we can shag." Winnie rubs her hands together in excitement.

"And Winnie can colour code all the stemware," adds Mina. "I promise to get drunk, trip over things, and drag Heathcliff up on stage to sing karaoke. There is karaoke, right?"

"It's not a karaoke kind of place. And I'm sorry, but no humans allowed unless you're offering your neck." Gideon licks his lips. "An offer I'd be foolish to refuse."

"You're not drinking from my friends," I growl, placing myself between Winnie and Gideon.

"Not even if Arabella agrees to dance there?" Winnie flicks her gaze to me.

"*Especially* not then. I'd want her all to myself." Gideon's eyes ignite at the edges. The fire burns all the way through my ice-encrusted heart.

"I cannot believe you were a dancer." Beth stares at the poster in disbelief.

"You said you worked in banking!" Isis cries.

I glare at her. "No, I said I worked *bankers*. And European royalty. And occasionally a vampire mobster or two. If you don't live your life in danger of being burned by the church for lascivious and immoral acts, then are you really living?"

The Nevermore Coven crowd around me, pushing Gideon out as they pepper me with a million questions. Quiet panic rises in my chest. I don't want the attention on me. Arabella Macquart is a woman from a century ago. I'm not her any longer, and I have very good reasons for ensuring she remains dead and buried. I have no intention of digging her up and making her dance for their amusement.

A wicked idea occurs to me; a way to distract from my past and inflict more pain where it's deserved. I grab Gideon's arm and drag him into the centre of the studio.

"Attention, everyone!" I clap my hands. People stop in the doorway, their heads turning back to me. "The grand opening isn't finished yet. Since Gideon Blake is so community-minded, he's agreed to demonstrate that *anyone* can enjoy one of Beth's classes. Gideon is excited about awakening his divine feminine, aren't you?"

Gideon's grin wobbles. "Um, I don't think I can—"

"Nonsense. A big, strapping man like you will have no trouble pole dancing." I wrap his fingers around the pole and stamp my heel on the floor. "Now, spin!"

Gideon throws out his hips in an exaggerated grinding motion that has everyone laughing. "Like this?"

Damn him. I forgot that Gideon is practically immune to embarrassment. I kick his foot. "Point those toes, Gideon Blake. We are creating magic here, not impersonating a herd of elephants. Now *climb.*"

Gideon was definitely not listening when Beth explained the mechanics of climbing the pole because he leaps into the air and wraps his legs around the chrome stick like a spider monkey. His whole face goes white with terror as he realises that he has no idea how to untangle himself.

I am giddy with delight.

"Now, swing!" I demonstrate by executing two perfect, pointy-toe climbs to give myself some height, before grabbing the pole in both hands and gracefully swinging my legs out from the pole and landing in a seat with chrome between my legs. I lean back, arching into a graceful pose.

"Easy!" Gideon hugs the pole for dear life as he inches his way higher. Beth looks on nervously. This is not what we're supposed to be doing on her opening night.

Once he's another foot off the ground, Gideon tries to copy my swing. He slams into the pole, catching the brunt of his weight right between his legs.

"Aaaaaah!" he wheezes.

Every woman in the audience cracks up laughing.

Every man winces.

Gideon slides down the pole with a sickening *screech*, his face twisting in pain. Beth runs over as he collapses at the base, clutching his ruined jewels.

Serves you right, Gideon Blake. You steal my jewels. I break yours.

"Are you okay?" Beth cries as she tries to get him to unclench his hands from his crotch. "Is there anything I can do? Perhaps a soothing massage. Or, I know, get into the tree pose. That will help align your chakras—"

"I need ... air ... " Gideon rolls onto his back, curling into a ball like a misunderstood hedgehog.

"Pole dancing is a dangerous business," I say. "Perhaps Gideon should be more careful."

Gideon tries to say something, but all that comes out is a gasp.

Maisie rushes over, clutching her pet duck in her arms. "You're so encouraging, Arabella. You know, the variety show fundraiser needs more acts. I think you'd be perfect."

I grit my teeth. I'd been planning to make an anonymous donation to fund the newspaper and keep Maisie's job, but before I could write the cheque, Beth and Maisie had concocted their absurd variety show plan. "I don't perform any more. Tonight was a favour to Beth."

"You wouldn't have to perform," Maisie nudges me. "You'd be the director! You put the show together, run the rehearsals, and create the overall vision. Please? As a favour to me? James Pond thinks you'd be amazing."

She holds up the duck. He's dressed in a sparkly bow tie and a hat with bobbing peacock feathers that makes me think of the feathers Catherina used to unfurl on stage.

"Quack?" James Pond begs, giving me big, duck eyes that match Maisie's.

"Please?" Maisie begs.

"No."

"PLEEEEASE?"

"No."

"With a cherry on top?" Maisie clasps her hands together over James's breast. "You'll be perfect. You're an actual showgirl."

"I wasn't merely a showgirl. I was an entrepreneur."

"Well, can you see your way to lending that damn fine entrepreneurial arse to managing this thing for me so I get to keep my job?"

"QUAAAACK?"

I sigh. "Fine."

Maisie does a double take. "You'll really do it?"

"Yes. I'll direct the bloody variety show. Anything to get the duck out of my face."

Maisie throws herself at me, wrapping me in her arms. "Thank you, thank you!"

"Quaaack!" James Pond flaps his wings in protest as he's trapped between us.

"Not so fast." I frown at her as I extract myself and pull duck feathers from down my sports bra. "I have two conditions. The first is that I'm not doing it on my own. I'm moving house. I have client work. I have to spy on Gideon. I'll need help."

"The Nevermore Coven can help with your move! Winnie could organise. I could pack boxes. Isis will cleanse the new house, and Celeste could bring us packing snacks when she finally gets back from her mum's—"

"That would require you all to enter my home, a thing that will absolutely not be happening."

"Fine, it was worth a shot. I'll find you an assistant. I promise." Maisie hugs James to her chest. "What's the second condition?"

A slow smile creeps across my face. "For the next three years, I expect every text message or conversation you start with me to begin with 'Arabella, O Magnificent One'."

"Deal." Maisie beams. "I'm sorry, I mean, we have a deal, Arabella, O Magnificent One."

What have I got myself in for now?

Message from the Conclave on the Sepulchrr App

Dearest subjects of the Midnight, Nightshade, and Dusk Courts,

The latest shocking news from Sanctus Estate: owner Gideon Blake was seen in the village of Argleton attending a pole dancing event, surrounded by scantily-clad dancers, both human and vampire! Alaric Valerian and his human consort were also in attendance, openly flaunting their disregard for our sacred laws.

This fiend clearly hasn't given up his criminal ways. Can we doubt Gideon's involvement in the huskings any longer? Upyr who associate with Gideon Blake and Sanctus Estate risk being drawn into activities that place the entire vampire community at risk.

We urge all vampires who are thinking of investing in or living on Sanctus Estate to reconsider.

The Conclave

19,021 Dig This   669 Resurrections

Message from Lord Hamish Aeturnus on the Sepulchrr App

To all my followers, I'm making a public statement about the Sanctus Estate project.

It has come to my attention that Gideon Blake, the billionaire real estate mogul in whom I have placed tremendous trust to see this project through, was for several decades the head of the infamous Vega crime family. He is responsible for numerous atrocities committed against our kin.

While we must all practise a certain amount of clemency regarding our past lives, I believe a leopard cannot change its spots. I no longer trust that Gideon Blake has the best interests of our people in his heart.

Effective immediately, I have pulled all my funding for the Sanctus project, and will no longer endorse it. For us to move forward as a society, we must have unity. While Gideon Blake has some innovative ideas, his real estate project ultimately serves to sow dissent among us. The only way we can maintain our unity is by embracing the court system that has served us well for hundreds of years.

Lord Hamish Aeternus, of the Blood Aeternus
    35,668 Dig This   1848 Resurrections

12

Gideon

Alyra: I'm so pleased I voted for Arabella to join the community. She'll liven things up around here, no pun intended. See if you can make her agree to do a vampire pole dancing class. I bet she'll have lots of attendees.

I don't care what's all over Sepulchrr. I adore living in Sanctus. You don't need Aeternus's money!

I hope your plums aren't too smushed. Can you send Sinead over to my place? I'm feeling a little peckish.

"Do you need anything else?" Sinead presses the icepack into my crotch.

"I'm fine, thanks." I try to shove her hand away, but she's relentless. My phone's been buzzing with a frantic screed of messages, but I haven't even been able to pick it up off the table. "What's not helping is you turning my gonads into a Scandinavian ice hotel."

Sinead pouts as she reluctantly removes the icepack. "I can't believe Arabella did this to you."

"Technically, I did it to myself."

"She cackled like a witch. She's evil."

"Sure, she's evil, but I'm her *favourite*." I go to roll off the couch, but she traps my thighs with hers, straddling me and grinding down a little, sending a fresh spasm of pain through my ruined gonads.

"Are you sure she's not Dusk Court? Because she's got you under her spell. I know what will help."

Sinead undoes the top button of her blouse and tugs down the fabric, offering her neck. It's the same move she pulled on me at her job interview, where she revealed she'd known about vampires for many years and was excited to work among us. I can see the faint scars from previous bites. I try to be careful and only open the same wounds when I drink from humans. Sinead's skin won't heal like ours, and she's too young and pretty to have a neck covered in puncture wounds. But some of our other members aren't as careful.

My stomach growls. I *am* thirsty. But for some reason, the idea of biting down on Sinead's neck while she moans in my arms is anything but tempting.

I try to duck under her, but she blocks me. "Come on, Gideon. You know you'll feel better after a drink."

"How many others have drunk from you today?"

"Only Alyra," she pauses. "Oh, and Duncan had a little nibble. And I guess Eleanor, as well. But I'm *fine*. I had a big slice of cake and an electrolyte drink."

That's three vampires. And while Alyra and Eleanor might've been delicate sippers, Duncan would have drunk deep. I warned her about this. "That's too much. You can get addicted."

"I know what I'm doing. I look after myself, and I gave my consent. Enthusiastically." Her eyes glaze over in anticipation as she leans closer. "Let me help you. You need your strength."

"I'm hardly an invalid. My ego hurts more than my testicles." Not strictly true. That pole was *brutal*. "Especially since you've done such a good job with the ice."

Sinead sticks out her lower lip. "Are you *refusing*?"

She says it as if I've somehow offended her.

"You're still my most trusted employee." I pat her arm as I push her gently off me. "I'm not myself today. I'll have something from the cellar tonight."

Sinead makes a face as she buttons up her shirt. I understand. I've been enjoying her neck for weeks now, and her little groans of ecstasy tell me that she's happy with this particular job perk.

But the idea of drinking from her has lost its appeal.

Which has me puzzled. Normally, I love the Upyr–Thrall connection, the way they melt into you as you share such an intimate moment, the taste of warm blood pulsing straight from the source, and their little noises that tell you they're enjoying themselves just as much as you are …

But I don't want to be close to a human like that, to share that kind of intimacy, unless …

Unless I'm sharing it with *her*.

From the moment Arabella's eyes locked on mine during her dance, I was gone. I've been a fool to think I could be this close to her without being pulled under her spell. I've told myself for one hundred and fifty years that I hate her for trying to have me killed. That I'm over her.

But it is a lie.

I'm madly, impossibly in love with Arabella Lestrange.

And she hates me. And my poor squashed testicles.

But a man can dream.

Just the thought of feeding with Arabella makes my crushed cock grow hard and ready. I push Sinead away and leap off the couch before she sees my arousal and thinks it's for her.

"Thank you for your help, Sinead. Have a good night."

Sinead gathers her things and leaves in a huff. I hope she does the sensible thing and goes home to bed, instead of what I suspect she'll do, which is head downstairs to Brimstone and find another of our members who needs a feed.

As she waits for the elevator, Sinead turns and flashes me a mirthless smile. "If you want my opinion, *Sir*, you should spend a little less time chasing after that cold bitch *courtesan* Arabella, and a little more time worrying about strengthening our battlements against the coming onslaught."

"Sinead, darling, a little word of advice." I let something of the old Gideon – the Gideon who ran a successful criminal empire for several decades – into my voice as I smile at her, making sure she can see my fangs. "If you want to keep your job here, and don't want to have to swallow any of Lilac's little potions, then you will do well not to say things like that about our members. Arabella's old life is no one's business but her own."

Her eyes immediately fall to the floor. *Good.* I won't tolerate anyone calling Arabella names or shaming her for her old profession.

In the background, my phone buzzes again.

My gaze falls on the large painting of waterlilies on my wall. "Incidentally, how do you know Arabella used to be a courtesan? You know all information about clients' past lives *must* be completely private. They have to trust us. If you've been snooping in my safe—"

She has the good sense to look ashamed. "I swear, I haven't! I wouldn't even know where to find your safe! I saw her on an ad for the pole dancing studio in the village – the owner has ripped off a famous Toulouse-Lautrec poster, and it's clearly of Arabella. And Paul Badica says he remembers her from her Parisian club. He remembers things he paid her and her girls to do to him. Depraved things, even by vampire standards. He's telling anyone at Sanctus who will listen, and posting about her on Sepulchrr, which isn't helping our reputation, especially not with Hamish blowing everything up—"

I stalk towards her. "What happened with Hamish Aeturnus?"

"See?" Sinead fixes me with a look that's half triumph, half exasperation. "You're so obsessed with her, you don't even *know*. Aeturnus pulled his investment. He doesn't want his name associated with a *criminal*. As of right now, unless you can come up with more money, Sanctus is over."

The elevator arrives and she stomps inside. The doors close with a final *DING*.

Shit.

That must be why my phone's been going off. With Aeturnus out, we're done. I barely have enough in the accounts to make payroll, let alone fund the next stage of the build. If only I could pay people in treasure …

Wretchedness twists my gut. I knew I was stretching myself building this place, and that I was taking a big risk by allowing vampires to pay for their homes with treasure instead of cash. I also knew that cutting out the Conclave would have consequences, but I had to do it or else everything Sanctus stands for would be a lie. How could I claim I built a sanctuary for Upyr if I let the Conclave control it?

I never imagined that Aeturnus would turn on me. The Conclave must have got to him, which means they see me as a threat. They won't stop until they destroy this place, which won't take them long. I've poured every cent of my fortune into Sanctus. I have nothing left.

I could ask Alaric for money. He has enough of it. But if word got out that he was an investor in Sanctus he'd lose any ground he's made on changing the human–vampire laws. Callista's out for the same reason.

I *hate* this. Why ruin something that Upyr need, something that's been nothing but good for vampires, because you can't have a slice of the pie?

I flop back down on the sofa, gingerly touching my crotch and thinking about how best to approach the implosion of my life's work and my new revelation that I'm absolutely besotted with Arabella Lestrange.

Again.

Still.

Arabella hates my guts, but that's only because she doesn't know the truth about what happened.

But I'm nothing if not determined.

I'm Gideon Blake.

I can save Sanctus.

And ... I can win Arabella back.

I just need to show her that I'm sorry I stole from her, and that we can pick up where we left things in Paris.

Not even her closest friends know her like I do. I've been privy to all the secrets she's hidden from them for so many years.

She trusted me once. All I have to do is win that trust back.

Ideas begin to sprout in my mind.

How hard can it be to sweep Arabella Lestrange off her feet?

But first, I need to remind myself of *exactly* who I am.

I grab my jacket from the back of the sofa and my favourite knife from the table.

Time for a chat with a certain unworthy human.

I circle the cottage twice, my brogues crunching on Dora's prize-winning flowerbeds as I peer in the darkened windows to be certain of what I'm seeing.

Mike is sitting at the kitchen table, alone, in the dark, staring at the kettle on the stove. The kettle is not on.

His odd behaviour is almost enough to make me get back into the Lamborghini and return to Sanctus. I drove past Spell The Tea on the way in, and spied Dora and Isis inside, sharing a bottle of wine while they stuffed herbs into hex bags. I'm pleased Mike hasn't stayed true to his threat of stopping Dora from seeing her sister. And he certainly doesn't look like a man who's proud of his outburst.

But I've seen far too many men like Mike ruin the lives of people I care about.

That look on his face at the pole studio reminded me of my father. I couldn't save my family from that rotten man, but I can help Dora.

Silently, I step up to the back door. It will take a flick of my wrist to break the ancient lock, but when I twist the handle, the door opens.

I pause at the threshold. Thankfully, the mythology of vampires requiring permission to cross a threshold is nonsense. Upyr like Alaric cling to an ancient code of politeness because they prefer not to frighten their food. But I like my prey afraid. From the moment I became an Upyr, my world was one of violence.

"Hello, Mike."

He raises his head, his whole body trembling as he tries to figure out how I appeared in his kitchen. "Y-y-y-you."

"Yes. Me."

I step towards him. I don't turn on the light. I see perfectly well in the dark and I want Mike afraid. He *should* be afraid.

Blake is not my second surname. I lost a bet with Allie so he named me after one of his grim poets. For several decades, I wore the name Gideon Vega – a name that causes women to swoon and the most ancient and powerful Upyr to quake in their slippers.

The chair makes a loud *SQUEEEAK* as I slide it out. Mike winces. He twists his hands into knots. I slide into the chair opposite him and set the knife on the table, blade pointed towards him.

We both stare at the knife for several tense, silent moments.

"You have nothing to fear," I say in my friendliest voice. "Not yet, at least. I'm here for a chat."

Mike's eyes flick to my face, then back to the knife. He doesn't utter a word.

Wise man.

I taste his fear on my tongue – hot and sticky and metallic. He smells much more appetising than he did at the pole studio. I can hear his pulse pounding erratically. He's terrified. *Good.*

I hadn't planned on drinking from him, but his fear smells delicious. *Perhaps it would teach him …*

No. I think of Hamish Aeturnus's message on the Sepulchrr app, the one that's now up to 50,000 Digs. The last thing I need right now is to prove Hamish and the Conclave right about me.

"I'm here to talk about your wife."

"You … s-s-stay away from Dora."

Mike's skin is bone white. He's trembling like a Christmas trifle on a foosball table.

I've still got it.

"Dora is a remarkable woman." I steeple my fingers like a wise man imparting important truths. "I'm sure you know this, or you wouldn't have married her. Women aren't our possessions, Mike. They're not unruly pets that need discipline, or faulty tools we send back to the shop if they don't work the way we want. Women are *mythological creatures*, and our only job on this earth is to worship them and get out of their way when they need to flatten a civilisation."

"W-w-why are you telling me this?" Mike sinks lower in his chair.

"Because I think you could use a little advice, man to man. I care about Dora very much, and you need to know that trying to control her is going to end badly for you."

"But ... but *she* already told me this!"

"She? Dora?"

"No." Mike's whole body convulses with fear. "The ... the tall, scary one. Arabella. She was here just before you. Sh-sh-she—"

"She *what*, Mike?"

He whimpers, shrinking into himself.

Arabella, you wild, beautiful, sadistic creature.

Mike's face twists with agony. "She has *fangs*—"

"You mean, like these?"

I smile. My fangs slide down, their sharpened points digging into my lip.

CRASH.

Mike falls off his chair. He hits the floor hard, crying out as his tailbone crunches on the tiles. He backs away from me, sobbing loudly. "You—"

"Yes." I stand. There is nothing more I can do here that Arabella hasn't already achieved. "I trust you'll think about what I've said. I'm watching you, Mike. And so is Arabella. Have a pleasant evening. I'll put the kettle on for you. I think you could do with a calming cup of tea."

I flick on the gas hob on my way out. As I step into Dora's fragrant garden, a tall, dark shape emerges from behind an old oak tree.

"You didn't need to do that." Arabella plucks the knife from my hand and admires the silver inlay along the blade.

"I did. It may surprise you to learn that I've come to care about the Nevermore Coven as much as you do. I don't like to see my friends hurt."

"Funny, it's never bothered you in the past." She twirls the knife in her long fingers. "I already took care of Mike. And I didn't need a blade to do it."

"What did you do?" I chuckle. "He's terrified."

Arabella smiles, her fangs sliding down. They're long and curved and elegant, like everything else about her. I grow hard at the sight of them. "Keep annoying me, Gideon Blake, and you'll find out."

"Can I ask you one thing?" I shift position, hiding my crotch behind a planter of geraniums so she can't see what her presence has done to me. "Why are *you* here? I thought Arabella Lestrange was only out for herself."

She blinks.

I press my advantage. "You send a scary fellow to cut my head off—"

"I did no such thing."

"—and then disappear from Paris, the only remnant of you a torn scrap of fabric in a burning theatre. And then you show up a hundred and fifty years later, a vampire with a successful finance business, only no one knows a thing about you after you left the City of Light. You have no court affiliation. And you're the same Arabella you were back then. Aloof. Distant. Independent. Except that you're not. Winnie says that you never miss a Nevermore Coven meeting. You agree to dance in Beth's pole studio opening, even though you think it's silly. Even though it risks exposing you. And tonight you show up here to terrify Mike so that he'll treat Dora better."

She huffs. "You've been pestering Alaric and Winnie for information about me."

"Well … yes. But only because I'm curious. I ask again, why are you here tonight?"

Arabella reaches down and uses my knife to slice off the largest geranium from the pot. She smirks as she crushes it in her fingers, while I try to force my body to behave and my not-inconsiderable appendage to stay hidden behind the remaining flowers.

"The problem with curiosity is that some people don't realise that they're the cat," she simpers.

"Fine. But I get to ask another question." Something brilliant has occurred to me.

Why didn't I think of this sooner?

"You are a masochist." The knife flashes in the moonlight.

"Maybe I'm just desperate." I close my eyes. "I need your expertise. As you may have seen on Sepulchrr, Sanctus Estate just lost our biggest investor. I need to raise money, fast, or we'll have to stop construction."

"What do you need me for? In case you've forgotten, you stole the one thing I owned of great value, and you're certainly not getting your mitts on my art collection."

There it is, that upward tick of her eyebrow. She *is* interested.

Arabella believes in Sanctus. If she didn't, she never would have bought a house.

"I wouldn't dare." I hold up my hands in mock surrender. "Lots of our members paid for their homes with items. Antiques. Rare coins. Bags of gold. One of them gave me an unused first-class ticket for the *Titanic*. I let them do it because it's the only way some of them can afford to buy in. I could afford it while I had Hamish Aeturnus's money, but—"

"Oh, Gideon." She clicks her tongue in disdain. "So you have a room full of useless vampire crap you want me to turn into fast cash?"

"Got it in one. I'll make it worth your while."

"Yes, you will." She taps the knife against her chin, thinking.

I'm terrified she's going to tell me that the price for her help is for me to leave her alone and never speak to her again. But if I've read Arabella right, she's not going to say that.

"I'll take fifteen—No, twenty per cent commission."

"Done."

"*I'm* not done. Maisie has guilted me into directing this absurd variety show." Arabella twirls my knife in her long fingers. "You're going to assist me. And by assist me, I mean, do all of the work."

"I'll be your willing servant."

"I like the sound of that. *And* you're going to be part of the show," she says. "I don't know what you'll be doing on stage yet, but suffice it to say that your role will be humiliating beyond comprehension. Perhaps it will involve a meerkat costume."

It's worth it if I can save Sanctus and bask in her presence. "I agree."

"*And* you're going to give my friends and me any information we need to help solve these murders."

I sigh. So much for keeping the humans safe from this monster. "Yes, fine. Callista wants me to unmask the husker—"

"But you're less amateur detective, more master debater?"

"Damn right. I am an exceptionally cunning linguist," I grin. Arabella groans. "But if the Nevermore Coven wants to swoop in and solve this mystery for me, I'll accept their help. Is that all?"

"For now."

"You drive one hell of a bargain."

"What can I say, Blake?" She plucks a second geranium from the pot and tucks it behind her ear. "I know my worth."

13

Arabella
Then

Miss Macquart, I am writing to conclude our business regarding the death of one Lord John Astor, Earl of Aylmere, last residing in Cairo, Egypt. Enclosed within is my report. You will find it thorough. I would usually leave out the more grotesque details in deference to the constitutions of my lady clients, but you have assured me you are no lady, so I have included such details as would lead you to the same conclusion as I.

After exhaustive investigation and one late-night excursion into a cemetery with shovel and pickaxe in hand, which I never wish to repeat, I can assure you that Lord John Astor is thoroughly dead.

I appreciate your business and your prompt payment of my expense claim for cleaning the grave dirt out of my best suit.

Please never contact me again.
Sincerely, C. Auguste Dupin

GIVEN HOW POORLY MEN HANDLE REJECTION, I EXPECT THAT TO be the last I see of Gideon, but he returns the following night.

I'm on the VIP balcony, schmoozing with a Hungarian cardinal who is considering taking two of my girls back to a confessional when

Gideon saunters into the theatre, his golden hair annoyingly tousled from the windy streets. He reeks of honey and human blood. Gideon pays the entrance fee and scans the room, those piercing eyes taking in the residents at each table before casting upward and settling on me.

"Arabella." He leaps the stairs two at a time. "I want to—"

I hold up my hand. "You cannot come up here."

"But you're up there."

"Yes, and this area is for our VIP clientele." I gesture to the cardinal, who is frowning into his purse, annoyed that Gideon has interrupted our business.

"What was last night, then?" Gideon's cobalt eyes twinkle.

"A mistake that cannot be repeated."

"Fine." He fishes out a battered purse from his pocket and tips coins into his hand. "What will it cost for you?"

I laugh. "I don't go to bed with theatre guests."

"When we go to bed together, Arabella Macquart, it will be because you beg me, not because I have paid for the pleasure." He grins as he holds out a pile of coins in his fist. "I wish to spend the evening in the pleasure of your company, even if I have to pay for the honour."

As if I would ever beg a man for anything.

I'd like to slap that self-righteous grin from his smart mouth, but the coins he casually drops into my palm are heavy and real. And I need them.

I spent most of my savings to pay Dupin, but it was a worthwhile expense. Now, I know for certain that my old sire has not somehow returned from the dead to claim what he feels is his. The creepy words and blood-soaked flowers were definitely Astor's style, but they must be from an admirer of one of my other ladies. I have offered Jacques an extra purse if he conducts a discreet investigation locally, asking around in the coffee houses and bistros of Montmartre about someone obsessed with the courtesans of La Petite Mort.

Whoever is writing these messages and leaving these gifts, we will find them, and I will deal with them.

But at least it is not Astor. Even a vampire as old and sadistic as Lord John Astor dies like a dog in the end.

In the meantime, I have my expenses and my new dress to pay for. And an evening with Gideon is more interesting to me than the cardinal's lecherous plans. I slip the coins into the folds of my dress and wrap my fingers around Gideon's wrist, pressing them a little firmly so that he remembers I have power over him here. I lead him to an empty confessional.

"What do you wish to do with our evening?" I ask as Séraphine brings our drinks. "Will you pepper me with more annoying questions about my personal life?"

"Will you refuse to answer them again?"

"I am in the business of creating enchantments, Monsieur Rougon. I am a blank canvas upon which men paint their dreams and fantasies. Knowing my history rather spoils the illusion."

"Not for me." He speaks with an intensity that leaves me breathless.

Perhaps my corset is too tight.

That must be it.

Gideon smiles, his face brighter than the freshly replenished oil lamps. "But no, I don't intend to unravel your mysteries tonight, Mademoiselle Macquart. I thought you might like to play a game."

"Are we not already playing a game?" I tilt my head to the side, enjoying the hard line of his jaw as he struggles to figure me out.

"If we are, I'm losing." He withdraws a backgammon box from the recesses of his suit. It's a beautiful set, inlaid with ivory and precious woods. He tips out the little pieces onto the velvet board and arranges them. "Do you always wear those jewels, even when you're not performing?"

I answer him with a question of my own. "When you fall asleep at the foot of your master's bed, do you keep a blade or pistol at your side?"

"Lucien isn't my master, and yes, of course. This is a dangerous city, and he is a man with enemies."

"This *is* a dangerous city, and I am a woman with enemies." I stroke my fingers over the jewels. "This collar is my blade."

Gideon purses his lips. He doesn't understand. How could he? He's a man. He's never had to do the things I've done.

"Are you performing tonight?" he asks.

"No. I take three nights a week off the stage to rest my body."

"It's a pity. You come alive when you dance." His gaze falls to the collar around my neck. "Not that you're not alive now. I just mean, you are different under the lights. I feel as though I can touch the moon when I watch you. Where did you learn to dance like that?"

I throw the ivory dice and move two of my men. Gideon shakes the dice and gets a double four. I watch his hand as he moves his four men, taking note of the tiny bones beneath the surface of his skin and the pulse of blood at his wrist. His honey and red cherry scent fills my nostrils, and I imagine drawing his wrist to my lips and supping my fill until we're both moaning for more …

"Are you alright?" Gideon tilts his head to the side. A golden curl flops over his eye. "You look like you're about to faint."

"Forgive me, I haven't eaten enough today." I sip my drink. The blood does little to sate my hunger for the man across from me. "Dancing is not something you learn. It's something you *are*. The music is in your veins, in your bones. I have always danced. I will always dance. That is something no one can ever take away from me. But if you mean, where did I learn to dance for men, to tempt and tease, to bring them to their knees, hoping for a taste of me? This I learned in Egypt, from my mother."

I snap my mouth shut. *Why did I say that?* I slam my men down on the board, sending two of his men to the bar at the centre.

"Then your mother is a true mistress of her craft, for your skills are immeasurable." Gideon's eyes warm. "I have a friend who is a performer of some renown in this city, an acquaintance of Lucien's, and I believe she would be eager to meet you. I hope I can arrange a meeting one day. Why did you choose this life, this theatre of the grotesque, instead of the stage at the Palais Garnier?"

"I thought you detested the opera."

"I do, but unlike me, you are a woman of refined taste."

With a smooth flick of his wrist, he tosses the dice and gets both his men off the bar, blotting one of mine. He grins at me, every perfect inch of him radiating the most infuriating sunshine.

I want to burn up in his light.

I raise my eyes to him, fixing him with my most devilish smile. I quirk my lip to the side, allowing him to see the tips of my fangs for a fraction of a second.

And I say something true.

"Because I can be myself here."

I know exactly what I expect. I know how a human should react to seeing a monster.

But that's not how Gideon reacts.

He leans *towards* me, tilting his head again. That infernal gold curl flops across his forehead. His eyes fix on the corner of my mouth, where I retracted my fang, but there is no fear in that peacock-blue gaze, only *hunger*.

"You are yourself when you cast enchantments on stage, drenched in faux blood," he whispers, his voice choked with awe.

Real blood.

"I am myself when I am both lover and horror, priestess and supplicant." I sip my drink, aware of a tingle in my lips where the blood stains them. "In my grandiose and completely correct opinion, nothing says romance like splitting open the rib cage of your lover and snuggling affectionately inside."

I'm testing him, pressing at the edges of what he'll accept from a *cocotte*.

Gideon shoves the table aside, scattering backgammon pieces across the thick Persian rug.

He falls to his knees, his hands finding my thighs. I grab his wrists, ready to toss him across the room for his insolence, but I find myself unable to separate myself from his warm, pulsing flesh.

Instead, I tighten my grip, drawing his warmth into myself, as if his fire can possibly thaw the ice from my immortal veins.

Gideon whispers. "Then allow me to present my rib cage for your pleasure, Mademoiselle."

Damn him.

Damn.

Him.

His lips are an inch from mine, full and wet from the juice I gave him. His scent swirls around me, syrupy-sweet cherry laced with the breathtaking tang of fresh, warm, vinous blood. My fingers itch to tuck that gods-damned curl back where it belongs.

We hover there, in that delicious, agonising space between acting and not acting, where every reason I shouldn't kiss him does battle against the one reason I should …

Because I *want* to.

Gideon leans in, eyes wide open, dark irises blown out with hunger.

I *want* him …

I draw back.

"Get yourself up off the floor before you crease that fine suit of yours."

Gideon sighs. His shoulders shudder as he stands, drawing himself away from me as if the act of doing so is physically painful. I see the evidence of his arousal in the tent of his trousers. *That is one impressive bulge.*

I wet my lips. What I wouldn't give to unwrap that gift …

"You should leave."

"If I return tomorrow night, will you see me?" he asks as he hovers in the doorway.

"That depends."

"On what?"

I offer him a tight-lipped smile, even as my whole body trembles. "On the state of your purse."

Messenger Chat Between Gideon Blake and Winnie Preston

Gideon: Winnie, I have a spot of lady trouble and I need your help.

Winnie: Isn't this something your bestie Alaric should help with?

Gideon: I already called him. He said, "I'm sorry, I can't hear you, the castle is going through a tunnel" and made chugging noises until I hung up.

Winnie: Before I agree to help you, you have to clear up one thing for me.

Winnie: Did you murder Danny or Patrick?

Gideon: No.

Winnie: You SURE about that?

Gideon: I think I'd remember if I'd killed someone.

Winnie: And you didn't pay someone to have them killed?

Gideon: Nope.

Winnie: If you're lying to me, I will send Alaric around with the testicle-severing knife. I'm happy to help. What's up?

Gideon: There's this lady that I'm madly in love with.

Winnie: Arabella.

Gideon: No.

Winnie: So, not Arabella? Hmmmm.

Winnie: Is her name Schmarabella?

Gideon: No.

Gideon: You don't know her.

Gideon: But I like her. A lot. And I want to show her how I feel about her, but she kind of hates me.

Gideon: Normally, my face is enough to have women throwing themselves at my feet. But this lady – whose name is absolutely NOT Arabella – is immune to my many charms.

Winnie: I think that we're going to need to call in the troops on this one.

Gideon: What? No.

Gideon: Winnie.

Gideon: Winnie, don't do this to me.

The Nevermore Murder Club and Smutty Book Coven Group Side Chat (without Arabella)

Winnie: Ladies, I'm reviving this side chat because Gideon has asked for my help in figuring out how best to woo Arabella. But I don't know her as well as you do.

Mina: Wait, why are we helping Gideon when we suspect he's a murderer?

Maisie: Yeah, aren't we putting our friend in danger?

Dora: Arabella thinks he's the murderer. There's a big difference.

Dora: And Arabella deserves great love.

Komal: Maybe if she had a good shag, she'd be less …

Beth: Abrasive?

Maisie: Caustic?

Mina: Terrifying?

Komal: I was going to say 'grumpy', but all of those fit.

Isis: Let's do it!

Messenger Chat Between Gideon Blake and Winnie Preston

Gideon: Winnie, darling, don't do what you're thinking of doing.

Isis, Dora, Beth, Komal, Mina and Maisie enter the chat.

Winnie: Too late!

Isis: Never fear, bloodsucker, the cavalry has arrived to save your love-life!

Gideon: That's what I'm afraid of.

Gideon: But I'll take any help I can get. What do you suggest?

Maisie: Flowers!

Isis: A pony!

Komal: The head of her number one enemy on a spike!

Gideon: What if I'm her number one enemy?

Komal: Hmmm. Good point. Hahaha. Good POINT. Get it?

Winnie: We ladies always swoon over a grand gesture.

Gideon: A grand gesture?

Komal: Because a spike ends in a point. It's hilarious.

Winnie: Yes, a grand gesture. It's in all the romance books. After the man messes up (and it's always the man who messes up), he performs a grand gesture that proves he's the one who knows her better than anyone else and that he loves her.

Komal: I am so clever. You could STAKE your reputation on me.

Gideon: And you think this grand gesture will work in real life as well as it does in romance books?

Mina: Arabella IS the only member of the Nevermore Murder Club and Smutty Book Coven who reads the book every week without fail.

Komal: And I happen to know she has a thing for the morally grey heroes, so if you break the law or the rules of common decency as part of the grand gesture, so much the better.

Winnie: But just a small law. Don't go crazy.

Maisie: We'll send you a reading list.

Gideon: Not that it's Arabella I'm trying to impress.

Winnie: Not at all.

14

Arabella

Sinead: All members are invited to attend the opening of the MIDNIGHT GARDEN AND SCULPTURE PARK – a jewel in the crown of Sanctus Estate. Our esteemed leader, Gideon Blake, will unveil the sculptures and introduce the artists. Entertainments provided. Thralls welcome. Open bar. The blood cocktails will be flowing all night.

Alyra: I'm at Sanctus Club, and someone has told me some utterly salacious stories about you and what you used to get up to. Naughty Arabella, the infamous Parisian courtesan. You are way too much fun to be hiding away. Come join us!

"Shouldn't you be overseeing your private kingdom at Sanctus Club?" I glare at Gideon as he greets me at the bar in Brimstone. The bar is packed, the music loud and *aggressively* vampiric – a haunted house soundtrack mixed with what sounds like a vending machine throwing up.

Cleo VII swings her head off my shoulder, opens one lazy eye, and flicks her tongue in excitement.

"Shouldn't you have that on a leash?" Gideon leans back in his chair and smirks at me. I hate how beautiful he looks tonight, his hair a glittering golden halo beneath the club lights, his black pinstripe suit perfectly fitted to accentuate his broad shoulders and lend him a slightly dangerous air, and the watch peeking from his cuff sparkling with real diamonds. The king among his fawning subjects. "Which Cleo are we up to, now?"

"Cleo VII and I come as a team. She's an excellent business partner. She weeds out the liars and time-wasters because she has no legs to pull."

Gideon laughs, his aquamarine eyes sparkling. "She's your business partner? Interesting. I had her pegged as a civil serpent."

"Only I may say snake puns. Say another snake pun and I will turn around and walk out of here right now and leave you to your fate."

"Woah. Don't throw a hissy fit." He grins. "Sorry, I couldn't help it. Can I make it up to you with a drink?"

"That depends *entirely* on the quality of the drink."

Gideon turns to the bar. He dismisses an Upyr who taps him on the shoulder and leans over to speak to Lilac, who is slinging her signature blood cocktails. Lilac's slime-green mohawk glows under the lights as she pours a glass of vintage blood for Gideon and mixes me a cocktail. She grins at me as she hands me my glass – it's a bloodsinthe, which is still my drink of choice. Some habits will never die. I'm shocked that Gideon remembers.

"Enjoy your evening. I hope to see you dance again soon." Lilac winks at me as she leans across the bar to deal with another customer.

I take a sip. The absinthe is sharp and fragrant, perfectly harmonising with the tang of the blood, with just enough sugar to take the edge off. Exactly the way I like it.

"That Lilac is a magician," I say. I don't have to yell over the music. It's one advantage of being a vampire with heightened hearing.

"I gave her the recipe." Gideon regards me over the top of his glass as he takes a sip. His glass holds blood only – some kind of royal vintage, judging by the deep claret colour. "We import the absinthe from a boutique distillery in France. Only the best will do."

"It is satisfactory." I set the drink down. "You want to do this *now*, with this raucous party in full swing?"

"There's always a raucous party at Sanctus. That's why you love it here. But truthfully, the sooner we get started, the sooner I can get the development back on track." Gideon glances around the room. Something like worry passes over his features. But I know Gideon Blake doesn't care enough to fear anything. "I'll take you to our vault."

I expect him to lead me to the elevator that goes to his private apartments. I've worked with enough rich Upyr to know that they prefer to keep their treasure close. So I'm surprised when he opens a nondescript door to a narrow staircase that leads down into a gloomy basement.

"This way."

I wrinkle my nose. "Hard pass."

"Arabella, this is where I keep the goods."

"You don't keep your valuables in your apartment? You hide the wealth of Sanctus down here with the …" I point at a dark shape dangling in the corner of the doorframe. "Spiders?"

"I *do* have a safe in my apartment, but that contains the heart of Sanctus – which, before you ask, is not a garish diamond necklace lost on the *Titanic* – as well as my personal treasures. This safe is for the regular, boring old treasure."

Gideon picks the spider from its web and holds it out for Cleo VII, who gobbles it up in one bite.

"You're just trying to butter her up."

"I don't need to. Unlike you, she's unarmed." Gideon pats Cleo's head. "Ladies first."

I descend the narrow stairs, every moment becoming more aware of how trapped and vulnerable I am down here, and how Gideon's body behind me blocks my only means of escape. He may claim that he's given up his crime lord ways, but he still exudes beautiful danger like a Valentino sample sale. Perhaps I should have told my friends where I was going tonight.

But that's ridiculous. Did I expect that Isis and Dora would drop their tarot cards and come to my rescue? Or that Winnie and Mina would give up spending the evenings with their lovers to skulk around a dusty basement with me?

But telling the others would mean questions, so many questions, especially from nosy Isis. And I might let slip that my purpose for accepting this job is to find what I need to ruin Gideon.

I don't need them. I have my knife strapped to my thigh and nearly two centuries of carefully honed vampire instincts. I can look after myself.

Even when you're alone with Gideon Blake? A dark voice in my head taunts me.

Especially then.

At the bottom of the staircase is a low-ceilinged corridor stretching in both directions. To the left, I see a loading dock and storage area. Gideon leads me right, past a series of locked rooms, to a heavy steel door. A sensor scans his fingerprints and retinas, and the door clicks open. He drags me inside.

I suppress a gasp as I take in the chaos. The vault is large – over twenty square metres – and every inch is crammed with furniture, rotting wooden chests, stacks of gold bars, and pyramids of hessian sacks. I touch one of the sacks and it topples over, sending a cascade of twelfth-century gold coins across the concrete floor.

This is *absurd*.

Why is Gideon trusting me with this treasure?

Surely he knows he's handing me the keys to his undoing?

I'm used to dealing with, at most, a few sacks of gold or random collections of religious relics.

This job doesn't require a financial advisor. It needs a vampiric Marie Kondo.

Good thing I know one of those.

I mentally revise the plan in my head. If I let Winnie take care of the sorting and cataloguing, that leaves me free for the scheming.

Gideon clasps his hands together, his eyes widening. He looks so *trusting*. "So, can you help?"

"Of course." I step over the pile of coins and inspect a stack of chairs. They bear the mark of Chippendale on the bottom. My mind swirls with all the possible ways to use this treasure hoard against him.

"But this isn't as easy as holding a jumble sale. All of this needs to be sorted and catalogued before I can start converting it into cash, and it can't hit the market all at once, or you'll have the authorities sniffing around. I need Winnie."

"Consider it done." Gideon whips out his phone and taps out a text message. "She says she'll be here in six minutes."

"How? Black Crag is fifteen miles out of the village, and she's got to navigate a precarious turret staircase *and* Alaric's desire to keep her in bed forever and ravish her body until she's a quivering mess."

I mean it jokingly, but my words sound harsh in the brutalist basement. As if I'm jealous of my friend and her happiness. As if I secretly long for a man with a cock like a one-eyed anaconda who could keep *me* satiated. As if such a man existed.

Gideon's eyes flash with heat. He steps towards me, his body caging me in so my back presses against the stack of Chippendale chairs. His gaze sweeps over my face, the colour of his irises deepening to a striking cobalt as he digests my words.

"If you ever need someone to turn you into a quivering mess—"

I snort. "I'd like to see you try."

That was supposed to be dismissive.

It came out like a challenge.

Like a *command*.

Maybe I am in over my head.

Cleo VII regards Gideon from my shoulder. I silently command her to bite him. Instead, she slithers off me to wrap herself around a chair leg. *Traitorous bitch.*

"I may have been a mere human last time we tumbled in the sheets." Gideon leans in. He doesn't touch me, leaving a space between us wide enough for my imagination to fill with all kinds of filthy promises. "But I seem to recall you enjoying yourself."

"It's my job to make little donkeys believe they are stallions." I glare up at him, defiant, determined to claw back control.

"Those little noises you made, and the way you bit down on me when you came so hard you broke your bed, was that all part of the act?" He's so close now that his breath brushes my naked neck. "I've had a hundred and fifty years to practise. I know a few tricks that might surprise even you."

"Somewhere in the woods, a tree is working hard to replace the oxygen you consumed with that absurd tale," I bite back. "You should apologise to it."

I want him to kiss me, so I have an excuse for castrating him.

Yup. That's the reason.

It has *nothing* to do with the tempting way his bottom lip puffs out, or the red cherry and poppy scent that swirls around me, making me light-headed and a heat flare between my thighs.

"You wound me, Arabella—"

A cold head drops between us.

Gideon yelps as Cleo VII expands her hood, her tongue flicking across his cheek. He staggers back, upsetting a cardboard box filled with Peruvian clay figurines, and adding them to the mess of coins on the floor.

Thank you, girl.

I hold out my arm and Cleo VII slithers around it, settling herself back around my neck. There's a bulge inside her length. She must've found a mouse hiding in the vault and had herself a snack. I stroke her cool skin affectionately. I am myself again.

Gideon is my enemy, my *mark*, and nothing more.

"We were talking about Winnie," I say coolly, enjoying how rattled he is as he tries to untangle himself from a bunch of gold chains.

"Yes. Winnie's actually already at Sanctus. One of our members hired Dracluttera to organise his possessions."

That's right. Winnie is doing a roaring trade as a professional organiser specialising in decluttering for Upyr. While I have made a habit of carefully curating my possessions over the years, many of my kin hold onto objects for centuries, which can create storage issues, especially when downsizing from a castle to a Sanctus "executive treehouse".

Gideon hops around, picking up Peruvian clay figurines. Thankfully, none appear broken. I move deeper into the vault, inspecting the objects and keeping as much distance between me and Gideon as possible. I pull out sacks of coins and notice some are much lighter than others.

I'm behind a towering pile of Eighteenth Dynasty statues when Winnie texts to say she's waiting upstairs.

"Never fear. Winnie's here to save the day," she calls out as I emerge into Brimstone. She's wearing one of her favourite organising outfits – lavender wide-leg trousers with a soft grey shirt. There's a smear of dust on her sleeve. Her eyes sparkle with excitement at the idea of tackling a new mess. A man turns from the bar to hand her a drink that matches her trousers. He sips a goblet of blood. "Gideon, Arabella, this is Paul Badica, my first client on Sanctus Estate. Over the centuries, he has amassed quite the collection of, er, pornographic woodcuts. I'm helping him to catalogue everything, and I'm trying to convince him to donate to the Prague sex museum so he can become a philanthropist instead of an, er, pervert."

"It *is* the best of all the sex museums," Gideon muses, stepping forwards to clink his own goblet with Winnie's.

I have strong opinions about the best sex museums, but I'm too busy staring at Paul to voice them.

"Hello, Arabella." Paul Badica waves, as if we're old friends and not … and *not* …

I knew it was all too good to be true.

Cleo VII senses my unease. She raises her body from my shoulder and expands her neck ribs into her hood. A low hiss escapes her.

"She's hissing at you," Gideon says to Badica, his eyes locking on mine.

"I'm not afraid of snakes."

"I'm not talking about the snake."

Gideon's right – I'm hissing under my breath.

Paul grins, but his lips wobble as he notices Gideon's expression, which has flipped from friendly to dangerous.

Gideon points to the door, the gesture sharper than any blade. His voice is low and dangerous when he says. "Your help isn't required, Badica. Go back to your woody woodcuts."

"But—"

Gideon snaps his fingers. Two hulking security goons appear and drag Badica to the exit. Patrons step out of their way. No one dares say a word in Badica's defence. That's the power Gideon Blake has at Sanctus – a power he wears as well as that exquisitely-tailored suit.

"That's my client!" Winnie plants her hands on her hips and glares at Gideon.

"He was my client, too." I stroke Cleo VII's back until she settles. "He used to frequent my theatre in Paris, back when he was a cardinal. I can assure you that whatever you saw in those woodcuts is tame compared to the things he made us *grandes horizontales* do." I glare at Gideon. "How could you let him in here?"

"Truthfully, I have no memory of him. When I was at La Petite Mort, I had eyes for only one vampire."

I fold my arms, refusing to acknowledge the delight fizzing in my stomach at his words. The depth of his feelings for me will only make my revenge that much sweeter. "He is a pervert and a scoundrel. He treated my girls appallingly."

He has seen too much. He will tell anyone who listens what I used to do. He's already told people.

I'm not ashamed of La Petite Mort. I'm not ashamed of being a sex worker, but I am ashamed that I ever had to take money from men like him, men who saw me and my girls as things he could possess.

He will ruin the life I've made for myself here.

He will ruin my revenge.

As much as the vampire community thinks it is inclusive and accepting, as much as Gideon has promised that Sanctus Estate is a place where our kin can be ourselves, they won't want their exclusive little enclave sullied by a *grandes horizontales*, especially not one who ousts their beloved leader.

"Your girls?" Winnie looks confused.

I glare at her until my words sink in and her cheeks redden.

Winnie's face falls. "Arabella, I'm so sorry. I didn't know. I was so excited to get my first Sanctus client, but I'm not working for someone like that. I'll drop him immediately."

Gideon's face darkens. "And I'll revoke his membership."

I raise an eyebrow. "Why would you do that? In case you've forgotten, you need his money."

"You have to feel safe here," he says simply.

The ice encasing my heart cracks open.

I don't know what safe feels like.

I've been hiding for so long, lying low, staying in the shadows, keeping myself small because I have to hold on to the thin sliver of freedom I've clawed out for myself. No matter how successful I am, no matter how much money I save, it never feels like enough, because I've lost it all before …

My heart feels too raw, too exposed. I can't meet Gideon's eyes. I can't bear the openness in his words. He's not supposed to *protect* me.

"Arabella?" Winnie asks. "Are you okay?"

I swallow. I'm finding it hard to breathe.

"I'm fine. It's the dust down in the vault." I drag her towards the entrance to the basement, my skin prickling with the awareness of Gideon's eyes on my back. "Winnie, you get started organising the coins. I'll create the inventory and make some calls to my buyers. Gideon, you stand out of the way and try not to break anything. Let's see if we can save Sanctus Estate."

And while we're at it, let's destroy Gideon Blake.

Only then will I truly be safe.

15

Gideon
Then

Darling Gideon, it was wonderful to see you again without blood on your shirt collar. I'd be delighted to meet your friend. I've heard so many delicious rumours about that theatre of hers.

We're having a little fete next Friday. Please bring her along, if you're certain she's not afraid of heights!

Your boss hasn't been to the Comédie-Française lately. Has he tired of me? I swear I shall fling myself from the grand staircase if that is so!

Yours, Sarah.

LUCIEN DROPS A HEAVY PURSE INTO MY HANDS. "MY COFFERS ARE not bottomless, Gideon. You are trying my patience."

"I apologise, Sir. Mademoiselle Macquart has expensive tastes. And as you did not wish me to hurt her, I must woo her if I'm to remove the collar from her neck."

Wooing Arabella is proving a challenge. Night after night I return to La Petite Mort. I bring Belgian chocolates and bottles of fine champagne and silk scarves from the *Samaritaine*. She refuses the chocolates and the wine but she accepts anything silky or glittering. It's like trying to tame a crow, if that crow were also a fussy eater and kept trying to peck my eyes out.

And I am acting like a besotted dandy, lavishing gifts upon a courtesan who indulges his whims only because he opens his purse for her. It's not even my purse.

But I cannot make myself stop.

Unlike the usual entanglement with a courtesan, I have not had so much as a kiss from Arabella Macquart in return. There was that one night when I knelt for her, and I felt certain she was about to kiss me, but instead, she gave me that smile, and a flash of tooth, and it must have been a trick of the light because she looked as though she had the most glorious *fangs* ...

I'm so enamoured with her that I'm hallucinating. But even if she did have fangs, I wouldn't care. Fangs suit her. I hope one day she bites me.

I am *sick*.

Her reluctance only makes me want her more. Every moment in her presence is foreplay.

Each night as I walk to La Petite Mort, I tell myself that tonight will be the night. I will find a way to take that necklace from Arabella's neck. I will complete the job and free myself and Jacob from Lucien's debt.

But then I walk beneath that velvet curtain, and I see her dancing, and every rational thought flees my body.

"I'm not so concerned with you hurting her as I am with her hurting *you*, Little Prince." Lucien glares as my fingers clasp over the purse. "But I am growing impatient. I have given you ample time and you have spent a king's ransom at La Petite Mort and still not secured the collar."

That damned collar. I've never once seen Arabella without those baubles around her neck. It's the worst tease of all. I long to see her dark skin exposed without those glittering jewels.

She says the collar is her armour. She certainly looks invincible wearing it – an impenetrable fortress of desire. I don't believe in magic or curses, but I can almost see the way Arabella weaves the necklace's good luck into her life, using the jewels to grow her business and to maintain her lifestyle of lavish clothing and expensive, disgusting red drinks.

The more time I spend with her, the less I want to do this job for Lucien. But I can't refuse him. He'll go out and find another soldier to do his dirty work, and that soldier may not take such an interest in Arabella's welfare. After all, it's easy enough to cut the jewels from a severed neck.

At least I can keep her safe.

But for how much longer?

Lucien is becoming suspicious. Soon his need for the necklace will outweigh the reasons for his caution, even though I understand neither.

I have to make a move.

Tonight.

"I have a plan." I tuck the purse into the pocket of my coat and smooth my lapels. I'm dressed in my opera finery. Lucien frowns at my outfit. He knows how much I hate the opera. "Fear not, if this necklace is worth what you say, then you will still make a tidy profit from this job."

Arabella descends the twisted staircase to greet me. She doesn't smile, but the sweep of her eyes over my sharp suit tells me she approves. I live for these moments when I feel the heat of her esteem, like the sun peeking through the clouds after months of winter rain.

I drop coins into her hand. Payment for her time. I never ask for so much as a kiss, and she never offers. Kisses are cheap compared to what I want from her, but I would pay a king's fortune for the rare glimpses of her true self, the woman she must hide to become the fantasy for her clients.

Unfortunately, my king's fortune is running dry, as is my king's patience.

Arabella wraps her strong fingers around my wrist, dark skin against light, and tugs me towards the confessional. I place my hand over hers. "Tonight I want to go out."

"Outside?"

She spits the word as if it's poison.

I incline my head in the direction of the street. "*Oui*. Outside these walls. I have a surprise for you."

"I cannot leave. The place doesn't run without me."

"Everyone here is too afraid of you to mess up while you're gone." I tug her towards the velvet curtain. "You can leave for one night."

Her mouth settles in a prim line. I'm certain that she's going to say no, but then she flashes me one of her rare, dazzling smiles. She slips her arm beneath mine.

"Very well. Let's get this over with."

I practically sprint outside, dragging Arabella behind me before she can change her mind. The night is clear, the sky a brilliant lapis blue, matching the jewels on her necklace. Without the cloud of opium smoke and the acrid, aniseed scent of free-flowing absinthe, fresh smells assault me. Warm bread and sweet pastries from street sellers, the cloying perfume of a gaggle of dandies heading into one of the other Montmartre cabarets, the crisp tang of dew-soaked flowers from crowded window boxes.

And sewage. Always sewage.

This is Paris, after all – a city of romance tinged with harsh reality.

We stroll along the Seine. Here, in the working-class immigrant heart of Paris, few people give a second glance to a white man strolling with a Black woman. Arabella relaxes a little. She tells me about fishing with her father in the village where she grew up. She doesn't say where that village is located, but she describes fierce, warm sunlight and a river so wide and deep that it felt like an ocean. "I was hopeless. I only ever caught one fish. It was about the size of my pinkie finger. My father fed it to a sweet ginger cat who used to hang around his market stall. The cat got violently sick the next day." She laughs. "I miss that cat."

The further we walk from La Petite Mort, the more she smiles. The moonlight kisses her ebony skin, making it shimmer. The jewels at her neck sparkle so brightly that heads turn on the street to bask in their brilliance, but to me, they are dull and pale when compared to the sparkle in her eyes.

"Why did you agree to come out with me tonight?" I ask, emboldened by the stars.

She looks out across the water to the glittering lights of the city. "Today is my ... birthday." There's an odd hesitation in her voice.

"*Bon anniversaire, ma chérie.*"

"It's not a happy day for me. Some years ago, a terrible thing happened to me on this day." Her voice is cold, emotionless. She doesn't look away from the water. "I cannot dance on my birthday. The music leaves me. I did not wish to sit in the dark and think of sad and evil things, so instead, I'm here with you."

She turns to me then, and the gold ring around her dark eyes is ablaze.

I tug her to me, pulling her against my body. My muscles burn with the desire to reach back through time and fix this.

"If I ever find out who hurt you," I growl, my lips against her hair. "I will *burn* them."

"I have nothing to fear from them anymore," she says, but her shoulders shake all the same.

We stay like that, my lips pressed to her soft, curly hair, the scarab beetle at the centre of her collar thrumming against my throat. Our hearts beat together through our ribs – mine races ahead of hers, spurred on by my rage and impotency.

I wish I could be the villain she needs.

She pulls away, breaking the spell that holds us, and drags me along the riverbank. Arabella stops to admire a painter as he works, hunched, shivering beneath a threadbare wool coat. When she realises it's Claude Monet painting scenes of people along the river, she plants a kiss on his cheek and orders me to buy him a loaf of bread and some cheese.

"Look." Claude shows us his work – a river scene rendered in dabs of colour, like prisms of light trapped in the paint. "I'm doing as you suggested, Gideon. I'm creating the impressionist movement. But still, no one will buy my paintings."

Looking at his work, I can kind of see why. Certainly, the colours are vivid and the composition dynamic, capturing a sense of fleeting movement ...

But will people want to hang these childish daubs of light in their homes?

Arabella stands in front of the canvas for many moments, and I wish I could take every cent in Lucien's purse and buy her all of Monet's paintings. "You are a painter of enchantments, Monsieur," she says, her voice choked with emotion. "Don't ever hide your magic away."

"I won't, Mademoiselle Macquart." He winks at me as he returns to his work. "You two enjoy your evening. It's good to see you both out *en plein air*."

It's good to be out with her, to know that Arabella exists outside the walls of La Petite Mort, and she isn't merely a dream conjured by my weary, desperate mind. But dream creature or real woman, she has caught the eye of Lucien Vega. I do not know whether Lucien believes the stories of the collar's magic or whether he simply wants to possess the jewels, but the why doesn't matter. Lucien requires his prize, or else he'll take it from her flesh, and he'll make me watch as he carves her up like a *poulet rôti*.

I can only hope that if I pull this off, Arabella won't need to know I'm the one who stole her jewels.

16

Gideon

Sinead: I've made the arrangements, and Mr Moriarty assures me that everything will work. All you have to do is get her back to Sanctus.

The smell hits me before I'm five feet from the door. Bergamot and patchouli assault my nostrils, bringing tears to my eyes. If this is human magic, then give me some of that Dusk Court blowing-the-world-to-smithereens nonsense any day. And to smithereens is the absolute worst way to get blown.

But this … this is *torture*.

I have to do it. For Arabella. For my grand gesture.

Arabella and Winnie have been working on the Sanctus finances for a week now. She's sorting coins, making calls, and driving up to London with stacks of treasure in the boot of her car. She returns empty-handed, but when I check my bank account, the number climbs at an alarming rate. Thanks to her contacts and astute deal-making skills, the treasures the vampires paid me are worth more than the value of their homes, and she's barely made a dent in the vault. At this rate, I'll be able to fund the rest of the project without having to court another investor.

I'm not surprised Arabella is brilliant. I *am* surprised that she agreed to help me save Sanctus. It's given me hope that maybe the Nevermore Coven's crazy plan for a grand gesture could work.

I'm about to find out.

It's after 7 pm. I've just woken from my daysleep and talked myself into coming here against my better judgement. The CLOSED sign is flipped over the door of Spell The Tea, but I can see Isis, Dora, and Komal at the counter, sharing a bottle of wine while they glare at a computer screen. Komal's laugh is audible even through the thick glass.

I'd intended to go straight to Celeste for assistance, since she's Arabella's closest friend in the Coven, but Winnie tells me Celeste is away visiting her mother and can't be reached, so I'm here to prostrate myself before these three intimidating women.

I knock on the window.

Isis's face lights up when she sees me. She's been fond of me ever since I carried her out of that secret room in Black Crag Castle after Baylor tried to husk her. She hurries over, her purple dress flaring out around her, and flings open the door.

"Gideon, come in, come in!" She grabs my wrist and yanks me inside.

A shop bell plays a tinny bar of "Black Magic Woman". Smells assail me from all sides, as if I've wandered into a Roman army camp after they pillaged a perfume shop. The mild woody scent of sandalwood mixes with fruity, floral ylang-ylang and the unmistakable tang of marijuana from the shop's clientele. And rising above it all, the delicious waft of human blood from the three Nevermore Coven members. I pinch my nose in an attempt to keep out the competing scents and follow Isis deeper into the shop, being careful not to knock over any of the precariously balanced crystals or grinning Buddha statues. I cannot afford any karmic retribution where Arabella is concerned. Ordinary, everyday Arabella retribution is hard enough on my poor vampire body.

"What can we do for you?" Isis breathes, her cheeks flushed. "Anything you need, on the house. I can tell your fortune if you like?"

"No thanks. I prefer to discover my future the old-fashioned way – by living it."

She shrugs. "Your loss. If you walk off a cliff tomorrow, don't come crying to me."

"You see me walking off a cliff?"

Isis smiles mysteriously and taps the side of her head. "I see many things, Gideon Blake."

"Mostly the bottom of this wine bottle." Komal sloshes the nearly empty pinot gris. The two girls cackle with glee.

"We're doing our taxes," Isis explains as she pulls out a bedazzled ottoman for me to sit on. "Well, Dora is doing our taxes. Komal and I are lending moral support."

"I'm plying Dora with Bollywood dances so she'll do my taxes, too!" Komal does a little shimmy, twisting her hands around her head like a dysfunctional helicopter. "I'm no Arabella, but I think it's working."

"It's not. Would you like a cup of tea, Gideon?" Dora calls from the back room. "I've just put on a fresh pot. We have a lovely tea for vampires distilled from dried blood."

"Tea would be brilliant, thank you," I call out.

"Sooooo," Isis leans over the counter, head resting on her palms. Her various necklaces clank and clatter together. "If not a reading, what are you here for? Are we going to talk about how to catch this killer? Or is this about a certain lady you want to impress?"

"Isis has some great penis enlargement spells," Komal giggles.

"I'm perfectly fine in that department, thank you."

"That's what all men who need the penis enlargement spell say." Komal tosses a small bag of herbs at my head. I catch it and toss it back at her. She ducks and it hits a display of tarot decks, knocking down cases like celestial dominoes.

"Hey, no throwing the merchandise." Isis picks up the herb bag. "Ever since the village started Speed Dating Tuesdays at the Rose & Wimple, the penis enlargement spells have been our top sellers."

"Don't mind the two of them. They're drunk." Dora emerges from the back room, balancing a tray with four steaming teacups and a small plate of biscuits. She looks happier than when I last saw her, and she's here hanging out with Isis and Komal, so the little chat Arabella and I had with Mike must've worked. It figures Mike's threats are as hollow as his head. But there's a cloak of sadness over her shoulders I haven't noticed before. People are probably so busy looking at Isis – the kooky, crazy sister – that they never notice Dora. But beneath her baggy sweater and severe ponytail, there is a woman with galaxies in her eyes. I hope one day someone notices them.

I accept the cup containing crimson-coloured liquid. I take a sip. It's quite good – it tastes of blood, with a lovely vanilla nose.

I set down the cup and meet their gaze. "I've been planning a grand gesture for a certain lady—"

"Arabella?" Komal claps her hands. "It's Arabella, right?"

"As I said on the group chat, I can neither confirm nor deny."

"What are you planning?" Komal's ponytail bounces behind her as she performs another classic dance move – the sideways camel having intercourse. "Did you read all those dark romance books Maisie sent you?"

"I did, and I have so *many* questions." I fix Komal with a look of utmost horror. "Since when are women fawning over men who don't take no for an answer?"

She shrugs. "What can I say? If he's a red flag in real life, he's hot AF in fiction. Sometimes all a girl wants is for a sexy hitman to tie her up in the back of a car and force her to do all kinds of depraved things … and like them."

"If you say so." All the hitmen I've known in my life have been ugly brutes and I wouldn't want these sweet ladies anywhere near them … mainly because the Nevermore Coven would have the hitmen quaking in their boots. "I've come up with something *mildly* unhinged. But I need your help with a little ambience."

"Name it." Dora sips her tea.

"Most human dates involve food. Vampires don't enjoy food the way humans do, but we are particularly attuned to scent. Especially …" I swallow down a memory that fights its way to the surface. "Especially *my* date. So I'm looking for some scented candles."

"We can help you there!" Isis drags me over to a shelf that's buckling under the weight of candles in every size, colour and shape. "What sort of scent are you interested in?"

"I don't know, exactly. The sort of scents you might smell in a movie theatre."

"Ooooh, if you're planning a movie date, this one is essential." Isis hands me a candle. I bury my nose in it, trying to block out all the other scents in the shop. Hot, buttery, salty popcorn. Perfect.

"And maybe something for dessert." Dora reaches over Isis's head to grab a blood-red candle. "Arabella loves red cherries."

I inhale the crimson candle. It smells sweet and fresh with a bright tang, like a warm Paris night. Even one hundred and fifty years later, it conjures up the taste of Arabella's lips, a taste I've never been able to forget.

"It's perfect," I breathe.

The ladies start tossing candles at me. By the time they're done, they've talked me into ten flavours, all of which they swear to me Arabella will love. While Isis skips off to wrap up my purchases, Dora clutches a small floral candle in her hand and stares intently at me.

"What?" I make a face. "Do I have someone in my teeth?"

"It's just that … do peonies, irises, waterlilies and apple blossoms hold significance to you?"

She holds the candle to my nose. My breath catches on my tongue. It's the *exact* scent of a certain garden where Arabella and I …

I swallow. "Yes. They mean something to me."

Dora frowns. "When I picked up this candle, I saw a vision of you and Arabella. Do you want to know it?"

"I thought Isis was the village clairvoyant?"

Dora glances over her shoulder, checking that Isis is occupied, doing battle with a wad of tissue paper. "You have no idea how badly I wish Isis was the one with the power. She loves all this witchy stuff. But we don't always get what we wish for. So do you want to—"

"Yes."

"Okay." Dora closes her eyes. "I see a necklace. No, it's more than a necklace, it's like a collar of gold, covered in glittering jewels. In the centre is a stone of the deepest blue, carved like a scarab."

My heart thuds against my chest.

"You're holding it in your hands," she says. "You're so happy. You're excited. You've never felt like this before. But I see other things, too. A dim parking lot. Tombstones. A phone with a blinking message. A dark presence. A painting made of light. And blood, so much blood ..."

"What does all that mean?"

"I don't know, I'm sorry. Believe me, I wish my visions came with a Wikipedia entry."

"And these visions are from the future? Not the past?"

Dora nods.

I step back, my mind reeling.

I'm holding the collar.

But that can't possibly be true. Unless …

Unless the collar has survived.

Unless I find it and bring it to Arabella.

I can undo all that went wrong between us.

There's no gesture grander than that.

My vampiric heart skips its languid beat. I grab Dora by the shoulders and kiss her square on the lips. "Dora, you are a marvel. I will write sonnets in your honour. I will name a dinosaur after you. I will build a statue to your brilliance—"

"Yes, yes, I'm glad you're so happy, given the amount of blood I've described. I forgot that vampires *like* blood. Just don't ask Alaric to carve the statue." Dora wriggles out of my grip and smooths down her sweater. "Winnie tells me he tossed another finished sculpture off the Black Crag parapet last night. Apparently, the pinkie finger had a microscopic chip."

I roll my eyes. "I swear, if he didn't have such a glorious arse, I'd have ended my friendship with that infuriating man a century ago."

"That's a lie and you know it. And Gideon?" Dora stares at her shoes. "Don't tell anyone where you got this vision. I can't have word getting out that I can …"

Her shoulders tense. I realise what she's not telling me.

Mike doesn't know.

I think about her husband's reddened face as he yelled at her in front of everyone. If he's that threatened by his wife dancing and having fun with her girlfriends, then what would he be like if he found out Dora sees visions of the future?

My fingers ball into a fist. If there's one thing I can't stand, it's any clothing made from polyester (natural fibre or naked, I always say). But a second thing I can't stand is weak, insecure men who bully and intimidate women because they want everything on their terms. I saw them every day on the streets and in the cabarets of Paris. I worked for one of them for far too long.

In my worst, darkest days, I fear I've become one of them.

As much as I want to put Alaric's testicle-severing sword to good use, I will not lift a finger against Mike until Dora asks. But *when* she asks (and I'm certain it's *when*), Alaric and I will delight in inventing several imaginative ways to teach Mike to respect women.

Maybe Komal's right and I'm more of an unhinged dark romance hero than I give myself credit for.

"Thank you, Dora." I take her hand and give it a reassuring squeeze. "Your secret is safe with me. But if you ever need a friend with sharp fangs and no morals, know that you can call me."

"Noted." She smiles sadly. "Good luck with your grand gesture, Gideon. I think you'll need it."

17

Arabella
Then

Mademoiselle Macquart, I have been asking around the neighbourhood about the mysterious goings-on at the theatre. The fishmonger witnessed a figure in a dark cloak fleeing down the street on the night the flowers were left, and a streetwalker reports what sounds like the same cloaked figure brushing past her, almost knocking her into the gutter. Although neither saw the figure's face, they believed it to be a man. I shall head to the coffee house after the theatre closes, knock some heads together, and see what falls out.

Yours, Jacques

W E BID GOODNIGHT TO MONSIEUR MONET, AND I ALLOW GIDEON to drag me through the streets of Montmartre. I've not spent much time outside at night since I first arrived in the city. People who look like me are not always given a warm welcome. Before I had an income and ready access to Thralled humans and vintage blood, I would hunt by moonlight, supping from drunks passed out in the alleys or the opium eaters as they emerged from their hollow dens. But now La Petite Mort demands everything from me during the midnight hours, and during the day I must have my daysleep. It leaves little time to slip into the heaving, pulsing streets of the city and feel her lifeblood.

But tonight – my Bloodeve – it feels right to be here, with him.

With my arm in Gideon's, the City of Light warms my cold veins once more. I remember the hope I felt when I first arrived with nothing but my two best dresses, the glittering collar hidden beneath my coat, and a heart cold with vengeance. I may be relatively new to immortality, but I'd already come to feel as though I'd drunk this city dry, until I saw it tonight through his eyes.

Gideon meanders all over Montmartre, stopping to sniff summer blooms or to throw coins at the street performers. He buys me candied fruits from one seller, and *café au lait* from another, both of which I toss in the Seine when his back is turned. He talks to everyone – the *insoumises* working in Rue Pigalle, the bohemians wafting merrily between cafes like leaves on the breeze, the footmen waiting by their carriages for their masters to finish in the brothels.

"You're so cold." Gideon wraps his coat around my shoulders, drawing me against him as we wander down yet another avenue.

"That's because I have no heart."

"I don't believe that. If you were heartless, you wouldn't have let me kneel for you. Come on!" He drags me forward, laughing. "We don't want to be late."

"Late for what?"

Gideon passes under a carved archway depicting cherubic angels, and into a wide grassed courtyard where a large contraption is tethered, bobbing gently in the breeze.

I stare up at it, confounded.

"It's a hot air balloon." Gideon drags me towards the wicker basket suspended beneath a large orange balloon. "When this envelope is inflated, it will fly us high above the city."

I struggle to form words. "But … *why?*"

"Because it's fun." He tugs my arm. "Haven't you ever wanted to fly?"

"Not really, no. I'm rather enamoured with the ground."

"It's perfectly safe. Consider it a birthday present."

"Your witty and learned arguments have filled me with assurance. I'm *not* flying in a picnic basket beneath a glorified carbuncle." I jab a finger towards the midnight sky. "Up there is the gravity."

"Technically, gravity isn't up there. It's—"

"I know what gravity is! Take me back to La Petite Mort this instant."

Gideon flashes me that cheeky grin. "Arabella Macquart isn't afraid, is she?"

If he thinks he knows how to get to me … he's right, damn him.

I fold my arms and glare at him as I step gingerly towards the contraption. A shadow darts in the garden behind the balloon, but I'm too distracted by my terror to discern it.

Probably just a stray cat hoping for a scrap of food.

Gideon's smile turns wicked as he reaches down to help me up. There is a small set of wooden steps placed next to the basket, enabling passengers (also known as "those who wish for death") to easily board the sky pufferfish.

Gideon's hand on my arm steadies me as I clamber up the narrow steps. "I swear it will be fun. Wait until you meet our aeronaut."

It's then that I realise there are three people already standing inside the basket. Two men and a woman. The woman waves cheerily at us and calls Gideon's name. She looks familiar.

"That's …"

My mouth falls open as the pilot beams down at me, golden curls tumbling from beneath her leather beret.

"You must be Arabella Macquart. I'm Sarah Bernhardt." The infamous actress extends an elegant gloved hand. "I'm so pleased to make your acquaintance. Giddy has told me so much about you. He's positively sung an aria to your flawless skin."

"Giddy?" I grin at Gideon. "Oh, thank you, Sarah, for this benevolent gift. I'm pleased *Giddy* introduced us."

"Wow, time goes so fast when you're being pushed out of a hot air balloon." Gideon hops up beside the greatest actress who has ever lived and extends his hand to me. "Are you coming?"

I take his hand.

Gideon's warmth pools in my chest as he helps me into the enormous basket, which creaks and groans with every movement. Sarah and her male companions rush around, fiddling with sandbags, lighting things, and muttering about wind speeds and compass directions. There is a picnic basket in the corner, brimming with foods that smell amazing – cheese, oranges, *tartines de foie gras* – which I can't eat.

With a huff and a jerk, the balloon is away. Gideon unloops the tethers. At first, I don't even realise we're moving. But then I look over the edge and see the tops of the buildings and the flickering streetlamps of Rue de l'Abreuvoir.

We're really flying.

My head spins from the wonder of it.

"Champagne?" Gideon holds out a glass. I accept it, taking a sip, knowing that I'll regret it later. The drink itself tastes like nothing, but the bubbles dance on my tongue, light and free, like me.

Up here, the city changes. Everything is so insignificant. The Seine is a periwinkle ribbon. Pieces of Bartholdi's Statue of Liberty are laid out at the workshops, the gargantuan limbs like shards of a broken doll.

Sarah leaves her two male friends to manage the envelope and sashays over to me. She wears a fashionable silk dress and a stuffed bat perched on her hat. "Giddy tells me you are the finest dancer in all of Paris."

"In all the world," Gideon adds.

"I am not in the same league as you." I feel like a little girl again, awed by the majesty of the grand houses where my mother worked and the ancient tombs she allowed me to wander. "I don't grace the stage for rapturous crowds. I dance for the pleasure of men. I say nothing except what they want to hear. What I do cannot be compared to your art."

"You should not shrink yourself so. Art is not about something. Art *is* something." Sarah runs her hands over her body. "Energy creates energy, Arabella. It is by spending myself that I become rich. If I recognise the collar you wear, you understand this better than most, I think."

Heat creeps across my cheeks at her words.

"I do as I wish," Sarah continues. "I sleep in a coffin because it amuses me. I keep cheetahs, a tiger, lion cubs and a monkey. I had a pet alligator called Ali-Gaga, who died of a milk and champagne overdose. But I only do these things because people wish to watch me. The actress or the dancer cannot exist without the audience. Pleasing others is the ultimate way to please ourselves. Do you agree?"

I raise my glass of champagne. "I agree thoroughly."

"Look!" Gideon points over the edge. "There's La Petite Mort."

I grip the edge of the basket and lean out, squinting where he points. From this angle, I can make out only the sharply steepled roof of the old church that now houses my theatre. Gideon's chest brushes my back as he leans in close behind me, pointing to other features of the city.

He turns, and his lips brush my earlobe, soft at first, so soft that I might believe it was an accident.

But then, he lingers.

The heat of him, the *scent* of him, sparks inside me like a lit fuse burning down, and I don't know what is going to happen when it gets to the end.

"What do you think you're doing?" I mean it to be a reprimand, but it comes out breathy.

He presses his lips against the edge of my jaw. I feel them curl back into a grin. "I think I'm trying to kiss an enchanting woman under the moonlight."

"Your friends can see us."

"Oh, darlings, please don't be shy." And then Sarah grabs me, tearing me from Gideon's grasp, and plants a kiss on my lips.

I've had several female clients over the years, so I'm familiar with all the different ways a woman's kiss can feel. But I've never kissed a woman I admire, nor a woman whose freedom to be herself makes my throat close in envy. Sarah's lips are soft, her scent floral and uplifting – the opposite of Gideon's bewitching darkness. Her hands cup my cheek, holding me in place, knocking me off-centre with her command of this interaction. Her tongue explores every corner of my mouth, brushing softly against mine before circling the tips of my fangs, which have already begun to drop, drawn down by Gideon's red cherry and poppy scent.

I expect her to pull away in disgust, but she continues to take her fill of me, while I wonder at the heady need she stirs in me, not to kiss her again, which is enjoyable, but for someone to take control away from me, to trust another enough to allow them to see who I am behind my mask.

When she does pull away, her breath is ragged and her eyes shimmer with lust.

"The night belongs to us, Arabella. We are too young and beautiful to hold ourselves back!" And before I can say a word, Sarah leaps onto the edge of the basket, making it sway. I grip the rim as we tilt downward, the world beneath us swaying across my vision.

"Sarah, get down!" Gideon growls, his arm going around my waist, holding me against him as the basket tips even further. Can vampires die from a great fall? I don't want to find out.

"Make me, *ma chérie!*"

Gideon grips the rope and looks down at me, his grey eyes sparkling. His arm tightens around my waist. I should be terrified of falling, but instead, I am *flying*. Laughter bubbles up in my chest. Up in the clouds, everything down there is so small and unimportant.

Sarah's other companions coax her down from the edge. She refills the champagne glasses. Gideon's hand never leaves my waist and I enjoy it too much to move it away. His breath on the back of my neck is a delicious torture.

We laugh and talk and laugh some more. Sarah sings a haunting aria. The men devour the goodies inside the picnic basket. The balloon bumps against the base of Gustave's Eiffel Tower, but we manage to push it away before we become trapped. Gideon doesn't try to kiss me again, and I am both disappointed and excited. I have made up my mind that I want to kiss this human. Sarah is right – I shouldn't hold myself back. I am safe here. My sire is dead and I can kiss a human if I want to.

But for now, I am enjoying the anticipation of this kiss. I intend to draw it out until we are both so desperate for it that we will burn in each other's passion. I've been in the business of sex long enough to know that anticipation is half the pleasure.

Sarah pulls another bottle of champagne from somewhere. I raise my glass to my lips. As I do, I notice my hand shaking.

I pull my attention inward, listening to my body. And it's telling me that I've made a terrible mistake.

I stagger to my feet. My legs give out from beneath me and I topple against the basket.

"Arabella?" Gideon wraps his arms around me, setting me lightly on the floor of the basket. "What's wrong? Are you sick?"

"Oh dear, she's had too much to drink." Sarah cries gleefully. "We can fix that with more champagne!"

I haven't had enough to drink.

My fangs slide down, their tips aching with thirst. Gideon is too close. He smells too good. And I'm fading fast. I haven't felt hunger like this since the night Lord Astor punished me by locking me outside as the sun rose—

No.

As I squint at the blurring world, I notice a hint of gold at the edge of my vision, the city beneath me unfurling into a glittering warmth.

This is not good.

All those months back in Egypt, I practised being able to stay awake during the sunlight hours, but since I arrived in Paris, I've let the skill lapse. And now I'm paying dearly. I won't stay awake much longer. I need to get home before I fall into the dreamless sleep, and my companions panic and take me to *l'hôpital*.

"Arabella, can you talk to me?" Gideon's mouth quivers with worry.

"Do you have … your pocket watch?" I slap Gideon's lapel, trying to reach into his pocket, but my fingers don't seem to be attached to my body.

"How forward of you—"

"I'm not joking. I need to know the time."

"I don't have it. I didn't bring it with me, in case I lost it over the edge during one of Sarah's mad dances. Arabella, what's wrong?"

The golden glow on the horizon. A glow I haven't seen for over a decade.

"I have to get down. Now." I tug on one of the ropes. The envelope collapses on one side. Sarah screams as we drop several feet before Gideon wrestles the rope from my hand.

"What's the hurry?" Sarah's friend drawls. "We have the sky all to ourselves. We were going to watch the sunrise and—"

"I can't." Panic clenches at my chest. My fangs bite into my lip. I slap Gideon's hands away, clawing at the basket, trying to drag myself upright. My skin is filled with stones and scorpions with scuttling legs and sharp, poisonous tails.

"*Ma chérie*, what's the rush—" Sarah's eyes darken as she scans my face. "Of course. We'll set down immediately."

"Arabella, what's wrong?" Gideon wraps his arms around me, pulling me against him.

"I can't explain. I can't—"

"Arabella?"

The world wobbles. The scorpions sting. The last thing I see before I pass out is Gideon's pale and worried face.

18

Arabella

Maisie: O Magnificent One, I've put up audition notices around the village – we're expecting a great crowd. Thank you again for doing this! See you tonight at book club!

"Something smells amazing." Winnie breathes deeply as she pushes open the door of Nevermore Bookshop. "That can only mean one thing."

"Celeste is back," I answer for her. Celeste has been running away to help her mum at least once a month now. As a vampire, I have no need of her sweet treats, but I miss Celeste when she's gone. She's a calming influence on my friends, even if only for the fact that it's difficult for Isis and Komal to infuriate me when they have their mouths filled with cheese scones.

"I smell butterscotch!" Maisie huffs as she runs up the steps behind us, her duck, James Pond, trotting alongside her, dressed in a Sherlock Holmes hat and matching capelet, and tugging imperiously on his lead. "Celeste is here!"

"Why is the duck at book club?" I ask.

"Yeah, I thought Heathcliff has a rule about no other feathered animals in the shop," adds Winnie.

"He'll have to deal this week. James Pond can't be left alone. He's stressed." Maisie hugs him to her chest. "He's worried that if we don't save the paper, I'll no longer be able to keep him in the manner to which he's become accustomed."

"You mean, he'll have to give up the duck Versailles you've built for him in your back garden and all those duck costumes he wears on his duck Instagram page and the fancy duck food you order in from Germany and he'll have to live in a communal pond with other pleb ducks?" I smirk. "However will he cope?"

"Quack," James Pond says mournfully, hanging his head.

"Don't remind him of the stakes." Maisie kisses his head. "But I'm sure, with you at the helm of the Zen and Tonic Variety Show, everything will be fine."

My stomach clenches. I should never have agreed to direct the show. I only did it because it seemed like a good opportunity to torture Gideon, but Maisie is putting a lot of hope into raising enough money to keep her job. Now, if the variety show is an abysmal failure, it'll be my fault and I won't be able to fix things with an anonymous donation if the council doesn't think the community is behind the paper being saved.

This is why I don't like doing things for other people.

"Let's go inside." I clench my jaw and turn the handle.

Laughter booms from the events room. We pass through the shop, Maisie holding James Pond's beak shut so he doesn't alert Heathcliff to his presence. When we step into the events room, Celeste bounces over and thrusts a tray into our faces.

"I made butterscotch tarts and cheese scones," she announces. The cupcake charms on her silver hoop earrings dance jauntily as she bobs her head. "You have to try them while they're still warm."

"Yes, carbs. Just the thing to distract me from my miserable existence." Maisie takes two scones. "How's your mum, Celeste?"

"She's going a little feral being stuck at home, but that's why she needs me so much." Celeste sets down a platter of mini quiches next to the scones. "I'll be back to help her again in a few weeks, but in the meantime, fill me in on everything I missed. How was the grand opening of Beth's pole studio?"

"Great!" Isis blurts out. "It turns out that Arabella used to be a dancer."

"She *invented* pole dancing at a Paris cabaret," Winnie explains. "Toulouse-Lautrec painted her portrait and everything."

He isn't the only one. I think of the painting that now has pride of place in my living room.

Celeste turns to me, her eyes wide, a silent question passing between us. "I'm not surprised. We all know Arabella is someone special."

"She is! She wowed the whole village and convinced a bunch of people to sign up to the studio. A group of her friends from Sanctus are now showing up for my vamp-friendly pole class and cashing in their ten per cent off vampire facials." Beth grins at me from her usual beanbag. "Although they keep asking if you're going to teach a class."

"I'd rather pull out my fangs with rusty tweezers."

"You'd be amazing."

"I'm already swamped with work and moving and plotting to disembowel Gideon, and now directing this bloody variety show *someone* signed me up for." I glare at Maisie. "No way do I have time to help a bunch of giggling vampires locate their divine feminine."

"Speaking of, who here is going to do an act? Arabella can't be our Simon Cowell without a few innocent souls to crush." Maisie beams at everyone.

Mina shakes her head. "Quoth and I have already agreed to help with costumes."

"I'm the MC," Komal says. "And I'm doing the promotion."

"Sorry, Arabella. I'm flat out behind the scenes at the studio," Beth says. "But I am helping with choreography for some of my students who want to perform."

"I'd love to, but I opened what I thought was a cupboard the other day and discovered a whole other wing of Black Crag that needs organising," Winnie moans. "Alaric has an *entire room* filled with Ancient Egyptian artefacts. I know everyone goes through an Ancient Egypt phase, but they usually grow out of it by age twelve and don't spend a small fortune collecting dusty old grave goods and then move on to their taxidermy era and *forget about them.* Who *forgets* about a room filled with mummies?"

"If Alaric needs help turning those mummies into cash, I know a guy," I say.

"If I can convince him to part with anything, I'll let you know," Winnie rolls her eyes.

"Dora and I are doing a routine," Isis pipes up. "I think we have a shot at first place."

"When did I agree to this?" Dora splutters.

"Last night. We were curled up on my sofa watching *Practical Magic*."

"I was asleep!"

"I didn't say you were awake when you agreed."

Dora glares at her sister. Her lip wobbles, and I know she's thinking about how her husband will react.

Add that to my list of director duties – make sure Mike is aware of the consequences should he make a fuss.

Celeste frowns at her phone. I assume she's looking at her calendar, but she has an astronomy app open. "I'm going to be at Mum's the week of the variety show. I'm so sorry, team. I've been letting everyone down lately."

"You haven't," Mina assures her. "Your mum needs you. Besides, we've got everything sorted."

"But the killer is still at large, and Maisie's on the brink of losing her job." Celeste's gaze falls to the floor. There's no reason for her to feel *guilty*. None of this is her fault. But Celeste always takes responsibility for others' pain. I've always said it's her greatest weakness. "And who knows what the vampire world is going to do with Winnie and Alaric—"

I sigh, attempting to change the subject before she spirals. "Can we actually talk about the book this week?"

"Yes, let's talk books! The first item of business – I have copies for all of us of next week's book." Mina holds up a paperback. She doesn't realise she's holding it backwards, but I recognise the design on the back cover as the choice I threw into the hat. *Freestyle* by Bea Paige.

"I finished the whole series," I tell her. "For those who haven't read it yet, i.e. every other member of this supposed *book club*, it's about a dancer who ends up with not one but four beautiful dancing men. It has the most amazing descriptions of movement—"

"Now I know why you chose that series." Mina's eyes sparkle. "All the hot dancers."

"*And* it's a second chance romance." I fold my arms. "My favourite kind."

"I'll bet." Winnie winks at me.

"Second chance is sooooo angsty." Isis makes a face. "And there are always too many flashbacks. I want a fun fake-dating story."

"No thanks." Winnie makes a face. "I don't want to read about my life. I'm still not over the trauma of trying to convince Alaric's mother not to eat me."

"I *love* the flashbacks, and I could use a little angst." Maisie grabs one of the paperback copies from the stack at Mina's feet. "It'll take my mind off the fact that I might not have a job in a month."

"I can't believe the council won't fund the paper," Celeste says.

Maisie slams her fist into a cushion. "Exactly. It's ridiculous, but they say subscriber numbers are too low for the resources we're allotted. People need local news! We inform the village about important things, except not a certain killer who's still at large, since only vampires know about that."

"Do we still think it's Gideon?" Celeste asks.

"No," Winnie and Dora say at the same time. I keep my lips firmly pursed because I'm not going to give Gideon a free pass on anything, even though I have to admit it's unlikely that he's the killer. For all his (considerable) faults, Gideon cares about Sanctus too much to risk putting it in the limelight by killing and husking ex-employees.

Winnie raises an eyebrow at me but doesn't say anything.

"But Gideon is letting us lead the investigation, and we *do* think the killer lives on Sanctus Estate," Mina adds, then explains what we know about the Thralled staff and Danny O'Hare. Maisie writes all the information we have up on a whiteboard for everyone to see, and dictates it into Mina's phone.

"So, what's our next step in the investigation?" Celeste crunches down on a butterscotch tart.

"We need to talk to the staff." Maisie is already back in investigative journalist mode now that she's sweet-talked me into being her director. "Maybe one of them will know if anything untoward is happening behind the scenes."

"Maybe we're going about this the wrong way." Isis glances over at the purple cloth covering the table in the corner. "We're thinking like amateur detectives when we could use magic—"

The other original members of the Nevermore Murder Club and Smutty Book Coven exchange weary glances.

"You've never told me what's underneath that purple cloth," Winnie says.

"Something that should not be discussed or disturbed under *any* circumstances," Dora says with finality.

"Remember the last time we used it?" Celeste wrings her hands, her cupcake earrings swinging wildly. "I still have nightmares."

"The *foxgloves*." Beth wraps her arms around herself.

"The *squirrels*." Maisie shudders.

"It's why we keep it here," Mina reminds everyone. "The bookshop is one of the few places in Argleton that has magic literally flowing in the pipes. It will keep the blasted thing safe from the wrong sorts of people and *us* safe from *it*."

"Fine." Isis pouts. "I'm just saying that we have other tools at our disposal."

"Let's save that one for when we're desperate," Beth says quickly. "And we're not desperate yet. So far, the killer seems to have gone into hibernation."

"Besides, you're magical, aren't you, Isis?" Komal says gently. "We don't need that when we have you."

I roll my eyes. Isis is as magical as a cinder block.

Isis's lip wobbles, but she shores up and breaks into a smile. "Exactly. If we need magic to help us, I can make that happen. But we're not there yet."

"Arabella, you keep leaning on Gideon, doing whatever you can to get more information from him," Maisie says.

"Yeah, Arabella." Komal nudges me. "You've got to dig *deep*, *pump* him for information, positively *deep throat* all his facts."

"And see if you and Winnie can talk to some of the staff," Mina adds, ignoring Komal's nonsense.

"That's not going to work. Everyone on the estate is an insufferable snob," I sigh. "Present company included. They'll be suspicious if a member of Sanctus starts asking them about their lives."

"Good point." Mina rubs her chin. "I know! Several of us are invited to the opening of Gideon's Midnight Garden next week—"

"For our sins," Winnie moans. "I'm drowning under broken sculptures and marble dust. Which reminds me. Celeste – Gideon's secretary wants to talk to you about catering for the human guests."

Celeste's face goes white. "For the vampire party? Um … I don't know, it's short notice—"

"You once made a three-tier cake shaped like Jason Momoa in forty-five minutes for Mrs Ellis's seventieth birthday," Dora reminds her. "You've got this."

"And Gideon will pay well," Winnie smiles. "Arabella's made sure of that."

"It's perfect!" Mina claps her hands. "Celeste is doing the food, Maisie is covering it for the paper, I'm there as Quoth's guest, Winnie's there with Alaric, and Arabella will be with her friends. We'll use the gala to talk to the staff and sniff out some secrets. With so many of us, we're bound to uncover something. Arabella shouldn't have to do all the work on this case."

I nod. "For once, we are in perfect agreement."

As the others chime in with ideas and theories, Celeste slumps down in her seat, her face miserable. I recall that Celeste had gone to her mother's house during Alaric's ball. Is she *deliberately* avoiding being around my kin?

For the first time, I look at my friend in a new light. I know Celeste has secrets, and no one respects her right to privacy more than me. But does Celeste know something she's not telling us?

I try to catch up with Celeste after the meeting, but she practically flees for the door before Mina has even finished wrapping up her plot summary of this week's book.

"Thank you again, Arabella, O Magnificent One." Maisie grins at me, but thankfully, she and her duck don't try to hug me again. "I'll see you at the auditions on Saturday."

"We'll see you there, too!" Isis waves as she drags a protesting Dora towards the door. "We're going to practise now."

"You'll need all the practice you can get because I won't be playing favourites."

"Don't worry. You will tremble before our talent and sheer audacity!"

"Exactly," Dora mumbles. "Behold our brilliance and despair."

Beth corners me as I help Winnie arrange the beanbags in colour-coded piles in the corner. "Maisie is so grateful for your help. I know you like to pretend you don't care about people, but you're a good friend, Arabella."

"I'm *not* teaching a vampire pole class," I growl.

"Why not?" she moans. "Don't you want to dance again? You love it."

I do love it.

But I'm never dancing again. It's too dangerous. Especially with ghosts from my past like Paul Badica and Gideon Blake around.

"I don't have to explain myself. I'm not doing it, and that's my final answer."

"It was worth a shot." Beth waves. "See you!"

After we've straightened the events room to Winnie's exacting standards, we say goodnight to Mina and the two of us walk up Butcher Street towards the Rose & Wimple, where Alaric is having a glass of blood with his Thrall, Reginald. I'd parked my car in the pub parking lot, but when I step into the space, it's gone.

"Someone stole my car!" Rage consumes me. How dare some punk touch my precious vehicle?

"Don't panic." Winnie pats my shoulder. "I'm sure it's around here somewhere."

"It's not like I've misplaced a sweater. I parked it right here, and now it's gone. When I find the person who did this, I'm going to lick off all their cartilage—"

Winnie rolls her eyes. "You vampires, always jumping straight to the stabbing and cartilage-licking. You gotta learn to *chill*. Why don't we just go up to the pub and hang out—"

"I'm not 'chill'. I don't 'hang out'. I swear unbreakable oaths. I eviscerate my enemies. I turn the blood of those who wrong me into delicious cocktails with tiny umbrellas made from their skin."

Winnie holds up her hands. "Okay, okay, I got it. No chill whatsoever. We'll call the police and make a report. Reginald can drive you home. I'm sure your car will turn up—"

A figure steps out of the shadows.

"Gideon?" I frown at him, suspicious. What's he doing in the village, skulking around near the alleyway where Danny O'Hare was found dead? He looks far too hot to be up to anything innocent in a pair of arse-hugging tailored trousers, a glittering Armani watch, and a cobalt silk shirt that matches his eyes rolled up to the elbows. "What are you doing here?"

"She means 'hello'," Winnie finishes.

"No, she doesn't," I snap.

"I've come to give you a ride back to Sanctus." He grins. "It's all part of our personal service for our members."

"Well, you can personal service yourself out of my way. I brought my car." *As soon as I locate the bastard who stole it and feast on their liver.*

"I know." His grin widens. "And a very nice ride it is, too. I had Sinead drive it home for you."

He *what?*

But how did she—

I dig in my wallet for my keys, but they're still there. "You *broke into my car?*"

Behind me, Winnie makes a choking noise.

"Technically, *Sinead* broke into your car. I merely provided her with the means to do it."

"You ... you—"

"I'm as cunning as ten foxes in a trench coat, each with a degree in cunning from Cambridge University. You're welcome. Shall we?" Gideon gestures to the Lamborghini looking completely out of place in the pub parking lot.

Is he on some kind of vampire drug? "Why would you imagine I'd want to get in a car with you after you've shown me that you have no respect for my property or agency?"

"Because I have an angelic face." He opens the passenger door. "And I have a surprise for you."

"If it's anything like the last surprise, I'll pass."

Winnie looks like she's trying not to laugh. "I'll just ... leave you to deal with this, Arabella. And don't forget your *special job* for the book club."

Oh, right. In the throes of discovering Gideon stole my car, I forgot that I'm supposed to find out more about Thralls at Sanctus.

My only other option for getting home is to take a taxi. Arabella Lestrange does not ride in taxis. And I haven't yet mastered the vampiric skill of turning into hundreds of bats when annoyed.

Think of your revenge. Think of how delightful it will be to watch Gideon's face collapse as he realises you've taken Sanctus from him.

I swallow back my annoyance and smile like I've already won. "Drive me back to Sanctus. But if you so much as breathe in my direction, I'm crunching your kneecaps like potato chips."

Wrath collects in the corners of his eyes. "I learned my lesson at the pole dance studio. Trust me, I'll be the perfect gentleman." Gideon gestures to the open door. "Your chariot awaits."

I slide into the luxurious leather seat. I want to find something to complain about but, honestly, the car is gorgeous. I'd been considering one before I bought my Alfa Romeo, but I didn't want to drive something conspicuous when I'm trying to lie low in Argleton.

Not that it did me any good. I need to deal with Paul Badica before he opens his big mouth and spoils everything I've built for myself.

I sink down in the seat, enjoying the way the leather hugs my body. Gideon slides into the driver's seat, plants his foot on the gas, and the car leaps away.

I must admit, I love the low rumble of the engine and the way it grips the road as we tear out of the village and into the farmland, heading the long way towards Sanctus' western gates. Gideon handles the winding country roads with ease. He oozes Bond villain energy as he allows the car to joyfully do what it does best – fly around corners and make my heart pound like my human friends' at a Black Friday book sale.

I pretend not to notice him glancing over at me every few seconds, or the way I keep having to tear my eyes away from the veins along his forearms.

As we careen down an avenue of ancient oaks, Gideon slows to a stop and pulls over on the side of the road.

"Do you want to drive?"

His wicked grin makes warmth pool in my chest.

"You'd let me behind the wheel?"

"I see the way you're biting your lip. You can hardly contain yourself. If Arabella Lestrange wants to tame this beast, then she's welcome to try." He pauses. "Just don't go too fast. This thing has a hair-trigger accelerator and it can run away with you—"

"Speed doesn't kill vampires, Gideon. It's suddenly becoming stationary that makes all the mess."

"Well, please don't make a mess. I have to keep the leather pristine or Winnie will never accept a ride from me again."

I momentarily forget how much I hate Gideon in my haste to scramble around to the other side of the car. He steps out and makes some grand gesture, which I ignore. I slide into the driver's seat, my feet finding the pedals. The leather hugs my curves like it was made for me.

Gideon opens the door to climb into the passenger seat, but I plant my foot and the car leaps away.

The wind slams the door shut, and I'm alone in the most beautiful machine humans have ever created. I cackle like a witch who's just discovered a self-cleaning cauldron.

I know I'm supposed to be seducing him, I know I'm waiting for my real revenge, but the look on his face as I left him in my dust was too good to resist.

I tear through the woodland path, carving up the corners and making the tyres squeal. My heart leaps in my throat, my breath hot and heavy as the rush of adrenaline warms my icy veins.

It's been a long time since I felt this free.

Not since the hot air balloon over Paris, or the night—

No. Don't think about that night. Don't let yourself believe this warmth in your veins or the pulse between your legs is because of Gideon.

He betrayed me.

He stole from me.

He burned my theatre.

He destroyed everything I built for myself.

Because of him, I had to start over from scratch. Again.

And he's so ready to believe that I'll forgive him. Leaving him on the side of the road is *nothing* compared to what he did.

I slow down as I pull up to the Sanctus gates and flash my ID at the security guard.

"Welcome home, Ms Lestrange. Um … isn't that Mr Blake's car?" The guard looks puzzled.

I smirk. "He lent it to me."

"Oh, um, yes. That isn't in my instructions." The guard glances down at some notes. "Mr Blake would have you go up to Sanctus House. I guess he's meeting you there in another vehicle?"

I'd like to see him try.

I park the car diagonally across three parking spaces. I can't resist having a little snoop around before I step out of the car. The glove compartment is filled with paperback dark romance novels – some of my favourites – with their edges dog-eared and notes scribbled in the margins. Most of the notes are simply, "WTF???"

Curious.

Sinead studies me as she meets me at the entrance, no doubt trying to puzzle out why Gideon isn't here. I can *taste* her loathing in the cool air. It's tiresome – I'm not going to stop Gideon nibbling on her neck. But she plasters a smile on her face as she ushers me inside.

Why does she look so familiar to me?

"Your car is parked in front of your property, Ms Lestrange."

"Thank you, Sinead. I appreciate your attentive and personal service." I lean in close, hissing in her ear. "If I find you have adjusted my seat, I will use your rib cage as a xylophone."

She swallows. "F-f-follow me. You and Gideon were supposed to arrive together, but I guess he'll be along shortly."

I wouldn't count on it.

She leads me away from the lively crowd gathering at Brimstone and down a wide hallway to a locked door with a RESERVED sign. Sinead pushes it open and ushers me inside. Gideon has set up two chairs in front of a large projector. A bottle of blood sits on the table with two glasses, and a series of candles are lined up beside them. The title screen for the film reads "Moulin Rouge".

Interesting – a film about the Paris cabaret that was one of my biggest competitors. I'll enjoy picking apart everything inferior to La Petite Mort, starting with the lack of blood.

I inspect the candles. They all bear a Spell The Tea label. Are my friends in on this? I sniff a red cherry candle, enjoying the notes of one of my favourite scents, although I prefer it when it's mixed with honey and poppy—

This is actually … sweet.

No, it's not.

It's … it's presumptuous. Why does Gideon think I'd like to spend an evening drinking blood and watching a movie with *him?* After he stole my car? It's the kind of thing that would be hot in a dark romance novel but in real life …

I can't stand Gideon.

Although … drinking blood and watching a movie *would* be the perfect chance to grill him about the Thralls on the estate.

Except that Gideon's not here because I left him on the side of the road.

Oh well, I'm not wasting a perfectly decent bottle of Duke. I settle into the nearest seat, slide the cork from the neck, and call out to Sinead, "Roll film!"

"I see you're enjoying your surprise."

I stretch languidly in my reclined seat and glance over my shoulder. Gideon leans against the doorframe, the warmth in his eyes edged with danger, just the way I like it. There are leaves in his hair and a smudge of dirt across his cheek. His once-immaculate trousers are torn.

He looks hot like this, like a forest nymph after a drunken revel.

"Took you long enough," I murmur, raising my nearly empty glass to my lips. Truthfully, it hasn't taken him long at all – most vampires can move much faster than humans when we want to. Sinead looks up from where she kneels at my feet, giving me the best massage I've ever had in my life. "What happened to your watch?"

He regards his naked wrist with wariness. "I lost it in a fierce battle with a badger."

I blink.

Gideon grins. "It was either give him my watch or he'd scratch up my beautiful face. What choice did I have? That badger is going to pull all the hot badger-ettes with his new bling."

Sinead untangles herself from my feet and throws herself at Gideon. "What happened to you, Sir?"

Gideon sinks into the chair beside me. "What happened, Sinead, is that I'm going to need another bottle of blood." He shakes the bottle I've been enjoying. The dregs slosh around. "Be a doll and fetch one for me."

Sinead shoots me a vile glare before storming out.

"Tsk, someone should teach Sinead that other women aren't her competition."

"She's upset because I'm not drinking from her," Gideon says. "And possibly because I smell like badger."

He doesn't smell like a badger, but he does smell like the woods and sweat and red cherries. I wave my hand. "I don't mind if you pop open one of Sinead's veins. You must be thirsty after your walk."

Gideon fixes his gaze on me. "There are a lot of marks on her neck. I think she's getting addicted. We've already had an incident—"

He cuts himself off.

"Danny?"

Gideon sighs. "Yes, Ms Nevermore Coven, I'm talking about Danny. We never had any complaints about Patrick Stock, and he wasn't a Thrall, so I don't think their deaths are linked to Sanctus, but your friends are determined to prove me wrong. Danny *was* a menace. Members were going off him – he was bothering the female residents, touching them inappropriately while they were feeding. Alyra made a complaint and we let him go, but he came back a couple of times, demanding we rehire him or he'd reveal our secrets. Lilac snuck one of her potions into his drink at the pub, but he was husked before we found out if it worked." Gideon accepts a bottle from Sinead and slides the cork out in a sensuous motion. "I'm sorry he was killed in such a brutal way, but I'm not sorry that he's no longer making women uncomfortable. Speaking of uncomfortable …"

He reaches beneath himself and draws out a long, gnarled twig, wincing as he tosses it into the corner of the room.

"I can't believe you walked back to Sanctus."

I wish I wasn't impressed, but I am.

Gideon pulls off a leaf stuck to his shoulder. "There was no phone reception on that road, and there aren't exactly many cars going past at this time of night. It was a pleasant walk. I got to catch up with my badger friend. What do you think of the movie so far?"

"The operatic excess of it appeals to me, but must we have all that *singing*?"

"I thought you loved opera."

"That was no opera."

He grins wickedly. "I knew you'd love it."

"It reminds me …" I trail off as a blur of tassels and corsetry and peacock feathers soaked in blood dance across my memories. I gesture to the line of scented candles on the table between us. "Why the candles?"

"Ah, now these are genius." Gideon leans forward and lights each one with a silver lighter pulled from the dark recesses of his suit. "We can enjoy the scents of a human movie theatre without having to *eat* the food or be around other people. That one is butter popcorn, that one is some sort of cherry-flavoured candy, and this one is foot odour from when other people take their shoes off. And this one reminds me of … well, you just have to smell it."

He holds the candle up to my nose. Notes of peony, iris, waterlily and apple blossom stir a bitter memory. I'm the woman in the painting, lying back on the stones, bathed in the scent of blooming flowers, my naked skin kissed by the moonlight, and Gideon …

I wrinkle my nose and set down the candle. "Why did you do this?"

"I thought it was obvious." Gideon shrugs. "It's my grand gesture."

"What?"

"My grand gesture. Like in the romance novels you love. Me and you … we were amazing together, remember?"

I fold my arms. "No."

He sighs. "I'm not denying that mistakes were made. We don't get to go back in time and fix the things that were broken, but this is the next best thing. A second chance to make this work. Hardly anyone gets that, but *we* do. Isn't that amazing?"

He looks so *earnest*, with all his dangerous edges softened by sentiment. This is exactly what I wanted. Gideon Blake is still completely besotted with me. This will make the moment I betray him that much sweeter.

But I can't let him think he's won me over so easily, or he'll know something is up.

"That's called being a vampire," I bite out. "Our lives are an eternity of second chances. It's rather tedious."

"That's a lie and you know it. You *love* what we are. You love never growing old, always being the most beautiful woman in the room, and getting to pull out all your vintage clothes once they become fashionable again." He pauses. "And you love to dance."

I snort. "I haven't danced since my theatre was taken from me."

"That doesn't mean you don't love it. What about at Zen and Tonic?" A note of something like awe enters Gideon's voice.

"I was doing a favour for Beth."

Gideon holds up a finger. "You love your friends."

I huff. This is becoming rather too personal for my liking. "My friends are the most ludicrous, most annoying—"

"And yet, you *chose* them. Winnie tells me you're at book club every week. You may huff and puff like a big bad wolf, but you're the one they count on." He leans back in his chair, folding his arms behind his head, and smirks at me with that same self-satisfied look that drew me to him one hundred and fifty years ago. "And you love fighting with me."

"I do not."

"You do. Admit it. You may be throwing darts at my face, but you're the one who put my picture on the target. No one goes to so much effort to hate someone who means nothing to them." Gideon grins.

My fingers curl into fists. I'm going to wipe that grin off his face. How *dare* he make up such a ridiculous story?

"You're *absurd*."

That infuriating grin makes his eyes sparkle. "You're the same Arabella. The music never left you."

Yes, it did. The music left me because you took it away.

I want to find a way to hurt him, to level things between us. Because if I'm the same Arabella, then he's the same Gideon – that warm, life-loving human boy who made me see the world as more than a cruel, harsh place to be endured.

I can't give him an inch. We're each as strong-willed as the other, and for some unknown reason, he seems to believe I'll give us another chance.

Gideon leans over, his hand brushing my thigh in the *exact* spot where he knelt for me, all those years ago.

Now he's a vampire, his skin should be cool, like mine. But everywhere he touches is fire.

For all he says that we're the same as we were back then, we're not.

I'm no longer a sex worker scrabbling to make a life for myself.

He's no longer human. No longer forbidden.

"You don't know how many times over the years I've thought of things I'd like to do with you," he murmurs. "Or to you. When this movie came out, all I could see when I closed my eyes was you lying on that huge, ridiculous bed of yours in your gold corset …"

His voice chokes.

I shake my head. I don't want to remember that corset, that night. The night I let Gideon Blake into my heart and he betrayed me.

He moves closer, his breath caressing my cheeks. "Haven't you thought of me over the last century?"

"Only when I took out the rubbish."

He is always so expressive, the complete opposite of me. I never want people to see how I feel. My emotions are secrets to be hidden away. Except for all those times when I let slip around him.

Not this time.

I was weak for Gideon Blake once before. I don't make the same mistake twice.

"I did think about all the different ways I might separate your head from your body," I add.

"That's a permanent solution to a rather handsome problem." Gideon rubs his chin. "I remember you saying something different last time we were alone together. You said—"

"We're not talking about the past." I don't want to know what I said. I *especially* don't want to know why Gideon remembers what I said to him over one hundred and fifty years ago. "Either watch the film in silence or leave me in peace."

Gideon leans back in his chair. I watch out of the corner of my eye as he brings the glass to his lips and takes a languid sip, as if he isn't bothered by my indifference. I want to bother him. I want my words to sting, yet he seems completely content to silently watch this movie.

I try to focus on the storyline, but I keep being drawn back to the man beside me.

What has he been doing since he left me in Paris?

How did he end up in Argleton, of all places? How did he become one of the most innovative property developers in the Upyr world? And how did he do it all without me knowing about him?

How did he end up an Upyr?

He *was* human when we had our liaison. A vampire can scent another of our kind. Besides, he'd been out during the day. That was how he arranged—

Stop thinking about it.

I try to focus on the film, but curiosity gnaws at me. I pinch the flame of the cherry candle between my fingers, savouring the slight sting of pain.

"When did you become an Upyr?"

"I thought we weren't talking about the past?" He raises an eyebrow.

"We're not talking about *our* past. But this—" I gesture at the general Gideon-ness of him. "—happened after you were with me."

"Lucien Vega made me an offer I couldn't refuse." Gideon's voice darkens. *Ah, so Gideon Blake isn't immune to secrets.* "What about you? You never did tell me how *you* became an Upyr in possession of a necklace worn by Queen Cleopatra herself."

I lean across the table and overturn the candle. He yelps as crimson wax drips down his face, hardening on his cool skin to create eldritch dribbles. I pick up my handbag and Gideon's car keys and leave without a word.

He doesn't get that piece of me.

Not until he's earned it.

And he'll never earn that secret.

EMAIL TO GIDEON BLAKE FROM ÉDOUARD MANET

Gideon, my dear friend. How positively *scandalous* to hear from you! After all the drama you've caused within the Conclave, I'm almost regretting not taking you up on the offer of a property at Sanctus.

Unfortunately, my muse does not respond to fog and drizzle. Speaking of which, I can't convince you to join us in Mykonos at the end of the summer? We're having a riotous time. You should see Nikola Tesla after he's been on the ouzo.

Of course, I remember Arabella from La Petite Mort. She was such a lovely addition to our little fete. Alas, I've had no contact with our seductive hostess. She disappeared along with the theatre, and I must admit that I've been distracted by, well, undead life. 150 years of it, and hasn't it been glorious? The art world has come a long way and made me obscenely rich. About time, I say! How I wish our dear friend Claude could have lived to see how beloved he became, or that Rodin finally managed to get into Renoir's pants. I offered them all the Kiss at various times over the years, but they were all too attached to the romance of death to take me up on it.

Artists, so temperamental! Am I right?

To your question. Yes, I recall Arabella's jewels. That silly curse has certainly proved true in Arabella's case, has it not?

I have followed news of the Antirhodos Collar over the years, not that there has been much news – only rumours about it resurfacing on the antiquities market in the 1920s before being snapped up by some mysterious wealthy collector.

If anyone can locate the jewels, it's me. If I do find them for you, you'd better be ready with absolute *piles* of money, because they will not be cheap. Give me some time to contact my sources.

In the meantime, if you truly wish to court the elusive and unpredictable Arabella, may I suggest speaking through art? It's always worked for me.

Yours, Édouard

19

Arabella
Then

BERNHARDT'S BALLOON MAKES EMERGENCY LANDING

In the early hours of this morning, the actress Sarah Bernhardt landed her hot air balloon in the Tuileries Garden, toppling a Rodin statue into the duck pond.

It's reported that a member of their party was rushed away from the scene, possibly taken ill from the airborne revelry. Bernhardt herself was spied drinking champagne from the mouth of a bottle and swinging a sword at passers-by. She is positively scandalous!

I'M DROWNING. I'M FIGHTING FOR AIR. HANDS WRAP AROUND MY neck, tugging, choking, fighting to free the jewels—

I wake with a wild jerk from the cold death of daysleep, my head pounding, my limbs weighed down by an invisible force.

Immediately, I know things are wrong. I'm not in my dark, windowless apartment in the coffin I have fashioned out of Parisian architecture. I am shrouded in silk, which is good. Arabella Macquart doesn't sleep in anything less. But candlelight flickers all around me.

And I *hurt*.

My limbs are made of a fire that bites and gnashes. My fangs scrape against my lip. They're heavy in my mouth, like I'm biting two coffin nails. My vision swirls, and I fight against the fogginess of my mind, searching for answers.

I force my hands to move, to rise to my throat and feel for the heavy weight of my collar.

It's still there. I still have my magic.

As the room comes into clarity, I don't see answers, but I do see Gideon. He peers down at me, a wobbly smile on his face. He looks a mess – his hair unkempt, his eyes ringed in dark circles, a line of stubble along his chin giving him a violent edge.

"You're awake." His smile cracks wide open. He calls over his shoulder, "She's awake!"

"Shoo, shoo!" A female voice cries out. My heart thuds against my ribs as Sarah Bernhardt – dressed in a flowing opera gown and fur stole – waves away a horde of medical men. She slams the door behind them.

Panic rises inside me. Those medical men must have examined me. They would have drawn my blood. Will they figure out what I am?

No. I have my necklace. The magic will protect me, as it has protected me all these years.

I wrestle with the silk sheets, frantically trying to untangle myself. Gideon reaches out to press me back into the bed, and I fling him across the room.

He crashes into a tea table, sending fine china and wood splinters in all directions.

Oops.

My breath heaves in my chest. My lungs are made of molten metal. They're not working as they should. I kick my legs out of the sheets. I have to get out of here. He smells too delicious …

"You should rest a while more," Sarah says breezily, as if all of this is completely normal. "You took quite a turn. Giddy has been nursing you for three days and nights."

He has?

Snatches of memory come back to me. We were in Sarah's hot air balloon, and I was having such a grand time, I didn't realise I'd stayed out too late until the sun peeked over the horizon. The last thing I remember is Gideon catching me as I collapsed and—

"Ow." Gideon picks himself up and rubs his head where he hit the table. "I brought you here. I didn't know what else to do. I have no idea where you live, and I didn't think you'd want anyone at La Petite Mort to see you like this."

I slump back against the pillows, my head spinning and my stomach growling with hunger. My sire made me all too aware of the effects of the sun. I've avoided it up until now, not wanting to put myself in a vulnerable position. But I was having such a good time that I became careless, and look what happened.

And Gideon … what does he think? Has he seen my fangs? Has he figured out what I am? He can't have, because if he had, he would have run far away or called the *commissaire de police*.

The magic is still protecting me.

I touch my collar as Gideon kneels beside the bed, his hand stroking my forehead. "You're still so cold. Should I have the fire lit?"

"Do stop fussing, Giddy. Let her catch her breath." Sarah floats across the room, picking up one of her lipsticks from the vanity and reapplying the crimson colour with intense concentration.

Gideon looks so worried. My chest pangs – a sharp pain that I'm afraid has nothing to do with my malaise. No one has cared about me like this since my mother.

I need to get out of here before I say or do something to reveal myself and place everything I've built in danger … but the simple act of sitting up against the silken pillows leaves me light-headed. Gideon places my hands in his. I don't have the strength or the desire to pull away.

"Arabella, what happened up there? We were having such a lovely night, but then you fainted. And your skin blistered." His voice cracks. "It was horrible. You looked as if you were burning, but I could see no fire. Sarah landed the balloon in the Tuileries Garden. We wrapped you in Sarah's furs and brought you here, but none of the doctors could help you. They forced all these horrible concoctions down your throat. They wouldn't tell me what was in them but they smelled *delightful*." He makes a face. "I thought I lost you."

"Drink." Sarah passes me a goblet.

Gideon's eyes widen. "She probably shouldn't have wine in her state."

"Give me that." My hands tremble as I lift the goblet to my lips. The scent of blood hits me in the face, and it's all I can do to sip like a lady instead of guzzling the whole thing. I finish the drink and wipe blood from my lips.

I needed that. It's not a miracle cure, but I do feel steady.

I glance up at Sarah. She winks at me. Gently, so that Gideon doesn't notice, she brushes her hand over the fur stole she wears around her neck, revealing twin dots of nearly healed fang marks.

Of course. Sarah moves in the same circles as Gideon's boss, Lucien Vega. While not a vampire herself – I would have smelled her – she is a Thrall. She felt my fangs when she kissed me and understood instantly what I was. Those doctors must know, as well. They must have been feeding me blood, trying to wake me up and hurry along the healing.

I run my fingers along my arms, over my neck. Gideon takes my hand in his and presses it to the swell of my breasts.

"It's a miracle," he breathes. "Your beautiful skin was so damaged, but you healed in just three short days. And you're awake. You came back to me."

Something cool slithers along my leg. I glance down, watching in numb fascination as the same something moves beneath the sheets, tipping over the discarded goblet.

Something that is very definitely not part of my personage.

"Cleo, *no*. That's naughty." Sarah leaps for the bedsheets and wrestles something out. My breath stills in my throat as a beautiful snake coils around her arm and undulates around her neck, its head raised and hood expanded to reveal a pattern of brightly coloured diamonds.

"This is Cleo II." Sarah holds out her arm and the snake rears its head back, regarding me with reptilian curiosity. "The naughty minx must have escaped her enclosure. She's intrigued by the scent of the wine."

I bet she is.

"Why Cleo II?" Gideon asks.

"Cleo after Queen Cleopatra, of course." Sarah pats the snake's head affectionately. Cleo's tongue flicks out. "She's an Egyptian Cobra, which is the snake Cleopatra likely used to kill herself. And she's Cleo II because she's my second snake. Cleo I sadly died when she swallowed an embroidered cushion. Snakes can be rather silly."

The snake regards me from Sarah's shoulder, her head gently swaying. She doesn't look silly at all. She is majestic, in charge of her fate, ready to bite anyone who crosses her. Like Sarah.

Like me.

Sarah holds out her hand. "Would you like to hold her?"

Gideon recoils, but I nod. Sarah places the snake on the corner of the bed. Cleo II slithers towards me, head raised, eyes watchful. I hold out my hand, knowing I have nothing to fear. If the snake bites me, she cannot kill me.

But she doesn't bite. Her cool body coils around my arm. I love the feeling of her muscles squeezing, her scaly skin sliding over mine, the beautiful diamond patterns shimmering in the candlelight.

"She likes you," Sarah says as she powders her cheeks. "You may keep her if you wish. I'm to sail to America for my tour within the week, and I'd like to know that she has a good home. She's nocturnal—"

Just like me.

"—although she enjoys sunning herself in the early mornings. Toads are her favourite food, but she's an excellent mouser and she will frighten away any unworthy suitors."

"That she will." Gideon's face is pale.

I hug Cleo II to my chest, my heart swelling, unable to believe how my life has expanded since Gideon walked into my theatre all those weeks ago. "I would be honoured to welcome Cleo to La Petite Mort."

Sarah leaves for her evening performance. Gideon sets out bowls of food in front of me. All of it smells disgusting.

I shove the bowls away. "Bring me wine."

He reaches for a white. I shake my head. "The bottle Sarah had before. The red."

He picks it off her vanity and sniffs, wrinkling his nose. "It's gone bad."

"That's the one I want, Gideon. *Please.*"

My voice cracks on the word. I've never asked for anything before. I never wanted to use that word with him.

I never asked for him to care for me like this.

Yet here he is.

Gideon rushes over with the bottle and pours me a tall glass. As I drink, he watches me intently. "You look so much better. I've been so worried."

"You never left my side?"

He nods. My heart does an uncomfortable fluttery thing.

"Lucien Vega must have loved that."

A shadow passes over Gideon's face. "He'll manage without me."

He sets the food aside and climbs up onto the bed, resting his head on the pink headboard and stretching his long legs out beside mine. He watches me as I drink the blood in long, hungry gulps. Cleo II slithers up to nestle along my side. Gideon shies away from her. "Are you going to keep that thing?"

"Don't call her a 'thing'." I stroke the snake's back, and she wriggles with delight. "Cleo and I have a lot in common. We're cold-blooded, wear diamonds, and will bite if attacked."

"I'm not frightened of you." He glares at the snake. "Either of you. Maybe I'd like to be bitten."

As if to prove it, he lays down beside me, wrapping his arms around my torso and pressing his body against me. Warmth radiates from his skin.

Cleo slithers over us. Gideon stiffens, but he doesn't flee. She curls up in a ball in the back of his thighs, seeking the warmth of his living flesh.

We have that in common, too.

He strokes my hair. "You don't have to be alone, Arabella. I'm here to take care of you."

I should bite him, drain him and run. Because he's wrong. I *have* to be alone. It's the only way I know I'll be safe.

Instead, I find myself sinking into his warmth, my head resting on the pillow as I fall into the dreamless sleep of a vampire who, for the first time, has someone to watch over her.

20

Gideon

Winnie: So that grand gesture was a bust. Perhaps a movie and candles weren't grand enough, or maybe the whole stealing her car thing was a bit TOO morally grey.

Yes, I know technically Sinead stole her car.

You're not giving up, are you? Maybe you just need to try something a little grander.

I sink into the soft leather seat of my car. A thick scent rises from the fabric, a chilly tang spiced with myrrh and ginger, like the first frost falling on fresh grass.

My car has been Arabella'd.

I breathe in deeply. I'm never washing this car again.

There's other evidence that she's been here, too.

Arabella has taken something sharp – possibly her fingernails – and scratched the words ARABELLA IS A SEXY BITCH into the dashboard.

It *is* true.

Humming, I turn the stereo up until my eardrums rattle and zip towards the village. Arabella has driven up to London to sell some religious relics to one of her contacts, so she won't be attempting to torment me tonight.

Thanks to Édouard's email, I'm one step closer to reuniting her with the Antirhodos Collar. He's also given me another idea to make Arabella see that destiny has brought us together again – for this, I need the help of my most trusted friend.

"If you've come about the sculptures, I'm not finished." Alaric frowns at the majestic raven taking flight from his workbench, every feather perfectly rendered in white marble. "And now I'll have to start this one again."

"What? Why?"

"Stop being polite." Alaric frowns at the sculpture. "I *know* you can see it. It's *obvious*. I cannot allow such an affront to the art of sculpture to see the light of day."

Before I can stop him, he kicks the sculpture off the workbench. It crashes to the ground. When the cloud of marble dust subsides, the raven is in five pieces.

Winnie, who is watching from the doorway, sighs.

"That's the fourth perfectly lovely sculpture he's destroyed this week," she tells me. "At this rate, you might need to hire Reginald to make sculptures out of margarine if you want anything to adorn your garden on opening night."

"My friend Alaric will come through for me."

I say it with more confidence than I feel. Even to this ex-criminal overlord, Alaric is *terrifying*. I prefer to stay on his good side.

Winnie makes a face. "Perhaps if he could *chill out* with the perfectionism and focus on *finishing* something."

Alaric frowns. "I don't need to chill out. I am a vampire. My blood is already cold—"

Winnie brightens. "Hey, I know, I'll bribe you! If you finish a sculpture and give it to Gideon, I'll do the thing you like …"

Alaric perks up immediately, but then stares glumly at the broken bits of raven at his feet. "Maybe this could count as *five* sculptures? Sort of a deconstructed sculpture park?"

"I'd prefer my park constructed, if it's all the same to you." I rub his shoulder. "I'm not here to bust your balls, Allie. I need your help. I have an idea for how to show Arabella that I've forgiven her for the whole trying-to-kill-me thing, and that I think she's beautiful and marvellous and I want to make her mine."

Winnie pipes up. "Is it gifting her a genuine Egyptian mummy? Because I can help with that."

Alaric looks pained. "I am not yet ready to part with my collection."

I grin. "Don't worry, friend. Your dusty old kings are safe from me. I'm going to create a sculpture of her for the garden."

Winnie claps her hands. "Oh, I love that idea! I think that could be just grand enough to work."

I plonk a worn, yellowed piece of paper on the table. "I want you to sculpt Arabella in this pose."

Alaric frowns at the poster. "Is this a Toulouse-Lautrec?"

Winnie runs over to look at the poster. "That's like the poster Beth had at her opening, except this one looks properly old. I still can't believe that's Arabella. Did she really wear those incredible jewels?"

"She did. Sadly, that necklace has been lost for over a century. But maybe not forever …" I shove the poster at Alaric. "So if you could just whip that up for me, Allie—"

Alaric folds his arms. "You do realise this isn't how art works. I'm not a dancing monkey who can carve you anything you like for a pat on the head."

I pat him on the head. "Well, what would you normally do?"

Alaric ducks under my arm and gestures to a fresh block of marble sitting on the workbench. "Normally, I would think of a pleasing form, and then I might trace a few lines on this block, and then I would take away the bits that aren't the pleasing form, and I'd be left with a likeness of my Winnie's beautiful figure."

"How am I going to win Arabella over with a sculpture of Winnie's tits?" I moan. "No offence, Winnie."

"None taken." Winnie's words are muffled by her hand over her mouth. Her shoulders shake. Is she *laughing*?

"I'm not sculpting any other woman's tits." Alaric folds his arms. "I am a man of honour."

"Give me that." I yank the chisel from his hand. "I'll do it. It will be more personal if it comes from me, anyway. Besides, it's just a hunk of rock. How hard can it be?"

21

Arabella

Celeste: I'm checking in on you – are you sure you're okay with this whole "pretend you're okay with Gideon to get close to him" plot? I want to find the killer as much as anyone but not if you have to do something you're uncomfortable with. The others would agree if you needed to back out. Know that I'm always here if you need anything.

"Maybe I can sneak out a couple of the larger coffins without him noticing. Or at least get you to help me sort through the chest of gold jewellery …"

I tap out a text to one of my coin merchants while I half-listen to Winnie talking through her issues with Alaric's surprise antiquities collection. When Winnie is struggling, she doesn't require a solution, just a warm body to help her work through her anxiety about towers of mummies falling on top of her. Her one-sided therapy session is preferable to her abominable heavy metal decluttering playlist, and gives me a chance to consider my options for taking Sanctus from Gideon.

The most logical course of action is to secretly alert the authorities to the definitely-not-legally-acquired artefacts hitting the antiquities markets. It *would* be nice and neat to get Gideon sent to prison for antiquities trafficking, but does run the risk of bringing down my network of contacts (and possibly me by association). I prefer this idea to spying for the Conclave, but that has—

"Arabella. You need to look at this."

That sounds bad. I rise and pick my way through clear storage containers filled with coins to where Winnie is working. She's started on the second row of coin sacks, but I can tell from the furrow in her brow that something's not right. She holds up one of the sacks and dumps out the contents.

It's filled with plastic packing beads.

"According to the manifest Gideon gave us, there are supposed to be two hundred and eighty-eight sacks of ancient coins of various denominations," Winnie says, her voice grave. "As far as I can tell, at least fifty of them have been emptied and filled with … *not* ancient coins. And that's not all. Most of those chests on the wall are empty. Gideon has a thief."

※

It takes me and Winnie hours to conduct a full inventory of the treasure vault. The results are as shocking as a villain dispatching a hero without a dramatic monologue.

Millions of pounds of treasure is missing.

Either Gideon hasn't been checking the treasure as it comes in, which doesn't seem like him, or someone on his staff has been ripping him off.

Winnie simmers with all the excitement of a volcano that's just discovered caffeine. "This could point us towards our killer. Perhaps Danny and Patrick caught the robber, who then killed them to keep their secret. Or … how about this? I wouldn't put it past Danny to be involved in this plot somehow. Wait until the other Nevermore Coven members hear about this."

As Winnie dials Mina and shouts her theories down the phone, I hide my smile behind the inventory list. What Winnie doesn't know is that her discovery has just handed me exactly what I wanted – a way to take Sanctus for myself.

I have you now, Gideon Blake.

Text Messages Between Komal and Maisie

Komal: You will not BELIEVE what Councillor Durant has done now.

Komal: He says that as tourism board director, I'm representing the council, so I'm not allowed to be involved in the variety show.

Maisie: What? But we need you to do the marketing. Otherwise, the audience will consist only of the Naughty Knitting Club and James Pond's duck friends.

Komal: No can do. Lord Future Mayor has handed down his decree. He's determined for this show to fail.

Maisie: That bastard! He's the reason we need the show! If he would just give the paper a proper budget, we'd be fine. I think he wants the Argleton Gazette shut down.

Komal: And that's not all. He's going to PERSONALLY oversee the chosen acts, and if there's anything too "licentious", he'll shut the whole thing down to preserve village "decency"!

Maisie: I'll give him village decency! And who even says "licentious" anymore?

Komal: Augustin Durant, and no one else. I can't believe he's going to be the mayor. He'll be terrible for the village, but there's no one qualified to run against him. I'm so mad. I'm going to fill his gym bag with onion bhajis. Want to join me?

Maisie: Hell yes.

22

Gideon
Then

Miss Arabella, I'm sending this note with Ms Bernhardt's messenger. I hope it reaches you in time. I need to tell you that Lucien Vega has returned to the theatre these last two nights in the company of two large, threatening men who were most anxious that I notice their silver-inlaid swords. He was MOST displeased when I said you weren't here. I've told them they're not to return to the theatre again, but I'm afraid if they do, I will not be able to stop them.

There have also been more bloody flowers left backstage, and a little songbird beheaded in your dressing-room.

Perhaps it is best if you remain away at this time.

Yours, Jacques

I STARE AT THE LETTER ON THE BEDSIDE TABLE WHILE ARABELLA sleeps. I *knew* Lucien would read into my disappearance, but I can't leave Arabella's side.

I swallow down my fear. I don't like the implication of the bloody flowers and beheaded songbird.

I hope he hasn't hurt Jacob.

He wants the necklace. Bring him the necklace and all of this will be over.

Jacob will be free. My business with Lucien Vega will be concluded. And Arabella will no longer be under threat from him.

But if I take the necklace, Arabella will know it was me. She'll never speak to me again. She'll send Jacques to break my kneecaps.

A dark voice inside me whispers, *Not if she's asleep.*

It could work. I'd pretend someone broke in, or one of Sarah's staff did it while my back was turned.

I curse myself for not taking the necklace from her when she passed out in the balloon. I could have pocketed it and told her it fell over the side. Truthfully, I'd been so worried about her that it never crossed my mind. Now that she's awake and has felt the jewels still intact, I missed my chance.

I have to try.

Around her neck rests the key to saving her, the key to freeing my stupid brother and me *and* her from Lucien Vega. All I have to do is avoid getting bitten by the snake and …

I reach for her slumbering figure. Cleo II is coiled into a ball in the crook of her arm. The cobra raises her head, her tongue flicking. I freeze. Cleo II lowers her head.

Heart pounding, I reach for Arabella's neck. My fingers brush the stones. They're as cool as her skin. I wonder if it's the necklace that keeps Arabella so cold, if these glittering jewels are a noose around her throat, draining her of life.

My fingers trail over the place where the jewels meet her skin. The tips of my fingers vibrate as if the stones themselves contain an energy.

Is the magic *real?*

I remember that flash of tooth she gave me when I knelt for her, and I could've sworn she had *fangs*. And this mysterious illness that blistered her skin but then healed over so completely I cannot tell she was hurt at all.

Something strange is going on, and it centres around the jewels.

Is Lucien after their value, or their magic?

What will a man like that do if he has infinite good luck?

And can I really take that away from Arabella?

Yes.

I don't care about magic. To save her life, to put her out of Lucien's path, I will do it in a heartbeat.

She has me now. She doesn't need luck.

I lay aside her thick hair, exposing the back of her neck. Three heavy gold clasps fasten the collar against her ebony skin. I lean in close, kissing the delicate skin behind her ear as I slide my fingers beneath the first clasp and—

She jerks away, her hands flying to the jewels at her neck. I quickly retract my hand, leaning in to graze my lips across her cheek as if that's what I intended to do all along.

Her eyes fix on mine as I press my lips to her skin. She tastes so sweet, like raspberries. I linger, meeting her fiery gaze, daring her to make the next move, while my heart beats a frantic dance in my chest.

A thousand moments hang in the air between us. She turns her head, the movement so slight, so precise, that I almost believe it was an accident. My lips glide over her silken skin and touch hers.

And we are kissing.

I don't know who started it, but one moment we are pressed together and the next, her hands are tangled in my hair and my tongue grazes her teeth and all I can taste is stardust and raspberry.

And I never, ever want to be anywhere else again.

I long to fold myself into her, to close the space between us until we are hot on cold, skin on skin. But I'm afraid that if I move, she'll realise that she's kissing me and stop.

And I can't stop. I don't ever want to stop tasting her.

As if hearing my wanton thoughts, she breaks our kiss and leans back against the pillows. Her breath comes out in ragged pants.

"Good evening." I lean in to kiss her again.

She plants her hands on my shoulders and shoves me away, but it's light, playful. I think. I don't go flying like I did the day she came back from her malaise. "You woke me up, *Giddy*."

"I beg your forgiveness." I sit up and give a quick bow. "You were lying there like Sleeping Beauty, and I wanted to be the one who woke you with a kiss."

She sits up, sliding one elegant leg to the floor, then the other. Cleo II follows her, slithering around her bare feet. "I want to leave this place. I'm sick of staring at these walls."

"You want to go back to La Petite Mort?" I still haven't shown her the letter. I don't want to upset her when she's unwell. I'm hoping I can get the necklace to Lucien before she even learns she's in danger.

"No. Not tonight. I want to be on the streets. With you."

Her eyes are golden rings of mischief, and my heart skips as I bring her a second glass of that foul-smelling wine. I hand her the dress she was wearing on the balloon ride, which Sarah had cleaned and pressed, but Arabella disregards it with a flap of her hand and instead disappears into Sarah's extensive closet, emerging a half hour later in a crimson evening gown that hugs her curves like a Titian painting.

Arabella perches at Sarah's vanity and does her makeup. Cleo II settles around her shoulders like a scarf. I watch, mesmerised by her grace and poise. In a different world, one where people of all skin colours shared the same rights and opportunities, Arabella would have been Sarah Bernhardt. She was born for a bigger stage than La Petite Mort.

When she's ready to leave, I offer her my arm (making sure to stay on the opposite side to the cobra's head). Together, we walk out of Sarah's apartment and into the streets.

This time, I lead her to the bottom of the Butte, along the Boulevard de Rochechouart, where the struggling artist Rodolphe Salis has opened a club called Le Chat Noir. We pass a lively crowd of artists, poets and musicians congregating around the mock medieval setting of threadbare tapestries, stained glass, and throne-like Louis XIII chairs. Arabella tugs on my arm, seeking out the *bonhomie*, but I have a different location in mind. I lead her around the corner to a secret garden Monet had spoken about. My lips still hum with the taste of her, and I long to see her bathed in moonlight among the flowers.

I find the garden's iron gates ajar, and we steal inside. We wander the meandering paths, taking in the ancient sculptures adorning the beds. Marbles from Italy and bronzes from Greece and Rome. Arabella stops for a long time in front of a granite statue of Cleopatra.

"The plaque says this was pulled from the waters in the Alexandrian harbour," I read. "They think it might be from her palace on Antirhodos."

At that word, Arabella squeezes my arm. Her other hand flies to her throat, caressing her jewels. Cleo II sizes up her namesake, slithering from Arabella's shoulder to circle the statue before settling herself on the pharaoh's headdress.

Arabella's fingers caress the curves of the famous queen. "She is *dazzling*."

"She is plain compared to you."

"She didn't cause the fall of Egypt because she was beautiful. She was so much more than that. She was an astute politician. She wanted what the men around her had – her only sin was wanting. And Rome destroyed her for it." Arabella steps back from the statue. "I will *never* be like her."

"Of course not. Your nose is much prettier." I take her hand. She lets me. "It's not a sin to want."

"I'm a *cocotte*, Gideon. Everything I do is a sin because I do it."

"Sin is a word used by people who are too afraid to live." I twirl her into my arms. "Dance with me."

She tries to wriggle out of my grasp. "You can't dance without music."

"Listen," I press my hand to the small of her back. "The music is here. It's in the wind in the trees, the clatter of carriages on the street beyond, the hum of people in the cafes. It's in this wonderful city. Dance this song with me. Show me the movements."

I spin her across the garden's wide boulevard. At first, she resists me, because she's Arabella Macquart and she must be in control at all times, but at some point, she lets go and allows me to spin and dip her. And then she is leading, forcing my feet into steps too complex to remember, sweeping me along as she writes the dance of the city. She throws back her head and laughs, and it's all over for me. I'm utterly *enthralled*.

"Thank you," she murmurs.

"For what?"

"For showing me what I've been missing. I've been so focused on surviving that I have not ever taken the time to see Paris, to hear her music. But I hear it now."

"Good." Something rustles behind us. "I hear something else, too. Is that Cleo?"

We both glance up at the snake, but she's sound asleep on top of Cleopatra's statue. Behind it, the hawthorn tree rustles.

"Who's there?" I call out into the gloom.

"Gideon, is that you?"

I grip Arabella's hand and drag her around the corner. The garden opens into a beautiful glade, each wildflower touched by pale moonlight. At the bottom of the slope is a long pool – a crystalline mirror reflecting the midnight sky. A man sits beside the pool, moonlight dappling his features as he hunches over an easel.

It's Claude.

"It *is* you, brother," he tips his beret. "And the lovely Arabella Macquart. We have missed you both at La Petite Mort. I am in debt to your brilliance. Ever since I started painting outside, I have found the voice. Now I *feel* the landscape. I can be bold and include every tone of pink and blue. It's enchanting. It's delicious! Pierre-Auguste, Berthe and I are putting together an exhibition to launch our new art movement. How can I ever repay you?"

"You should paint Arabella," I suggest.

"He doesn't want to do that," Arabella snaps.

"I do. Very much." Claude stands and kisses Arabella's hand. "It's been a long time since you last sat for me, Mademoiselle Macquart. You were always my favourite model. The light has never looked more perfect than at this exact moment, and with that necklace around your neck, you are already a queen. Will you honour me by sitting?"

"Very well, if I must." Arabella sighs, but there's a musicality to it that lets me know she's pleased. "Where do you want me?"

"Perhaps there?" Claude points to a statue comprised of several fallen pillars, arranged to look like a Greek temple half-submerged with waterlilies collecting at the base. Before I can do anything, Arabella climbs over the side of the pool and wades towards the statue. She settles herself among the columns and shrugs off the crimson dress.

I gasp as her full nakedness is revealed in the moonlight.

She is resplendent. She is *poetry*.

Every curve of her is music, every limb an exquisite dance of flesh and bone. She catches my eye, and I cannot hide my awe. The corner of her mouth quirks up into a satisfied smirk.

It's that little smirk, more than anything, that makes me hard.

How is this woman real?

Arabella drapes herself over the ruins like a panther sunning herself on a savannah. Only, there is no sun beating down, just the inky moonlight that makes her skin shimmer like a galaxy and rings her eyes in gold.

My breath hitches as her fingers trace the jewels around her neck. My cock strains painfully against my trousers as I follow the swell of her breast, the curve of her hip, to the enticing mound between her thighs.

I'm seeing her.

Naked in body *and* heart.

Arabella Macquart, free from the constraints of her station, free of the position society and prejudice have laid out for her, free of her own rules, is a force of nature. I feel the way an archaeologist must when unlocking the door to an ancient tomb – a witness to history, the first to uncover a precious treasure.

Claude bends towards his canvas and picks up his brush as if he hasn't at all noticed that he's in the presence of a goddess.

My body is wrecked with wanting, with all the ways that this woman is so far beyond me.

The only sounds are the stroke of Claude's brush and the pounding of my heart in my ears.

I have no idea how long I sit beside the painter, my cock a rigid, painful thing, refusing to touch myself and ruin the spell she has over me. Every moment is an exquisite torture, especially when her gaze falls on my tented trousers, and that satisfied smile tugs at her lips.

Finally, Claude stands, brushing off his overalls and carefully tucking the canvas beneath his arm. "Now, we must wait for the paint to dry. I shall bring the finished work to La Petite Mort once I am satisfied."

I get to my feet, painfully, and draw my purse, but he waves my hand away.

"This is my gift. Perhaps, one day, if this impressionism idea ever takes off, it might even be worth something." He waves at Arabella as he bustles off. "Good evening, Mademoiselle Macquart."

"A pleasure as always, Monsieur Monet."

Arabella starts to get up, but I hold up a hand.

"Don't move."

My command pulses through her body. I *smell* the pleasure it causes her to lie back again, to obey, to give me this tiny sliver of herself. The night air thickens with myrrh and ginger, and the slightest tang of raspberry.

Arabella wets her lips.

I hurl myself over the edge of the pond. The water is a welcome shock to my stiff, lust-addled body. I wade across to her, pulling myself up onto the columns, my clothing soaked through, my skin almost as cool as hers.

"You will ruin that fancy Italian suit," she scolds me, raising up on her elbows, allowing me to drink in her beauty – her slender neck and narrow shoulders, draped with glittering jewels, the delicious dip of her navel, her small, round breasts with their large dark nipples, and the dark triangle between her thighs.

I smile down at her. "Maybe I'm ready to be ruined."

I cup her chin in my hand. Her skin is cool from the evening air. I should offer her my coat, which is still mostly dry, bundle her up and take her somewhere warm. But I'm too enchanted by her.

I cannot go another moment without kissing her.

So I don't.

I bend down, and I press my lips to hers.

I hold my breath for a moment, half expecting her to disappear into fog.

Instead, she kisses me back.

Her lips are cool against mine, and soft – so soft that my chest aches. I part them with my tongue and explore her, tasting raspberries and moonlight. A mewling sound escapes her, and she is no longer soft, but a tiger, fierce and hungry with wild need, devouring me whole.

Our bodies move together. The wretched longing that has twisted inside me – since the night I first saw her dance – unfurls. I think I wanted her before I even knew she existed.

"You were right about coming out tonight," I moan against her.

"I know I'm right," she gasps between kisses. "I'm right about everything. I'm right about things you haven't even *heard* of yet."

I laugh as I smother her mouth in mine.

Arabella presses her hand against my chest, fisting my shirt, pulling me closer. She might as well be squeezing my heart. She could tear it from my chest and eat it in front of me, and I wouldn't care. Whatever she wants, I'll give it to her …

"Monsieur Rougon, it is you!"

Arabella curses, biting my lip. I feel a sharp prick and taste my own blood. She sucks on my lip, but I pull away, turning towards the sound of the voice and the revolver I keep in my coat, thinking only to protect Arabella.

"Who goes there?" I yell into the gloom.

A shadow moves along the edge of the pond. A familiar voice calls out, "It is I, Monsieur Rodin. I'm sorry for interrupting you." Auguste Rodin steps into the moonlight and bows his head. He carries a sketchbook under one arm and something clenched tight in his fist. "I was sketching in another corner of the garden when I heard you in conversation with Claude. I did not wish to disturb you."

"An excellent idea," I call back.

He doesn't get the hint. "I'm creating a large work that I'm thinking of calling *The Gates of Hell*. This sculpture will represent the tragic love story of Paolo and Francesca from Dante's *Divine Comedy*. I wandered past after Claude left, and something of your love story captured me." He nods to the sketchbook in his hands. "I have been struggling with how to capture the raw beauty and tragic desperation of the kiss. But when I saw the two of you, the work came to me in a flash."

"But our love story isn't tragic," I say.

"All love stories are tragic," Auguste shouts back. "I thought you should know that I'm not the only one watching you."

My blood runs cold. "No?"

He nods towards the sycamore trees. "There was a fellow in the bushes there. He ran away when he saw me. And Gideon?"

"Yes?"

"He left this behind." Auguste opens his hand, revealing the butchered body of a songbird. The head is nowhere to be seen. "And he had a dagger in his hand."

23

Arabella

Gideon: Paul Badica has been reminded that the contract he signed when he and his new wife purchased their Sanctus property forbids him from talking about past interactions with members. And when I say "reminded", I mean, "reminded with Alaric's testicle-severing sword". I am eagerly awaiting your presence this evening. I have a surprise for you.

Winnie: Celeste, Mina, Maisie and I will be there tonight. We're so excited to see Sanctus up close! (And Mina is excited to do a bit of snooping.)

Celeste: What's better for Thralls after they've had a vampire nibbling on their neck – whiskey chocolate ganache or coconut praline?

I finish applying my lipstick and study my reflection in the mirror. I want to look positively *fearsome* tonight when I deliver the bad news to Gideon.

Normally, the idea of spending an entire evening in the company of vampires would turn my stomach – especially with Paul Badica and his new wife in attendance – but I cannot miss this opportunity to let Gideon know I'm his only hope to save Sanctus and lord it over him all night long.

Besides, Mina's right – this will be the best opportunity to get the gossip on the Sanctus community and their Thralls, if there are any staff members acting suspiciously, as well as the issues Gideon is having with the Conclave.

I've chosen an emerald green dress in a beautiful, cascading velvet. If I must be in nature, then I am going to be the most beautiful flower in the garden tonight.

As I pass through the living room, I glance up at my painting. Tonight, the woman appears smug, haughty, her neck extended to show off her jewels. It's some of Claude's finest work. Several times over the last century, I have been tempted to sell the painting. It certainly would have made my life easier during that terrible period when I slept on the streets and hunted in the dark like a shadow. But I refuse to let a man – even one of the world's most renowned artists – provide for me when I can do it myself.

I touch my bare neck.

Even though it's been one hundred and fifty years since I wore them last, I miss those jewels.

I miss the certainty of wearing them, the knowledge that their magic made me invincible – that for once, no man could ruin what I'd built.

Until a man did.

I circle my neck with my hands.

After I rebuilt my fortune post-WWII as an intermediary, allowing Upyr to turn their old antiques and stores of gold into modern cash, I visited a jeweller in Italy and had them make me a replica of the Antirhodos Collar. Of course, I have no photographs of the piece, but I had this painting, the Toulouse-Lautrec poster and a couple of portraits from Édouard Manet and his circle.

The jeweller toiled for weeks on the piece, making sure each detail was perfect. When he presented me with the finished product, he wept. He said it was the most beautiful thing he'd ever made.

It was beautiful, but it wasn't *my* necklace. It was missing something. No heart. No soul.

No magic.

I sold it the next week in Vienna and used the money to buy myself passage to America. They don't have courts, which meant I could live and work in peace. Until … my past caught up to me once more. An old client made a menace of himself, and I had to become a shadow again. That's how I found myself in the tiny, vampire-free village of Argleton.

I thought I could be safe here, but then Gideon Blake showed up.

And he wants to *surprise* me.

As if his very existence isn't the worst kind of surprise.

I return to my room and fish around in my jewellery box, locating a gold necklace dripping with emeralds. I fasten it around my neck. The metal feels cool and heavy against my skin. It's not the same, but it will do.

I grab my purse and exit my home, keying in the code to lock the doors. I wander through the winding woodland path, past the completed houses sitting back from the road, half-hidden in the trees. Windows reflect the starry night sky.

I follow the sound of voices and music into the Midnight Garden, which occupies an area between the executive homes and a block of smaller two-bedroom townhouses. It looks like every vampire in Sanctus is here, plus a few invited human guests. I grab a glass of blood from a tray held out by a human member of the Sanctus staff. I notice the distinct bruises on her neck.

I sweep into the garden, admiring the world Gideon has created. A stream runs through the middle, but it's been corralled into a mosaic trench with little steps and sculpted corners to create a pleasing babble of water. Little bridges and stepping stones enable visitors to cross over without wetting their feet. The crowd mills around on the crisp white stone pathways, lit at the edges by LED strips that change colours, while night-flowering plants burst into bloom from the beds. Large braziers at either end of the garden take the chill off the evening, and the air swirls with inviting floral scents. It's modern and clean and so far removed from the dazzling gothic finery of the courts, and I love it. Gideon has—

No, don't give Gideon credit for this.

Gideon hires people who dream up this stuff for him and then stands in the spotlight and lets everyone congratulate him for his genius. Gideon is currently on the brink of total financial ruin. Gideon is vampire enemy number one because many of our kin think he's trying to establish his own court in Sanctus, which, looking around, isn't too far from the truth.

He doesn't build things. He doesn't create.

He destroys.

But this time, I'll destroy him first.

Ten sculptures stand on plinths down the length of the garden, each one covered in a black cloth, ready for its big unveiling. Near the bar, a quartet of human classical musicians – three men in decadent Baroque ensembles and demonic face paint, and a woman in a flowing red gown – play a strange and eerie composition that sends a delicious shiver down my spine. I would have hired them at La Petite Mort …

"That's Broken Muse," Alyra whispers as she appears at my side and hands me a blood cocktail. "Gideon knows them. He flew them off their European tour specifically for this event. They're exquisite, especially the violinist. I'd like to have a nibble on that gorgeous neck."

I seethe internally as I sip my drink. Of course, Gideon hangs out with rockstars. This life of his should have been mine.

It can still be mine. Once I take Sanctus from him.

Out of the corner of my eye, I notice Mina and one of her husbands, Moriarty, cornering one of the servers, who keeps touching her neck. I spy Celeste at the catering table, fussing over the dishes, and Winnie is rubbing Alaric's back and whispering encouragingly in his ear as he stares at the covered sculptures with a mixture of terror and derision.

"We shouldn't talk about humans as if they're meat for the slaughter," Alyra's companion says stiffly. "If we create a culture of othering them, then it becomes difficult to reconcile our issues with consent—"

"But they *are* other," Alyra rolls her eyes. "They're *food*, and occasionally entertainment, like cat videos on the internet. But they hardly deserve our *respect*."

"We were all human once—"

Alyra laughs and hugs her friend close. "I'm teasing, you silly goose. Arabella, I'd love you to meet my friends, Luminita Le Fey and Eleanor Mock, both of the Blood Alexandre. Ladies, this is Arabella Lestrange, of the Blood, er—"

"Just Arabella," I interrupt.

Alyra's smile freezes, but she doesn't make a fuss over why I refuse to give my blood allegiance. "Eleanor is our resident activist. She's working on a campaign to raise awareness of the issue of illegal siring. She wants every vampire who sired without consent to face trial. Isn't that absurd?"

"I think that's a wonderful idea." I lean in to air kiss Eleanor's cheeks. She does the same, and when she steps back, she looks excited.

"I'm so pleased you agree. If you like, you can come along to our first meeting. It's next month in Brimstone." She fishes around in her handbag. "Let me find you a flyer—"

"She doesn't want a flyer, Eleanor. She's just being polite. Arabella, welcome to Sanctus." Luminita leans in for an air kiss. "You're a friend of Beth Duncan. I saw you dance at her studio opening. You were sublime."

"I was helping out my friend. I don't do that sort of dancing."

Anymore.

"Oh, *please*, Arabella." Luminita's tinkling laugh grates my nerves. "Modesty is useless for a vampire. We've all had our bad girl century – Alyra can tell you about that time we stowed away with Sir Francis Drake."

"Those jolly days on the *Golden Hinde* … he should have named that ship the Golden Behind for how much that man worshipped my derrière." Alyra laughs.

Luminita hoots, "Pirates do love their booty."

I smirk.

Alyra nudges her friend. "But nothing can beat Luminita here. Why, she once left some rather graphic graffiti on a pillar in the Hanging Gardens of Babylon."

"You did?" I give Luminita a second glance. I'd have guessed her a younger vampire, Kissed fewer than a hundred years ago. Even by vampiric standards, she is *startlingly* beautiful. Vampires don't age as humans do, with wrinkles and grey hairs, but time leaves its marks on us. We develop a deathly pallor, as if we are turning to stone. Our eyes grow hard, crystalline. And we become *monstrous*, less empathetic to the cycle of life and death after existing outside it for so long. I've known such vampires in my life, and they are terrifying and dangerous. It had already begun to happen to Alaric before Winnie came along and made him reconnect with the world again.

But Luminita is so fresh and vivid and *alive*.

"Don't look so shocked, Arabella. This is all thanks to your friend." Luminita touches her hand to her cheek. "Alyra and I both have a weekly standing facial appointment at Zen and Tonic. We swear by Beth's beauty elixirs."

Beth *is* a miracle worker.

Maybe I should have my own standing appointment.

Luminita and Alyra flitter off to speak with Dalton La Rue, leaving me and Eleanor together.

"I'm interested in hearing more about your cause." I lift my blood cocktail to my lips.

"The courts give us so many rules. They tell us they are for our safety, but are they not really about control? 'Vampires and humans must never copulate', except that we know contraception can eliminate the risk of Dhampir. 'We must never drink from our kin, because of the sacredness of a vampire's blood', but we know that drinking from a vampire grants the drinker some of their power, so is this *most sacred law* really about ensuring no one of us becomes too powerful? And what happens if a vampire chooses not to obey? Your friends Winnie and Alaric are prime examples of flouting our sacred laws," Eleanor sniffs.

I jump to my friends' defence. "Winnie and Alaric shouldn't be punished because the Conclave is too slow to keep up with contraceptive innovations."

I worry for my friends. At the moment, people are too afraid of Alaric's mother, the Lady of Agony, to openly condemn their relationship, but Alaric's friendship with Gideon is turning their betrothal into another Sanctus Estate controversy. It would make their lives easier if Winnie agreed to become one of us, but she's not ready, and Alaric respects that. Even in the Upyr world, consent is sexy as fuck.

And I worry for me, too. Alaric isn't the only vampire who hasn't obeyed our laws. Too many women have woken up with bite marks on their necks and an insatiable hunger, bound to the very monster who Kissed them. Lord John Astor made it clear to me that he knew he'd never be punished. If anyone ever found out what I did to him …

"Gideon built Sanctus so we could be safe," Eleanor continues. "But how many Upyr view that as their licence to act out their darkest, most depraved fantasies? You know all about these horrible husking murders in the village! How can we stop siring abuse when we allow things like that to happen to innocent humans? Or like this!" Eleanor frowns as she indicates a vampire leading one of the servers behind a bush, his hand pressing against her neck.

"The Sanctus staff have all agreed to be Thralls." My heart pounds in my ears.

She sniffs. "That may be so, but if your employer can Thrall you, isn't that an abuse of power?"

A fair point.

Eleanor smiles sadly. "I apologise for bringing down the mood with my passions. If you'd like to discuss it further, you can come to our meeting—"

She's interrupted by a familiar, smooth, deep, annoying voice.

"Arabella," Gideon breathes as his eyes devour me. I nod, satisfied that my outfit choice has had the desired effect, especially considering he's wearing a suit that's an impeccably tailored existential crisis.

"Gideon, just the man I wanted to see. Take a walk with me." I grab his arm, nod farewell to Eleanor, and lead him away from the crowd. I hiss in his ear. "You have a problem."

"I do. I think my heart's stopped." He places his hand over his chest. "That dress is the reason warning labels were invented."

"I need you to be serious. Someone is stealing from you."

He laughs, a curl of golden hair flopping over his face. "That's absurd. No one would *dare*."

How easily a man with power and notoriety assumes he is safe.

"Oh, they dared." I struggle to hide the glee in my voice as his face freezes mid-laugh. "That vault of yours has been decimated. Most of those sacks of coins are stuffed with packing peanuts. The chests are empty, although they left behind most of the ugly old furniture. Whoever did this has gone to great pains to only smuggle out small items and leave the vault looking exactly as you left it. If you hadn't hired me, no one would have ever noticed."

For a moment, Gideon's mask of easy confidence collapses, and the full force of his rage burns across his features. He glances around, and I realise that the fear darkening his cobalt eyes isn't for himself – it's for *them*. For every vampire who trusts him to keep them safe within Sanctus' walls.

I feel a flicker of unease at what I'm doing, but I stamp it down. I'm not going to destroy Sanctus. I know better than most how needed it is. I'm making certain Gideon Blake doesn't get a second chance to fuck it up.

Gideon whips out his phone. "I'll need to brief the security team. Every one of them worked for me when I was Gideon Vega. They know what to do with traitors."

The unease flickers higher this time. "I'm afraid you have bigger problems than catching the thief. I can sell the furniture and what coins we have left, but that will give you only a fraction of the money you need. You don't have enough left in the vault to keep Sanctus open."

Gideon swallows. His phone drops through his fingers and clatters on the cobbles before landing in the stream with a *plop*.

"I … I …" He swallows again. "Do I have any options?"

Oh, I *am* enjoying this. "There's only one thing that will save Sanctus now. A new investor."

He shakes his head. "There's no one else. Not since the Conclave put a target on my back—"

"You have me."

A hundred different emotions pass across Gideon's features. "You … you have that kind of money?"

"Why are you questioning the only person offering to help you? I told you, I am very good at my job."

"I believe it." He puffs out his cheeks. "This is ... I can't believe it. I truly am the luckiest vampire to have you back in my life."

You keep believing you're the lucky one. Meanwhile, I'm going to enjoy my revenge.

"I want Sanctus to succeed as much as anyone." I shrug, as if this isn't a big deal, as if I'm not putting my life's savings on the line to ensure he suffers for what he did to me. "Of course, as majority shareholder, I'll be taking an active role in management decisions."

"Yes, yes, whatever you want." His eyes sparkle, and for a moment, I almost wish I *was* going to work together with him to improve Sanctus. I picture the two of us bickering over his enormous desk, and then I picture him flinging everything off the top and bending me over it ...

I quickly banish *that* fantasy, which has no place whatsoever inside my revenge plot, no matter how my skin heats at the thought of his hand sliding up my thigh as he presses me into that cool mahogany ...

"I've already drawn up the paperwork. You'll find it in your inbox ..." I stare meaningfully down at his phone bobbing its way downstream. "Later. As soon as you sign, I'll have the funds transferred."

"Arabella, I can't thank you enough for this. I know things between us are—"

"Fraught?" I suggest. "Violent?"

"Extraordinary," he corrects me, and there's a mischievous gleam in his eyes that I don't like. It looks a little too much like hope. "But this is truly remarkable. Know that I *want* your ideas. I truly believe Sanctus could be the start of freeing *all* vampires from court control. With you at my side, we can make this place—"

"Gideon, *there* you are."

Sinead steps over the trickling stream. She glares at me before turning her attention to her boss. "I've been texting you. We're ready for your presentation now. Your friend Lord Valerian says that if you don't hurry up and unveil his statues, he'll be forced to do it himself, using your intestine for the ribbon-cutting ceremony—"

"Tell Allie to hold his murderous thoughts. I'm on my way." Gideon smooths down the front of his devastating suit, then reaches out and shakes my hand. "Thank you again. I can't express in words what this means to me. And luckily, I don't have to, because I'm about to unveil my surprise."

Great, Gideon's surprise. I was hoping he'd forgotten about it.

Gideon skips away. Sinead fixes me with one final glare before taking off in the direction of the trees, glass of blood in hand to deliver to some Upyr. I find Celeste and Winnie in the crowd, and we elbow our way to the front.

"Welcome, residents and staff, to the first of many events to be held in our new Midnight Garden." Gideon beams from the small makeshift stage. The band have set down their instruments, and every eye at the party is on him. He struts the length of the stage, twirling the microphone in his fingers, loving the attention. My gaze trails down his exquisite Armani suit to his shiny patent leather Brionis. Why do clothes have to look so good on him? "I envisioned this space as a place of quiet solitude and contemplation. A good friend of mine once said that when he started painting outside, he could, in his words, '... *feel* the landscape. It's enchanting. It's delicious!'"

How *dare* he steal Claude's words? I want to shove my wine glass down his throat and twist until it pops out of his ear.

"Unfortunately, Claude Monet refused the gift of the Kiss and remained a human, so he's not able to be here tonight," Gideon says with a laugh, his eyes settling on my face, the irises blowing out to darken their cobalt rims. "But I'd like to think he'd be proud to know I remember his words and I'm trying to keep his spirit alive by offering these art commissions to scrappy up-and-coming artists with fresh ideas. Without further ado, let's begin with the first piece by a local artist who goes by the name of Quoth. His piece is titled *Gone*."

Gideon whips off the first cloth to reveal a large wrought-iron birdcage, bedecked with steel creepers and roses. The door hangs open. There is nothing inside the cage except for a couple of steel bones. The piece has a powerful, forlorn quality to it.

The crowd clap in appreciation. Quoth looks like he's going to be sick. Mina squeezes his hand and beams. Behind them, Heathcliff downs a blood cocktail and promptly spits it out all over his rumpled black shirt.

Gideon moves down the line of sculptures, giving a short introduction to each piece before unveiling it. Quoth has contributed three pieces in total, all of them variations on the theme of cages. His work is stunning, and it no doubt helped ease Gideon's fears that Alaric wouldn't come through with enough pieces.

Not that I care if Gideon is afraid of anything.

Alaric's sculptures are next. People gasp when Gideon reveals them one by one. They are studies of the Upyr form from our various myths, each more beautiful than the last. There is something of Rodin in Alaric's technique – a sense of passion and tragedy and the breadth of human experience.

Finally, Gideon pauses at the last sculpture. His gaze sweeps the crowd, but he stops when his eyes land on mine. "This final piece is from a creator who is a little ashamed to have his work displayed alongside these two other amazing artists. This is his first ever sculptural work, but what he lacks in technique I hope you can agree he makes up in passion for his subject."

Gideon yanks off the sheet, revealing …

What is *that?*

It's an abomination to the craft of sculpting. A travesty in travertine.

Bulbous blobs protrude from a lopsided base that looks in danger of toppling over beneath the weight of its creator's ineptitude.

It might be said to *vaguely* resemble a woman's torso if the model were made out of potatoes and you were feeling extremely generous.

Beside me, Eleanor winces.

Winnie covers her mouth with her hands. "Oh no, he somehow made it *worse.*"

She looks over at me, and something tells me I need to take a closer look at that sculpture.

I rush over just as Celeste bends down to examine the plinth. "Um, this sculpture is called *Arabella.*"

"Is that supposed to be you?" Alyra asks me.

My mouth falls open. Who would create a horrific sculpture and name it after me?

Is this a sick joke?

Gideon glides over to me, a blood cocktail resting casually in his fingers.

"Do you like it?" he asks.

"Do I …" Realisation dawns as I take in his expectant smile. "*You* made this?"

"Of course! Alaric helped me. Well, he tried to help, but I told him I had to do it myself." Gideon gestures to the abomination behind him. "I wanted to show you how I feel about you, that even though one hundred and fifty years have passed, I still remember every curve of your body—"

"Clearly you don't, because my curves don't resemble the Elephant Man!"

His smile freezes on his pouty lips.

"I can't believe this. You thought putting an ugly sculpture of my naked form in the garden of the estate where I live would *win me back?*" I glare at him. "You're even more clueless than I thought. I don't want you back."

Gideon's face freezes. "You still have feelings for me. I can tell. Why else would you help me?"

"Oh, I have *feelings*. But I won't repeat them in polite company," I hiss. "Why do you think I want to help you keep this place open? Why did I buy a house in Sanctus in the first place? Because you promised discretion. You promised *safety*. I don't want to be reminded of what I had and lost because of you. I don't want this—" I gesture at the monstrous effigy. "Reminding people that I used to dance naked and sell my body for money. I want you to stop trying to win me back and accept my eternal hatred like a man." I whirl on my heel and storm away.

"Arabella, wait!"

My friends call after me, too, but I ignore them. I cross the babbling stream and rush up the winding path towards my house as fast as my Louboutins will carry me.

"Arabella!" Celeste jogs up alongside me, her short brown bob with the red streaks flying around her face, and her cupcake earrings jangling as her dress rides up over her ample breasts.

I don't slow down. "How come you're not puffing?"

"You think that because I run a bakery and eat raw cookie dough every day, I'm not in shape?" Celeste leaps in front of me, forcing me to stop so I don't plough into her. She thrusts her hands on her hips. "You know I run in the woods near the Old Mill most days. What I want to know is, why are you so upset?"

"Wouldn't you be upset if someone created a hideous naked statue of you and put it up for the whole neighbourhood to see?"

"Only if they were someone I cared about."

"I don't *care* about Gideon. I hate everything about him, from his stupid face and his ridiculous smile to that suit he's wearing and—" Something behind Celeste's head catches my eye. I dart around her and step onto the path that leads to the front door of my house.

"Arabella, what is that?"

But I can't tell her. Because I have *no idea* why there is a beheaded songbird nailed to my brand-new front door, with a message beneath, scrawled in what looks suspiciously like blood, that says:

MINE.

24

Arabella
Then

Gideon and Auguste search the trees for the man watching us while I pull on my skirts and lace my corset. I don't know why he's so surprised. I was a naked woman in a fountain, kissing a man. At La Petite Mort, one would pay handsomely for such a show. This fellow leaving blood-soaked flowers and possessive notes is trying to get the show for free. I should be more concerned, but I'm too light from Gideon's kisses. The magic of my collar protects me.

The men emerge from the trees as I tug the silk over my corset. Gideon wraps his arms around me, his grip possessive. He glares at the trees as if he's a wild god attempting to fell them with the power of his disdain.

"Let's get away from here." Gideon's lips brush my earlobe. I nod, desperate to finish what we started.

We return to the Cleopatra statue. I hold out my arm and Cleo II coils around me, her body squeezing gently as she slithers back to my shoulders. My fingers entwine in Gideon's as we bid goodnight to Rodin and wind our way back through the Paris streets. Gideon twirls me around corners and pushes me up against lampposts, his human lips thrilling every time they brush mine – warm as an Egyptian evening lying in the shadow of the pyramids, warm as the memories of my mother's arms around me.

We're almost at La Petite Mort when Gideon tugs me to a standstill at the top of the street. From here, I can see the entrance to my beloved theatre. And what I see makes my cold veins chill over with ice.

Two burly Upyr toss Jacques into the street. Catherina hurls herself at the nearest vampire, beating him with her tiny fists. He grabs her and sinks his teeth into her neck, with not a care for who might see on the street or for the laws against drinking from another Upyr.

Catherina slumps to the ground as the euphoria of the bite consumes her. The vampires disappear inside. Gideon's fingers crush my hand.

I've seen those men before.

"Those are Lucien Vega's henchmen," I whisper. Gideon nods, his lips moving in a silent curse.

A moment later, we hear screams. Our patrons rush into the streets. Édouard Manet struggles to replace his beret. Blood trickles from a nasty cut across his cheek.

A cut from a silver-edged blade.

Séraphine screams. Jacques drags himself across the ground and into the crowd, trying to direct everyone to safety. One of the henchmen grabs Jacques' face, raising him up by his skull. Jacques' eyes widen with fear as the henchman flicks his wrist and twists his head like the top of a medicine bottle. Jacques flops to the ground, his sightless eyes gleaming from the wrong side of his head.

Jacques, no.

I rush forward, panic gripping me. My hand flies to my throat. They killed Jacques. What's happening? How can this be? The necklace is supposed to protect all of us.

I have to stop them.

Gideon grabs my wrist, jerking me back. "Arabella, we can't go in there."

"You saw what they did to Jacques. I have to help my girls!"

"Catherina's okay. Look, she's lifting her head. You can't let them see you." Gideon looks pale, confused. He shakes my wrist, leading me away. Normally, I could break his grip without working up a sweat, but I'm so shocked and frightened that I let myself be led away.

Gideon pulls me behind an opium den. His hand goes to my cheek, caressing my cold skin as if I'm the one who's been cut.

"What's going on?" I demand, slapping his hand away. "Why are your boss' men destroying my theatre? Why did they kill Jacques?"

"I'm so sorry, Arabella." Gideon's face twists in pain. "They've come for me."

His words whip away my breath.

"What?"

"They think I've stolen something that belongs to Lucien. I haven't, but because I didn't show up when I was supposed to, they think …" He winces. "Never mind. It's not important. I'm going to fix it. Tomorrow, I swear. I promise that after tomorrow, they will never bother you again, and I will go to Jacques' family and make certain they are looked after. But we have to survive tonight, just until the sun rises. We have to hide somewhere they can't find us. Do you trust me to keep you safe?"

I meet his eyes, drowning in those sumptuous pools of cobalt, luxuriating in the sincerity in his voice.

Since the night I became a vampire, I've never trusted another soul, and certainly never a man.

It's served me well. I'm alive. My head is attached to my shoulders. My beautiful theatre is – *was* – thriving.

But my chest is a hollow ache of loneliness – a dark cupboard where I've locked away my heart.

And Gideon Rougon looks at me as if he possesses the key.

I swallow. "I know where we can hide."

My apartment is three blocks from La Petite Mort, on the top storey of a rambling tenement. Gideon wraps Sarah's fur stole tight around my neck, hiding the glitter of the collar and Cleo II's scaly body, and he keeps his head bent low as I drag him through the streets, past the overflowing cafes and chocolate houses, past the crowds emerging from the more respectable opera houses and the less respectable cabarets. To any stranger on the street, we are a young bohemian couple rushing to our next adventure.

Our feet clatter on the crooked wooden stairs. I unlock my door and drag him inside. Gideon crosses the room as I run around lighting the lamps. Our building does not yet have electricity installed.

"You have no windows?" he asks, skirting the perimeter of my sitting room, ducking where the eaves of the ceiling make it impossible for him to stand.

"The rent is cheaper without them." It's a nice half-truth.

"It would have been good to keep watch on the street. At any rate, I don't think they'll find us here. As soon as the sun rises, I will sort this out. I promise." Gideon sinks into my chaise longue. "So this is where you live. It's … exactly as I pictured."

My home may be modest, as I spent much of my accumulated fortune opening La Petite Mort, but I regard my precious objects – the sumptuous embroidered cushions, the inlaid credenzas, the lavish vanity table – with a critical eye. I surround myself in luxury, but no one would know that I pilfered many of these pieces from empty mansions during the Commune, or rescued them from the rubble of burning buildings, or that they were gifts from lovers or men who wished to be lovers. Like everything about my life, this luxury has been hard-won, and I will defend it with my life if I need to.

Cleo II peeks out from beneath my fur. She slithers across the floor before winding her way up the coat rack and hanging there like a reptilian scarf.

"You're the first man to see this place."

Gideon's eyebrow arches with surprise.

"Don't look so scandalised," I smirk. "You know the work I do. Although I mostly manage the theatre now, I have had my share of private clients. I keep opulent rooms in Pigalle where I've had men, and women, and all combinations thereof, if the price is right and the fancy so strikes me, or the rent needs to be paid. But never here. Never in *my* space."

"I'm the first?" His words are a whisper. His eyes are wide with awe.

I can't believe it, either.

I should hate having him here, his broad shoulders and irksome smile sucking all the air from the room. I should hate the way he runs his fingers over my carefully collected possessions, and the imprints of his soles on my thick Persian rug.

Instead, he feels like a missing piece that's finally been found.

Gideon stands and closes the space between us, his cobalt eyes fused to mine.

He stops with an inch between us, an electric fission of air that threatens to pull us together like two stars colliding.

My heart pounds so loud Cleopatra herself could hear it from her tomb.

"I want to kiss you, Arabella," he whispers. "I want to kiss you because you are brilliant, and beautiful, and infuriating, and beguiling. I want to kiss you because a cobra is glaring at me from the coat rack. May I kiss you?"

I've had enough of him treating me tenderly, like a flower with broken petals. I shift my body closer, pressing myself against him.

He's a human. He's mortal. He's dangerous—

I kiss him.

The moment my lips touch his, it's as if the room ceases to exist. It's just him and me, floating in a world of our own.

The last time Gideon kissed me, it was delicate, the way someone might approach a horse he's afraid will bolt. But this time, Gideon kisses like he can't get close enough, like he has to crawl inside my skin.

I kiss him like I want him to.

He tastes exquisite, sweet as honey and red cherries, with the sinful tang of poppy and blood.

Blood.

His pulse hammers in my ears. My eyes draw downward to the vein in his neck and the sweetest nectar pulsing just beneath the surface. I could bite him now and send both of us to the heights of ecstasy. My fangs itch to taste him, and they start to slide down …

I force them back up. I'm not ready for him to know the monster in me. The monster doesn't dine tonight. I want to be *Arabella*.

Besides, the delighted little noises Gideon makes assure me that he's enjoying himself *plenty*. He presses his body to mine, arms banding protectively around me as he walks me across the floor and pushes me through the doorway to my boudoir.

His eyes remain open. All the cobalt is nearly consumed by the black of his pupils – only a thin ring of colour remains. Usually, at this stage, men close their eyes, believing they are safe and secure in the hands of a weaker creature. If they are human, this is usually when I pounce and take the blood I need to survive. Once, I used this moment to draw a dagger – a monster slaying a monster.

But tonight, all I want is to fall into that ring of cobalt and drown myself.

The backs of my legs hit the bed. Gideon's eyes briefly break their lock on mine to gaze at my large, four-poster throne.

As they should.

My bed is a true masterpiece, fit for a queen.

It's bedecked in gold silk curtains, with an Egyptian god and raunchy cherubs carved in fine mahogany by some reclusive vampire in England named Lord Valerian. It was acquired by me at great personal expense because I deserve a bed fit for a queen.

Gideon's nimble fingers graze over the wood as if it's delicate tissue.

Terror plunges a cold knife into my chest at the thought that he'll laugh at me – at this *cocotte* who dares to live like a queen, at the shabby facade of my life.

I realise with a start that he's the first person whose opinion I care about.

Am I ... *falling* for this human?

"This is ... quite something." Gideon's peacock eyes flash with amusement. "I don't know how you sleep at night with this giant crocodile-headed monster leering down at you."

"I sleep like a little babe, and don't you forget it." I glance towards the coat rack in the other room. "Or I shall have Cleo II remind you."

"What I meant to say is, terrifying animal-headed gods aside, this bed is beautiful." Gideon reaches for me. "But not as beautiful as you.

You are a mythological creature, Arabella. I can't believe you're real. I can't believe you're here in my arms."

I expect him to kiss me then, to seal those fiery words with his tongue, but he hovers just out of reach, fanning my lips with his warm breath, making me mad with wanting him.

"Here you are, in the boudoir of a goddess. And yet you aren't giving her what she desires." I trail my fingers down the buttons of his shirt, letting him feel the faintest bite of my sharp, red-painted nails.

Gideon sucks in a breath as I smile. I glance down at his trousers, pleased to see his cock already hardening beneath them.

"And what is it you desire?" Gideon's words are a whisper on my lips. "I know what I desire. I want to spread you across this enormous, ridiculous bed. I want to slowly unlace your corset until the very sensation of silk ribbons pulling across your skin sets you on edge. I want to crawl on my knees between your thighs and worship you. I want you to scream my name until the night burns into the day. I want to kiss every infuriating insult from your gorgeous, poison-filled lips."

"Then—"

"That's not all I want." Delicately, he puts his hand to my cheek, his warm fingers sliding along my sensitive skin and down my neck, resting right above the jewels of my necklace. "I want to wake up beside you, not just today, but every day. I want to trace my name on your skin. I want to watch your belly swell with my child. I want to be a man worthy of being looked at the way you look at me now. I'm greedy, but I want all of you, *ma petite déesse.*"

My little goddess.

His breath catches, his words dripping with want and a kind of aching sadness.

How I ache for those things, too, for things that can never be, for a future with this man that was stolen from me decades ago on a hot Egyptian night.

But my sire can't take this night from me.

For one night, I can let go.

I can surrender.

I can be *his*.

"Then have me," I whisper before crushing my lips to his.

His lips are so warm, so soft, his tongue a hot demand against mine. My fingers thread through his golden hair, fingering the locks with my nails as I pull him closer, our bodies pressing together. I taste every strained breath and smell every thump of his pulse surging in his neck.

Gideon's hands roam over my body. His fingers reach behind me, working loose the lacing of my corset. He moves slowly, keeping his promise of drawing out the torture of laces dragging across my skin as though he's unwrapping a gift he's anticipated all year. And he's right, damn him – by the time he loosens the final lacing and tugs the golden corset over my head, I am a mess of want.

Beneath, I'm wearing a gold silk chemise with delicate Chantilly lace along the hem. The loose fabric kisses my skin as I shift beneath him. His breath hitches when he slides the straps over my shoulders, revealing a hint of my breasts, framed in the glittering jewels of my collar. He palms one breast and feels the nipple hard beneath the fabric.

Gideon traces the hard bud with his fingers, and I squirm against him from the delicious agony of sensation. The strangled moan that escapes his lips is pure, delicious, *evil*.

He tugs on one nipple, then moves to the other, rolling it beneath the fabric until pleasure and pain dance with each other. I didn't even know this is something I enjoy, because I'm so used to pretending and performing for clients that I no longer know my own body. In Gideon's hands, I'm rediscovering myself.

I'm learning that I have *wanted* for years, for decades. That, for all the good luck my collar has brought me, it has never sated the hunger that grows and gnaws inside me. That pretty jewels and a queen's magic can never replace who I am inside. That in his deep eyes I see myself as I truly am, and I'm ready to unleash her.

As much as I want to have all of him now, I take my time, slowly unbuttoning his shirt and letting it fall to the floor before my fingers roam the planes of his muscular arms.

I intend to memorise every inch of his beautiful body. He must be thinking the same as he peels away the golden silk to reveal my breasts. His hands graze my skin, soft but certain – an experienced lover.

It's been so long since someone took care of me, since I wasn't the one doing all the work.

An ache builds in my bones – they're kindling stacked for an inferno.

Gideon breaks our kiss to trail his lips down my neck, tugging my chemise lower still. He scrapes his teeth along the edge of the collar before moving to my bare breast. His pulse throbs and I'm so aware of how vulnerable he's made himself to me, and he doesn't even know it.

He's not the only one vulnerable.

I gasp as his tongue swirls around a hardened bud. His knees hit the floor with a thud, and he looks up at me, his eyes anchoring on mine. My chest is a raw wound of need and desire and *honour* that I'm the one he's chosen to kneel for, that I might be worthy of him.

I moan, tangling my fingers through his hair and arching into him as he sucks me into his hot mouth. No matter how much he gives me, no matter how he splinters his chest open to reveal more of his gooey human heart, it will never be enough. I'm lying to myself that I will be able to give him up.

He's human, he's human, he's human …

What of it? whispers the evil, monstrous side of me. *So what if it's forbidden by Upyr law? Where were they when you were taken against your will? Did they help you when you were broken? Why care for their laws when this is something you want?*

If I offer him the Kiss, he may choose it.

I choose him. I *want* him.

I don't want tonight to end.

Gideon takes his time with each nipple, making sure to give them equal attention before his lips trail down my stomach, pushing my chemise down to the floor as he moves along my body. He remains kneeling, a supplicant at his altar. Gently, he pushes me back onto the bed, his kisses trailing fire over my thighs as they near the aching need between my legs.

Men rarely go down on me. When they do, it's to satisfy their egos. They get off knowing they can make me crazy. I've perfected the art of wriggling beneath their furious lappings and clamping my thighs around their faces as I scream through a fake orgasm. Once, I forgot my strength and made a client pass out. Jacques dumped him in the street, where he'd have assumed his wretched state was from the absinthe he'd imbibed. (I kept his coin. I am a businesswoman.)

But usually, my pleasure is not even a distant thought. They expect me to blow their tiny dicks and if they don't finish then I have to ride it and pretend I enjoyed it. Most of the time I do – there are far worse jobs on this earth than fucking a man who worships you – but I'm there for the coin.

Gideon is different.

He lays me back on the bed and slides an embroidered pillow beneath my head so I can watch. I think he likes me watching. His eyes never leave mine. They're dark as night and hooded with desire.

He kneels between my legs, his warm hands pressing into my knees, driving my legs apart and holding me in place. His breath kisses my core, warm puffs of wanting as his restraint thins. Fire licks me from the inside.

With deft fingers, Gideon pushes aside my silk underthings before sliding his tongue over me.

His tongue is molten sin.

I gasp. When he strokes my clit again, I have no control over the way I writhe or the curses that fall from my lips. He laughs against me as he devours me like a starving man at a banquet.

I rake my fingers through his golden hair as my arousal perfumes the air, mingling with the metallic scent of his blood to create a libertine bouquet. His tongue writes poetry against me. Everything about his touch has my body on fire, and when he adds a finger along with his expert tongue, I buck my hips against his mouth, desperate for more.

"Did you want something, *ma petite déesse?*" he murmurs, raising his other hand to play with a nipple, rolling it between his fingers while he curls his other finger inside me, stroking over a spot that makes my body feel like it's seen the sun for the first time in decades.

Gasping, I buck my hips closer to his awaiting mouth.

"I'm afraid that I can't quite hear you," he murmurs, lifting his head so I can see that cheeky grin spreading across his features. "You'll need to speak up."

"Gideon, you b-b-b—" I gasp, the insult not quite able to slip past my lips as he kisses hot air against my needy flesh.

"Gideon, you beautiful, generous, magnificent specimen of manhood," he finishes for me. "May I …?"

"Make me come now, you *bastard*, or I will force you to eat your own—"

My threats become a scream as he thrusts a second finger inside me and sucks my clit into his mouth. My body explodes with sensation, sparks flying through my limbs as I ride out my pleasure on his face.

"Such lovely manners. You're so beautiful when you come, *ma petite déesse*," he growls against my pussy.

"Then let me do it again on your cock," I command, gripping the back of his golden hair.

"Mmmmm, but what if I want to taste you again? What if I want to feast between your legs until the sun rises?"

"Gideon Rougon, give me your cock *now*."

The snap in my voice makes him sit up, his darkened eyes hooding with lust. The air crackles between us, heated by the clash of our wills and scented with the headiness of blood and sex. My jewels feel heavy around my neck, cutting off my air. Or maybe that's the way he makes me feel when he looks at me like *that* – breathless and choking on things I dare not say.

"Since you ask so nicely, *ma petite déesse*."

I'm not opposed to that name.

Gideon stands up and leans over me, kneeling on the bed, fitting his knees between mine. His forearms cage my face as he crushes my lips with his. I taste my pleasure on his tongue, sharp and sweet. My fangs itch to slide down and pierce him, to taste him as he's tasted me, but I refrain. For now.

Between our frantic kisses, I strip off the rest of his clothes, letting my fingers roam over the hard planes of his body and down to his cock. He's as big as I guessed, his shaft thick with a pleasing halo of veins. Gideon shudders as I rake the tips of my nails down his length, touching the bead of precum gathered at the swollen head.

Normally, a man has to pay extra to have my mouth anywhere near his cock. These days, I make Catherina get on her knees for them. That woman has a mouth like a steam injector.

But for Gideon … I cannot *wait* to taste him.

It takes no effort at all to throw him beneath me. He cries out in surprise, but I hold him down as I slide down his body. I don't give him time to protest as I lick his shaft, tracing the thick veins around his head before laying a trail of feathery kisses that leave him panting.

He sucks in sharply as I take him into my mouth. He tastes exquisite – warm and fresh and so very human. His blood pulses just beneath the surface as I slide my lips down him, taking him deep into my throat. My fangs slide down and the hunger gnaws at me. It's been so long since I tasted fresh human. And if I pierced him here, now, he'd probably faint from the ecstasy of it …

But as much as I want Gideon at my mercy, I don't wish him unconscious. I have *plans* for this cock.

So I stamp down the hunger, curl my lips over my fangs, and stroke him slowly until he wriggles and moans and grabs my shoulders, his fingers digging into the collar.

"Arabella," he breathes, his fingers sliding through my hair and down to my neck. "If you keep that up, you won't get your cock. I want to be inside you. Please …"

I laugh, my lips vibrating around his shaft before I pull back, running my fingers down my breasts and stomach.

"Since you asked so nicely …" I shuffle up his body, lining up my entrance with his shaft. As much as I'm shaking with the need to sink down onto him, I like teasing him more, so I rub myself along his tip, enjoying the curses falling from his lips as he tries to hold himself back.

"Wait …" A line appears between his eyes as he grips my hips, holding me. "I want you bare for me, you have no idea how much, but aren't there rules …"

I assume he's talking about the sheaths us *grandes horizontales* are expected to wear by the *brigade des mœurs* to help prevent diseases and unwanted pregnancies. But I don't need to use them, as he can't give me any vile human disease nor make me pregnant, not even with a Dhampir.

"I *am* bare for you, Gideon. Trust me, it's safe."

The cruel grin tugs at his mouth. His fingers slowly lift my hair, grazing the clasp of my collar. His eyes drop to the bright jewels.

I stiffen.

"I want you completely bare."

I swallow. My fingers tremble. I've never taken it off. Never. Not since the night I lifted it from my sire's cold, bloody fingers. The magic has kept me safe and helped me build a life for myself. If that magic goes away …

"Why?" I ask, running my fingers over the scarab.

He leans forward, his breath on my lips as he splays his hands on my thighs, his fingers rubbing against my sensitive skin. "I told you. I want all of you."

Yes.

I trust you.

Yes.

Keeping my eyes locked on his, I slowly unhook the collar. My fingers tremble. Cleopatra's jewels fall into my hands, heavy and cool to the touch. I imagine I can feel them humming against my fingers. I lean over and drape them over a velvet jewellery box on my vanity.

I swallow. Without the heavy collar of jewels, I'm naked in a way I haven't been in a long time. I'm used to men seeing me without my clothes on. I'm used to faking intimacy to get what I want.

I'm not used to being so *exposed*.

"You're even more beautiful without those heavy stones," Gideon murmurs before running his tongue down my neck as his hand slips between my legs.

A deep, unsteady breath fills my lungs and I gouge deep welts down his chest with my nails as he uses his fingers to rub my already punished clit.

But if he can torture me, I can just as easily torture him. I hover above his waiting cock, sinking down just enough to tease his tip with my entrance.

He groans, gripping my hip with his free hand while he rubs harder. "Are you trying to torture me?"

"Yes," I say with a smile, sinking way down so he fills me completely. "It's all part of the La Petite Mort full service. Afterwards, I'll drink your blood."

"I'd like that."

He shouldn't say that to me, not when he smells so delicious and the veins in his neck pulse with excitement. But not now, not this first time. I want him to be fully in charge of his faculties when I break him apart.

He feels amazing inside me, hot and hard and so big that I ride on the edge of pain.

Gideon lets out a ragged breath but I don't move, just sit there, letting my body get used to the feel of him.

It takes all the strength I have to hold back. I only break when he reaches up, wrapping his hand around my bare neck, and crushes his lips to mine.

I rock my hips to meet his over and over again. He drives up into me, desperate and wild, whispering sweet words of longing as he punishes me with his cock. He's a mess of contradictions, this human who loves life yet tethers himself to a king of the undead, this man who hates opera and loves art, who craves wealth and yet wants me even without my jewels.

We're more alike than I care to admit.

Our breathing and our bodies were always meant to meet this way. We match each other, every piece of him designed by the bountiful gods to fit perfectly against me. And when he thrusts into me … I see stars behind my eyes.

His thumb rubs my clit in perfect rhythm with his thrusts. His cobalt eyes never leave mine, always calling me back from my pleasure to focus on him, on us, on the dance of our bodies.

My orgasm builds slowly. I savour it, moving against Gideon's body, drinking in the intensity of his gaze as blood and red cherry swirl inside my skull.

He must sense my body clenching because he grips my hips in his hand and whispers, "That's it. Fall apart for me, Arabella. We'll come together."

At his words, my whole body shivers then explodes as I cry out his name, riding my orgasm on his cock, clawing at the skin of his shoulders.

"Oh, Arabella." He cries my name like a prayer as he digs his fingers into my hips and spills inside of me.

He pulls me against him as the throes of pleasure leave his body. I rest my head against his shoulder, breathing in his scent as we lie together, a tangle of limbs beneath the watchful eyes of the goddesses on my bed, our breathing as one.

"May I stay with you tonight?" he whispers before leaving a trail of kisses down my ear and bare neck. "May I keep you safe and warm?"

"That is acceptable," I murmur.

Safe and warm.

The last time I was safe and warm was in my mother's arms, before she was cruelly taken from me, before I followed her into a life of sin, before my sire stole the warmth from my veins and I was forced to break the most sacred vampire law.

I never thought I'd be safe or warm again.

But now, for the first time in decades, I'm warm, inside and out.

My body senses the sun approaching the horizon, even though I cannot see it. Soon, I will fall into the dreamless sleep of the Upyr, the sleep of death. I'm not afraid of Gideon seeing me in my most vulnerable state. I almost relish this knife edge I walk with him. I wonder if I could become addicted to the intoxication of trust, as I've seen so many others fall under the spell of opium.

Weariness clasps my limbs. I settle into his body, his cock still wet and warm inside me. He kisses my ears, his fingers trailing over my naked throat, whispering words I barely hear, as I slip into sleep …

25

Gideon

Sinead: I've just been informed of a little blip in the security system, but it seems to have righted itself. Carlton thinks it's probably due to the stream being diverted over some of the network cables.

I MOVE AWAY FROM THE PARTY, MY HEAD HUNG IN SHAME.
What was I thinking? I never should have put that sculpture on display.

I thought I knew Arabella. She used to love pomp and pageantry. She belongs on a stage, baring her soul when she dances, not buttoned up in her designer suits, moving money around for rich, pompous vampires who are utterly beneath her. (I include myself in that list.)

I thought the sculpture would say that.

But maybe I don't know her at all.

She offered to save Sanctus.

I realise I'm not alone. Members of the Nevermore Coven surround me.

Winnie pats my shoulder. "I'm sorry, Gideon. I thought she'd love the statue. But I didn't realise just how *abysmal* it was."

"Thanks, Winnie. That makes me feel so much better," I mutter.

Alaric pats me on the shoulder. "It certainly made a statement."

"What kind of statement?"

"That you are blind to her beauty and filled with rage."

"So it's not a *literal* copy of her figure," I snap. "Art doesn't always have to look like stuff, right? That's what the impressionists were always saying. Maybe it's a metaphor?"

"It is a metaphor," Maisie adds. "It's a metaphor for 'the person who inspired this statue is someone I hate'."

"Are you going to talk to her now?" Isis asks.

"I don't know if I should." Arabella's words bounce off the inside of my skull. "I don't think she wants to talk to me ever again."

Which means not only have I lost my chance with Arabella, but I've lost Sanctus, too.

Celeste comes running up to the group, her bright hair whipping around her face. "Someone defaced Arabella's house."

"What?"

"I walked her home, and she was fuming about the sculpture …" Celeste flashes me a sympathetic look. "But then we saw someone pinned a beheaded bird to her door and wrote 'MINE' underneath. It looks like it's written in *blood*."

My heart hammers against my ribs.

"But that's impossible. Sanctus security would never allow that to happen …" I reach for my phone but realise that it's in the stream. "Is Arabella okay?"

"She's grumpy, so I fear for the life of the perpetrator when she gets her claws into him."

"She shouldn't have to dirty her claws. I'll take great pleasure in gutting this bastard myself."

It can't be Lucien. He's long gone. I made certain of that.

But it could be another vampire who knows about my past with Lucien, trying to intimidate me into giving over Sanctus to the Conclave by threatening Arabella …

Maybe it's this same member of staff who has been robbing me.

"She doesn't want you to know about it. Please don't let on that

I told you," Celeste begs. "And don't worry about Arabella. We'll make sure she's safe."

Her eyes flash with venom, and I believe her. Celeste Lucas may be a sweet, apple-cheeked baker, but there's always been something about her. She has an odd smell – not vampiric, not magical like Dora, but kind of earthy and wild. The scent of someone who will go *feral* to protect her friends. And she does have an impressive collection of kitchen knives.

I hold Maisie back as the others run off to check on Arabella. "Maisie, I'm so sorry, but I'm not going to be able to help with the variety show."

She stops in her tracks. "What? Why not?"

"You heard Arabella tonight. She doesn't want anything to do with me." My shoulders slump. "I've already crossed her boundaries, and there's a whole history between us. I have to respect what she wants."

And if this is someone connected to Lucien, and they're trying to get to me through her, then she's safer if I'm nowhere near her.

"Arabella says things she doesn't mean all the time. The other week, she told Isis that the reason everything goes wrong in her life is because her shower singing angers the gods. But she still shows up to book club every week. Without fail. If Arabella didn't want you in her life, she'd be drinking her coffee from your skull right now, not demanding you help her direct a variety show. She cares about you in her own caustic, Arabella way."

"Vampires can't drink coffee."

"How do you survive eternity without coffee? Coffee is *life*. You have to do the variety show." Maisie lowers her voice. "In case you haven't noticed, the village is a little wary of this brand-new development filled with rich toffs, especially with the recent spate of murders. I think the variety show will bring the community together, and Sanctus Estate should be part of it."

"Can't I just clip tickets or something?" I brighten. "I'll know. I'll pull a rabbit out of a hat. I'd need to find a rabbit. And a hat …"

"I *need* you to do this. Please, Gideon."

If I'm close to Arabella, I can protect her. Even if she hates me for it.

I sigh. "Okay, fine. But only if Arabella is okay with it. Because if I show up and she doesn't want me there, she'll kill me, and then you, and then me again. And you know how much she hates getting blood on her shoes."

"I'll manage Arabella, I promise." Maisie hugs me. "You're the best."

No. I'm not.

But I'm trying. Maybe Maisie's right. Arabella is helping me with the Sanctus finances. And she hasn't tried to kill me again.

If someone is trying to hurt her at Sanctus, I will *present their skull to her as a trophy.*

And if Édouard finds her necklace and I get it back, like in Dora's vision, then she'll have to forgive me.

Right?

The Nevermore Murder Club and Smutty Book Coven Group Chat

Celeste: You should tell Gideon what happened.

Arabella: No.

Maisie: She's right, O Magnificent One. Gideon should know that someone is leaving dead birds on your door.

Komal: He could step up security around your house.

Arabella: I'm not having Gideon's goons vamp-sit me because some ex-client thinks I owe them favours.

Celeste: Then maybe we could help. One of us could stay with you at all times.

Arabella: Hard no.

Celeste: Arabella, this is serious! We've been thinking the two huskings were connected to Sanctus Estate, but what if they're about *you*?

Arabella: That's absurd. I never met Winnie's ex, and I wouldn't give that rat Danny O'Hare a second glance. His family tree is a circle.

Mina: Celeste makes a good point. If this killer is stalking you, they've probably been listening to our meetings. They know that we hated Patrick for hurting Winnie. And all of us have had run-ins with Danny. He spilt beer on your Versace dress two weeks before he died, remember?

Arabella: Vividly.

Komal: I just thought of something. Remember that book club meeting a few weeks ago, when Winnie swore she heard someone moving in the bushes outside?

Winnie: Er … that was Alaric being adorably creepy, as only he can.

Komal: Oh.

Mina: Alaric's adorable creepiness PROVES that any vampire could have been hiding outside, listening to our every word, trying to get intel on Arabella.

Isis: I wish a man would be adorably creepy for me!

Celeste: No, you don't. This is serious. This guy could be trying to please Arabella with these deaths, but now he's turned against her. We have to protect her.

Celeste: I think the killer is someone at Sanctus Estate. Do you think they're worried we might expose them? We were asking a lot of questions at the Midnight Garden opening.

Mina: I don't think so, otherwise the message would have said "STOP SNOOPING", not "MINE".

Beth: Yeah, this seems like a stretch. It's probably something to do with Arabella's past.

Arabella: I agree, and I'm going to make him pay.

Celeste: I think I'm onto something.

Beth: Sorry, Celeste, but this whole theory seems far-fetched. Someone at Sanctus Estate covering up an illegal Thrall operation seems much more likely. We need to do more snooping.

Winnie: Speaking of snooping, one of the servers told me Alyra Maythorn was feeding at Brimstone one night when Patrick walked in and saw them. Gideon offered Patrick a permanent job at Sanctus as chief architect, with a huge bonus package, but Patrick refused. So Gideon asked Lilac to make Patrick a drink so he'd forget, but he ran away and got himself killed before he could take it.

Mina: That's the second time Alyra's name has come up in connection to a victim.

Arabella: But if Lilac's potions work, why would Alyra – or anyone – need to kill Patrick?

Winnie: That's a good point, but it definitely warrants more investigation. She's your client. See what you can find out.

Arabella: I see we've cycled back to "Arabella, do all the work".

Celeste: You won't let us help!

Arabella: That's because you're all useless.

Beth: We love you, too.

26

Arabella

Maisie: O Magnificent One, I can't tell you how much I appreciate you doing this! Have fun at the auditions tonight.

A SINGLE WORD FLASHES ACROSS MY MIND AS I PULL INTO THE Zen and Tonic Pole Studio parking lot.

MINE.

The back of my neck crawls with the horrible feeling that I'm being watched. It's been over a week since the Midnight Garden party, but no matter how hard I try, I can't get that message out of my head. Especially because I recognise the handwriting.

It's the same loopy, spiky letters that were written on the mirror at La Petite Mort.

After I lost the theatre, I forgot all about the bloodstained flowers and dead birds and creepy messages left backstage. I had bigger concerns, like finding enough blood to stay alive and getting the fuck out of Paris. I assumed it was one of Catherina's admirers. We had problems with them from time to time.

But the same handwriting showing up on my door one hundred and fifty years later? This isn't about Catherina, who is long dead. This is about *me*.

Someone who tried to terrorise La Petite Mort is *here,* in Sanctus Estate, and they want me afraid.

My blood turns to ice.

It's no accident that this happened after I gave that little performance at Beth's studio. I was a fool. I got caught up in the music, the encouragement from my friends, and the idea of seeing Gideon Blake sweating, and I revealed myself. This is *exactly* why I've had to be so careful. This is why Sanctus' NDA and strict privacy rules appealed to me. Many of the vampires who used to frequent La Petite Mort are still alive and kicking, and they don't want their modern lives ruined by what they might've got up to in the past. Someone wants to shut me up or keep me for themselves.

This is America all over again.

No, it's not. This is my home. No one is driving me away this time.

In the car, I pull up the footage from my security cameras again, only to see the same error message stating that the feeds had conveniently gone dark just before the incident. A message on the Sanctus app informs everyone of a security glitch that lasted only ten minutes, and that, as far as their team know, nothing happened, but to report anything unusual to Gideon.

Like hell I'm telling Gideon about this. I'm not going to have him sweep in and solve my problems for me. Especially not now that he's signed off on me becoming Sanctus Estate's largest shareholder, apparently without even reading the contract. (I'm surmising here. If he read it, he definitely wouldn't have signed it. Everything I need to oust him is right there in legalese. I just need him to mess up one final time, and Sanctus is *mine*.)

And he's already given me all the ammunition I need. The Sanctus notification I set up on Sepulchrr is already going nuts, with Upyr Digging and Resurrecting the news that Sanctus security has been compromised. Conclave officials are using it to demonstrate that Sanctus is too dangerous without court oversight. They're putting together a contingent of officials to come in the flesh to demand an inspection.

When I swoop in and flush Gideon, I'll be praised. *Worshipped.* And the Conclave won't have anything to complain about anymore.

Their witch-hunt against Sanctus will fizzle out and this place can become a sanctuary once more.

I hope.

I might want to dunk Gideon in a vat of molten gold and have him mounted on my car as a hood ornament, but I don't want Sanctus to fall. In this *one single thing*, I'm on his side.

Provided he never goes anywhere near a block of marble again.

Luckily, I have a good idea of who is responsible for the word on my door – the same person stirring up rumours about me on the app. I'm arranging a special surprise for him.

But first, I have to make it through this painful evening.

I can't believe I let Maisie talk me into this.

I once created the best, most avant-garde, most *exclusive* burlesque theatre in Paris. And now I'm reduced to amateur theatre. All for the sake of helping out a friend who might not care so much about her job loss if she'd acquired a little more compound interest and spent a little less on expensive duck toys.

And now, since I prematurely told Gideon never to speak to me again, I'll have to do it all on my own.

I walk into the pole studio and take in the sorry bunch of ragamuffins waiting nervously for the auditions to begin. This is no Belle Époque theatre filled with young women hungry to be the next Sarah Bernhardt. I have my work cut out for me.

They fall silent as I step into the centre of the room.

"The auditions will begin at precisely eight pm," I announce. "Line up stage right. You will have exactly two minutes to impress me. Do not waste them."

While the would-be actors line up in the wings (changing rooms) of the makeshift stage (a bare area of floor with two poles that Beth has demarcated with black tape). Half of them go to the wrong side because they don't know where stage right is. As I gather the health and safety forms Maisie had them fill out, I notice three juggling pins on the prop table. Nothing good can come of that.

A table has been set up for me in front of the next row of poles. A water pitcher and two glasses. Two pads of legal paper and a handful of pens. Handwritten signs on each chair read DIRECTOR and DOGSBODY.

I fold myself into the DIRECTOR chair and glare down at the judging sheet.

Fine. I'll do it all myself. As usual.

"First act," I bark, pulling the pad towards me. "Your time starts now."

Isis drags a protesting Dora out onto stage, holding a wimple in place over her unruly hair. "We're doing a sister act. Get it?"

"I do not." I fold my arms.

"I … I just need a minute." Dora stammers. She crosses her arms, shoving her hands into her armpits as she gazes out into the audience, her face a picture of abject terror.

"Your minute is coming out of your performance time."

"Dora's *fine*. She's just being a scaredy-cat." Isis sets down her phone on the corner of the stage and jabs at the screen with her finger. "She'll get into it once I start the song. Hang on, the wi-fi dropped out. I'll just—"

BANG.

Dora shrieks. Several actors dive for cover. But it's only the studio doors banging open to admit a figure in a dapper pinstripe suit.

Gideon-bloody-Blake.

"Sorry, I'm late." Gideon skulks up to me. His fingers graze the edge of my table, inches from my arm. I feel every place he doesn't touch. "My, what a stunning batch of talent we have assembled before us. We have our work cut out for us whittling down the list."

"No conversing with the judges before the auditions." I glare at Gideon. "Get in line and take a number—"

"I'm not auditioning. I'm a helpful behind-the-scenes type, providing comic relief and endless back massages …" Gideon whirls around to glare at Maisie. "You didn't ask her, did you?"

Maisie looks sheepish. "Not as such."

"That's why steam is coming out of her ears. When you said that she still wanted me to turn up today, even though she *explicitly* told me she never wanted to see me again …"

Maisie sinks into her seat. "I may have fudged the truth a little."

Gideon's eyes flash. "You said she'd be *excited* to see me."

"Yes, well …" Maisie shifts uncomfortably. "I thought she would be. I may have underestimated the depth of Arabella's ire. But it's for a good cause! Can't you two work it out for the sake of the show?"

Maisie makes puppy dog eyes at Gideon, who looks like a hot air balloon after one of Sarah Bernhardt's raucous champagne parties over Paris – deflated, lifeless, kind of shell-shocked.

Gideon twists to face me, and the pain in his eyes shocks the retort from my lips. "I only came today because Maisie asked me. I thought you wanted me here, and that maybe this event would help make Sanctus more a part of the community. I never intended to make you uncomfortable. I'll leave right now."

"Wait!" Beth stalks across the room, swiping my water glass and taking a long sip. "You're not going anywhere. As the variety show organiser, I have a say. And I say that unless Gideon works on this, I'll withdraw my sponsorship."

Now Beth is grinning at me. *Oh, I get it.* They think that if Gideon and I work together, I'll be able to get more information out of him about the murders.

Is there no part of my life free from his incessant Gideon-ness?

Apparently not.

"Fine," I huff. "You stay. But you're not the director. *I* am. I'm not interested in discourse. I am correct in all matters. Understand?"

Gideon's shoulders sag. He slumps into the DOGSBODY chair beside me. His leg brushes mine, sending an unexpected jolt of warmth through my body.

He jerks his legs away.

"I swear, I didn't set this up," he whispers as he pulls the stack of audition sheets towards himself. "I promise, you won't even know I'm here."

Gideon lied.

I've been stuck in this room with him for three and a half hours, and not only am I aware of his existence, but I want to commit crimes against him.

Many crimes. All the crimes.

At last, we made it through the final act – Richard from the Rose & Wimple playing "Don't Fear the Reaper" on pint glasses. I collapse on top of my judging pad, my fingers aching from the number of times I've written OH HELL NO in my notes. Beth and Maisie usher the would-be performers out of the theatre, and the four of us pull up chairs to deliberate over our final line-up.

"So far, we've got the Argleton Volunteer Firefighters, Reverend Kirkpatrick and the church choir, Maisie and James Pond, and the Naughty Knitting Club's rendition of 'No Scrubs'." Beth glances down at her list. "And absolutely no jugglers."

"Are we sure we don't want even one juggler?" Gideon raises an eyebrow. "I thought the fellow with the chickens was quite—"

"No jugglers," I growl.

"But they were such *happy* chickens."

"No jugglers."

"No jugglers." Beth consults her list. "So, crunch time. If we add Dora and Isis—"

"We can't add them. Dora threw up before she even sang a word."

"She'll get there," Beth says. "I have a calming elixir that will help her."

I very much doubt that. I think Dora's reluctance to perform has more to do with the possibility of what her husband will say. But Gideon and Beth seem to have decided that they're running this show, so what I say doesn't matter. I add Dora and Beth's names to our cast list.

"So with Isis and Dora in, I think we're almost there." Beth scribbles in her notes. "But we need at least one more act for the second half."

"That's obvious. Arabella has to perform," Gideon says.

"I'm the director."

"That never stopped you at La Petite Mort." His eyes shimmer. "You want to be on stage again. You know it."

"You could do a pole routine!" Beth grins. "It will be the perfect advertisement for my studio!"

I fold my arms and glare at them both. "That's not happening."

The last thing I need is another client seeing me dance – or worse, someone in the audience films me and puts it on the internet.

"Go on, Arabella." Gideon's eyes shimmer. "Don't you want to show all these amateurs how a professional does it?"

"All the ladies in the book club will be there!" Beth grins. "We'd cheer you on!"

Gideon leans over and whispers, "Admit it. You want to be back on stage again, every eye in the village on you while you captivate them. Don't you remember what it felt like to be the most famous, most notorious dancer in Paris?"

He's right.

Damn him.

My pulse quickens, which has absolutely nothing to do with the whiff of honey and red cherry I smell when Gideon leans close.

Seeing these rank amateurs ruining the stage has made me long to darken the floorboards once more. I'm already mentally hunting through the folder called "dance costume insp" I'll never admit is on my computer.

And I can find a way to hide my face and ensure that people are too distracted to notice who I am.

"Fine. I'll perform. On one condition."

Gideon lets out a ragged breath. "Name it. Anything."

"Gideon must agree to be part of my routine." I steeple my fingers. "*And* he promises to perform any role I give him without complaint."

"Oh no. No no no. You're going to make me dress like a banana, or force me to act as a giant baby and suck on a dummy or … or …" Gideon's face crumples as he contemplates all the horrific things I might do to him.

"I was actually thinking of appearing as Marie Antoinette and cutting off your testicles with the world's tiniest guillotine, but I'm intrigued by the dummy idea."

"Go on, Gideon!" Beth slaps his shoulder. "It'll be fun. I'm sure Arabella is kidding about the guillotine."

"She is not." Gideon swallows. "But of course. I'll be your humble servant."

"Good." I write our names down on Beth's studio booking form. "We've filled all our slots. Maisie, you contact our performers and make sure they have the rehearsal schedule. Gideon, you will be here, on the dot, at seven pm Friday, so we can begin working on our routine. Beth, I'm going to need some private practice time …"

Message from the Conclave on the Sepulchrr App

SECURITY CONCERNS AT SANCTUS ESTATE

An inside source at Sanctus informs us that on the eve of the Midnight Garden sculpture party, where un-Thralled humans were invited onto the estate to mingle with Upyr residents, the security system broke down for several minutes. We cannot confirm if anyone entered the property without detection, and no security breaches have been reported, but Upyr should be concerned that Gideon Blake's security is not as impenetrable as he would have you believe.

This is particularly alarming given the husker is still on the loose. Humans and vampires should not be socialising freely without regard for our rules. We should not stand for these threats to our safety and secrecy.

Yet another lie fed to innocent Upyr by a man who wants to steal your money!

The Conclave

    1255 Dig This   122 Resurrections

Gideon
Then

Gideon, I hope this letter finds you well. I do not know your residence so I left this missive with Claude in the hopes he will get it to you. I've had to flee the city. It has become dangerous for me to hang around La Petite Mort. I wish I could tell you why, but you are not yet ready to know. Hopefully, you'll never need know the truth.

I write to you as a friend, with some less-than-friendly advice. You must break off your affair with Arabella. I fear it will be the death of you.

I know the idea of losing her seems as unthinkable as losing your left thumb. I say this as a man who's had more than his fair share of affairs. A woman may occupy your thoughts, wholly and completely, for a time. You cannot paint, you cannot think, you cannot breathe. They are beneath your skin, and you cannot imagine excising them without cutting out pieces of yourself.

But when it's over, it is like crossing the border into another country. They become distant memories — languages you no longer speak, landmarks you remember only as flowery sentences in your diary.

You can learn to live and paint again without a thumb. But you cannot live without a heart, and she will surely take yours.

Please don't look for me, but know I wish you well.

Edouard

A RABELLA'S HEAD LOLLS AGAINST MY SHOULDER, HER LIPS PARTING slightly.

She's asleep.

I know from watching her when she was sick that she's a proper mistress of the night. The moment the sun peeks over the horizon, she falls into a dead slumber. Not even Sarah singing show tunes would wake her.

Now's my chance.

I slide my arm out from beneath Arabella and gaze down at a goddess in her golden chemise, the only blemish on her skin a tiny, perfect mole on her inner thigh. I drown myself in her beauty one final time before I roll away from her. I rise from her bed and search for my clothes, popping a button from my shirt in my haste. I gingerly touch the claw marks on my back.

Sex with Arabella is even more wanton and dangerous than I could have imagined, and I have a vast and graphic imagination.

She is no mere woman. She is a *goddess*.

And I'm about to steal from her.

To save her life. To save my brother.

The necklace rests on top of the velvet box on her dresser. Now that it's separated from her neck, the stones appear dull, the gold tarnished. I pick it up, amazed at how light it feels.

All this fuss over such a tiny, breakable thing? I find it hard to believe it was ever magical.

I wanted to wait for the perfect moment when I could make it look like someone else had stolen it, but I'm out of time. I have to hope that once I pay my debt to Lucien and we're free, I can explain things to Arabella. She'll hate me, but I'll happily be hated by her as long as she's alive.

I stuff the jewels down my trousers, wince as I tug my jacket over the wounds across my shoulders, and make a run for it.

At her door, I pause, my heart in my throat. I look back at her sleeping. She hasn't stirred. Her chest doesn't even look as though it's rising. She's so beautiful like this, all her walls crumbled to dust.

I contemplate leaving a note, but I know her well enough by now to know she wouldn't read it. Better for me to return once I'm free of Lucien's influence and explain myself.

I slip away into the sunlight.

I know there is no point returning to Lucien while the sun is high. He sleeps like the dead and no matter the urgency, the guard on duty during daylight – the one with the sadistic streak and the scarf pulled tightly around his neck – won't let me in to see him. So I wander, distraught, through the streets of Paris, my pocket heavy with jewels and betrayal.

When I return in the evening, Lucien has only one guard at the apartment. I'm so familiar with the habits of Lucien's soldiers that it's easy for me to slip past him when he goes to the basement for more wine. My brother's snores tremble the basement stairs – at least that means Jacob is still alive.

Silently, I push open the door to Lucien's boudoir, blocking the exit and squinting to make him out in the gloom.

Lucien's head snaps up from where he's tangled in the sheets with a youth cradled in his arms. I haven't said a thing, but he knows I'm there. He's always had a canny sense like that. Lucien drops the boy, who murmurs as he hugs the sheets, his neck bruised and smeared with dry blood—

My back hits the wall with a *CRACK* like a revolver shot.

I gasp for breath. Lucien's smooth, cool hand closes around my throat. He pushed me, but how? How did he cross the room that fast?

"Little Prince, you dare show your face here?" Lucien's eye bore into mine, cold as death and twice as dangerous.

"I told you I would handle it, and I did." I gasp out.

"You have it?" he whispers, his breath reeking of blood and nightmares.

His fingers close tighter in excitement. I manage to choke out a sound of assent.

"Leave us!" Lucien commands. The youth crawls away, his eyes blinking slowly, lost in an opium daze. Lucien lets go of my throat. I drop in a heap, gasping for air.

"Show me." Lucien sits on the edge of the bed, his limbs jittering with excitement.

With trembling hands and still gasping for breath, I pull the necklace out of my trouser pocket and lay it across his waiting palms.

He stares at the collar with a hunger so raw and greedy I half expect him to stuff the jewels into his mouth and start chewing. I've been so sick with the need to keep Arabella and Jacob safe that I've forgotten that if the collar truly is magic, I've handed Lucien a powerful weapon.

"Our business is concluded," I say. "I'll take cash now, and the key to my brother's restraints. We'll be out of the city before you've even put on trousers."

"Oh, sweet, innocent Little Prince." Lucien stands. At his full height, he's nearly a head taller than me, and even though he's naked and I have a knife and revolver concealed, every hard line of his body speaks of danger. His hand circles my wrist, his fingers squeezing together until I wince with pain. "I told you, you're *mine*. I'm not done with you yet."

"I don't even need the money. I just want my brother." I look up into his eyes, but they are fathomless black holes. There's nothing human inside him, no softness, no empathy. "I got you the necklace, so Jacob's debts are wiped and we're both free."

"Tsk, tsk." His fingers tighten their grip. A whimper rises in my throat. I buck against him, trying to free my hand, but it's like fighting a brick wall. His skin is so cold, like touching ice. "That was never our deal. I promised only that your brother's debts would be wiped. He may of course go free. But I cannot allow someone with such a talent for this business to leave me. You are mine, Little Prince, and that makes you the luckiest of men. I will give you the world. I will give you *immortality*."

His eyes flash with cold, monstrous *possessiveness*, and the last thing I see as a human is a pair of long, gleaming fangs sliding from his upper jaw and sinking into my neck.

28

Arabella

Gideon: I truly am sorry about showing up for the auditions. I know that you're sick of me.

But I'm not sorry we're performing together, even though I know you're going to use it to torture me.

I enjoy being tortured by you, ma petite déesse.

And I'm also not sorry that we're now in business together. Welcome to the Sanctus family, my not-so-silent investor.

In the interests of full investor disclosure, I should let you know that as well as stealing from the vault, someone has been leaking information about Sanctus to the Conclave – like a teeny tiny security breach on the night of the Midnight Garden launch party. I've determined the leak to be Paul Badica, and I've taken care of him. I thought you'd like to know.

I HURL THE PHONE AT THE WALL. IT BOUNCES OFF AND SKIDS ACROSS the tiles, the screen shattering. Cleo VII slithers to safety. There's now a phone-corner-shaped dent in my brand new wall.

He's not allowed to do this to me.

He's not allowed to steal my revenge. *Mine.*

He's not allowed to use that name, to remind me of that night.

Especially not tonight, of all nights. My Bloodeve.

I sink into my sofa.

I can't think about Gideon. I can't think about the man who sired me and how satisfying it was to carve him to pieces. I have an issue to deal with. A songbird's corpse sits on my coffee table, the word "MINE" scrawled with its blood by a careless finger. I found it there when I came downstairs after my daysleep. A brief message on the Sanctus app referred to another security glitch.

I don't know how Badica did it, as he would have had to come during the day. He and his wife have a private Thrall, so I'm guessing that's how. And if that Thrall has staff access to the security system, they could also be stealing from the vault …

All I know is Badica is about to find out what happens when someone tries to terrorise Arabella Lestrange—

My phone beeps. A text from one of my favourite clients in London.

It is done.

A satisfied smile plays across my face. Maybe Gideon hasn't beaten me after all. Cleo VII coils herself into a ball beside me as I search through the Sanctus directory for a number. It's answered after three rings. The male voice on the other end sounds cautiously optimistic.

"Who is this?"

"You know who it is, Paul Badica. Or should I call you Cardinal?"

"Arabella." He pants into the phone. "I wondered when I'd hear from you. Are you as excited as I am to relive our old times? When I saw you had found a place in Sanctus, I thought it must be fate. I'll introduce you to all my friends. They're already so excited to meet you. You'll be a rich woman with all the business we'll give you."

"I'm already a rich woman." I pat Cleo VII's scaly back. "I just wanted you to know that I got your messages."

"Messages? What messages?" He lowers his voice. "I have to be careful, so my wife doesn't find out. I'm supposed to be a respectable man now."

I can't help the unladylike snort that escapes my mouth. I don't have to be polite to men like him anymore. "As opposed to when you were a man of the cloth."

Badica doesn't catch my sarcasm. He's speaking in a whisper, his voice strained with desire. "If you want to arrange a meeting next week, then send me a message on Sepulchrr. And send me photographs. You know the sort of thing I like. I'll pay whatever you ask."

Out the window, beneath the cool light of the full moon, I see members of the Sanctus security team rush past.

"That's good to know, Paul, because my price is *everything*."

"What?"

"I want everything you have, and I'm not asking. I've already taken it. Your accounts are empty. Check them now. You'll see I'm not lying."

"Arabella, what is this?" I hear frantic tapping as he searches the app. Paul's tone changes. "You *bitch*. What have you done?"

"You made our private business public," I say. "And I haven't forgotten how you terrorised my dancers after we kicked you out of La Petite Mort. So I made your money mine. Well, I'm not certain it's all your money, but that's a conversation for when Gideon's goons come knocking. Oh, and since you collect antique erotica, you might be interested in some rather raunchy sketches from my personal collection that I've posted on Sepulchrr. They already have several thousand Digs and Resurrections, and more every minute as people recognise the cardinal at the centre of the scenes. My friend, the artist Berthe Morisot, had a real knack for capturing the realities of life in Montmartre."

"I never did anything to your dancers that they weren't begging for, you crazy bitch," he yells. "You can't do this to me!"

"I already did."

"Just wait a second." His tone switches to pleading. In the background, I hear knocking. "It doesn't have to go down like this. We can work something out—"

"The way you *waited* before you opened your mouth about me at Sanctus and defaced my property?" I sneer. "I don't think so. You may have known me on my back when my job required me to be sweet and demure, but don't for one second underestimate me." The knocking becomes louder, more insistent. "And you shouldn't have underestimated Gideon Blake. You may have heard rumours about the kind of man he was before he opened Sanctus. Those rumours are true, and you broke his rules. I suspect that's the Sanctus security team. I hear they're all members of the Vega family."

"But I didn't—"

I hear the splintering of Norwegian larch and harsh voices shouting. Paul Badica sobs into the phone.

"That will be them now. Goodbye, Paul."

I hang up. A few moments later, the security team return past my windows, dragging a man in silver handcuffs. Paul Badica's bloody face is visible beneath a shaft of moonlight.

I cross my legs, sipping my glass of blood and enjoying the show. Paul won't be defacing my property or stealing from Sanctus ever again. Gideon may be a scoundrel, but he has some sense of justice.

And Paul Badica's wealth has nicely refilled my coffers after buying this house. I may even do a good thing and drop a sizable chunk into the Sanctus construction account, since that's probably where most of the funds came from.

Not because I care about Gideon. At all. But because I like living here, and I want to see it succeed.

As soon as I've pushed Gideon out and taken Sanctus for myself, I can get started on my ideas to improve this place.

I take another sip of blood. This is a decent vintage I opened for the occasion – a WWI British Soldier from the Sanctus cellar, full-bodied and earthy, like the mud of the trenches – but it would be even better fresh.

It's been a long time since I've tasted fresh blood directly from the source. I lived on it after La Petite Mort was destroyed, when I had no money and no other options. And so, when I made a new fortune, I decided that I'd never again return to dragging victims from the street like a beast, supping my fill of drunks and addicts, tasting the sour notes of their vices in their blood.

Humans – *consenting* humans – on tap is very tempting.

It's my Bloodeve. Maybe I deserve a treat.

My fingers hover over the Sanctus app and its list of Thralled staff members available for feedings. Sinead's name is at the top of the list, with 82 5-star ratings. "Oozes sophistication with notes of lime, fresh pear and honeysuckle leading towards a succulent finish," one review says.

Mmmm. Sounds divine.

But no, I don't want to spend my Bloodeve sucking on the neck of a woman who dislikes me.

I scroll down and see Danny O'Hare's name, with a 2.4-star rating. I'm about to click on his reviews when my doorbell rings.

Annoyance sours the blood on my tongue. I'm not expecting visitors. I prefer to be alone on my Bloodeve. The only time I ever broke that rule was the night Gideon took me out on Sarah Bernhardt's hot air balloon, and I won't have a repeat of how *that* turned out. No one in the Nevermore Coven would be able to breach Sanctus gates without me being alerted, so it must be someone on the estate.

I glance down at the Sanctus app, thinking I must have clicked on a Thrall order by accident. But no.

Who could be at my house? Is it the security team coming to tell me they've kicked out Paul?

Or another ex-client, here to make a nuisance of himself?

My gaze falls back to the dead bird on the table. The back of my neck prickles.

As my finger swipes through my phone, searching for the security feed, a movement out the window catches my eye. Something rustles in the bushes. A dark shape passes along the edge of my garden.

I gasp as the shape moves beneath a shaft of moonlight and I glimpse its form.

A wolf.

A *giant* wolf with a piece of jewellery dangling from its ear – a distinctive gold hoop with a cupcake on it.

29

Arabella
Then

I WAKE SHROUDED IN SILK, MY BODY WARM WITH THE GLOW OF LOVE.
It's been so long since I felt *warm*.

I open one sleepy eye, drawing out the pleasure of emerging from the night into his arms—

He's not here.

My other eye flies open. I grasp the cold sheets beside me.

He's not here.

I roll from my bed and survey my apartment, my heart hammering against my ribs faster than it has in decades. Part of me hopes this is a cruel joke, that he's hiding beneath my bed or behind the *commode*, preparing to jump out and surprise me with one of his silly gifts or …

It's then I notice my baubles and makeup containers flung carelessly across the marble surface of my *toilette*.

The collar is gone.

No.

I've been a fool. I've been so stupid. I thought he loved me. I thought he was different from all the rest. But he's just another man come to take from me, come to destroy everything I've fought for.

I won't cry.

I will never shed a single tear for Gideon Rougon.

He has my necklace. My magic is gone, and everything I've built is in danger—

"My theatre," I whisper, as I tug my best fur coat over my shoulders and fly for the door.

Cleopatra's curse is swift and cruel. By the time I arrive at La Petite Mort, the blaze is already so intense that I cannot even cross the street. *Sapeurs-pompiers* fight the fire with water pumped from the Seine, while a crowd gathers to gossip over the flames. Many of them jeer at my beautiful burning theatre, pleased to see a house of ill-repute receive such godly vengeance.

I hear that one of the lamps wasn't properly extinguished and it set fire to the curtains.

But I don't believe this explanation for a moment. I know why my theatre is burning. Lucien Vega is behind this. And his servant, Gideon Blake.

Gideon did this.

He took my collar and burned my theatre.

The good fortune that has been with me ever since I left Egypt is fleeing from me, undoing everything it helped create. As I fall to my knees, stupefied with horror, the wooden beams that hold the roof come crashing down, and the outer stone wall of my theatre collapses inward.

Please, let all of my girls be tucked safe into their beds ...

As if hearing a cue from the devil himself, a *pompier* drags a dark shape from the rubble. My hand flies to my mouth as I recognise Catherina's favourite scarlet gown. The *pompier* dumps the body on the road and returns to the pumps.

The body is without a head.

There are only three ways to kill a vampire. Burning, draining completely of blood, and severing the head from the body. Our kind can survive burning, if we're unlucky. But never a severed head ...

I'm so sorry, Catherina.

Fear and sadness choke me. I bow my head, no longer wishing to see the misery my hubris has caused. Instead, I'm confronted with the shimmering golden silk of my chemise – the one Gideon so reverently tugged from my body mere hours ago.

I believed I was safe. I believed that no man could ever take away what I built. And then I went and opened my heart to Gideon Rougon, and he proved me wrong.

I touch my hand to my throat. But instead of the heavy reassurance of my jewels, my fingers brush bare, cold skin.

As cold as Gideon will be when I catch him.

The loose chemise fits too tight. It's choking me. His scent rises from my skin, now part of the fabric. I want nothing more than to burn it away, as he has burned everything I loved about him. I tear at the chemise. Silk rips in my hands – long, jagged ribbons like the bandages of a mummy. I tear and tear, tossing them into the fire as hot tears of rage burn down my cheeks.

I have nothing left now, except *vengeance—*

"Arabella Macquart."

I whip my head around, aware with a cold rush of fear that I'm kneeling in a fur coat and ragged chemise that now barely covers my body. The stern voice belongs to an officer of the *brigade des mœurs*. The officer grins at me, revealing a row of rotting teeth. "You're coming with us."

"On what charge?" I leap to my feet, preparing to run. But another officer slams into me from behind and shackles my wrists. "I've done nothing illegal."

The first officer laughs. "As if you don't know, you naughty minx. You haven't shown up for your venereal disease check-ups. And look at ye – darty eyed, blood on your lip, roaming the streets in naught but a fur coat. Looks like hysteria with a touch of syphilis to me! We can't have you infecting the good men of this city."

"This is preposterous." I strain against the shackles, but they must be inlaid with silver, because I can't break them. "We had an exemption. Your boss—"

"Not anymore, you don't. You should have been more generous, sweetheart." He breathes smoke into my face. "You thought you were special, but you're just one more *cocotte* who's going to learn her place."

30

Arabella

I watch the wolf from above.

She watches me back, sitting upright, ears pricked, brown eyes alert. The more I study her features, the more I'm certain of it – that wolf is my friend.

She has Celeste's red streaks in her auburn coat, her kind eyes, and a feral regality to her features. And there is the matter of that earring. The wolf didn't pierce her own ear.

Plus, wild wolves haven't been seen in England since before I was given the Kiss. And while I believe it likely many members of Sanctus lay claim to exotic pets, this she-werewolf isn't a pet.

She's my friend.

I'm contemplating what to do with this new information when the wolf's head whips around, her snout in the air, sniffing some new scent. A moment later, there's another knock on my door.

The wolf leaps into the bushes, heading closer to the stairs leading to the house, body low to the ground.

Hunting.

My heart thuds against my chest. I pull across the tablet that controls the features of the house and bring up the security camera. A figure stands on my doorstep, one hand casually wrapped around a bottle of blood while the other swipes through his phone.

It's Gideon.

And coming up right behind him is Celeste.

Gideon has his head bent down, focusing on his phone. He has a tote bag from a gaming shop slung under his arm. A moment later, a text beeps on my screen.

> **Gideon:** I'm here to work on our routine before tomorrow's rehearsal. I promise I'll even let you dress me as a meerkat.

I text back as quickly as I can.

> **Arabella:** You fool, get out of here.

I search my memories for what I know about werewolves, which isn't much. They exist only as rumours among our kind – fairytale stories about a time long forgotten. All I know is that every full moon, a werewolf transforms into their wolf form, with all the wolfish instincts and proclivities that entails. A single werewolf can terrorise a whole village when their shift overtakes them, and they are driven by their hunger, their need to eat and to protect their territory. If they ever did exist, I've been told, they were hunted to extinction a long time ago.

But that can't be true. Because Celeste is *here*, stalking towards Gideon, and one thing I *do* know about werewolves is that in their wolf form they are vicious, and their hunger knows no limits.

My phone beeps again.

> **Gideon:** Is that any way to talk to the greatest meerkat to ever grace the stage? Please let me in. Don't make me press my beautiful face pathetically against the window.

As quickly as I can, I grab the dead songbird (*don't think about bird guts between your fingers*) and the tablet, punching the button to open the living room window.

"Hey, Celeste," I call out. "You don't want him. He'll be stringy. No flavour."

I toss the poor songbird out the window. I have many talents, but underarm bowling is not one of them. The bird *splats* against the sculptural fountain in my garden, spilling blood and bits across the white tiles. The scent hits my nostrils, and a flash of raw hunger surges in me. But Celeste doesn't even slow down. The bushes rustle as she sneaks closer to Gideon.

I've got Gideon's attention, at least. He steps out from the entrance, gaze trained on the bits of bird. "Arabella, what's going on?"

Shit.

The wolf growls. I slam the window shut as Gideon hollers. He whirls around, searching for something that could fend off a wolf. Celeste leaps for Gideon. I sprint to the front door, punching the button to open it as I grab an umbrella from the stand.

Gideon's on the ground, his hands around Celeste's neck. In the harsh glare of the entrance light, I get my first up-close look at Celeste in her wolf form.

She is *terrifying* – larger than any wolf has business being, with vicious claws that swipe at Gideon's arms and chest. Powerful jaws snap at his face, and I know that even with his vampiric strength, Gideon will lose this battle.

"Argggh!" Gideon wrestles with her. Blood gushes from claw wounds in his arm.

"Celeste!"

At the sound of my voice, Celeste's back straightens. She sits back and glances over at me, teeth bared, stained with Gideon's blood. Her eyes narrow. She doesn't seem aggressive towards me.

Is she here to protect me?

Raw fear punches through me. I can't let Celeste hurt Gideon.

I step forward, placing my body between them.

"Arabella, no." Gideon hisses.

"He's part of our pack," I growl, brandishing the umbrella. "We don't hurt our own."

Celeste growls back, the sound so deep and dark that it rumbles in my stomach. I think she's telling me to move … or else.

She lunges straight at me, those horrible teeth bared. I swing the umbrella through the air, knowing with horror that it's not going to stop a huge, salivating wolf with a heroine complex.

A long shape darts between my legs.

Cleo VII rears up, fangs bared, hood extended, hissing a warning. Celeste twists midair to escape the snake, hitting the flagstones on her side. She whimpers, rolling into my garden bed, crushing the flowers.

Cleo VII advances. Celeste scrabbles onto all fours and slinks off into the bushes.

"Cleo, you beautiful creature." I hold out my arm, and she coils around my shoulders, her tongue flicking as she fixes her eyes on the spot where Celeste entered the woods.

"Arabella …"

I turn at the forlorn sound. Gideon lies, clutching his arm, blood staining the flagstones beneath him. *Shit*.

"I can't leave you out here to attract more delightful wildlife." I grab Gideon under his shoulders and drag him inside, leaving a trail of blood across my front porch. I'll be sending him a bill to clean that later.

Once inside, I'm confronted with the scale of my problem. There is absolutely nowhere in my vast and pristine new property where I want a bleeding, moaning Gideon. I settle for dumping him on the kitchen tiles while I search for something to clean him up with.

"Ow." Gideon crawls towards the living room. "Why didn't you put me on the couch?"

"That couch is Hermès. You're not getting anywhere near it until those wounds are healed over."

"That blasted wolf has ruined a perfectly decent suit." Gideon coughs blood on my Scandinavian larch floorboards.

"Don't pretend like you don't love an excuse to go back to Savile Row."

"Did you just save my life?"

"Technically, Cleo VII saved your life. But don't let it go to your head. She still doesn't trust you." I toss him a damp tea towel. "You're bleeding on my new rug. Fix that."

Gideon wraps the towel around his arm. He fishes his phone out of his pocket as I open my fridge and pull out a bottle of vintage blood I'd been saving for tonight – a Steamboat Captain (full-bodied, sea-salt flavour). "I'd better call the security team and tell them we have a wolf problem."

I whip the phone out of his hand. "Don't do that."

Gideon tilts his head to the side. "And why wouldn't I? Are you hoping that beast comes back for another bite?"

"Perhaps." My heart hammers against my ribs as I debate what I should tell him. I wipe off two glasses and pour blood right to the rims. I hand him his glass and settle on the truth. "Drink. You'll need it. That's no ordinary wolf. It's Celeste."

"Celeste? As in, that human cutie from the bakery?" Gideon gulps down his blood. His wounds still aren't closing.

"The very same. Didn't you see the earring in her ear?"

"I was a little busy trying not to get my face ripped off."

"Well, she was wearing Celeste's earrings. And she's trying to protect me, so I don't want your guys to hurt her. Besides, aren't they busy with Paul Badica?"

Gideon smiles ruefully. "They may be."

"Celeste told you, didn't she?"

"She's just trying to protect you." Gideon winces as he leans against my larch cabinets, empty wine glass clutched so tight his knuckles are white. "And I take it from the delightful treat you tried to distract her with that you received another message."

"I sure did. It must have been his Thrall, because I found it on my table when I woke up. But I don't need a fuss. I've already taken care of Badica myself. I suggest you take a look at his accounts. If his Thrall can mess with the security system, they're probably the one stealing from you."

"Stealing from *us*," he corrects with a groan. "That occurred to me too. My team checked his accounts, but we didn't find any evidence, and now they've been completely cleared out. Not that you'd know anything about that."

I smirk. "The clergy are always losing their wallets in the most inconvenient places."

"We'll keep digging, but his crimes are enough for me to make certain Badica will never step foot inside Sanctus again. This place only works if everyone inside it feels safe. Which is why Badica's Thrall is gone, too, and I'm doubling security. But don't change the subject. Celeste is a werewolf?"

"It appears so." I slump down on the sofa, tossing Gideon's phone on the table beside the scrawled word, and sipping my blood.

"I wondered why she smelled … not entirely human."

I know exactly the scent he's talking about. It's always clung to Celeste, this … wildness. I thought it was from all that running in the woods.

"This wound isn't closing. It must be something to do with werewolf magic. No wonder our kin hunted them." Gideon crawls across the floor, reaching for his phone. I kick his hand out of the way. "I *have* to, Arabella. What if she attacks one of our residents?"

"Celeste wouldn't do that."

"She was just about to gut me!"

"She thought she was protecting me. Besides, good luck finding her. Her species has eluded capture for, oh, thousands of years."

"You have my word that my men won't hurt her. They'll keep her secret. We'll contain her until the full moon is over. She'll turn back into a human, and we can find out exactly what's going on. I know you have every right not to trust me, but I'm asking you to *try* it for your friend's sake. If she's allowed to roam these woods and another Upyr sees her … you know our kin get a little stabby when confronted by ancient enemies they thought long dead."

I sigh and kick his phone off the edge of the table. It skids across the floor towards him. He makes the call to Sinead.

"A werewolf." Gideon slumps back on the floor once he hangs up. "Of course you're friends with a werewolf …"

His voice trails off. His cobalt eyes fix on a spot behind me.

Oh, right.

I don't need to turn around to know what he's looking at. I hung Claude's painting behind my sofa. I like entering my home to be greeted by my naked figure reclining over the ruins of a Greek temple – Aspasia clad in moonlight, with the jewels of a queen at her throat.

I especially like the reaction it stirs in Gideon. His body is frozen, the only movement his Adam's apple bobbing at his throat. Red cherry, poppy and honey scent the air, and I'm aware that once again, Gideon has wormed his way across my threshold into my sanctum.

"You kept it," Gideon whispers.

"It would be a sin to destroy something so beautiful," I say.

"On that, we agree." Gideon tears his eyes from my naked form, those luminous aquamarine orbs fixing on me. "Arabella, this—"

"*All* it means is that I enjoy torturing you with what you'll never have again. Take a good, long look at that painting, because that's as close as you'll ever get to *this* Aspasia." Lights break through the trees outside. "You'd better pick your jaw up off the floor. The cavalry has arrived."

∞

I watch from the window as Gideon's security team moves through the woods. There's some snarling, trees rustling, and a lot of lights moving quickly. It looks like a scene from *Jurassic Park*, only Gideon is more annoying than Jeff Goldblum.

"Thanks for the update, Sinead. We're going to keep her overnight, until the full moon is over." Gideon appears by my side, his mobile phone in his hand. He's taken off his jacket and rolled up the sleeves of his shirt, revealing surprisingly muscled forearms that absolutely do not make my lady parts tingle. "They've got her. She's alive and unhurt. Sinead says they're loading her into a secure cell now."

I don't like Sinead knowing Celeste's secret, but Gideon assures me she's trustworthy, and Sinead being Thralled to Sanctus gives a measure of protection. "I want to see her."

Gideon glances towards the garden, where his security team are hefting a dark shape into the back of a vehicle. "I don't think Celeste would want you to see her like this."

"Tough. She's my *friend*. I know that concept means nothing to you, but she's important to me. Besides, I'm not in danger anymore. I took care of Paul Badica."

"*I* took care of Badica."

"If you say so." I shrug, knowing it's infuriating him that he has no idea what I did. But I've already lost interest in my so-called stalker.

How has Celeste been transforming into this beast every full moon, and we haven't noticed? The Nevermore Coven prides itself on sniffing out a supernatural mystery, and yet she's kept this from us the whole time. How much control does she have over her shifting? Does she only eat raw meat? Is she immortal?

I have so many questions, I sound like Isis.

"Celeste is dangerous. She's already tried to eat two of my men. And me." Gideon points to his wound.

"Don't punish her for her excellent palette."

"Are you saying I taste good?" Gideon smiles, his fangs visible, long and curved, a beautiful shape. "You would know."

I sigh, already forgetting the way his forearms made me feel.

"Are you going to listen to me if I insist you stay with one of the Nevermore Coven members tonight?"

"Staying at Black Crag or Dora's cottage would require far too much explanation, and this isn't my secret to spill."

"Riiiiight, and Arabella Lestrange wouldn't want to spend her Bloodeve with her friends."

I have to carefully arrange my face to hide my surprise. "You remembered."

"I would never forget," he says, checking the wound. It's stopped bleeding but is still an ugly, jagged gash in his perfect skin. "When I found out you were Upyr, I figured that what you told me was your birthday was really your Bloodeve. Working on our act was merely a pretence to get me in the door so I could give you your surprise."

"Please, no more surprises."

"You're going to like this one, I promise."

"You sound awfully certain."

"That's because I know one thing for a fact." Gideon grins wickedly as he collects his now-bloodied tote bag. "Arabella Lestrange cannot walk away from a game."

31

Gideon
Then

Days pass in agony. I writhe in bed, every bone in my body feeling as though it's been shoved through a meat grinder. My veins burn from the inside. My teeth hang heavy in my mouth, like lead nails shoved through my gums.

Lucien visits me each day, opening the vein on his wrist and forcing me to drink. He says his blood will heal me quicker. He wears the necklace around his neck, beneath his shirt, the jewels making his throat appear lumpy, sickly. He's anxious to leave the city. There's been trouble in Montmartre, but he can't leave until I'm able to control the monster I've become.

Until I'm just like him.

I need to find Arabella. I need to explain what's happened. I did this to save her, to save my brother, but I didn't know the kind of monster Lucien truly was.

But first, I need to be able to stand without my veins burning.

Finally, I'm able to sit up in bed. Lucien opens his veins to me a final time, but he allows only a sip. The thirst burns in my throat. I lunge for him, but he shoves me away, patting the top of my head like a dog.

"Patience, Little Prince. Put on your best clothing. Tonight, we hunt."

I tug on my frock coat. The rustle of fabric against my skin sends me reeling with ecstasy. Everything is so much sharper – pleasure, pain, longing. Arabella is constant in my thoughts.

First, Lucien shows me that he's kept his promise. My brother is no longer chained in the basement. Lucien hands me the stub of a steamer ticket to England. Jacob is safe and far away from me. It's up to him to make his own fortune now.

We head out, to everyone on the streets a pair of merry bachelors. But inside my skin, a monster claws, desperate to escape. The people passing by – ladies in their dazzling dresses, the men in their top hats and opera gloves – are but tempting fruits ripe for the plucking. Colours swirl behind my eyelids. I'm drowning in one of Claude's paintings.

Lucien's first stop is a meeting with the owner of a loud, busy *brasserie à femmes*, the air so thick with cigar smoke that were I still human, I would barely be able to see my sire – my *master*, I suppose, now – through the fog. Men thump their tables and women dressed in provocative provincial costumes slam down glasses of cheap alcohol. The owner's face pales when he sees Lucien striding through his establishment, but he greets the vampire with a smile and invites him back to his office. Lucien leaves me outside the door while he disappears inside, touching the jewels at his throat to trigger the good fortune that – were it not for me – should still belong to Arabella.

I have paid the ultimate price for my betrayal – my humanity. Now that Lucien's got what he wanted, he'll forget all about Arabella.

I should forget her, too, but I cannot. I must warn her of the monsters who hunt at night, the very monsters who now count me among their ranks. I have to tell her that I'm sorry for stealing her collar, and that I love her, and—

But how to get to her without drawing Lucien closer to her? I stand, still as a statue, hunger gnawing my insides as a dozen frantic escape plans compete for my attention. The smell of fresh blood pumping just beneath the skin of the brasserie's clientele, mixed with the cloying scent of cheap wine and rich meat, makes my head spin, which explains why I don't notice a dark-suited shadow in the crowd until he's literally in my face.

"Gideon Rougon," the shadow hisses.

I startle at my name. Something about the shadowy figure is familiar, but I can't place them. The shadow beckons with a bony finger. I catch the scent of a predator – he's a vampire, like me.

I follow him into the street. He walks briskly, floating through the crowds like a ghost. I jog to keep up with him, aware that even with the speed Lucien's blood has given me, I can't keep up.

He stops near the dilapidated *bouquinistes* along the bank of the Seine. He steps beneath one of the gaslamps and pulls down his hood, revealing his features in stark relief. I suspect he was once handsome, but his sharp cheekbones and high, noble forehead are slashed with deep, messy scars. One eye is sewn shut, the other a bulging, lizard-like orb. His nose barely exists. His lips are a ruin of torn skin. I smell blood on him.

A chill runs down my spine as I recognise him. He's a patron of La Petite Mort, usually seated at one of the corner booths, his scarred, horrible face cast in darkness.

The shadow smiles, pulling back those hateful lips to reveal long, sharp fangs.

"Do we know each other?" I ask, my fingers moving to the knife in my pocket. I assume he's an associate of Lucien, perhaps thinking he can get to my sire through me. I will snap him like an overcooked frog's leg.

The monster's mouth tugs into a grotesque shape that might be a smile. "We are not yet acquainted, but I am familiar with you, and you are intimately familiar with one of my possessions – one Arabella Macquart."

My throat closes over. I don't want this rotten creature anywhere near her. "Arabella is no one's *possession*."

"Oh, little mouse," he chuckles. "You have no idea about the world in which you live. My Arabella has been naughty. She likes to play these games of hers. Running away to Paris, hosting her little parties, dancing for other men to make me jealous. She likes to tease, as I'm sure you're aware. But she always knows to whom she belongs. I'm here to take home my property and make sure that no little mice from this cursed city follow us."

He's lying. Arabella would never love a monster such as this. She would never consent to being possessed. "Arabella is not your property."

He laughs. "How she will laugh when I describe the expression on your face! How that eyebrow of hers will twitch! Of course she is mine. She has always been mine. You are merely the next in a long line of her toys – pretty distractions I allow her because it's fun for us both to watch a cat play with its food. *She* sent me to you, little mouse. She told me where to find you. She's informed me of your pathetic attempts to woo her with hot air balloon rides and naked paintings by that upstart Monet. All the while, she returns each night to my bed and I kiss the little mole on her upper thigh, and we laugh at you. What is it you call her? *Ma petite déesse.* So sweet! She wants her property back – a collar of dazzling Egyptian jewels. Return this trifle to me and we shall have no more business together."

How does he know about the hot air balloon? About Claude's painting? About the mole?

He could only know if Arabella *told* him. If she's had him in her bed.

She'd never reveal such personal details, unless …

… unless he's telling me the truth.

… unless she is his.

My heart – heavy and racing with Lucien's blood – ices over. Frost creeps through my swollen arteries. I am cold, bitten by poison, dead inside and out.

None of it was real.

She was never mine.

I think of the jewels hanging around Lucien's neck, hidden beneath the silk of his shirt, gifting him with wealth and power. Jewels that I stole from the woman I love. A woman who has been *laughing* at me this entire time with this … *thing.*

And my cold, dead heart senses a way out of my nightmare. A way to cure me of Lucien's poison. If I can't have Arabella, then I can have *revenge.*

He wants Arabella's collar. He can have it.

"My boss has the jewels," I say. "His name is Lucien Vega, and he should still be in that brasserie where you found me. He is very strong, very powerful. If you and I—"

But the shadow has already decided on the outcome of our meeting.

He moves with impossible speed. In the blink of an eye, he is upon me, his hands about my throat. I fly backwards, the breath forced from my lungs. My spine crunches in agony as he slams me against something hard. The world spins as he tips me back. I smell fish and sewage. A cold gust sweeps my face, as cold as the ice of my heart.

We're on a bridge. The shadow holds me over the water, my hands dangling uselessly, my feet flailing for purchase. His reptile eye glints with triumph, and he leans in close, those hideous lips of his drawing back to reveal his fangs, and I know he means to drink me dry and leave me for dead. And in my rage and pain and grief I cling to the frozen monster inside of me.

I do the only thing I can think to do.

I sink my teeth into his neck first.

Breaking his skin is like biting through steel. My fangs ring inside my skull. But the points are new and sharp, and they break through with a *pop*. His blood pools in my mouth.

"You ..." he gasps. "You are Upyr ..."

He tastes *sublime*. Better than Lucien, better than any pleasure I could possibly imagine, better even than the night I spent between Arabella's thighs. If Arabella tasted of sunlight, then this creature is like climbing to the sun itself.

I'm aware, then, with a knowledge that has been gifted to me along with Lucien's blood, that the vampire I drink from is not some lowly brute like Lucien but an ancient beast of incredible power.

Somehow, my bite has disarmed him. He did not realise I am newly Kissed. With his ruined nose, he did not smell me as I did him. He cries out as he realises his mistake.

He is slow and sluggish in my arms. I cling to him, sucking and gulping down the liquid ecstasy of his veins, and manage to bring my feet back to the ground. Salvation and damnation entwine on my tongue, in my gut, lighting every part of me on fire as I drink, too much and too quickly, all the things Lucien warned me not to do.

But I can't stop.

I bargained with a devil to save my brother, but I would carve Jacob to pieces right now if it meant I could have more of *this*.

Between feedings, Lucien has explained the laws of monsters – laws that vampires must obey. Do not copulate with a human woman, because of the risk of Dhampir. Do not get caught outside in the sunlight. And *never* drink from the blood of your kin outside of the Kiss. He said that draining a vampire of blood is one of the few ways to kill them, but it also changes your blood. You take on some of their magic, their power. And that's more than dangerous – it is a *sin*. If a vampire is found to have drained another, they will be executed.

No Upyr is meant to have that kind of power.

Now I know why.

I *taste* the shadow's power – the dark, heady bite to his blood that no human delicacy will ever match. I think of how easily my father and brother sold their souls to a devil in a bottle when they could have had *this* ecstasy instead. His blood flows down my throat and fills my stomach and seeps into my veins. Already it's changing me. Already his ancient magic stirs within me.

And then, the tap runs dry.

I suckle at the messy pulp of his neck – I've not yet learned how to make a neat bite – but only manage a few meagre drops. His body hangs from my arms – limp, lifeless. I pull back and my fangs slide from his slack skin with a satisfying *plop*.

I've barely been a vampire for a week and I've already committed the ultimate sin.

Oh well. Start how you mean to continue, I suppose.

I won't feel guilty for draining this creature who treated Arabella as his property, not even if she loved him the way I wish she loved me.

I glance around, listening to the shadows with my now superior hearing. The bridge is deserted. I fling the broken monster against the stone and shove him off the bridge.

He topples over the edge into the waters below. The last thing I see before he sinks beneath the surface is that single eye glaring back at me.

I sink down into the gutter, gasping, willing my body back under my control. My veins are on fire and I long to touch the edges of the power his blood has given me, but my ruined heart is a frigid ball of pain.

Arabella sent this creature after me.

She meant for him to kill *me—*

"There you are, Little Prince."

Lucien's voice breaks through my agony. I look up to see him descend upon me, his lips curled back into a satisfied smirk. There are two drops of blood on his starched collar. He gives no indication that he saw what happened.

He picks me up by the arm and dusts off my suit.

"Are you determined to embarrass me, Little Prince? You shouldn't have run from the brasserie, but I forgive you. It's been a long time since the bloodlust was new in me. I've forgotten the thrill of it. You've been hunting, I see. There's blood all over you, and you smell sublime. Are you sated?"

I shake my head, too numb to register what he's asking.

Arabella tried to have me killed by a monster.

I thought I could make her see the truth of why I took the collar, but we can't come back from this.

"Then we must begin our lesson." Lucien claps a hand on my shoulder, shoving me forward. "I know just the place. A perfect hunting ground."

I follow him like a dog trotting after its master. Lucien chats amicably about the gift he's given me, the life I can expect to enjoy at his side. I don't hear a word, so lost am I in memories of gold-rimmed eyes and the taste of raspberries. So lost that I don't notice until it's too late that Lucien has led us to a familiar Montmartre neighbourhood.

"Come and see what's become of your courtesan!" Lucien laughs, tugging me along.

Even before we reach the old church, I know something is wrong. My vampiric senses pick up a tang of smoke in the air. Arabella's ginger and myrrh scent clings to the pavement, but it's sickly with fear. Lucien laughs to himself as we round the corner.

No.

I don't believe what I'm seeing. It's a trick of this disease Lucien infected me with. It's the magic trying to seduce me to ruin. I'm seeing my nightmares come to life.

But it's real. The stone facade of La Petite Mort is a pile of rubble and charred wooden beams. The statue of Jesus peeks out from beneath the broken remnants of the stage. Fire-stained air stings my throat. The blaze has long since been extinguished. The exposed guts of the building remain – a carcass strewn across the ground.

La Petite Mort is no more.

The street is eerily silent, no revellers or bohemians lined up outside, no haunting music or moans of ecstasy from the VIP confessionals.

Where is Arabella?

What did Lucien do to her?

She wished me dead. I should hate her.

But I can't bear to see this place she loved as a charred ruin.

My fangs dig into my lip. I taste blood. I taste *rage*.

The magic whispers a single, intoxicating word.

Vengeance.

Lucien looks like the cat who found a bowl of cream. He touches the necklace beneath his shirt. "Your little *cocotte's* luck ran out."

This can't be because of the necklace. That's impossible. That would mean that its magic is real—

But monsters are real, because I am one, and magic is real, because I taste it on my tongue, because it's whispering to me that Lucien doesn't deserve to be my master.

I have to find Arabella.

Even if she wants me dead, even if she hates me for what I did, even if she never felt anything for me other than pity or scorn, I need to know she's okay.

I have to make sure she knows what Lucien is, and what the scarred creature who claimed her as his own truly wanted from her. She is surrounded by monsters and if I do nothing else with my wretched life, I will keep her safe from them.

A crisp breeze gusts from the direction of the river, sending ash and debris billowing down the street. Something slippery and golden wraps itself around my leg. I reach down to free it.

My breath stills.

It's from Arabella's chemise.

The same chemise I tore from her body, before I became a monster and she … and she …

She came here.

Grief shatters the ice around my heart, and my heart with it. There is nothing in my chest but raw, pulped meat within a hollow shell of hate.

Vengeance.

"It's all very tragic." Lucien's hand clamps on my shoulder, his fingers digging into my flesh. "I'm told that no one inside the theatre survived."

That *night*, that beautiful night when we lay on golden sheets and showed each other slivers of our true selves, wasn't supposed to be the last time I saw her. I was supposed to win her over with my charms and help her and Jacob escape Paris and marry her on the stage at a theatre in Vienna and stand in the wings holding her furs while she toured the world bringing audiences to tears with her dancing, and every night I would kneel at her feet and worship her until she screamed my name like she might grant me godhood if only I'd give her one more orgasm.

She can't just be *gone*.

There isn't supposed to be a world without Arabella Macquart in it. Even if she never stopped hating me, at least the venom of her hatred would have flowed in my veins, and I'd carry that piece of her with me everywhere.

Now all I have left is a singed ribbon of gold and a whisper of hate in my veins.

The fabric slips through my fingers, dancing across the cobbles.

"What is that you have there?" Lucien asks. "A little souvenir?"

I snatch up the silk before he can kick it away. I bring it to my face and breathe in. Ginger and myrrh fill my head, chased by the faintest scent of raspberry.

I turn away, not wanting Lucien to see me cry. He grabs me, his grip like steel, steering me along the street towards another lively cabaret.

"My poor sad Little Prince. I brought you here to teach you a lesson about being one of us – you can no longer tie yourself to the mortal world. You cannot love your food. I know you are sad to lose your *cocotte*, but it will pass. Nothing cures sadness like the power now flowing in your immortal veins. That is what you must experience tonight. Obliterate her memory with the hunt."

He pulls me into a dark alley, surveying the street beyond with the steely intent of a predator.

My stomach churns. I am hungry. *Starving.* The blood of that scarred creature churns inside me, its whispers growing louder. I do not feel *right*. I do not know what is me and what is Lucien and what is a darker, older magic. The hunger rises like a beast clawing at my chest, giving me the briefest respite from my grief.

"There." Lucien points at a woman in a dirty green dress who tarries in the entrance of the alley, calling out a list of her services to the men who hurry past. "She is tonight's feast. Streetwalkers are easy pickings, because no one will stop to investigate their cries of pleasure, nor believe them when they wail about a client sucking on their neck. But you have to be careful not to drink too deep. You can't take enough to kill. If we leave a trail of dead bodies behind us, sooner or later, we end up on the end of a stake."

He nudges me towards the woman.

"Go, Little Prince. She is yours. Take her. Embrace the gift I've given you."

My fangs slide down. The hunger burns in my veins. My whole body trembles with heat and grief and rage as I grasp skin and pull my prey towards me.

"Very good, Little Prince," Lucien praises me as my fangs descend on his neck. "But you must practise on the human."

Lucien's body jerks as my fangs sink into his flesh. His blood floods my mouth. I gulp him down, blood spilling over my lips as his crimson river flows faster than I can drink. I'm drowning in him, and it is nothing like the human blood he's fed me from bottles these past days, or the dribbles from his veins to ease my transition from man to monster. He tries to shove me away, but he's no match for me. Now that I'm at full strength, now that the scarred shadow's ancient blood courses through me, I taste *more* than Lucien's claret. I'm swept away on a molten river of Lucien's essence. I lose myself in the rush of his avarice, his cruelty, his quest for power. I *am* him, his blood is my life now, and I think of the love he's taken away from me and I take more, more, more for her …

"Gideon, stop! I told you, we don't drink the blood of our kin."

I don't let go. I suck harder.

"She's getting away," Lucien snaps.

I'm faintly aware of a woman screaming in the alley, of footsteps scuttling away. Lucien jerks in my arms but the bite holds him captive and I won't let him go.

This is for Arabella.

Lucien's struggles grow feeble. "Gideon, you must *stop*. You are draining me. Gideon … you will *burn* for this sin …"

Then let me burn.

I don't stop. My rage bubbles to the surface, mingling with the pleasure arcing through my veins. Lucien struggles one final time, and then he sags, his eyelids fluttering closed and his lips puffing with ecstasy. And then he doesn't move at all.

When I'm done, he's a dead weight in my arms, his blood cold and stale. I drop him into the gutter, exactly where he belongs. I fumble at his neck and remove the collar. The jewels glitter in the moonlight, pale imitations of their true beauty now that they're no longer adorning Arabella's neck. I pocket the necklace and, on impulse, slide the signet ring from Lucien's finger – the symbol of his hold on the criminal kingdom. I slip it over my own.

Then I take my thin, silver-inlaid blade, and hack off his head.

Some minutes later, I step out of the alley into the busy street, a monster among the throngs of humans. The collar weighs heavy in my pocket. I wipe the blood from my mouth with my sleeve. For now, at least, my hunger is sated.

My heart is crowded with whispers of blood magic. But at least they drown out the grief.

I wind my way back through the streets to the Seine, where Arabella and I spent evenings walking, laughing, enjoying each other. My fist curls around cold stones. I stare down at the collar in my hands. I don't even remember taking it from my pocket. The jewels glitter in the moonlight, dappling prisms of pale light across the lapping waters below. Claude would have been smitten with the colours.

I wish I could cut out my mangled, rotten heart.

Arabella never loved me. I was nothing but a *distraction* to her. And now, because of this damned necklace, I'll never get the truth from her.

I draw back my arm and hurl the necklace as hard as I can. It sails in a graceful arc before landing with a faint splash, joining that ancient monster in his watery grave.

Tears prickle the corners of my eyes. I don't blink them away. I let them fall. I indulge my stupidity.

I turn back to the city, a city that belongs to me now. The only jewellery left on my person is Lucien's signet ring – a key to a new life. His empire is without an heir and here I am, with nothing left to hope for and the blood of two monsters singing in my veins.

I hope Édouard is right. That one day, loving Arabella will feel like a distant memory of a forgotten country. Because right now, loving her is a poison that burns from the inside, and the whole world will feel the bite of her loss.

32

Gideon

Sinead: The wolf is now contained. Incidentally, WHY is there a wolf requiring containment? When I signed up for this job, I was promised the toughest thing I'd have to deal with was entitled vampires demanding I wax their coffins, not an enormous bloodthirsty wolf wearing cute cupcake earrings.

AFTER A QUICK TRIP UP TO MY APARTMENT TO COLLECT THE sword Allie made for me, I lead Arabella down the maintenance stairs into the sub-basement level beneath Sanctus House. Her jaw is set in a firm line. She looks ready to swallow my testicles whole, but I know it's only because she's afraid for her friend.

At least, I hope that's why. I'm personally quite a fan of my testicles. "This way."

Arabella stalks beside me as I navigate around a bunch of supplies to a locked door. I scan my thumbprint and the door pops open. "She has the dungeon to herself tonight."

"One question." Arabella's jaw clenches tighter. "Why did you even *build* a dungeon in your fancy upmarket vampire property development?"

"I may be an astute businessman, but I'm also an Upyr." I hold the door open for her. "If things go wrong out here, we won't be able to call the police for help. I need somewhere to keep troublesome vamps until we can administer the Mora."

Fear trickles down my spine. I'm holding the first werewolf seen in thousands of years. What will the Conclave do to Celeste when they learn she attacked the two of us?

Nothing. Because they don't need to know.

From the look on Arabella's face, she's thinking the same thing. I lead her into the small holding area with a grey tiled floor and two thick steel doors with small hatches. Beside each door is a video feed, showing the room on the right empty and the room on the left—

Arabella doesn't flinch as Celeste hurls her body at the door. Thanks to the "revealing secrets" charm Lilac placed in the walls of the cells, Celeste's human features are clearer through the fur on her face. I'd think her a CGI creation for a B-grade horror film if I hadn't felt her very real, very *sharp* claws tear apart my flesh.

I glance down. The cuts are no longer bleeding, but they still haven't disappeared. It makes sense – vampires and werewolves are ancient enemies because we both have the power to hurt each other. That's what makes us the monsters and humans the food.

Arabella steps up to the door. She slides open the hatch, revealing a narrow slit of thick, bulletproof glass.

"Hello, Celeste."

The wolf hurls herself against the cage. She is beautiful, and terrifying.

Arabella steps back, her eyes flicking to me. "What's the plan now?"

I know what she's not asking me. *Are you going to call the Conclave?*

I check the astrology app on my phone. "The full moon finishes in the morning. According to my super speedy and totally factual internet research on werewolves, once the sun rises, your friend should revert back to her human form within a few hours. Apparently, it takes that long for the wolfishness to wear off. Maybe then she can give us some answers."

"Us?" Arabella smirks. "As if you'll be awake then. When the sun comes up, you will be tucked in your bed like a good little Upyr."

The magic of two monsters whispers in my veins. Over the years, I've dared to test the edges of what their blood has gifted me – superior strength, a high pain threshold, and an extreme tolerance to sunlight. I'm confident this is a battle I can win. "Excuse me, what kind of weak old vampire do you take me for? I'm in peak physical and mental condition. I have been training for this very challenge ever since my Kiss. I can resist the glowing orb of vampiric doom."

"Is that so?" Mischief glints in her eye. "I bet I can survive for longer."

"I doubt it. Me and the sun are the best of friends." I pretend to flex.

She scoffs. "I once trained for *months* to withstand the rising sun. It may have been some years ago now, but I can assure you that you have no hope of beating me."

"Fancy a wager?" I ask. "We will wait together for Celeste to turn back. The first one to fall into the dreamless sleep owes a favour to the other."

She licks her upper lip. "What kind of favour?"

"Whatever the other person wants. Within the bounds of Upyr decency, of course," I say quickly. "I'm not going to demand a kiss."

"I'm not concerned whether you are or not, since I'll be the one who triumphs."

"I *told* you that Arabella Macquart can't resist a challenge." I hold out my hand.

Her eyes flash. "Fine. But when I win, I will make you *pay*."

I grin. "Is that a promise?"

Her fingers close around mine, cool and soft and determined. Her firm handshake jolts my injured arm in its socket.

"Sweet Gideon, I love it when you state the obvious with such a sense of discovery. It is a promise *and* a threat."

Arabella orders my staff to fetch two comfy chairs from Brimstone and place them in front of the cell. She doesn't seem bothered by her friend snarling and hurling herself at the door. She slips down into a chair, pulls a slim eReader from her purse, and starts reading.

After ten minutes of watching her brow furrow in concentration, I cannot bear the silence. "What are you reading?"

She holds up a finger without looking up. "None of your business."

"Is it something for the book club? Something full of smut and red flag men? Komal explained to me the appeal of red flag men, which is why I stole your car."

"I like romance heroes who don't annoy me while I'm reading."

"Fine. Maybe I'll write my own romance about a red flag heroine, based on you."

She snorts. "We both know my red flag is that I'm too good to be true."

I laugh.

Another ten silent minutes go by.

"Hey, Arabella?"

"Be *quiet*. I can't hear myself losing the will to live."

I cup my hands over my crotch, ready to defend myself if necessary. "I want to know what you've been doing with yourself since that night we spent betwixt your golden sheets …"

She looks up from her eReader with a huff. "You think I'm going to engage you in conversation, as if we're two old friends? This is my Bloodeve. I don't talk to anyone on my Bloodeve."

I shrug. "Fine. I'll go first. I left your apartment with the necklace. I took it to Lucien Vega because he was holding my brother captive and slowly draining him dry, and giving Lucien the necklace was supposed to free me and Jacob from under his thumb. Instead, as thanks for my troubles, Vega gave me the Kiss."

Arabella doesn't move, or even glance up from her book, but I catch the briefest flicker of interest in the corner of her eye.

I knew it.

"I had some inkling of what Lucien was, or what he *believed* he was. Truthfully, I thought the vampire thing was a role he played to terrify his enemies, a kink he'd taken so far that he believed his own lie. I thought that right up until he sank his fangs into my neck and made me just like him."

She turns the page.

"Immortality suits me." I rub my jaw. "I'm lucky he did it when he did. It would have been a travesty to ruin this face with old age."

"The tragedy is that you think I care." Arabella still won't look up from her book.

"Mmmm." I know I have her. "So where was I? Ah, yes. As soon as I recovered, I was determined to find you. I needed to beg your forgiveness, explain that I'd become a monster, and make sure you were safe from all the other monsters out there. But then you sent a monster of your own after me."

"I did no such thing."

"You *did*. Ugly fellow, long scar across his face, used to hang out in the corner of La Petite Mort. He said you belonged to him, like you were his *possession*. He knew things about you, about us, that only you could have told him. He said you'd sent him to retrieve the necklace. He nearly killed me, but he didn't realise I was newly turned and I managed to overpower him."

I pause, teetering on the edge of my secret. And then, because I can never control myself around this woman, I *fall*. "When I drained him, his blood tasted heavenly. So different to Lucien's. I think he was ancient, even by our standards."

My breath hitches. I've just revealed something that she could take to the Conclave and have me killed instantly. If she cared for that ancient vampire, she will react to my crime.

"I don't know who you're talking about." She turns another page. "Men often believe they are paying to own me – that's part of the illusion. But I'd remember a suitor with a scar on his face, especially an ancient Upyr. I've only known one ancient in my life, and I have no desire to know another ever again. I did not send this man to kill you. I was a little preoccupied at the time."

I wait for her to elaborate. She does not. So I continue.

"You heard what I said. I drained him *dry*."

"I heard, Gideon."

I let out my breath. "So if you didn't know him, how did he know intimate things about you? About us? He knew about the mole you have on your inner thigh."

She sighs. "I danced naked on stage every night. There's every chance he saw that mole. As for other details, Auguste said someone was watching us in the park. Upyr, as you know, can hide in plain sight. Some have tremendous powers of persuasion over humans. I've no doubt this ancient you met was just another jealous man who wanted to steal from me."

I feel so foolish. I never should have believed that monster. I'd been too certain of my guilt; I wanted Arabella to hate me more than I hated myself, and he gave me exactly what I wanted. "I never meant to steal from you. I wanted you to be free."

"You should have told me about Lucien. I had a right to defend my own affairs. The only reason Lucien used you is because he knew of the long line of scoundrels who attempted to take the collar from me. Not one of them lived." She taps her nails on her eReader. "I would have taken care of Lucien."

"I never should have underestimated you," I say. "I think Lucien is the one who burned La Petite Mort. He took me to see it. He gloated when he showed me the fire. He said there were no survivors. I thought you were *dead*." I swallow as the lump of grief I've carried since that day rises through my esophagus. "That's why I husked Lucien and took the necklace from him."

She *has* to react to that. It's not simply that I drained two vampires. Killing your sire is one of the most abhorrent acts in Upyr culture. Arabella would be within her rights to have me thrown into the cell for Celeste to finish off.

That's why I've never told anyone what I did to Lucien.

Until now.

Her reaction is not what I expect. She rests the eReader on her knee. When she turns to me, there's a warmth in her eyes I've never seen before. Not pity, not revulsion, but *understanding*.

My heart is a jackhammer against my ribs.

"Say something," I beg her.

"What do you want me to say? That I appreciate you extracting a bloody revenge on my behalf?" Arabella's lips curl back into a smirk. "No, thanks. I prefer my vengeance firsthand."

"I believe it. All I wanted was to see you again, and you were gone. I had no choice but to endure, so I—"

"Do you still have it?"

She leans in close, her eyes ablaze.

"Do you have my collar?" Her words are a choked whisper.

I shake my head. "I'm sorry. After your scar-face boyfriend tried to kill me and I thought I lost you to the flames, I couldn't bear to keep it. I threw it into the Seine."

"The ancient wasn't my boyfriend."

"He said you were his, that he'd come to take you home." His laughter reaches through the past to squeeze around my heart.

"I've never belonged to anybody."

"What about your sire?" The relationship between vampires and their sires can often be close.

Arabella's eyes narrow. "It wasn't my sire."

"But maybe—"

"It couldn't be my sire, because I killed him."

Her words hang in the air between us, charged with electricity. Arabella holds firm, daring me to comment.

She killed her sire.

I turn over every tiny snippet of personal information she's let slip past her defences, every little piece of herself she's gifted me, and I weigh them against her words. I remember her and Eleanor Mock talking in low voices about non-consensual siring. And I think I know why she did it.

She was turned without consent, same as me.

This is why she hates her Bloodeve.

We are both sinners.

We are the same.

I know that the words I say next are the most important I'll ever say.

"He must have deserved it."

"He did."

She doesn't elaborate. Her silence is curated. I know better than to ask.

Stillness envelops us, broken only by Celeste's frantic scrabbling.

Arabella sighs, her talons trailing along the edge of her eReader. "I was born in Egypt, on the banks of the Nile. My mother had fled her own country because she was pregnant out of wedlock. She found a wealthy benefactor in Cairo and set about establishing herself as the city's most formidable courtesan. She worked hard to give me an education, dance lessons and art classes, to introduce me to the right people. She wanted me to marry, to have a family, to have what she didn't. But I saw her freedom and I craved it. It's no surprise that I went into the same line of business, even after I lost her to cholera in my teens.

"I became a favourite in diplomatic circles. I knew enough about history, literature and art that I could provide the kind of scintillating conversation that attracts powerful men. I had many suitors showering me with exquisite gifts. Some of whom begged me to become theirs exclusively."

"Him?"

My fingers claw the arm of my chair. I can already tell from her detached speech and the way she stares straight ahead at the dungeon door, refusing to meet my eyes, that I will hate this story.

She nods. "*He* was Lord John Astor, a British diplomat who lived in Cairo. He had a wife and children back in London, but he barely spoke of them. He took me to all the finest parties. He introduced me to the pleasures of opium. And …" She pauses. "He made me his Thrall."

I push out a breath. That is not what I expected her to say.

She waves a dismissive hand. "You are a white man. You cannot understand. Even the kind of freedom I enjoyed was precarious. I could not own property. I was rich with gifted wealth, but what is given can always be taken away. When Lord Astor showed me the kind of power he wielded over this secret underworld of vampires, I saw a way to ensure my future. I saw a secret that I could use against him when I needed it. I can't deny that the ecstasy of his bite was immeasurable, but I didn't choose it because of that. I chose it because women like me deal in the currency of secrets, and he'd gifted me a winning hand.

"For a time, we were happy, but as his star rose within Cairo society, and mine alongside it, his proclivities grew darker, more sadistic. He became fiercely possessive – he would rage when he saw me so much as speak to another man. He wanted to keep me as his. He offered me the Kiss. I refused. I didn't want to tie myself to him. But Lord Astor was not used to being refused …" She swallows. "He Kissed me anyway."

No.

My hand flies to her knee. I want to hold her. It was so long ago now, but my raw need to eviscerate this guy is as strong as if he did this to her yesterday.

"When I woke from the stupor, changed forever into a monster, there was Astor, expecting me to thank him for this gift. He was so pleased with himself for creating me. He tied the Antirhodos Collar around my neck and told me that I would be his good luck charm, forever by his side. From that day onward, he never allowed me to take off the necklace, and he never let me out of his sight. It felt like a noose around my neck. All I could think of was the choice he'd taken from me, that all this freedom he promised was an illusion. I belonged to him. I was his property. My desires mattered not, as long as he got what he wanted. The jewels around my neck weighed as heavy as lead."

I squeeze her knee. Arabella places her hand over mine, as if she's the one comforting me. "I want to know what you did next. I want to hear how you made him pay for this."

"I did what women must always do – I pretended to be happy he had changed me. I laughed merrily and kissed ardently and learned everything I could about my new powers. I trained myself a little each day to stay awake as the sun rose. I *schemed*. And one night, I sensed my chance. We were alone in the house – rare, as he was always entertaining Upyr delegates from other countries. He had even lent out his Thralled maid to another Upyr. I took him to bed one final time, occupying him until the last possible moment. As the sun rose over the ancient city, he had us crawl into his coffin to sleep entwined.

He would lock the coffin from the inside, keeping the key around his neck. I remained awake, and when he slipped into the dreamless sleep, I drew my dagger."

She bends down and withdraws a long, silver-inlaid dagger from her boot. I can't help staring at it. It is such a small, elegant thing, but deadly to our kin. Not unlike her.

"At first, I went for his heart, but in the gloom of the coffin, I missed, piercing through his ribs into his lungs and waking him. He thrashed, weak but still dangerous. His hands went around my throat, but he couldn't get a good grip on me because of the collar. I swiped at his face, again and again, eventually drawing open a wound across his neck. His blood gushed over me. I drank deeply, knowing I needed the burst of strength to finish him off. His hands loosened, and I hacked at his neck until his head rolled away. Then I curled up beside him and fell asleep."

The horror of it strikes me like a match, lit and burning bright – trapped in a coffin with the monster you just killed and the dreamless sleep calling you under.

I squeeze her hand. She doesn't pull away.

"When I woke, he was still and cold. I licked the old blood from the silk lining. I knew I'd need all the strength I could find to flee before my crime was discovered. I found the key around his neck and climbed out of the coffin, all while the ancient magic of his blood whispered in my veins. As I cleaned myself and dressed in my finest gown, I noticed the collar of jewels around my neck – not a single delicate setting had been broken during the struggle, nor was there a drop of Astor's blood to be seen.

"I always intended to leave the collar behind. Who would carry their noose with them? It was too easily identifiable and would be impossible for me to sell once word got around about Lord Astor's murder. But as I ran my fingers over those sparkling jewels, for the first time I *felt* the magic in the stones rising up to meet the magic humming in my veins. The collar did bring good fortune, but not to Astor. It had protected me in the coffin. Perhaps it would protect me during whatever came next.

"I threw a fur coat over my dress, buttoned it high to hide the collar, filled a trunk with fine dresses and silk scarves, stuffed every hidden pocket and fold with Astor's jewels and cash, and held a candle to the wooden coffin until it caught alight. Burned, drained, and beheaded – the only three ways to kill a vampire, and I'd done them all to ensure I was rid of him. I escaped from the house before Astor's maid returned. I made it to the port and purchased a berth on a merchant ship sailing for Marseille. From there, I made my way to Paris. I intended to sell my fine clothing and the jewels I took from Lord Astor, and use the proceeds to find myself a little cottage in the country. But on my first night, I saw a poster for Sarah Bernhardt performing at La Comédie-Française. I snuck into the theatre and watched her from a secret spot in the lighting rig as she enthralled the audience. I was determined that I could be like her. So I went back to my old trade, selectively selling off some of my riches and saving my coin until I could afford a theatre of my own. And La Petite Mort was born."

Arabella touches her hand to her throat, almost as if she can still feel the heavy weight of the collar. "That collar was more than jewels to me. I don't care about the legend. It was a symbol of when I took my life into my own hands, when I freed myself from a man's shackles. And you took it from me."

I hang my head. "I am so sorry. If I'd known, I—"

"You what? You never would have taken it?"

I pause. She's right. I still would have done what I did to save my brother. To save her.

"Exactly." She shakes her head. "I would not have expected any less. On the scale of my pride versus your brother's life, your brother would always win. This is our problem, Gideon. We are who we are. We may be guilty of the same sin, but we will always be at cross purposes. What became of your brother?"

"He was shot over a card game in a Whitechapel pub. He died a pauper," I pause. "He died free."

She contemplates this. "You said you had a surprise for me."

"Ah, yes. A Bloodeve surprise – a game of skill and chance."

She taps her nails. "Not backgammon again."

"No. Far too boring for the great Arabella Lestrange. All that frowning at the board like every decision is life-or-death." I pull out the game store bag from behind my chair. "We play Catan. Are you in?"

"I win again!" Arabella throws her cards on the table, that triumphant glint in her eye. "Longest road! I've been amassing an empire while you're over there crying like a little bitch over your ore mines!"

"Urgh, fine. You are ore-inspiring in your talents."

"Gideon."

"I'm in ore of your majesty."

"*Gideon.*"

"You give me wood—"

She hurls a city at my head.

Small confession: I let her win. Arabella is hopeless at this game. She holds everything too close to her chest and utterly refuses to trade. She's determined to do everything herself, and because of that, she spreads herself too thin and allows me to monopolise ore and wood. I could have won three times over.

But I like seeing her smile and laugh and dance around. Letting Arabella win means we both get exactly what we want.

There are no windows in the dungeon. I glance down at my watch. I checked the time of today's sunrise – 4.43 am. I'd normally be crawling into bed by 4 am. It's now 6.59 and Celeste is still a wolf. Dreamless sleep tugs at my limbs, but I can't imagine closing my eyes while in Arabella's presence. Partly because I think she'll do something unspeakable to me while I'm unconscious. (She does have prior form.)

But mostly, I don't want to spend a single moment asleep around her.

"Are we playing again?" I reset the board. "Do you fancy a little rule change? Strip Catan? Every time one of us builds a city, the other loses a layer. I can promise you plentiful wood—"

"Make *one more resource pun* and I will do something unspeakable to you."

I lean close and hold up a sheep card. "It's a baaaaaad idea to keep flirting with me like that."

I expect her to slap me, but she doesn't. We stay like this a beat too long, our noses practically touching.

"You never needed jewels or fine dresses," I whisper. "You shine so brightly you make the moon jealous."

"Will you *shut up?*"

"Make me."

I brace myself for her to thrust a city into my eyeball. Instead, her lips brush mine, so light and soft that I almost can't believe it's real, that she's real.

But it's all the permission I need.

Catan pieces fly everywhere as I throw aside the table. I pull her from her chair and settle her over my knees. She kneels on me, grinding herself down against me.

"I *will* make you," she growls. "I will make you come apart so you will never annoy me again."

"I am *wheat* for you," I manage to groan out.

She grinds down harder, her fangs knocking against mine. Her tongue is vicious, stealing any further puns I've saved. My cock strains as she brushes me through my trousers, desperate to discard the fabric between us.

The spark that flares when we kiss wakes the magic in my veins. The blood of ancient vampires pulse within us, whispering of sins that taste like heaven. *We are the same.*

She cups my cheeks, her sharp nails digging in. My fingers roam over the planes of her body that I memorised on our first night together. The ones I've hungered for ever since.

Arabella breaks our kiss abruptly, her breathing heavy as she narrows her eyes, staring me down. "This means nothing. It's like scratching an itch, you understand? I still hate you."

I smile, trailing my fingers down the length of her until I cup her clothed pussy. The heat in my hand is almost more than a vampire can bear.

"You're kind of ruining the vibe when I'm about to build my longest road to your settlement."

"You …" Her eyes drift downward to my straining cock and my finger running over her through the fabric of her tailored linen trousers. "I can't believe you're still using Catan puns. It's as if you're asking me to punish you."

"They're turning you on," I whisper, leaning forward and running my lips down her neck.

"That's a stretch," she says through a laugh.

"I mean, I'm not judging you. To wheat her own—"

She grips my shoulder, wrenching herself off my lap. The chair hits the door of Celeste's cell and shatters into splinters as Arabella presses my back against the wall, holding me with her talons at my throat. She melts against me, her curves fitting perfectly as she holds me beneath her spell, exactly where I want to be.

The smile barely touches her lips as she leans forward, her words a cool breath against my cheek. "Why do you like to play with fire, Gideon Blake? I could easily take your life right now and disappear forever, and no one would even know. I could run to Alaric's mother or the Conclave with word of your crimes. So why aren't you afraid of me?"

"Is that what you want, for me to fear you?" I reach up, placing my hand beneath her chin, tilting her head up so she has no choice but to meet my gaze. "Now that you've come back to me, the only thing I'm afraid of is losing you again."

"Then you should probably stop making terrible Catan puns."

"Probably," I nibble her bottom lip. "But you said I couldn't make snake puns, so I don't know what else to do with my talents. Plus, I enjoy being afraid. That's how I know I'm still alive. From the way your heart is beating in time with mine, I know we're the same."

Her hands slowly trail down the front of my shirt. I suck in a breath as she slides them below my trousers, running the very sharp points of her fingernails over my hard shaft. "We're nothing alike."

Her bottom lip quivers. I pull it between my teeth, tasting her lip gloss. Our shared heartbeat thrums madly with fear, with ecstasy. "We both killed our sires. We both crave wealth and comfort and safety. We both like to be in control of everything, including Sanctus. We both know that you're a goddess who demands supplication. And I have been waiting a century and a half to show you how I can worship you."

She doesn't pull away when I kiss her again. Her hand in my trousers strokes harder, and the other goes to the back of my neck, pulling my hair so she can take in more of my mouth. Our tongues caress one another. I can't even breathe because every time I do, I just take in more of her scent.

Memories from our night in her bed mingle with the here and now, so that the scrape of rock behind my back feels like the softness of her ridiculous bed and her hand on my crotch feels like the first time. But this is not *then*, this is *now*. Our old selves have died, and now we have nothing left to lose.

Hungry growls escape my throat as I let my fingers trail down her back, the tips still dancing from the memory of the heat, the *wetness*, between her legs. Now that she's in control I can no longer touch her pussy, but I still feel every inch of her through her clothes.

I need to find a way to get the blasted things off her.

She must have read my mind, as her fingers make quick work of unbuttoning my shirt and tossing it aside. Next goes the leather belt and scabbard for my sword, which clatters loudly as it hits the floor. In her bed in Paris, she was languid, sensual – a nymph that might slip through my fingers and disappear. Here, she is not nymph but monster, hunger gnawing at her belly, teeth bared, taking what she wants.

I want her however she chooses to be. I want the bloodthirsty woman who killed for freedom and the sensual goddess who enchanted all of Paris and the terrifying vampire who agrees to partake in silly town variety shows to help her friends. I want the Arabella who must do everything alone and the monster who will devour the world for the people she loves. I want to be worthy of her loyalty, her passion, her *love*.

I want every side of her. But if tonight all I get is the monster, then so be it.

She barely breaks our kiss to toss her shirt and bra to the side, undressing herself, robbing me of the pleasure. Her skin shimmers in the low light. My hands go first to the slope of her shoulders, the dip of her collarbone – beautiful bare skin, where there should be jewels.

I draw my touch lower, feeling the peaks of her nipples as they harden under my fingertips. She moans into my mouth, her hips pressing closer to me so her heat drags against my hard cock. Our teeth clash as we war for dominance, as our twin monsters dance.

Gripping her arse, I lift her and she wraps her legs around my waist. I spin her so now she's the one flat against the wall. Her breasts are at the perfect height so I trail my kisses down to them, swirling my tongue around each hardened bud until she is mewling like a black cat begging to be let in from the rain.

Her skin against my lips is *exquisite*. She tastes exactly as I remember – like wild raspberries, like sweetness and danger. She threads her hands through my hair, tugging enough that it hurts, holding my mouth against her nipple, demanding the pleasure that is her due.

I kiss her like a fool who believes he could belong to her.

Sliding my hand between us, while keeping her balanced against the wall, I dip my fingers into the waistband of her tailored trousers, the button popping free as I push aside lace and silk to cup her. I hiss between my teeth to feel her slickness beneath my fingers.

I want to see Arabella, I want to know if she looks the same as my dreams. I want to smell raspberries and touch my lips to her wet heat and lick over that tiny mole high on her inner thigh. But I don't dare break the kiss, lest she comes up with a reason why this is a bad idea.

I love a bad idea when it feels this good.

I curl a finger, teasing her entrance before sliding into perfect softness. She plunders my mouth with such vicious need that I'm not certain if she's kissing me or punishing me.

I can't breathe. I don't *want* to breathe. Raspberries scent the air as I swirl my fingers over Arabella's clit, her legs quivering, her talons clawing at my skin. Her little moans are the perfect music. And her sweet, sweet pussy …

She grinds against my hand, demanding more, but instead of giving it to her, I slide deeper, plunging two fingers inside her as another teases her other hole.

I murmur against her lips. "I'd love to utilise this two-for-one port."

I can't resist.

It's too perfect.

Her whole body shakes, not from orgasm, but from laughter, her lips purring against mine.

"No more cheesy Catan puns. Let me *come*."

Her eyes are commanding but her voice is rough, husky, the inflection faintly questioning.

"Is Arabella Lestrange *begging?*" I ask, utterly unable to keep the satisfaction from my voice even though I know she'll make me pay for it. Or perhaps *because* she'll make me pay for it.

"I … don't … beg …" She digs her nails into my back as she arches against me. I pound the tips of my fingers into her clit and this time when she trembles, it's because pleasure has finally claimed her.

Holding Arabella while she comes apart is a privilege, one I never dreamed I'd get to have again. I slide two fingers deep inside her, breathing through the tightening of her walls around them, trying not to lose my shit at the thought that I could be inside her—

"What was that?" Arabella breathes as she slumps against me.

"Probably Celeste's stomach rumbling because she couldn't finish me off. We've got time." I twist my fingers inside of her. Can I give her one more before we—

"It sounded like someone calling my name." She grips my wrist, stopping my movements. "Come on."

Pushing me away, she grabs our discarded clothes, sliding on her shirt and bra before I could even wipe away her scent from my hand. Her lips are swollen, her hair dishevelled, her lipstick smeared across her cheek. She looks enchanting.

I shove my twitching, desperate cock back into my pants as he reminds me *painfully* that he isn't going to get any release tonight.

Cockblocked by a werewolf with *earrings*.

A timid voice calls from the cell. "Hello? Arabella? Is that you?"

"I'm here." Arabella struggles into her coat, finds the key among the detritus of our Catan game, and unlocks the cell door. I step to the side, my hand resting on the sword Allie made for me, ready to act in a moment if she's in danger.

Celeste – in human form – rushes Arabella, wrapping her in a huge hug. Arabella doesn't normally like displays of intimacy, but she squeezes her friend back, resting her head on Celeste's shoulder.

Her very *naked* shoulder.

"I'm so sorry I didn't tell you—" Celeste's eyes fly open, and she sees me. "Argh! Man!"

It takes me a moment to step back from the intimacy of the scene and realise that Celeste is stark naked. Her eyes widen as she realises this too, and she yelps and attempts to cover her lady bits with Arabella's body. Only Arabella is tall and willowy and Celeste is a rather lovely but very different shape.

"Gideon," Arabella snaps. "Can you give her some privacy?"

"Of course." I cover my eyes with my hands. "I didn't know—"

"You didn't know werewolves don't shift with their clothes? This isn't a shifter romance novel where logical inconsistencies are explained away by magic. That's not how it works." Celeste grumbles as I try not to peek through my fingers. I fail, but only because I'm looking at Arabella, not her.

Arabella shrugs off her designer trench coat and tosses it to Celeste, who wraps it around her voluptuous figure. From what little I've seen of her, that woman will stop hearts. Not mine, of course. My undead heart beats for one woman, and it's the one glaring at me.

"You can lower your hands now, Gideon. How did I get here?" Celeste ties the trench coat around her waist. She's shorter than Arabella, so it brushes her ankles. "And *where* is here?"

"You're in the dungeon Gideon installed in the basement of Sanctus Estate, because he's a weirdo who assumed he'd need a dungeon."

"I *did* need a dungeon." I gesture at the claw marks Celeste has raked in the wall. "Vindication is mine."

Arabella ignores me. "And as for why you're here … What do you remember?"

"I thought I was helping but I guess I … er, got a little wolfy," she admits. "The truth is, ever since the Midnight Garden party, I've been sneaking into the woods near your house and watching over you. I knew you'd be safe during the day because the vampire killer would be asleep, too, so I'd come at night and guard you. Outside of the full moon I have control over my shifting. I can move between my wolf and human forms at will. But during the full moon I go full wolf. I run on instinct. I'm in control, but who I am changes, if that makes sense? Usually, I lock myself away during the full moon, but I thought I would still be okay to watch you because the wolf inside me recognises you as part of my pack, but the fact I'm in here suggests maybe not."

"It didn't look that way," Arabella says. "So when you go to your mother's house for a week every month, you are actually—"

"Locked away in a grain silo up at the Old Mill so I don't hurt anyone. I shouldn't have risked it! But no one else was looking out for you and you refused to let me tell Gideon. I don't even know what happened last night. I can only ever remember fleeting snippets during the full moon. I stayed later than usual, after you woke up, because I smelled something off in the trees, something that reminded me of the smell on your door when we found the graffiti. I remember seeing you through the window, Arabella. I was worried for your safety. I remember eyes in the gloom. I remember trees, woods, exciting smells, scraping my claws into vampire flesh. I remember tasting fresh meat."

"That was me." I wave my injured arm. "Hi. Thanks for the trauma."

"I'm so sorry, Gideon." Celeste winces.

"Don't be," Arabella assures her. "Whatever your reason for taking a chunk out of him, he deserved it."

"She's right. I was probably the eyes you saw. I came to see Arabella to wish her a happy—" Arabella makes a throat-slashing motion and I quickly amend my words. "To work on our performance for the variety show. I was standing on her porch when you … er …" I don't think I'll be popular if I say *attacked me*. "Gave me a lovebite."

"I really am sorry." Celeste lowers her head. "I should have recognised your scent, but I'd just managed to scratch the killer and I had his scent and then you stepped out and it seemed like you were covered in his scent—"

"Hold on a second." I've been distracted by Arabella's beautiful legs and how dizzy I am after staying up past sunrise, and I missed half the conversation. "What killer? You mean the killer who husked Patrick and Danny?"

Arabella waves a hand impatiently. "Celeste has this absurd theory that the killer is after me, despite there being absolutely no evidence."

"It's not absurd, and there's tonnes of evidence."

The two women have a whole conversation with their eyebrows before Celeste shrinks into herself and smiles sheepishly at me.

I'm not amused. Not amused at all. "What evidence do you have for this?"

"I guess … I guess I don't really have any evidence," Celeste says. "There was a vampire in the woods near Arabella's house, but that could have been anyone who lives on the estate. I've just been paranoid because I've been wolfing out."

I don't believe her, but I'm not going to get any information out of her while Arabella is around. She still doesn't trust me. Well, she doesn't have to trust me for me to save her adorable arse from getting slaughtered by a husker. I have resources. I can make sure she's safe without her even knowing.

But it's best I don't reveal this plan to Arabella, so I shrug, as if I believe Celeste's bullshit excuse. "Okay, then, as long as you're certain."

"Oh, I am. I am!" Celeste bites her nails. "I hate the full moon. It's as if my wolf wakes up, my human body goes to sleep, and everything that happens is just a dream. Or a nightmare."

"How long has this werewolf business been going on?" Arabella leans against the doorframe.

"Since I was thirteen." Celeste scratches behind her ear. "I mean, I guess I've been a werewolf all my life? Contrary to what horror movie lore tells us, werewolves aren't turned from a bite, like you guys. It's a gene that's passed down from your parents. But you don't start shifting until you hit puberty. Which, let me tell you, when you're a girl and you start sprouting body hair in random places, is heaps of fun."

"We know some things from the internet." I wave my phone.

"But vampires either consider werewolves a myth or a species that died out years ago. Are there a bunch of werewolves living in Argleton?"

"Werewolves usually live together in isolated communities," Celeste says. "That's why you don't hear about us. We keep to ourselves. My parents live in the wilderness in Snowdonia. They can roam freely without risking tourists reporting them or trying to pet them. At least, I assume that's where they are. I haven't seen them since I left."

"You left?" Arabella's eyebrow twitches. She's curious. I am, too, truthfully. I still can't believe werewolves actually *exist*.

"I want to be *human*. I don't want to live in the dirty woods and cold mountains and eat raw rabbit meat I have to catch myself. When we weren't in our wolf forms, we stayed in a remote cabin, so remote that we could only get two television channels. I longed for cosy sweaters and dessert cocktails and movie popcorn and friends to gossip about celebrities with, but that's not the life a werewolf is supposed to want. I was obsessed with cooking shows. Something about making delicious, sweet, extravagant things for your friends is just so beautiful and fun and human to me. When I told my parents I wanted to be a chef, they laughed. Werewolves don't do that, they told me. We have itinerant jobs. We keep to ourselves. We stick with the pack.

"But I couldn't stand the idea of that being my life, so when I was sixteen, I ran away. I figured that as long as I hide my condition and didn't hurt anyone, I could live in the world just fine. And I've done that for twelve years! All through chef training, I lived in a pokey London flat with a lockable storage room downstairs. I lost my bond when I left because of all the claw marks in the storage room walls. But I never once escaped. After I graduated, I got a job doing the catering up at Lachlan Hall, and then I opened the bakery, and my parents were wrong. Everything's been fine." Celeste looks between me and Arabella, her expression miserable. "Until now."

"There's only one thing to do." Arabella sways a little on her feet. "You have to tell the book club the truth. Mina, Maisie and Isis will be able to figure out—"

"I can't tell them!" Celeste wails. "You have to keep my secret. Promise me you will. Please, Arabella?"

Celeste tugs on Arabella's arm, but it flops in her hands. Arabella's eyes flutter shut, and she slumps against Celeste, her body becoming dead weight in Celeste's arms.

"What's wrong with her?" Celeste shrugs Arabella's head off her shoulder and lays her down on the floor.

"She's asleep."

"Why—Oh, of course. The sun's out. But why aren't you asleep?"

"As well as being the viciously handsome vampire of everyone's dreams, I have some immunity from the sun's curse. You know what this means?" I ask her.

"That we have to get her to a coffin before she turns to dust?"

"No." I can't stop grinning. "It means that I've won the bet."

33

The Killer

I watch from the edge of the woods as Gideon hurries across the estate with Arabella in his arms. He looks a mess, his legs wobbling and his skin blistering from sun exposure. But thanks to the ancient blood in his veins – *my* ancient blood – he has some immunity.

She looks like an angel, perfectly still beneath the umbrella he holds for her, her elegant features calm and serene. Her neck is bare, but I know the necklace must be close. I can sense it.

My Arabella wouldn't risk that magic falling into the wrong hands.

My own dreamless sleep presses against my eyelids as I watch her, limp and vulnerable, in Gideon Blake's arms. She may be proud of her ability to withstand the sun longer than most, but both he and I surpass her. It was a must, given what I have had to endure.

I reach down to touch the tear in the fabric of my sleeve. Tsk, tsk, that dirty wolf got far too close. Usually, I can evade it, but in my haste to be with Arabella on her Bloodeve, I'd forgotten about the full moon.

My skin has almost healed. It's taken all night. Disgusting creature. One day soon – once the necklace is mine again – I'll have that she-wolf skinned and made into a fine fur coat.

But for now, the wolf is a problem. She's tasted me. She has my scent. I won't be able to hide in the woods any longer. I need a new tactic.

I think of the little studio in the village where Arabella and Gideon plan to dance. I think of their names scrawled on the practice schedule that my Thrall handed to me. I think of the three ways to kill a vampire, and which one will taste the sweetest.

My little gifts have set the stage. It's time for Arabella to obey. I need to take back what's mine.

34

Arabella

Celeste: ARABELLA, PICK UP YOUR PHONE. EMERGENCY!

My eyes flutter open. It feels like an annoyingly cheerful capybara is doing a dance inside my skull. I tug the bamboo duvet over my head. Unlike other vampires, I do not go in for the traditional coffin aesthetic. I like being able to spread out in a real bed, to sleep without four walls feeling like they're closing in on me.

Arabella Lestrange doesn't follow old-fashioned Upyr traditions. She *sets* trends.

I reach over and look at the phone. 7.44 pm. I've slept in. I hardly ever sleep in.

I'm also late. Gideon and I are supposed to start rehearsing our act for the variety show at 7—

Gideon.

In a flash, it all comes back to me. Saving Gideon from Celeste, locking her in the dungeon beneath Sanctus. Finding out she's a *werewolf.* Finding out Gideon drained *two* vampires. Playing Catan with Gideon. And …

I kissed Gideon.

Then, we took things further.

I took things further.

And ... wow.

I thought I'd misremembered how good he was back in Paris, that my memory was torturing me out of pure sadism. But no. The man is not without talent.

And the way his face changed when Celeste nearly spilled the beans on her absurd theory about the killer being after me ... The golden boy looked positively *feral*.

If I didn't hate him so much, it would be quite delicious.

But then, how did I end up back in my bed? I remember talking to Celeste and then ... nothing. I must've passed out.

I lost our bet.

I cast my eyes around my room. A note is pinned to a bottle of blood on the nightstand. I pick it up and read:

If you're wondering who tucked you into bed, it was me. Well, I carried you here in my arms, like a hero of legend, and then I collapsed from exhaustion and sun exposure, so Sinead had to do the actual undressing and tucking, lucky woman.

All appreciation gift baskets can be sent to me via Sanctus House.

Gideon

PS. I know we're supposed to be rehearsing our routine this evening, but I propose we put it off until tomorrow so we can both have a lie-in. And also so I can talk you out of making me wear a meerkat costume.

PPS. I am eagerly awaiting cashing in my prize for winning our very legitimate, no-take-backsies bet. You wheat some, you lose some.

That's an awfully long note. I touch the paper. It smells of him, all fruity and zesty.

I pick up my phone. There are a million messages from the

Nevermore Coven, but it's probably Komal freaking out about Augustin Durant's latest stunt.

The phone buzzes. Winnie's calling.

"Hello," I cradle the phone against my cheek as I flop back onto my pillows. Gideon's scent rises from the note, and I slip into a dreamy memory of his fingers drawing out such *pleasure* …

"Arabella, where are you?"

"Still in bed. You won't believe the night I've had—"

"You'd better come quickly. Beth's studio is on fire."

I smell the blaze before I see it.

I'm driving Gideon's car with the windows down, and the smell of burning brings up a memory I've tried hard to forget – my beautiful theatre a ruinous sacrifice to Lucien Vega's empire.

In my chest, my heart is a charred, broken thing.

Gideon sits in the passenger seat beside me, his hands folded in his lap. He jiggles one leg until I snap at him that I'll cut it off. For years I thought him responsible for La Petite Mort burning. Now, after everything he told me, I'm forced to adjust my opinion of him.

He's still a rat bastard, but maybe not quite as ratty or bastardly as I thought.

And judging from his jackhammer leg and the way his cobalt eyes have clouded over with worry, he cares about the future of Beth's pole studio and the village variety show just as much as I do.

Not that I care. At all.

We exit the estate and the high trees that provide our sanctuary give way to low hedgerows and rolling fields. The village looms above us, a plume of smoke rising from the centre.

I put my foot down and race along narrow, winding streets lined with Victorian townhouses and thatched-roof cottages, thankful for the sports car's impressive grip as I tear around the village green and pull to a stop in front of the inferno that was once the historic wattle-and-daub stables.

My throat burns as I clamber out of the car. The building is beyond saving. The fire has already caved in the roof. Villagers gather at the edge of the lot, staring mutely.

Beth stands in her yoga clothes, arms folded across her chest, staring into the flames with a look of despair and ire so deep that not even a mushroom smoothie could fix it.

"Beth …" I'm speechless. I can't think of a single thing to say that will comfort my friend while her dreams go up in flames. I know all too well the desolation that brings.

Beth nods, but doesn't look away from the flames.

Maisie jogs over, her reporter's notebook clenched tightly in her fist. "I'm so happy to see both of you. We were worried. And before you ask, Chief Baker is saying it's arson. You and Gideon were both booked in to practise your variety show act. You should have been inside when the building went up. I'm so grateful you cancelled."

I glance at Gideon, my heart hammering against my chest.

We were supposed to be in there.

If we hadn't been with Celeste in the dungeon, if we hadn't had that silly bet to stay up all night, Gideon and I would have been practising in the studio. Our names were printed clearly on the schedule sent to all the performers. Anyone could have found out when we meant to be there.

Celeste's warning rings in my ears. Maybe I've been foolish to ignore it.

I turn to Gideon. "Where's Badica?"

He looks surprised by the question. "He's on a train back to his family seat at Nightshade Court. I sent a note to Alaric's mother, who will deal with him once he arrives."

"And there's no chance that he could have snuck off that train and come back here?"

"None whatsoever. I left him in the care of two of my most trustworthy men." Gideon looks puzzled. "What's this about?"

"Whoever did this knew you and Arabella would be using the hall tonight," Celeste pipes up. "They nailed shut the doors and windows. Lilac says there's some kind of spell around the building so a vampire wouldn't be able to escape. They intended to kill you both, just like they killed Danny and Patrick."

I glare at Celeste.

Gideon turns to me. "Are you being stalked by a crazed killer and you didn't think to tell me?"

"Celeste is being alarmist," I hiss through gritted teeth.

"I'm not being alarmist. They tried to burn down a building with you inside!" Celeste yells. Tears stream down her cheeks. Beth pulls her in for a hug, her eyes still fixed on her burning studio.

I turn away, but Gideon's grip around my arm is a vise. He tugs me to the edge of the green, out of earshot from any human villagers. "You should have told me."

"I can take care of myself. This isn't the first time I've run into people from my past." I frown. "They usually calm down after they realise I'm not going to expose their secret kinks to their current business interests. Badica was a special case—"

"Does this look calm to you?" Gideon waves his arm at the smouldering remains. "Someone tried to *burn you alive*, which is supposed to be the worst imaginable way to kill a vampire. If something happens to you, I can't—"

"You can't *what?*"

My charred heart flutters with life.

His long eyelashes tangle together as he squeezes his eyes shut. "It doesn't matter. What matters is that we catch the person who did this before they hurt you or anyone else."

"On that we are agreed," Maisie groans, as the members of the Nevermore Coven crowd around us. "Completely aside from the threat to your lives, Zen and Tonic was the only venue in the village where we could host the variety show. We're going to have to cancel, and without it …"

"Maisie, how can you be thinking about your job when Arabella was almost killed?" Dora scolds her.

"I'm sorry, Arabella," Maisie says glumly, dropping her gaze to her colourful sneakers. "It's just that being a journalist is the only thing I've ever wanted to do. This fire feels personal somehow. This killer is attacking people in the village, including *my* friends, and they're also trying to ensure I can't write about it."

"It sure does feel personal," Beth whispers. Celeste hugs her tightly.

Dora and Komal berate Maisie as she shrinks into herself, but I'm silent. What she said about only ever wanting to be a journalist … She's worked so hard to drum up support for the village variety show, and Beth's worked even harder to open her own studio, and as annoying as I find the whole thing, I will confess that my friends have done everything they can to make the show a success, including hiring me to direct it.

I too have had something I built destroyed by fire. If this killer is after me, then so be it. But he will *not* drag my friends into his vicious game.

I'll find a way to fix this for Beth and Maisie and the village. Somehow.

I drift back to the conversation and notice Gideon studying me, his plump lips in an unusually serious line. I suppose he was also supposed to die in tonight's fire. Even Gideon Blake feels unsettled when threatened with roasting to death.

The thought makes my chest fill with heat and my steely pulse thump in my ears. As pissed as I am at this killer turning his sights on me and the perfectly innocent pole studio, when I think of Gideon being hurt, I'm filled with rage.

I just got those skilled hands and that naughty tongue of his back in my life, and if I'm being honest, I'm not as upset about it as I let him believe. No one is killing Gideon Blake – that pleasure should be all mine.

So who did this? Whose neck am I severing?

They have to be a member at Sanctus Estate, and they're going around husking innocent humans. They need to be put down.

If Paul Badica isn't the one who gave me those songbirds and burned down the hall, then who did?

Who hates me this much?

35

Arabella

ANON: Thank you for your service to the Conclave. That information about the Sanctus security leaks has been most useful. If you have any more dirt on Gideon Blake that the Conclave could use to gain control over Sanctus Estate, we would love to hear it.

I tap my talons against the steering wheel as I pull into the parking lot at the Rose & Wimple, the text from my Conclave contact burning in my mind.

Gideon Blake has given me more than enough information to hang him. If the Conclave test his blood, they'll know he drained a vampire. Everyone – even the Sanctus members – would turn on him.

But if Gideon goes down for draining the blood of his kin, Sanctus will crumble. As much as I love revenge, I won't do it that way.

What interests me is how easily he trusted me with that secret, knowing that I could destroy him.

Do I even still want to destroy him?

And *why* did I decide to trust him back?

That's the question that haunts me as I drop my keys into my purse and pick up the object I've brought along, and my copy of this week's book club read – Sierra Simone's *Priest*, a taboo, forbidden and delicious romance between a man of the cloth and the woman who tempted him to break his vow on the altar of his church. Something about their story appeals to the sinner in me.

Tonight, I'm breaking a vow with myself.

Staying silent isn't protecting me any longer. My silence cost Beth her pole studio, and it put Celeste in the path of a killer, and it nearly took Gideon from me.

This isn't about me anymore.

When I turn the corner into Butcher Street, the object heavy under my arm, I blink in surprise. *If they cancelled this week's meeting and forgot to tell me, heads are going to roll.* The lights in Nevermore Bookshop are on, but I can't hear any laughter or gossip, or smell Celeste's baking. I hesitate on the street, shifting my object to the other arm. Winnie appears at the window and waves at me. I let myself inside, careful not to bang the object against the narrow shelves as I navigate through the dusty shop. When I enter the room, I nearly drop it in horror.

The Nevermore Coven is a *mess*. Everyone is silent, dishevelled, shells of the vibrant women I secretly adore. The murder board is scattered in pieces across the floor, surrounded by a fortification of overfilled wine glasses that no one has touched. Only Beth is on her feet. She paces the length of the room, wringing her hands and muttering under her breath. Her usual slick ponytail is sagging, with wispy strands floating around her face. The bags under her eyes need to be checked as oversized luggage.

No. This won't do.

I stride over and drop the object onto the floor in the middle of the circle. Mina jumps as books and murder board pictures go flying. Beth shrieks.

"Argh, you spilled my wine!" Komal cries.

"Arabella, what gives—" Isis's eyes blow wide as she takes in the painting that's face up in front of her. "Is that … Is that you?"

Every member of the Nevermore Coven leans in to get a good look. I thrust my hands on my hips and wait.

"Arabella, *why* is there a naked painting of you with what looks suspiciously like Claude Monet's signature in the corner?" Winnie asks.

Eight pairs of eyes turn to me.

I take a deep breath.

"I'm going to tell you all why. But first, I have one condition." I glare at Isis. "When I'm done, I will not be taking questions."

"But—"

"*No questions.* This is new for me. I need to keep some pieces of myself." I close my eyes. "*Please.*"

For a moment, all is still around me. Then a warm hand closes on my arm and Isis says, "Arabella, sit. We're here for you."

I open my eyes and look down at eight women who, despite my best efforts, know me better than anyone and still want to be my friends.

I sit.

And with a lump in my throat the size of a Birkin bag, I spill every secret.

I give them every raw and aching memory of my long life.

I give them all the shattered icicles they've chipped off my heart.

As I talk, Celeste creeps closer to me, until her arms go around me. I don't shrug her away. On my other side, Winnie squeezes my knee. At some point, possibly around the time I tell them about waking up and finding Gideon and my necklace gone, Dora reaches up and brushes a tear from my cheek.

I should have trusted them a long time ago.

When I'm done, I'm not the only one crying. I straighten up, push Celeste lightly off me, and fix them with my most vicious Arabella glare. "I'm telling you all of this because we need to catch the killer, and if Celeste is right and he's after me, I'll need your help."

"You have my sword." Winnie leans in, eyes damp with tears and wild with potential mischief. "Well, *Alaric's* sword, if he ever lets me have one again after I accidentally cut open his first edition Churchill biographies."

"And you have my ..." Celeste mimes wolf claws at me, but says for the benefit of the Nevermore Coven, "Rolling pin."

"And my yoga mat." Beth leans forward. "Whoever burned my studio is going to regret the day they crossed the Nevermore Coven."

The room stirs with life once more as the Nevermore Coven get to work.

"It's obvious where our search begins." Mina sloshes wine from her too-full glass as she steps into her role as lead amateur sleuth. "Your present and your past are colliding. This scarred man – the one watching you at your club – he must've been the one leaving you those bloody flowers and decapitated songbirds backstage. I bet he's the one who burned La Petite Mort and now he's burned Beth's studio—"

"*Lucien Vega* burned La Petite Mort," I growl.

"Do we know that for a fact?" Mina makes a face. "I hope this doesn't break your no question rule. I'm just trying to build a new murder board."

I suppose we don't know it for a fact, but I don't see why it matters. "Both this shadow creature and Lucien Vega are *dead*, so we can eliminate them as suspects."

Komal raises a thick eyebrow. "Aren't vampires the experts on coming back from the dead?"

"A vampire can't survive—" I start to shoot her down, but pause. There have been rumours, over the decades. Tales of powerful Dusk Court vampires who twist their magic into something so dark and profane that they can cheat their own death. The problem with Dusk Court is that their rites are so exclusive and secretive that such rumours will circulate, and it serves their purposes to be viewed as great sorcerers. The most impressive magic I've ever seen a Dust Court vampire wield is Lilac's superior mixology skills.

"I think it unlikely," I say finally. "But if a vampire was born with the kind of power that they knight you for in Dusk Court, and was very, very lucky, it might *theoretically* be possible."

"It might be worth chatting to Lilac about how theoretical it is. She's Dusk Court, right?" Mina taps something on her Braille-note. "In the meantime, if you can rack your brain for anyone else from your past. Have you not recognised anyone at Sanctus?"

"No one apart from Badica, who we've ruled out. It was so long ago," I say. "And I haven't really been socialising with the other members.

Plus, vampires can alter their appearance as humans can, if they have the right kind of money."

"Aren't you now the main Sanctus investor?" Maisie says. "Wouldn't that give you access to files on the members? We could cross-reference them against your memories of La Petite Mort."

I hadn't thought of that. Once my money landed in the Sanctus account, new permissions and folders appeared on the app, giving me access to deeper layers of the organisation.

The reason I hadn't thought of it is because it's a huge invasion of the privacy of Sanctus members, the very privacy I wish to protect. I shouldn't be giving the Nevermore Coven access to the personal files of hundreds of Upyr. But finding this killer is more important. It *has* to be.

Gideon won't see it that way.

And that's why Gideon hasn't done anything to catch the killer beyond get the Nevermore Coven involved. Because he's afraid that what he's built is rotten from the inside out. He can't touch those files without breaking an oath. But I can.

"I'll see what I can find out," I say.

"Good. In the meantime, we need to keep you safe."

Celeste and I exchange a glance. "What do you mean?" I ask carefully.

"Clearly, this killer is well established at Sanctus and has figured out how to get around Gideon's security systems. We need to increase security in a way the killer isn't expecting. Good thing I happen to be married to the world's foremost fictional criminal mastermind." Mina cups her hands over her mouth and yells at the ceiling, "Oh, Moriarty! Can you come down here?"

Messages Between Arabella and Morrie

Arabella: I require your skills.

Morrie: Hello, Arabella. I presume you've messaged me privately because you want to do something dastardly and illegal and my wife doesn't know anything about it?

Arabella: You are amazingly perceptive for one so young and human. As you know, you're coming to Sanctus tomorrow evening to check over my home's security system, given that it's POSSIBLE I am the killer's next target.

Morrie: Sounds sensible.

Arabella: Oh yes, very sensible.

Arabella: But I have another job in mind.

Morrie: I'm intrigued.

The Nevermore Murder Club and Smutty Book Coven Group Side Chat (without Arabella)

Winnie: Hi everyone. I know we're all reeling from the fire and trying to investigate, but I think we need a fun distraction. Gideon informs me that he managed to kiss Arabella last night and she didn't behead him immediately, so he must be good at it. However, he's not good at grand gestures. They've all been an abysmal failure so far and he needs our help.

Gideon: Hello.

Isis: Hi, abysmal failure.

Gideon: So, the thing is, Arabella lost a bet with me, so she has to agree to anything I want. This is my last chance to show her how I feel, but I don't know what to do.

Celeste: Hmmm, the thing about grand gestures is, they can be hot in fiction, but in real life, they come off a bit creepy.

Winnie: Like that statue thing.

Gideon: I now see how I went wrong there.

Gideon: What do you suggest?

Winnie: Instead of horrifying her with more sacrilege to the art of sculpture, maybe you should apologise for whatever it was you did that made her hate you with the fire of a thousand suns.

Celeste: In a good second-chance romance, the heroine usually falls for the hero when he does something vulnerable, when he shows her a piece of his heart that no one else gets to see.

Gideon: But what if the hero is rakishly good-looking but not very good at being vulnerable? What if he spent several decades grieving this woman he thought he lost forever and is a TINY BIT terrified that he'll mess everything up?

Komal: Even better.

Maisie: If he cries, that will seal the deal.

Gideon: I'm starting to think that none of you have any idea what you're talking about.

36

Arabella

Gideon: Lovely Arabella, I've decided on how I'll make you suffer for losing our bet. You must endure a date with me. Ha, am I evil? YES I AM. Meet me at the elevators to Sanctus Club tomorrow night at the stroke of midnight. Wear something devastating.

"Everything looks in order." Morrie stands up from where he's been inspecting my home security system and taps the screen of his tablet. "I'll run some checks on the camera feeds, but after I install my additional measures, no one will be able to get within a foot of this house without your express approval. Plus, I've taken the liberty of installing a booby trap in your garden. It's simple, but should be effective against even the most bloodthirsty vampire."

"Moriarty, you are a wonder." I shake his hand while extending my other arm so Cleo VII can slither into her favourite position, draped over my shoulders like a scarf. "And just what exciting trap have you installed?"

"For legal reasons, it's better you don't know. All I'll tell you is not to stand in your fountain. Now …" He cracks his knuckles. "Onto that other little task you wanted me to tackle."

For several minutes, he taps away on his tablet. The conceited smirk tugs downward as he frowns at the screen.

"Hmmm."

"What?" Cleo VII and I look over his shoulder but I don't understand what I'm seeing.

"I'm inside the Sanctus network, at the deepest possible permission level. None of the members' personal files are here."

"Someone deleted them?"

"No. It means they're not stored on this system. Members are identified by numbers only, which seems like a complicated way to manage a property development. Hmmmm. A company might do that as an extreme safeguard in case someone hacks their system. That way, hackers wouldn't get access to sensitive personal information."

Like intimate details about the vampiric lives of their members.

"But there have to be files, right? Gideon couldn't have built all this without them. Are they on paper?"

"Doubtful. More likely they're on a completely external system – a server or a hard drive that's not connected to the Sanctus network. If you found the hard drive, I could poke around in it for you."

I think back to something Gideon said when I deigned to accept him as a client. He has a safe in his apartment where he keeps the "heart of Sanctus".

He must mean the hard drive.

Even with my powers of persuasion, I'll never get Gideon to hand it over. His whole reputation is built on keeping the secrets of Sanctus members, and I'm coming to learn that when it comes to Sanctus, Gideon is a man of his word.

Which means that I need to find a way to steal it.

By looking at the hard drive, I can cross Alyra off the list. Or not.

Or Gideon.

The thought invades before I can stop it. Gideon *was* the head of the Vega crime family for decades. He has incurred the wrath of the Conclave. We know the killer knows everything that goes on at Sanctus.

I have to cross Gideon off our suspect list once and for all because the Conclave are making him their scapegoat …

Because I *want* to go on this absurd date with him.

Because he's melting away the ice encasing my heart.

But before he thaws me completely, I need to know I can trust him. He's broken my trust before. And if you're not in my circle of trust, you're in my pyramid of suspicion or rhombus of revenge.

Because, if he's innocent, maybe I don't need to take Sanctus from him any longer.

Maybe he's the right person to create this sanctuary, after all.

But I'm still Arabella Lestrange, and he wronged me.

A little *light* revenge is good for the complexion.

I turn back to Morrie, who's been waiting with an amused smirk on his face while I did my thinking. "I can get you the hard drive."

After Morrie leaves, I send off a text to Celeste, explaining what I need from her. Once I have a reply that she and Beth will help me, I head straight for my closet. I ignore the way my heart twists in my chest, like it's being wrung out by an overenthusiastic washer woman, as I plot how to bring down Gideon with fashion.

I don't believe in dressing for a man. I buy my clothes for me. But as I run my fingers through the racks, I can't help imagining which fabric Gideon will peel off me tonight.

There it is.

The dress.

I bought it on a trip to Paris about ten years ago. I love that travelling to Europe is cheap, and fashion is always calling. I usually go to Paris, Milan, Berlin and Vienna a few times a year to meet some of my contacts, sell some Merovingian gold, and fill my suitcase with exquisite clothing. I enjoy the trips, but … I always go alone.

A memory surges, unbidden, of Gideon dragging me through the streets of Montmartre, twirling me beneath the moonlight, holding out treats that I could never eat, climbing into a fountain to kiss me …

The ladies in the Nevermore Coven are always talking about going on a weekend trip to Paris. Sometimes I imagine taking them to my old haunts – blowing Celeste's tastebuds with my favourite viennoiserie pastries, shopping for gorgeous books and art with Beth at *les bouquinistes* along the banks of the Seine, taking Isis on a ghost tour of Montmartre, showing Winnie all the paintings in the Louvre I posed for (seventeen in all), walking with Mina and Oscar down the avenues at Père Lachaise and helping her to touch the tomb engravings on some of my past suitors.

But I've never offered. I couldn't be in Paris with them and not reveal my secrets.

They know your secrets now, a dissenting voice whispers. *But that was never the issue, was it? The reason you kept it a secret in the first place is because you're afraid that when they get to know you – really know you in your bones – they'll find you unworthy of their friendship.*

I finger the neckline of the dress.

I don't want to do this.

Revenge should be a pleasure, like savouring a fine vintage blood. But this feels like pushing my icicle heart over the edge of a balcony.

I'm falling, about to shatter and bleed everywhere, and I can't do a thing to stop it.

I force the edges of my heart to harden, to freeze over again. This isn't about Gideon or our history. It's about protecting the people I love from the monster in our midst.

I need every weapon I have. I need to get into that safe.

I step out of my slacks and pull on the dress. It fits perfectly. I find a pair of heels that look like they could sever an artery, and, thus attired, finish my makeup and hang a pendant of a silver-inlaid sword around my neck, briefly enjoying the way the blood-red garnets in the hilt sparkle against my skin. I kiss Cleo VII on her cold, scaly head and lock her away in her enclosure, and stroll over to Sanctus House as if I'm not about to shatter another vampire's glass heart tonight.

Sanctus House is eerily silent as I approach the lobby doors. The downstairs bar is empty. Sinead walks beside me to the private elevator. Gideon is nowhere in sight.

"Mr Blake says you can wait here for him. He's been held up."

"Where is everyone?" Suspicion clings to my throat. *Does he suspect—*

"Mr Blake ordered the entire building empty tonight." Sinead's lip curls in what might've been disgust. "He says you might be embarrassed when everyone hears you scream in pleasure."

Oh, sweet Gideon. You may be good, but it's you who'll be screaming.

Sinead's phone beeps. She checks her notifications, and I see a series of orders on the Sanctus app. Requests for her blood. She clicks on Alyra's name, then pockets her phone when she sees me looking, spins on her heel, and stomps off.

With every minute that goes by standing in that empty hallway, the ice around my heart grows stalactites that dig into my ribs. Just as I'm about to tear the sword from my neck and run back to my place, the elevator doors slide open, and there he is.

Gideon steps out, looking absolutely *sinful*, in a dark suit that's pure 1930s Parisian gangster chic. I'm reminded of the first night he caught my eye at my theatre, a human unaware that he was the mouse trapped in a cage for the amusement of the cats.

And now …

Now he is a feline, sleek and predatory.

"You're ten minutes late." I frown as he holds the elevator door open with his hand. A Cartier watch glitters on his wrist. "That means you forfeit your prize."

"We never agreed to those rules." He pouts. "Besides, I was always taught to show up fashionably late to pick up a lady. It gives her extra time to primp and hide the dagger in her purse."

"Joke's on you, Blake. I'm not carrying a purse. I have no intention of paying for a single part of tonight's escapades."

He frowns. "Then where will you keep your revenge dagger?"

I smirk, and the stalactites melt. Just a little. I cover the pendant on my throat with my hand. "That's for me to know and you to find out."

"I love it when you talk dirty."

He gestures to the elevator. I step inside, willing my glass heart not to shatter too early, no matter what Gideon does or says. I need to withstand the onslaught of his charms, or I'll talk myself out of this. It shouldn't be too difficult. It is *Gideon*, after all.

Gideon gets in behind me and presses his hand into the small of my back, shifting me aside so he can press his thumb to the small electronic pad.

Warmth fizzes up my spine, something that happens too often when Gideon is touching me. The elevator starts so smoothly that I hardly notice the movement.

My tongue is glued to the roof of my mouth. The sword necklace weighs a hundred kilos.

"You said you had something to show me." I need to fill the silence with bickering before I scream at him to run from me. "What grand gesture have you prepared tonight? Are you going to fly me by helicopter to the top of the Great Pyramid, where you have blood cocktails for two waiting?"

"No grand gesture." Gideon tries to smile, but it comes out wobbly. "Although I'm taking notes about the pyramid date."

"Please don't. I don't appreciate sand in my blood."

"Noted." He runs a hand through his golden hair. "Actually, maybe tonight *is* a grand gesture. But it wasn't meant to be. I mean, maybe I did mean it, in my dreams, when I wished so fervently that I'd get a second chance."

"You're babbling."

"I'm nervous."

"Intriguing." I straighten as the doors slide open. "I like you nervous."

At first, I'm greeted with a darkness so gloomy and complete that I'm certain the elevator has taken us to the wrong floor. But then the lights slowly go up, revealing Gideon's private Sanctus Club – a piece of his soul he's offered me.

No, not a piece of *his* soul.

A piece of *mine*.

I suck in a breath as I step into the club, taking in the details that are so familiar to me even after all this time. The velvet sofas trimmed with gold. The crystal absinthe fountains sitting on tables inlaid with tortoiseshell. The white grand piano beneath one spotlight and the red clawfoot bathtub where Catherina and I once performed the Countess

Bathory routine. The curtained confessional booths that surround the narrow balcony with the ironwork railing. Dark corners and romantic nooks begging to be sullied with wanton acts. Monstrous stone sculptures of saints and gods above the empty stage.

It's impossible.

It can't be.

"Arabella." Gideon's breath is a whisper on my neck. "Please, say something."

I can't. I don't have words for this. How can I speak when my heart is shattering?

Gideon steps out of the elevator, sweeping his hand around the room. His smile is just as smug as always but his eyes fix on mine, raw and panicked. "Welcome to Sanctus Club. Otherwise known as La Petite Mort, version two."

37

Gideon

Celeste: You're going to be amazing tonight. I think she'll love it!

Alaric: If you hurt her, I have the testicle-severing blade ready.

A RABELLA GLARES AROUND THE REPLICA OF HER THEATRE, HER lips pursed tightly together.

"I've stunned the great Arabella Lestrange into silence." I try to sound flippant, but my pitch rises, betraying my fear. I don't know yet if this is good speechless or if she's going to use her sword necklace to carve out my spleen and force me to eat it.

Her obsidian eyes narrow on me. "How?"

The question throws me. In the gaping chasm of secrets between us, she's opted to grasp for something almost … benign. "I remembered."

"*How?*" she repeats, stepping into the club, her fingers grasping the back of a velvet-clad sofa. "I *created* La Petite Mort and I don't remember it this well."

I shrug. "A hundred and fifty years of dreaming about this place, of grieving the woman who owned it, of wishing I could be back here with you, of hoping foolishly for a second chance to make it right.

Alaric helped me to translate my memories into pictures. Claude and Édouard left behind sketches of some of the interiors, and they helped fill in the blanks."

"You did this."

Her words are a serpent kissing my skin, cold and dripping with venom.

"Before you rip my head off and pickle it in absinthe, please, let me ask you a question. Why do you think I built Sanctus Estate?"

She scoffs. "To make millions of dollars. It's precisely what I would have done if I had the resources to achieve it."

"I'm touched by how little you think of me." I flop down on one of the velvet sofas so she won't notice how much my legs are trembling. "The money is a part of it. I won't lie. I like nice things. I like feeling safe in a world that hasn't always been safe for us. But the reason I built this place is because of you."

"Me?"

I pick up an absinthe glass and fill it with soda. I need something to do with my hands so they'll stop shaking. "Everything in my life has been penance for what I did to you. When Lucien turned me into a vampire, it messed me up because I always thought I had the power. But for women, it's all so normal as to be completely mundane."

"What's normal?"

"Someone taking what isn't theirs. For you to then have to rely on that person. For you to scream into the night but no one hears you, or they hear you but they don't care. I thought about you, and about everything you'd said about La Petite Mort being your home, something you created for yourself, and I realised that even if you'd sent that scarred creature after me—"

"I didn't."

"—that you did it because you'd been trying to build something without him, and I ruined it all. I met vampires in Vega's business who were there not because they wanted an afterlife of crime but because they had no other option if they wouldn't – or couldn't – be part of a court. I tried to give them options. My own home had never been a place of sanctuary, so I tried to offer sanctuary for those who were outcasts even among our kind. And yes, along the way I busted a few kneecaps and turned a few enemies' skulls into fine tea sets. When this land came up for sale, I sold all my shares in Vega Enterprises and founded Sanctus. I wanted it to be a place where all vampires could feel *safe*. And meanwhile, you were out there, alive, doing such amazing things that you put my little efforts to shame."

Her voice tinges with sadness. "I make rich vampires richer, Gideon. I'm hardly creating world peace."

"That's not what I heard." I grin. "I googled *la dame fléau de la Salpêtrière*."

Arabella lets out a slow breath. Her body stills, her hand clasping the sword at her throat.

"Arabella."

"Yes?"

"When you got sent away for being an unregistered courtesan, did you slay every doctor and nurse in that institution so you could free the female inmates?"

"Perhaps."

I grin. "You are *so* beautiful."

My compliment doesn't have the usual effect. Her eyelashes flutter shut. She almost looks like she wants to cry. I quickly add a shot of blood to my drink and take a long sip. *That's better.* I feel more like myself with blood on my tongue.

"When I was designing Sanctus, I couldn't stop thinking about La Petite Mort. It was my sanctuary. The happiest nights of my life were spent in that confessional booth, playing backgammon with you and spilling my secrets, or sitting with the artists, mesmerised by Claude's brush or Victor's sharp wit or *you*. Mostly you. I thought you *died*, and I wanted to keep this piece of you alive."

I bite back a rising panic, a sense that I'm walking along the edge of a bridge and below me are the turgid waters of the Seine. One false step and I could fall, and Arabella would be torn away from me again.

Arabella glares at the empty stage, eyebrow twitching.

"It's not an exact copy." I hurry on before I try to take back my words. "But I did hunt down an antiques dealer in Paris who was selling off the statues that survived the fire, and I even found one of the old confessional booths. Alaric carved these others for me."

Arabella frowns at the gleaming marble bar and the giant gilded cage hanging over the dance floor. "I see you've modernised."

"I made some improvements."

"You've *modernised*."

"We couldn't very well have gas lamps and privies. I'd have a vampire revolt on my hands. Usually, this place is pumping, but tonight it's just ours. Cocktail?" I gesture to the ornate absinthe fountain on the bar behind us. "We've painstakingly recreated the bloodsinthe you used to serve, right down to finding the perfect brand of French absinthe."

Arabella still hasn't said anything. Reluctantly, I turn away from her to perform the traditional *la louche* ritual she loves. I place her bloodsinthe on a tray next to a single shot of blood for me. Arabella takes both glasses. She swallows the shot in one quick motion, and holds the bloodsinthe to her lips and takes a long sip.

I pour myself another blood shot and take a sip as she asks, "Why didn't you tell me sooner?"

I swallow. "Because I was afraid of hurting you. You didn't want to remember the past, and here I am with this effigy of it. I didn't want you to hate me."

"Nothing's changed. I still don't want to live in the past, and I still hate you."

She says it without venom, and my foolish heart dares to hope.

"*Everything's* changed. You need a place to hold the variety show. I know you're only directing it because Beth and Maisie twisted your arm, but I thought you could have it here."

Arabella turns away, playing with the sword around her neck. I hear the rush of air as she breathes out, straightening her shoulders, steadying herself. Have I messed up again? I wasn't even trying to win her over. I just want to help and—

"Let me make sure I understand this," she says. "You want to invite the village of halfwits, future murder victims, and extras in the next terrible teen vampire novel adaptation into your super secret exclusive vampire club? You want Beth trying to sell everyone her beauty elixirs while Isis Meriwether traipses all over the estate pretending to tell fortunes and Komal and Augustin Durant finally either eviscerate each other or fuck on the DJ booth? Why?"

"Because it will make you smile."

"Hmm." She stands up and whips my drink from my hands. I reach up to grab it back, but she spins away. Her heels clack on the floor as she steps up the narrow staircase onto the stage. "I'll show you what will make me smile."

38

Arabella

Alyra: Arabella, I assume you're out with Gideon, but if you could be a dear and slip away to meet me, I'd appreciate it. I have something important to tell you, and it cannot wait. It is a most distressing and scintillating piece of gossip, and I'm afraid my mind won't be at ease until you know.

Beth: Celeste is waiting in the getaway car. I'm finishing up with a couple of clients and then I'll be downstairs with your disguise. Be careful. We don't know what a vampire like Gideon will do when he finds out you crossed him.

MY HEELS CLACK AGAINST HARDWOOD AS I STEP ONTO THE STAGE. A gleaming stainless steel pole stretches from the floor up into the fly tower and grid, secured at both ends. It calls me like a siren leading sailors to their ruin. I've certainly used a pole like this to lead men to ruin.

"What's this doing here?" I ask, without looking back at Gideon.

"Oh, that old thing," he says mildly, as if he didn't order Sinead to have it installed in time for tonight. "It's just lying around, waiting for a goddess to return."

"You'd better hold this." I hand him my drink. As I do, I run the tip of my finger over his lips. They part ever so slightly, and his cool breath touches the pad. I love the way his lips feel, soft and cool. His hand lingers on mine before he raises the glass to his lips and takes a long, luxurious drink, and it takes everything I have to hold his gaze, knowing what I intend to do to him.

This is the only way.

I'm *supposed* to be alone.

It's no less than he deserves.

If only I could make myself believe that.

I pull away from him before those cobalt eyes change my mind. I sashay across the stage to the pole. I run my hands over the cool metal like I have so many times before. If tonight is all I have left of him, I intend to make it count.

My fingers go to the zipper of my dress. Slowly, revelling in every moan and whisper from Gideon behind me, I pull it down, sliding the dress from my shoulders and stepping out of the fabric. I'm not wearing a bra – only a golden G-string and my gold heels.

Every inch of my skin sings with the knowledge of what I'm doing to him. The song is both triumphant and mournful. Tonight could have been the start of something. Instead, it's the end.

But Arabella Lestrange never leaves the stage until the final curtain falls.

My fingers slide down the cold metal. My muscles wake up and *remember.*

The music in my bones, in my skin and sinew, flares to life. I fling myself into a dance, dipping and spinning, pulling my legs in so I spin faster. There's no music playing through the club's speakers, but I don't need it. I dance to the song inside me – a song of love and loss and hope shattered and reborn – and the sharp intake of breath as Gideon watches. I spin and dip and toss my head as I dance the story of us.

This isn't like Beth's pole studio – a series of movements designed to titillate. This time, I'm not back in Paris. I'm here, *now*, and every movement is for me. For *him*.

This is me dancing through the complicated feelings I have, using my body to figure out what my heart won't resolve. I have to hurt Gideon tonight, and I don't want to. But that's only because I've been foolish. I've got too close. I've let him inside my heart again.

I dance to force him out. I dance to say goodbye.

My body says the things I can't speak aloud.

I think I'm in love with you, but I'm afraid.

I'm going to hurt you, and I want you to push me away, and I want you to hold me close.

I climb to the top of the pole, spinning faster, faster, so fast the club is colour and light around me, an aurora with me at the centre – except for two pinpricks of cobalt light that never leave me.

All my life has been about proving that I don't need anyone else. I'm alone, up here at the top of the world, but all I feel is the gaping chasm of space between me and the man sitting on a burgundy ottoman, his eyes following my every movement.

I never needed Gideon Blake to complete my life, and that's why he's special.

He's the only person I've ever *wanted*.

And the wanting feels like weakness. Hating him is so much easier than admitting to myself that maybe I don't want to be alone, that maybe his infuriating face wouldn't be so terrible to wake up next to every evening.

The necklace swings out, the speed of my spin dragging the chain tight around my neck, reminding me of the weight of the collar I once wore.

I let go.

Gideon gasps as I drop right to the base of the pole. For a flicker of time I'm falling, and he rushes the stage with his arms out as if he can catch me. At the last moment, I catch myself, gracefully twisting off the pole and sliding across the floor, coming to a stop on my knees in front of him, palms upward. A goddess dethroned.

With a groan of desire, he sinks to his knees in front of me, one hand going to my cheek. His touch is poison and antidote.

"I thought you were falling," he whispers, his voice choking.

"I was," I whisper back.

I *am*.

His fingers dig into my cheek in a way that hurts so good. His other hand possessively grips the back of my neck as he brings me closer. His lips brush mine.

And then we're kissing, and it's raw and desperate and so, so hot. I've never kissed someone the way I kiss Gideon, as if I'm tasting salvation.

I'm still falling, my body collapsing like a dying star, ready to return to dust after aeons of burning bright. How does his touch feel like a return? Like coming home?

Gideon breaks our kiss, sitting back on his knees, his eyes sweeping over me. The fear in them has been replaced by hunger.

I'm not strong enough to push him away.

When he kisses me again, sweeping me into his arms and pushing me back against the pole, my heart leaps as though I'm dancing. He hears the same song I do – of love and loss and hope and redemption.

His hands leave my body to unknot his tie. He grins against my lips as he slides his fingers down the inside of my arm, wrapping them around my wrist and raising it above my head.

"What do you think you're doing?"

He holds up the tie. "May I?"

"May you *what*?"

"Everything in your life is about being in control. It's why you won't admit what your friends mean to you, and why you refuse to acknowledge the real reason you agreed to direct the variety show. It's why you keep pushing me away."

It's why I won't ask you for the hard drive.

Gideon searches my face, waiting for me to deny it. I don't. Vulnerability flickers in his eyes, and the edge of his mouth turns downward before being tugged into his easy, satisfied smirk. "I want to show you what happens when you let go."

He doesn't know that I've already let go, that something in his kiss has sent me over the edge and he's the only one to catch my fall.

It's always been him.

So I let him knot his tie around my hands and lift them over my head. Usually, this sort of play is not something I enjoy. I never let my clients or paramours leave me vulnerable – I learned that lesson at the hands of Lord Astor. But I can't refuse Gideon. I don't *want* to refuse him. The idea of making my body vulnerable to him is oddly appealing.

I've already opened my chest and laid my heart bare.

His face is close to mine as he works on the knot. Gideon Blake is no sailor, but he secures me tightly. I search his eyes for any sign that he guesses my intentions. They're as clear and bright as ever.

Gideon gives the tie one last tug. Both my hands are secured above my head, pushing out my chest and making my breasts point up. I can feel my nipples hardening from the cool air and the heat of his gaze.

He cups my cheek, pulling my face to his to kiss me. His hands roam over my body, sliding over my skin, skimming my hardened nipples until I am bending my back to chase the thrill of his touch.

"How does it feel to be at my mercy for once?" Gideon's breath is a whisper on my cheek. I open my mouth to answer, but then he kisses my skin so softly, so all that escapes is a quiet moan.

"That's the right answer." He steps back, admiring his work.

I'm aware of how obscene I appear – tied with my hands above my head, breasts thrust forward, legs spread wide, wearing only my G-string, heels, and a dagger at my throat.

Every atom of me is alight. The air between us hums with the ghosts of my dance.

"What do you plan on doing with me, Gideon?" I ask, my voice coming out husky, betraying how much I'm enjoying this.

He smiles, taking a step back off the stage and running his hand along the edge. "Remember when I said I made some improvements to La Petite Mort?"

He pushes a hidden spring. A small compartment opens in the stage, the lid facing me so I can't see inside. Gideon rifles around and grabs something, hiding it behind his back as he kicks the lid closed.

"In the hundred and fifty years since La Petite Mort, very little has changed. Upyr crave only three things in their immortal lives – power, profit, and pleasure. Like you, I aim to facilitate all three. But one thing *has* changed – sex toys are really fucking brilliant now."

"You keep a cache of sex toys in a hole in the stage? For anyone to use? Is that hygienic?"

"Sinead and her team clean and replace them after every party," he says casually. Cool air caresses my body as he stalks towards me, wearing a suit so sharp it wouldn't be allowed on an airship, his hands hiding some secret object behind his back. I'm nearly completely naked while the only thing he's taken off is his tie, and that has me off balance. But every minute that I enjoy his game is a minute closer to getting that hard drive.

"I'm sure Sinead loves that part of her job."

"Sinead has been on the receiving end of many of these toys," Gideon says. "The parties we host here can get a little ... raucous. There's a reason Sanctus has an eager team of Thralls. Blood and sex are a potent combination."

As the word *blood* falls casually from his lips, I lose myself in fantasy. The last time I knew Gideon, I had to hide my true nature from him. But we are both Upyr now. Visions come to me unbidden of the two of us sharing a Thrall, taking turns to sip from their neck while we tease each other and kiss with their sweet blood on our lips.

You know, wholesome family stuff.

I banish the vision. After tonight, it will never happen. Gideon will hate me, the way I hated him after he betrayed me. All I have left is this moment. And I will sup every last drop of pleasure from it before I destroy our second chance.

Gideon's free hand slides slowly down my body, stopping over my lingerie. He strokes his fingers idly over the fabric, and I am utterly at his mercy.

"You're soaked," he whispers with awe. "For *me*."

"Will you stop with that false modesty? It's annoying."

That grin again – the grin that undoes me. "If you wish."

From behind his back, something vibrates. At first, I think he's getting a phone call, but then Gideon whips his hand out. He's holding a small beige cone about the size of his palm. The ripples surge as he moves it closer to my clothed pussy. "This is my favourite. It can either go inside of you, or I can find other ways of using it."

"*Gideon.*"

He lightly presses the vibrating toy to my skin and even through my panties I feel a jolt. My hips jut forward, chasing the release.

"You like that, Arabella? You want more of this against your pussy?" He slides aside my underwear and brushes the cone over my clit. It vibrates against the sensitive skin, just enough to drive me wild, but not enough to give me any kind of satisfaction.

"You're trying to make me beg," I grit out.

"Maybe." He takes the cone away. I buck my hips forward. My orgasm teeters on the edge of spilling over.

"I hate you. You are the vampire form of crumbs in a coffin."

"Is that any way to talk to the man who controls this little toy?" Gideon grins as he presses the cone against my clit, hard enough to make the vibrations echo through my body and carve out a hole in my belly before taking it away again.

My legs tremble. My veins are on fire. I'm *this* close and that rat bastard …

"Everyone who ever loved you was wrong!" I scream at him. "Put it back or I'll curse your entire bloodline."

"Too late for curses, I'm afraid. If you would only ask nicely." Gideon swipes the cone lightly over me, making my hips jerk.

That bastard. That bastard. *I take back every nice thing I thought about him.*

"Gideon?" I manage to breathe. "Please …"

"Please, what?"

"Please … let me come."

"How would I do that? Are you wanting me to hold this against your clit?" he asks, running the tip of the cone along my pussy lips.

"Y-y-yes." My voice quivers.

"Hmmm. And are you going to be a good girl for me if I let you have this orgasm?" He slides the silicone toy into my entrance, not deep enough for any relief, just making me want it more.

"I'm no girl, and I've never been good, so I don't intend to start now."

"Pity," he tsks. "That's not the answer I wanted."

He steps away, bending as if he's going to put the device away. *Rat bastard.*

"Please? Please! I'll be your good girl."

"Pardon? I can't hear you."

"I'll be good. Just let me come!"

"That's my *very* good girl." Gideon's hand goes around my neck, angling my head up to devour my mouth as he turns the vibrating cone up high and plunges it against my awaiting clit.

My orgasm bursts from the well of my stomach, fire racing along my veins. I strain against the tie as my body jolts. Gideon wraps one arm protectively around my waist, his lips never leaving mine. He swallows my scream with *far* too much satisfaction.

He doesn't remove the cone, but moves it across my clit again and again until I come a second time with several hard, shuddering spasms that eventually recede into an unfamiliar warmth in my stomach and thighs. But it's nothing compared to the warmth in a pair of cobalt eyes as they regard me with awe.

"You're so beautiful when you come for me." Gideon pumps the toy in and out of me, driving me towards a third orgasm. But just as the wave of pleasure begins to crest, he abruptly pulls the toy out, letting it fall on the floor.

I whimper. "I was so close."

Gideon crushes his lips to mine as he kicks off his trousers. Next are his boxers. His cock springs free. He's as long and hard and beautiful as I remember, his tip purple and glistening with precum.

"*You* are close?" he groans, taking himself in his hand as he kisses a trail of fire along my neck. "You need this? You have no idea what need even is. You like this … alive and perfect and all wrapped up for me like a gift – it's all I've ever wanted. It's the wish I fall asleep to and the dream that wouldn't die. We're not soulmates, Arabella. The gods didn't bring us together. I *willed* you back to me. I knitted the threads of fate together with the sheer force of my desire to see you again."

He squeezes my arse in his hands, pushing me up to deepen our kiss.

"You are insufferable," I groan against his lips. "Shut up and fuck me."

"Gladly."

His hand on my arse grabs the string of my G-string and snaps it. He tosses the fabric away as if it offends him. He's just ruined the most expensive square inch of Italian silk and lace, but I don't yell at him. It did the job I wanted it to – it brought Gideon Blake to his knees.

Both his hands go beneath my derrière, lifting me and pressing my back into the pole. He wraps my legs around him. I lock my ankles together, bringing his hard cock against my bare pussy. I can't help but stare down at the space between us, the place where we are almost joined, skin to skin and heart to heart.

And then Gideon's hand is no longer underneath me but on my chin, a single finger lifting my head, forcing me to drown in those cobalt eyes.

In one firm stroke, he thrusts forward, and he's inside me.

The century and a half between our last meeting and now narrow to a single point. I'd forgotten how good he felt, and I remember *everything*. I remember the way he bites his lower lip when he's fucking, and the way his body wraps around mine as if it's a Worth gown made to my exact measurements.

I remember all the ways going to bed with Gideon feels like dancing, like losing myself in the music. His cock inside me is a symphony, his little groans an opera written just for me.

"Gideon," I growl, and then his name is all I can say, over and over as his cock slams into me, stretching and taking and giving. "*Gideon.*"

Am I begging forgiveness? Am I demanding more? Am I saying goodbye?

"You said to Winnie once that you're not chill," he whispers against my lips as his hips buck against mine. "Lucky for you, I *am* chill. Every time you say my name like that, I want to braid our bones together. That's chill."

"Oh yes, the chillest."

The pole creaks as I hang my weight from my arms while Gideon Blake thrusts into me with all the force of a vampire coming undone. Sweat rolls down his cheek, gathering at the rumpled collar of the silk shirt he still wears. I slide my hands beneath it, feeling the hard planes of his body and the muscles straining and working as his cock does glorious things between my legs.

And then he thrusts his hand between us, pressing his fingers to my clit, stroking that sensitive bud until I see light behind my eyes.

"Give me another one, Arabella," he purrs. "Come with me so I can feel you squeeze my cock while I fill you." Gideon strokes my clit with those sure, experienced fingers. I squeeze my thighs around him, drawing him deeper, even though I'm worried that he's too deep already, that he lives inside me now, and I'll never be able to scour his memory away once he hates me for betraying him.

This orgasm doesn't begin in a hollow place in my stomach, but in my chest. It's a dull, warm pain thawing the icicles around my heart and spreading through my limbs as my body arches and contracts around Gideon. An otherworldly noise tears from my throat, and Gideon swallows it down as he moans his orgasm back at me.

We kiss and we hold each other as our bodies tremble, as he thrusts so deep that I see the cosmos, as his lips slip from mine but find me again. I taste blood and touch the sharp point of his fangs with my tongue and he touches mine and both of our lips are bleeding, immortal blood mingling, heightening the pleasure until it seems as if Gideon is correct and I must be a goddess, because I've made the earth stop spinning and invented a whole new level of pleasure hitherto unknown.

We reach that level again, and again, the hours falling away as Gideon looks up at me with eyes filled with worship.

Finally, I drop my legs from around him. I can't feel my toes. We've moved to one of the velvet couches, and as he tightens his arm around me so I don't slip off, I notice the time on his watch. It's an hour past sunrise. I just have to hold on a little longer.

Gideon may have outlasted me before, but this time, I've used every one of my considerable tricks to wear him down. His arm weighs heavy across my stomach.

I sit up, testing my shaky legs, then stagger towards the bar. "More blood?"

Gideon tries to follow me, but his legs won't take his weight. He flops back down on the sofa.

"Mmm, yes, please. You're not the only one whose legs don't work," he murmurs, his words slurring a little as I hand him a glass. He tucks me under his arm, pulling me against him, the same way he once curled his body around me when I was recovering in Sarah Bernhardt's bed.

I turn so that I'm facing him, our legs tangled together. It's there now – a white film at the corners of his eyes.

I don't want this. I don't want to think about those beautiful things he said to me, or the ache between my thighs or the way my clit is utterly punished, unable to have another orgasm even if I tried. I don't want to know that I'm walking away from all this, from *him*.

But it's too late.

I can't fight the sunlight, or my own nature.

"Hey, don't look so sad." Gideon touches my cheek. When he pulls his fingers away, I see the tips are wet. I'm crying. *Why am I crying?*

He looks shocked by the tears, too. His arms circle me, and he pulls me against him, and all I want to do is freeze time.

"I've got you, Arabella," he murmurs. "The sun will set again, and I'll be right here beside you. I'm not ever going to let you go again. I love you."

39

Gideon

Sinead: I know you're busy shagging Arabella, but I'm just letting you know that Alyra is looking for her. She seems rather distressed.

A RABELLA STILLS IN MY ARMS.

I don't dare to breathe, certain I've said too much, that she's going to run again. My head feels as though it's floating away from my body. Dreamless sleep hangs heavy in my limbs.

But I won't take the words back. I won't pretend I didn't mean them. Because they're real. This, right now, she and I – *this* is real. I love her and I'll put everything on the line for her, and if she rejects me now, then so be it.

I've grieved her once, and it nearly broke me. But I would rather grieve her again than pretend for another *moment* that she isn't my whole world.

"Arabella, did you hear what I said? I love you." Every word struggles past my sleeping tongue, my body so close to collapse, but I refuse to succumb until she hears this. "I've loved you from the first moment I walked into La Petite Mort. All the years since, when I thought I lost you, I've been a shadow wandering the earth with a hole in my heart shaped like you. I know things with us aren't simple, have never been simple, and maybe the destructive parts of our nature enjoy that. But one thing *is* a simple, immutable truth – I love you, and I always will. Please, can you say something?"

"*Gideon.*" My name, again. How I wish I could hear her say it over and over until the end of time.

"Please …" I try to say more, but my tongue is stuck and everything is moving slowly and too fast, all at once. My head spins. Stupid sun.

"I'm never myself," she whispers, her face buried in my shoulder. "Except when I'm with you. I show you who I truly am, and you never run away. You never cower. Instead, you lean a little closer and beg for more. That's addictive, but I don't know where the edges are. I'm afraid that you'll look so deep into me that you'll see something that will make you run away, and I won't survive it."

She looks up at me, and her expression is something I never expected to see. Sorrow. Another tear rolls down her cheek. I'm transfixed by it. I never thought I'd see Arabella so vulnerable. Are those tears really for me?

"Are you okay? Why are you crying?"

She shakes her head.

I try to catch the tear on my finger, but my hand doesn't obey the messages from my brain, and I jab her in the nose instead. How late into the morning is it?

"Please, say something. I just told you I love you. Surely you have an opinion on that. You might want to share it quickly, before we fall asleep."

"I've already said everything I came to say."

Her dance.

The way she twisted herself around that pole … the way her eyes locked on mine even though she was spinning crazily out of control, as if I were what kept her grounded and safe … that terrifying drop where I thought she'd crash to the ground but she caught herself just in time. Everything about her dance said, *I am here, and I trust you, but I'm afraid.*

That makes two of us.

"Being here with you brings back memories," she says, her eyes flicking over the bar again. "Not all of them are pleasant."

"Maybe it's a good thing that we host the variety show here," I suggest, trying to pull her away from deeper things. Just because I said the words, doesn't mean she's ready to say them back. She's right – she's given me so much of herself already. "You can do over shum of the bad parts with a shappy— Er, I mean *happy* memory."

My words sound slurred, drunken.

You can do this. Just stay awake a few moments longer.

Arabella scoffs. "There is nothing happy about listening to Isis Meriwether warble her way through show tunes."

"Fair, but won't it be nice to shee La Petite Mort full of people again? I know it son't be the wame. I mean, won't see the game. I mean, won't be the shame, but—"

She rests her head on my chest. Behind her head, the lights swim in my eyes, an aurora of colour against her dark skin. "It's going to mean a bunch of humans traipsing unbidden around Sanctus Estate. Our members won't appreciate it."

"They'll get over it." It sounds like I'm speaking with my mouth full of soap. "This killer wants humans to know their place. They believe Upyr are so superior that we can do whatever we like. Winnie and Alaric have already made people shee that we can change, that maybe humans and Upyr can be closer, more intimate. Maybe the variety show is the start of something beautiful. What do you think?"

"I don't think anything. I *know* it's going to be a disaster." Arabella tilts her head to the side. "But it shall be amusing. Are you feeling all right? Sun not too bright?"

"I feel like a man who's getting his second wind." I tug her to her feet. "Shall we have another dance?"

I reach out my arms to her. Arabella steps towards me, but then she tilts away, and with a *THWACK* that jerks through my body, I find myself embracing the floor.

It takes me a moment to comprehend that I've fallen.

I try to lift my head, but my neck is made of jelly and won't co-operate. At first, I think I must be drunk. I'm assaulted by vivid, blurry memories of dragging my father to bed after he'd collapsed from drink, of carrying my brother home after he got into drunken brawls.

No, I can't be drunk, because I don't touch alcohol, and I'm a vampire. A vampire who has stayed up far, far too late, and is now caught on the edge of his dreamless sleep …

"Ah—" I try to speak, but my jaw won't work.

Arabella leans down to inspect me. "Only a few moments more."

What does she mean?

I try to pull her against me, but she flinches away.

"I'm sorry about this, Gideon. Truly, I am." She does look sorry. At least, I think she does. Her face has gone all wobbly. "You may have the power of two vampires in your veins, but I can still outlast you. I don't want to do this, but I have to protect my friends, and you have to protect your reputation for Sanctus. This is the only way it can be. Consider this payback for taking what's mine."

Payback? But …

Everything goes black.

40

Arabella

Alyra: I'm going to insist you leave that delicious toy boy and see me. I'm going to try your house again and then I'll see if that snooty Thrall will let me up to Gideon's apartment. If you don't want me to burst in on you dressing Gideon up in a meerkat costume and pulling his tail, I suggest that you answer my messages!

Celeste: I'm outside in the car ready to wolf out if you need me. I want it on record that I disapprove of this plan. You should have just asked him for the hard drive.

I DRAG GIDEON'S BODY BACK ONTO THE SOFA. A SMALL STAIN OF blood dots the edge of his lip. I resist the urge to swipe it away with my finger.

Instead, I give him a swift kick between his legs.

His body jerks from the force of my blow, but he doesn't react.

He's out cold. I glare down at him as I pull on my dress, but my gaze is drawn from his sleeping form to the glitter and velvet of Sanctus Club. Framed Toulouse-Lautrec posters adorn the walls, including a very familiar print in pride of place above the bar.

It's me, smiling down from the past, over the bar that should have been mine.

The corner of the poster is burned away. This isn't a copy. It was one of the posters on the wall outside when La Petite Mort burned. Has Gideon had it all this time?

I reach up and trace the outline of the collar. My free hand grazes my neck, my wrist stinging a little from where Gideon's tie dug in.

He made all of this to remember me ...

I look back over my shoulder at his slumped form. I should feel triumphant. I'm doing exactly what he did to me. Instead, regret churns in my stomach.

I don't like this feeling. I don't like not being in control of my emotions. Gideon Rougon shouldn't tie me up in knots. I'm supposed to tie *him* in knots.

Er, Gideon Blake. I mean Gideon Blake, of course.

On impulse, I untie his shoelaces and tie them together.

Now that's done, and I'm in control again. On to the next stage of the plan. I pull out a clever little device that Moriarty gave me and hold it over Gideon's thumbprint. It scans his thumb and creates a 3D skin. I pull my phone from the hidden slip in my dress and send a text to Morrie. Once he confirms that Sanctus security is down, I cross the bar, smooth down my dress, and call the elevator.

I hold the device up to the scanner in the elevator, and after a short ride, the doors open right into Gideon's apartment, which takes up the whole of the top floor of Sanctus House.

The apartment is pure Gideon – the furniture stark and modern, but softened with luxe fabrics and clever lighting that comes on automatically as I move through the space. Everywhere I look, my eyes fall on exquisite art.

Gideon may not be an artist, but he understands them. He's as touched by art as I am.

The man has *taste*.

Well, mostly.

The hideous bust he made of me stands in the corner beside the window. I grab an Hermès throw from the sofa and toss it over the statue.

As much as I'd love to spend hours investigating Gideon's art collection, discovering where each piece came from and the story behind it, I have a job to do. I glance around, searching for a hiding place for a safe. It has to be large. The hard drive will be tiny but Gideon said he stored his "treasure" here – his private fortune will be substantial.

I wander through the rooms, pressing back against the nausea and dizziness of my approaching daysleep as I study the walls. There aren't many of them. In the kitchen, I inspect the high-end blood cellar, but I can't find a hidden safe. I check his bedroom and gasp at the obscene rotating *coffin-shaped* bed that overlooks floor-to-ceiling windows for a 240-degree view over the woods and the estate. Everything about this bedroom is pure Gideon. My fingers itch to run over the sheets, to check if they're high-count Egyptian cotton, but I think about Gideon lying passed out downstairs while I ransack his private apartments, and I move on quickly.

I shouldn't feel bad. This is exactly what he did to my boudoir.

The thought doesn't fill me with my usual righteous indignation.

After checking the closet and resisting the urge to run my fingers along the row of suits and drench myself in his cologne (he wears Mischief, by the famed Upyr designer Vesper, of course), and discounting the office and media room for their lack of wall space, I turn to the long wall on the right of the living area, where a large painting that looks like one of Claude's takes pride of place. I stand at the end of the wall, which separates the living room from the kitchen – and notice that it tapers outward, forming a triangle thicker on one end than the other.

Aha. Found you.

I study the wall, but can't see a seam or hidden panel. I turn to the painting. This is the bit I'm unsure about. I had no way of knowing what kind of security system I'd face. Morrie has furnished me with a small kit, but I couldn't hide it anywhere on my body or Gideon would have found it, which suggests that when I came out tonight, at least part of me knew that if he kissed me, I wouldn't be able to resist him.

What does it say about me that I'll happily go to bed with a man I intend to rob?

It says that I'm still the same Arabella Macquart. I can separate matters of the heart from matters of business. And right now, my business is saving my friends. It's stopping a husker from exposing vampires and destroying everything Gideon is trying to build.

My limbs are stiff and heavy as I take down the painting. Sure enough, behind it is a recessed door and complicated-looking lock. I snap a picture on my phone and text it to Morrie. A moment later, he texts back detailed instructions.

I return to the kitchen for a salad fork. (Luckily, Gideon has drawers filled with cutlery, even though he won't use any of it. I try not to wonder if that means he often has Thralls over for dinner.) I work for a few minutes and the door swings open, revealing a narrow, triangular room, the walls lined with empty shelves and niches.

I have no idea if, right now, a silent alarm is going off. I have to hope that Morrie is as effective at disabling Sanctus' security as he says he is, giving me a short window to get this done.

My legs wobble as I step inside.

The room is long and narrow, barely a metre from wall to wall at the long end of the triangle, designed so that someone visiting the apartment wouldn't notice its presence. I expect the niches to be filled with Gideon's "treasure", but they're all empty and coated in dust, except for two.

The first contains a hard drive.

I've got you now, Gideon Blake. All your secrets are mine.

I peer into the second niche. It contains a small object.

It's a torn ribbon of fabric.

Golden fabric, singed with ash and stained with blood.

The corner of my chemise.

What … what is that doing here?

41

Arabella

Morrie: Arabella, update me. Is everything okay? I can only keep the security system offline for another two minutes. And the sun is pretty high. You need to get out.

Celeste: I saw the lights go on in Gideon's apartment. Are you okay? Update, please!

The fabric falls through my fingers. Even now, I remember the dress, the night, the way his body felt against mine, as if we were made for each other. I remember the bone-deep betrayal when I found my necklace gone and my theatre on fire. I remember tearing the fabric in rage and hurling it into the flames.

He said he thought I was dead.
He must have saved it from the flames.
All this time, he kept it.
What am I doing?
I don't want this lie. I don't want to be alone.
I want *him*.
I want the infuriating, beautiful man downstairs. I want him by my

side, between my legs, in my arms. I want to fight huskers and killers and the Conclave *with* him.

I've done this all wrong.

Tears well in my eyes. The ice around my heart shatters, jagged pieces of my foolish pride stabbing through my ribs.

My phone beeps again. I don't have to look at it to know it's Morrie, giving me a one-minute warning.

Everything is ruined now.

And I can't blame anyone but myself.

I stuff the hard drive and fabric down the front of my dress, turn on my heel, and leave Gideon's apartment for the last time.

42

Gideon

Sinead: WHERE ARE YOU ANSWER ME NOW.

"Wake up, Gideon, you absolute *tool*."

Tiny hands shake me from dreamless slumber. My eyelids are glued together. I try to reach up to prise them open, but someone has glued my hands to my sides.

What's going on?

Why can't I move?

Hazy memories come back to me. Arabella waiting at the elevator, wearing a devastating dress and the attitude of a woman who's never been told no. Walking her through Sanctus Club and seeing her go from shock to rage to delight. Her dancing her fears for me on stage. And telling her I love her, and instead of eviscerating me, she cried. And then she … she …

Cold water slams in my face.

I jerk upright, spluttering.

"That got your attention." Sinead crouches down beside me, tossing aside the jug she used to drown me.

"This shirt is *silk*," I growl. Or try to growl. My mouth doesn't work properly. What comes out is, "Thisssssurtissssssilk."

"I don't care about your shirt. I care about the fact that my boss is lying asleep on the floor of his ridiculous club, completely oblivious to the fact he's been robbed."

"Wobbed?"

"Yes. Robbed. Early this morning *someone* waited until you fell asleep, then broke into your safe and took the hard drive."

My blood runs colder than the ice water now dribbling its way down my spine. "Thatsssssimpossible. We upgraded the security system after those glitches. It's foolproof."

"Impossible or not, it's happened."

I shove up onto my feet. "We must—"

My legs don't agree that we must do anything. They collapse under me and I crumple into a damp and undignified heap. Sinead steps back so I don't drool on her Jimmy Choos.

"The thief tied your shoelaces together." She frowns. "Stop squirming and I'll fix them."

I moan as she goes to work on my laces. Why does my head feel like it's had a disagreement with Vlad Tepes' impaling stick?

The whole point of being a vampire is never having a hangover again.

"What happened to me?" I rub my temples.

"My guess is that she used her pussy to tire you out, then waited until you fell asleep. How else do you explain the state of you?" Sinead re-knots my laces. "It's not quite sunset yet. I found you like this when I came to clean up before we open. Come on. Use my shoulder."

If it's still daytime, no wonder I'm out of it. I crawl up Sinead until I'm sort of standing. She half walks, half drags me into the elevator. When we emerge into my apartment, my heart sinks into my squelching shoes. The door to my safe stands open.

I don't have to check inside to know the hard drive is gone.

"She took that little scrap of fabric you were keeping, too."

"What?" The jolt of raw, visceral grief at losing that silk sinks me to my knees. "Who took them?"

Sinead glares at me. "Are you thick? Arabella. We have her on security footage wearing a fedora, fake moustache and black cape, staggering out of the gates in full sun with one of her Nevermore Coven friends. I warned you about her, but you wouldn't listen."

Arabella?

She did this? She drugged me and robbed me. After all the things we said to each other. I thought—

I've been a fool. When I created Sanctus Club, I meant only to honour her. I wanted to surround myself with things that remind me of her. But I should have realised that she would see the club as me taking something from her.

Yet another man destroying everything she built.

Those tears last night weren't for me, they were for everything she lost.

I'm not angry that she robbed me. I'm impressed.

A wave of sadness washes over me, and the hole inside me I thought she had filled opens wide, a gaping maw of loneliness.

I told her I *love* her. I opened my heart to her, and all this time, she'd intended to get even.

Everything about last night – the dance, the sex, the tears – they were all lies.

What's on that hard drive is enough to destroy me. I don't even care. It's what I deserve.

But this isn't about me.

With that hard drive, she could go to the Conclave with all of Sanctus' secrets. She'll destroy me and probably get a knighthood for her troubles. But innocent vampires will have their lives ruined – vampires who trusted me with their secrets.

As much as it hurts, as much as I'll destroy every hope I have of winning Arabella back, I have to reclaim that hard drive.

"What do you want me to do?" Sinead asks, her hand cradling her phone as someone on the team barks at her through the speaker.

"Call security," I moan, staggering to my feet. "No, don't bother. I'll find her."

"That's not what we—"

"*I'll take care of it.*"

"No, Gideon, you won't." Sinead lowers her phone. "The security team are already responding to an incident. The husker has struck again."

The Nevermore Murder Club and Smutty Book Coven Group Side Chat (without Arabella)

Mina: Everyone, get to Nevermore Bookshop NOW. Arabella stole a hard drive from Gideon and brought it here. She's asleep on my sofa and Morrie is trying to extract the data.

Mina: And Celeste and Beth are here for some reason.

Beth: Hiiiiii.

Winnie: What? WHY?

Mina: I don't know. I woke up and found them all here.

Komal: But Gideon was doing his final grand gesture last night?

Maisie: I guess it didn't work. Maybe Arabella really does hate him.

Winnie: You're wrong. Arabella loves him, I know it. She's just afraid that being in love will make her weak.

Komal: So she commits robbery? That makes sense.

Winnie: It does to Arabella.

Celeste: Okay, so ... Beth and I MAY have helped Arabella steal the hard drive from Gideon.

Mina: WHAT?

Celeste: She called me in need of a getaway car. Beth was at Sanctus doing some at-home vampire beauty treatments, so we hung around after the sun came up. Beth helped her sneak out the gates and I drove us back to the village and we got her upstairs.

Isis: But how did Arabella walk around in the sun?

Mina: Isis! We can't worry about narrative inconsistencies when our friend just committed a crime and tanked her one chance at romantic happiness with the hot vampire billionaire!

43

Arabella

Winnie: You tied his shoelaces together? You ARE evil. Why didn't you just ASK him for the hard drive?

"Can you get your bony elbow out of my ribs?" Komal moans.

"Where do you suggest I move my elbow? Off my arm?" Beth shoots back.

"We could move the computer to the coffee table," Maisie suggests. "Then we could all see."

"But the cord won't stretch that far, and the Nevermore Bookshop wi-fi is so terrible because of all the weird magic in the air," Mina points out.

"I'm not 'weird magic'." Isis sticks out her tongue. "That's insulting."

"Beth, move your elbow before I turn *you* into a beauty elixir."

"*Croak!*" The shop raven – actually Mina's husband, Quoth – flaps his wings dramatically, trying to make them all shut up.

"*Quack!*" Maisie's duck hops around the room, not wanting to be left out.

"Ladies and birds! I know that being this close to me drives everyone mad with lust, but if you give me some room, I'll be able to get this done faster." Morrie types furiously. The Nevermore Coven doesn't hear him over their bickering.

I stare at my phone, flicking idly through headshots of Sanctus members Morrie sent me, looking for someone I recognise. Every face blurs together. I expected to feel triumphant after I pulled off this heist. It's exactly what Gideon did to me all those years ago. But I can't stop thinking about his expression when he lay next to me, the way being in his arms felt like coming home. The tenderness in his voice when he told me that he was giving Sanctus Club to me for the variety show.

He wants to knit our bones together.

He says he *loves* me.

I pull the torn piece of fabric from my pocket, running my fingers over the charred edge. *His precious treasure.* He kept this in his safe. He said that he'd grieved me, past tense, but if he kept this fabric and made the club from memory, did his grieving ever end?

Even though remembering me made him sad, he chose to live in that sadness every night so that he could keep one foot in the only world I existed in – his memories.

And I thought that if I asked him for the hard drive, he'd refuse me?

I don't understand Gideon Blake at all.

For the first time since becoming a vampire, I'm confronted by the curse of our long life – that there is no end to suffering, not even the relief of time. I spent a century and a half hating Gideon. And he spent that same time turning my memory into something bold and useful – creating beauty from his loneliness instead of encasing it in spite.

Which of us is the greater evil?

"Morrieeeee," Mina whines, dragging me back to the present. "Can you give us an update on what you're seeing? Beth is clawing my arm off."

"Sorry, I'm just excited to finally figure out who this husker is so we can deal with them."

Beth does look excited – her face flushed, her skin glowing. This is as much her revenge as it is mine. She was thrilled when I asked for her help in my heist. She caught me as I collapsed at the doors to Sanctus

House, dressed me in an absurd disguise that shielded my precious skin from the sunlight, and dragged me out the gates using her visitor ID and into Celeste's waiting car. Hopefully, it will all be worth it, and we'll find out who burned her theatre and husked Danny and Patrick.

"Fine, fine. In the interest of saving your beautiful skin for my little games …" Morrie leans back in his chair. "Most of this is information on the Sanctus members – personal, private data about some of the most important vampires in the world. Family histories, bloodlines, court affiliations, investment portfolios … it's all here and protected by several layers of encryption. Gideon's clever, I'll give him that. Not clever enough for me, but as well as being the Napoleon of Crime, I am also the Charlemagne of Clever, the Julius Caesar of Cunning, and the Marie Antoinette of Avarice—"

"Yes, yes." Mina elbows him. "Can you stop with the epithets and start with the case-breaking info? We need a list of everyone at Sanctus who could potentially be our killer."

"I've already forwarded headshots to Arabella. She's looking through those for anyone she met in her previous career. Meanwhile, I'm looking for anything that jumps out as unusual, which isn't as simple as you think, because I don't know what I'm looking for, but hmmm … this is interesting."

"What's interesting?" Beth leans closer.

"It's records of emails sent between Gideon and Augustin Durant."

Komal leans forward. "What did you say?"

"These emails go back to the start of the Sanctus project. A lot of it is arranging meetings with the council about the planning application, which is all perfectly above board. But here …" Morrie taps the screen. "Gideon has sent a significant amount of money to Augustin Durant for 'Consulting Services'. It looks as though Durant used that money to bribe members of the council to approve the Sanctus Estate planning application."

Komal leaps into the middle of the rug and starts turning in wild circles, her arms flapping at her sides.

"What are you doing?" I snap. "Are you possessed by a demonic chicken?"

"This is my victory dance," Komal yells. "After all these years of torture from that prick Augustin Durant, after all of my projects being delayed or denied or stonewalled by his stupid pretty face, I *finally* have something to get him with."

"Komal," Dora says softly. "You can't use these emails against Durant."

Komal freezes mid-twerk. "Oh, I'm using them. That corrupt wanker is gunning for the mayor's job, where he will make my life miserable. I've *earned* this."

Mina shakes her head. "We all want to see Durant toppled from his throne, but if you go to the press with this, you'll expose all of Sanctus Estate as vampires."

"No, I won't. Maisie can write the story. She'll keep all the vampire stuff out of it."

"I can't do that." Maisie hugs James Pond to her chest. "That's not the actions of an ethical journalist. This story would get into the wider media, and they'd demand my sources. I'd have to give up these files with all the private information about vampires, or say I don't have a source. Not only would it throw the *Argleton Gazette* into disrepute, but I'd never work again."

"Why are you pretending to be an ethical journalist now?" Komal shouts. "Remember when you wrote that exposé about the supposed witch's curse on that lovely old cottage so Dora could buy it at below market value?"

"That curse is real," Maisie cries. "Once, I was having tea at Dora's house when the shelf over the sink came crashing down without either of us touching it. What's that if not a curse?"

"Mike's shoddy handyman skills?" Beth asks, one eyebrow raised.

"Remember when you implied people got listeriosis from drinking your ex Mark's cider, and he had to close down the family mill and move away?" Isis adds.

"That was performing a public service! I've sometimes abused my journalistic powers, and every time I've said I'll never do it again." Maisie clutches James Pond to her chest. "But if I break this story, every human journalist in the country will be looking at Sanctus. One of them will uncover something. There's too much at risk, especially with the killer still at large. Don't forget that Arabella lives there."

Maybe not, once Gideon discovers what I've done.

"I'll make sure that no one finds out …" Komal's face falls. "Oh no, you're right. It would expose everyone." She flops onto the sofa. "It's not faaaair."

"You know," Beth says. "Arabella's friend Alyra was my first client yesterday evening for her weekly at-home facial scrub and beauty elixir infusion. She said she saw Durant outside the Sanctus gates. He was very angry, yelling all sorts of insults and foul things at the gates, as if someone was listening to him. Perhaps it's related?"

Interesting. I noticed a few missed calls from Alyra last night, but with everything going on, I didn't think it was urgent. Maybe she overheard Durant say something that she couldn't repeat in front of a human. I locate Alyra's name in my phone and hit *call*. It connects on the third ring.

"Alyra, I'm sorry I missed you last night. I wondered if you could tell me what you know about Augustin Durant—"

"Arabella." Gideon's voice forces my heart into my throat.

He sounds scratchy, wary. I guess I can't blame him.

I should have done this all differently.

"Gideon?" I force myself to remain calm. All around me, members of the Nevermore Coven turn towards me, faces rapt with interest. "Why do you have Alyra's phone?"

"Because I'm standing over Alyra's body in the Midnight Garden. She's been husked, and the killer has written MINE, ARABELLA on the path in her blood."

44

Gideon

Arabella: I know you're dealing with Alyra's death right now, but I think we should talk about last night.

"The thing is," Jo says. "I've never done a vampire autopsy before. I don't know what's normal."

Jo Southcombe is a friend of Mina's. After much convincing, she's agreed to act as Sanctus Estate's resident vampire criminal investigator – a new role that I've created this evening after our first Sanctus Estate homicide. Usually, I would call an Upyr representative from Alyra's court, but I need to keep Conclave loyalists far away from Sanctus. Jo's the best in the business, and she also won't tell the human police about the dead body I'm keeping in the basement of Sanctus House.

"So you can't help us?"

"I didn't say that." Jo rolls up her sleeves. "It's every medical examiner's dream to be called out of their Lesbian Film Club in the early hours of Sunday morning to perform a vampire autopsy. Just consider yourselves lucky I keep my portable autopsy kit on me at all times."

"Oh." I brighten. "That *is* convenient."

"I'm kidding, you idiot. I'm going to have to improvise. I don't suppose you have a bone saw handy?"

"Drat our luck. I left my bone saw in my other trousers."

"Then go to your kitchen and find me a knife. A *large* knife."

"I'll get you anything you need." I wring my hands. "Spare no expense. Sinead!"

Sinead brings the knife and a few other things that Jo requests. I lock the basement door and slump against the stone wall, fighting to catch my breath.

I'm still woozy from lack of sleep and the shock of Arabella robbing me and Alyra turning up dead. My phone dings again. It might be Arabella. I reach for it, then drop the phone back into my pocket.

I thought I'd rather risk losing her again than go another night without telling her how I feel. I thought I had to give her the chance to admit that there is something deeper between us than two profoundly beautiful people wanting to hate-fuck each other into oblivion. But I was wrong.

I'm so, so tired of being wrong.

The pain in my chest is worse than grief, because this time I'm not grieving a woman I lost, but a woman I thought I'd found again. The dream of Arabella I've carried with me for a century and a half isn't real. It's my foolish heart burnishing off her edges and softening her dark soul and making me believe she's someone she's not.

I bared my soul to her. I gave her everything I have to give. And she still hates me.

That's it. There's nothing else I can do. I told her I loved her and she threw it back in my face. She robbed me and took the talisman I've carried since her reported death.

And I know I deserve all of it, but that doesn't make it hurt any less.

I'm not good enough.

I wasn't good enough for my father not to beat me. I couldn't save my brother from the bottle. I couldn't stop Lucien from turning me into a monster. I couldn't stop myself from being so blinded by grief that I *embraced* that monster.

And now Arabella has the hard drive, and with it, every secret that Sanctus is built on. The record of every sordid and illegal thing I did to make this sanctuary happen. Every bribe, every favour owed, every rotten cheque written.

When that gets out, the only good and right thing I've ever done in my whole sorry life will fall, too.

It's right that my ruin is at her hands. Maybe we're just destined to ruin each other, over and over through eternity. But who else will she bring down with me?

"Are you squeamish, Sir?"

A soft voice breaks me from my spiralling thoughts. I look up through grief-soaked eyes. Sinead stands in the narrow corridor, regarding me with pity.

She points her elbow at the closed door, from which emanates a distinctive scraping noise. "You're not sitting in on the autopsy?"

I shudder. "I'll pass."

"Weren't you in a vampire gang back in the day?"

"I *ran* the vampire gang, thank you very much. The great thing about being the boss is that someone else does the bone sawing."

Sinead folds her arms. "Sir, if I might be frank. We need to do something about Arabella. Alyra was trying to get hold of Arabella all night. It can't be a coincidence that Alyra was killed the same night Arabella robbed you. She's probably in the village right now, with her human friends from that meddling book club. I knew it was a mistake to involve them in anything to do with our community. Not only have they not found the killer, Arabella could *be* the killer! And now they've stolen our most secret files. They could expose everyone on the estate! We need to contain this—"

"I spoke to Arabella. She and the Nevermore Coven are on their way to return the hard drive. Alyra was her *friend*. She didn't do this."

"You're in love with her. You're not thinking straight. She's dangerous."

"That will be all, Sinead."

"You can't let her get away with this—"

"*That will be all.*"

Sinead lets out a growl of frustration and storms away, leaving me alone with my dark thoughts. I stare at Arabella's message on my phone. She wants to talk. What is there to say?

I can't force her to love me.

I can't keep flaying my heart open for her to stomp on it with her Louboutins.

I can't—

There's commotion in the corridor. A cascade of women fill the narrow space, tripping over each other as they rush towards me.

"Gideon." Winnie throws her arms around me. "Are you okay?"

"I'm not the one lying on a slab, so yes, I'm as dapper and delightful as ever," I answer, my breath hitching as I catch Arabella's eye. She quickly looks away.

"It's not easy to kill a vampire, right? How did this even happen?"

"I guess we can cross Alyra off our list of suspects," Mina says. "We'll have to review all the information once Jo gives us a report, and redo our murder board *again* …"

"We should wear our vampire-repelling charms," Isis pipes up. "For added protection. Oh, and maybe you should hire me to cleanse the estate of bad magic, just in case—"

Dora grabs her sister and shoots Arabella a meaningful look. "I think what Isis is *trying* to say is that we should get in there, in case there's an important clue."

"Er, right, yes." Isis pumps her fist in the air. "Ladies, to the vampire autopsy!"

The Nevermore Coven shove their way through the door, leaving me and Arabella in the empty basement corridor. A memory flashes – another time we were stuck in this basement together, with scattered board game pieces and her body quivering beneath me …

"No Catan puns?" Arabella asks, her voice the lightest I've ever heard it. "I was expecting a 'wood-n't you know it'?"

"Alyra's *dead*," I snap. "She died within the walls of Sanctus. This place was supposed to be a sanctuary. I was supposed to keep her safe, and instead I was passed out on the floor of my empty bar while the woman I love stole from me—"

"Gideon," Arabella says.

For once, my name on her lips doesn't affect me. My whole body is numb.

"Gideon, please, can we—"

The door opens with a creak, cutting her off. Winnie pokes her head out, shooting me an apologetic look. "Jo says she's finished, if you want to hear her conclusions."

"I have some interesting things to report," Jo says.

Jo has Alyra's body beneath a white sheet on top of a large trolley used for transporting supplies from the loading bay. The Nevermore Coven gathers around, shoulder to shoulder. Winnie hugs me, resting her head on my chest in a way that would have Alaric brandishing his testicle-severing sword if he were here. Iris's face is as white as the sheet. Maisie has her pad and pencil ready to take notes.

Jo looks haggard. She clears her throat and wipes a smear of blood on her PPE. "Okay. Unlike the last two victims, who were human and easy for a vampire to overpower, Alyra was Upyr, and an older model at that." Jo glances down at the corpse. "Although she looked amazing for her age."

"She's a long-time client," Beth pipes up, her face pinched. "My beauty elixirs work wonders for vampires as well as humans, and my latest formulation is set to revolutionise skincare—"

"*Beth*," Dora hisses.

"Sorry."

"The cause of death is simple." Jo lifts the edge of the sheet to reveal two fang marks in Alyra's neck. "Exsanguination. Alyra has been husked, just like the others."

Winnie buries her face deeper into my chest. Across the room, behind a horrified Komal, Arabella's eyes bore into mine. I look away from her, down at Alyra's body. Her eyes are closed, and she looks peaceful, like she's asleep.

She was supposed to be safe here.

This is all my fault.

Jo consults her notes. "One of the questions I had was how the killer overpowered Alyra, considering there are no visible signs of a struggle. I know that vampires heal quickly, but I'd expect to see something – a torn sleeve, rumpled clothing, blood splatter, but there's nothing. So my hypothesis is that she was drugged."

My stomach drops. "Drugged?"

"An analysis of her stomach contents will tell me which drug, but that's going to take a few weeks because I'll have to somehow sneak the sample through our lab. It would help if you knew some vampire chemist with a handy lab I could use."

I think of Lilac. "And what's the second thing?"

"This is what I wanted to show you." Jo points to the fang marks. "Around the fang wounds are these other marks. Here and here. They're very faint. I've gone back to my autopsy photos of Danny and Patrick, and I can see these same faint marks with an identical pattern. I think we can say that these three people were killed by the same killer."

"Which means that there's a killer at Sanctus." Beth glares at me. But she can't make me feel worse than I already do.

The Nevermore Coven all start talking at once, arguing over how best to approach solving the crime. Arabella flicks her gaze towards the door. I follow her back into the hall, but we're blocked by Sinead and a tall woman in a black suit.

"This is Dani, the funeral director," Sinead snaps, her eyes never leaving Arabella's face.

"Hello, Gideon. I'm so sorry for your loss." Dani holds out her hand, giving mine a firm shake. "I understand the deceased is a vampire? Lucky for you, our company is used to dealing with the strange and unusual. This will be my first vampire funeral, but hopefully not my last. Er …" Dani's lip wobbles. "I think that was the wrong thing to say. You're supposed to live forever, aren't you?"

"That's the goal." I gesture to the room behind me. "Sinead will show you to the body, if you can get past all the amateur sleuths."

"Ah, the Nevermore Coven is here." Dani peers around me. "I'm friends with Mina, so I've met them already. Don't you worry, I'll make sure Alyra gets our best service without any Coven interference."

Sinead and Dani disappear into the basement, leaving me alone in the corridor with Arabella.

"Here." She thrusts the hard drive into my hands.

I stare down at it, marvelling at how something so small can hold so many secrets. Every member of Sanctus trusted me to keep their identities safe, and in a single evening, this woman found my weakness and destroyed everything.

"Why?" I grind out.

"Why did I take it? Because I think someone at Sanctus is the killer, and they knew me in my old life," she says. "I needed to look at all of their faces, check their past names and information, and find the arrogant bastard who thinks he can scare me into submission and hurt my friends."

I look up at her, as if seeing her for the first time. *Does she think so little of me?* "If you'd asked me, I would have helped you do that. Why did you think I wouldn't?"

She looks at a spot past my shoulder. "I didn't want you to break the promises you've made to the members. I want Sanctus to succeed just as much as you. People like you and me – we *need* sanctuary, and I've come to believe that you're the one who can make this work without the courts. If members found out that you helped me dig through their files, no one would trust you again. But if I did it on my own, it absolves you."

"I'm not absolved!" I jab my finger at the room behind me. "If I'd caught this killer, instead of being distracted, Alyra would still be alive."

"Then it's a good thing you won't have me around as a distraction anymore." Her eyes flutter shut. "I broke every rule Sanctus has. I know I'm being kicked out. I know I'm losing my home. I don't care anymore. I didn't even find what I was looking for. Paul Badica is the only Upyr I recognise, and he's long gone. We're back where we started, with no clues about the killer. But at least you'll be able to keep Sanctus open. The Nevermore Coven will help you find the killer. Get justice for Alyra. I've done enough damage. I won't be a *distraction* any longer."

"You can't leave." My fingers clench around the hard drive. "I can't do this without you."

"Gideon, this mess is my fault. Don't punish yourself for it. I fucked it up it myself, the same way I fuck up everything in my life. I'm done blaming you for my mistakes. At least this way, I'm the only one who gets hurt." She juts out her chin, as if to say that she has so little left to be proud of, but she's proud of that.

You're not the only one hurt. "Is this everything you have to say to me?"

Arabella bites her lip.

Tell me that you love me.

Tell me you love me, and we can figure this out.

She shakes her head. "I'm sorry."

I push myself off the wall and back into the room. Arabella's eyes follow me, the golden halo at the edges eclipsed by the gloom at the centre. Her lip quivers, and normally that would be enough to send me to her, on my knees if necessary, to take her pain away.

Slowly, I shut the door in her face.

45

Arabella

Sinead: Gideon has graciously decided to allow you to remain at Sanctus. We will keep the robbery and security breach a secret so it doesn't cause more issues with the Conclave. Personally, I think we should be performing the Mora on you right now, scattering nine pieces of your dismembered corpse to all corners of the earth. Consider yourself warned.

E̶veryone in Sanctus Estate stands as Alyra's coffin is carried into the Midnight Garden. For many Upyr, it's the first funeral they've attended since being given the Kiss. Vampires are rarely slain these days. That's why this husker has everyone so afraid.

One of our own is dead.

I gather beside Eleanor and my friends while Father Simon, an Upyr priest who once served in the court of King James II, gives the last rites. I search the mourning faces. Someone in this crowd killed and husked Alyra, along with two other humans. They probably attended Alaric's vampire ball and watched us condemn an innocent man for their crimes.

Baylor was far from innocent.

I look around at my friends. Every member of the Nevermore Murder Club and Smutty Book Coven is in attendance as special guests of Gideon. The only humans invited into our sanctified rites. They all wear tasteful black and have their heads bowed – except for Celeste, who told the others she couldn't make it, but instead stalks around the perimeter of the woods in her wolf form, sniffing, searching for the scent she smelled in the woods that night.

A scent she couldn't smell on Alyra ... but the body had been outside for a whole day.

I will do anything to protect them. I will not see one of my friends in a mahogany box because of this beast.

When the rites are over and the servers light the fragrant braziers and pass around trays of blood cocktails, I notice Gideon standing beside the empty plinth that once held his bust of me. Instead of being surrounded by his usual gaggle of sycophants, he's alone, his fingers drumming against a glass of pure vintage blood.

He smiles at me – although it doesn't reach his eyes – and beckons me with a finger. I float away from my friends, crossing the stepping stones over the babbling stream, and step up beside him.

"A sad day," I say.

"Yes."

This isn't the Gideon I know. He fidgets. He looks everywhere but my eyes.

I swallow. "You didn't have to let me stay at Sanctus."

"It's easier this way. If the Conclave found out about the robbery, Sanctus would be finished. Besides, you still need to sell the rest of the Sanctus treasure, and find out who's been stealing from me." He sucks in a shuddering breath. "Something tells me I'll need every Merovingian coin for what's coming."

"I'm already looking for a new house. I'll be gone just as soon as I can sell my Sanctus place."

"You don't have to do that. Just because we're not ... *anything*, doesn't mean you should lose Sanctus. It's supposed to be your sanctuary, too." His shoulders sag. "Arabella, hear me out. I swear it's the last time."

The seriousness in his tone snaps my gaze to his.

"I want to apologise. I've been harassing you. For over a hundred years, I thought you were dead, I thought that I'd lost the love of my life, and I let that loss define me and every decision I made afterwards – and they weren't all good, noble decisions. When you showed up in that supermarket looking like a Bond villain on sabbatical, I thought, this is the universe giving me another chance. This time, I wouldn't let anyone take you away from me. I thought that if I could just make you see that I've changed, that I wouldn't hurt you like I did back then, I'd finally be redeemed. I wouldn't be the monster everyone says I am, the monster I've always believed myself to be.

"But all this time, I've disregarded your feelings. You've told me that you don't want me, and I didn't listen. I thought I read flirtation behind your barbs, because that was always how things were between us, but in honouring my grief, I haven't respected yours. You have a right to hate me, Arabella, and if I truly care about you, I have to respect that. So, this is the last time you'll hear from me. I'm signing over ownership of Sanctus to you."

"What?"

Did I hear that right?

"Sanctus is yours. I may have built it, but the Conclave hates me too much. I'm a liability. Sanctus deserves a chance to thrive without me."

"I don't want to own this place. What are you talking about?"

"Yes, you do. That's been your plan all along, yes? That's why you agreed to bail me out, and then reported on me to the Conclave. I took La Petite Mort from you, so you take Sanctus from me. I know it's not as much fun if I hand it over, but …" He shrugs. "You've beaten me. You've won."

"This is a trick."

"No trick. I'm keeping my promise. I'm giving up."

I puff out my lip. "Gideon Blake doesn't *give up*."

"He does when he realises he's been a complete arse. I love you, Arabella. I've made no secret of that, but I can't charm you into loving me back. You've made it clear that you won't be happy until you have your revenge. And I want you to be happy. So if that means giving you Sanctus …" He shrugs again. "It's yours. I know you'll take care of this place in a way I can't. As soon as the arrangements are done, I'm leaving. In the meantime, I won't speak to you except for Sanctus business. I'm having Sinead redecorate Sanctus Club so it no longer resembles La Petite Mort." Tears roll down his cheeks. "This feels like tearing off my arm and eating it, but that's the least of what I deserve. I'll do what I should have done from the moment I saw you again and stay out of your way."

I'm too stunned to speak.

He's leaving? He's walking away?

He's giving me Sanctus?

"Unless there's a reason I shouldn't?" Gideon's cobalt eyes search mine for a sign that he's got this wrong, for a last shred of hope for what we once had.

But I can't give it to him.

I almost ruined this place. Even after I learned the truth about our past, I almost destroyed this sanctuary out of some misplaced need for vengeance.

We're no good for each other. Gideon is better off without me. And I'm better off alone.

So I say nothing.

With a nod of his head – as if he finally sees me for the cold creature he should have run from all those years ago – Gideon bows his head and walks away.

Anonymous Message on the Sepulchrr App

Friends, this is Gideon Blake. I'm forced to create an anonymous account to leave this message because the Conclave have revoked Sanctus' access.

I wanted to let you all know that, effective immediately, I'm stepping down as director of Sanctus Estate.

The project will continue without me — with an exceptional new leader. I'll let her introduce herself in her own time. We've built a wonderful community in the trees, with world-class amenities, a tranquil sculpture garden, and the latest in anti-sun technology. New houses are going up right now. I invite you to come and see our sanctuary for yourself.

All Upyr have the right to feel safe, and not everyone does when the courts do nothing about illegal siring and refuse to revisit ancient laws that no longer serve us. Upyr have always had the choice of whether they want to join a court. Over the centuries, the Conclave have manipulated us until there is no real choice. I wanted to give you an alternative. We only have one life, and it's long and hard and filled with beauty. Choose what makes you happy.

I'm leaving not because I don't believe in Sanctus, but because I don't want my past to destroy your future. If we cannot forgive each other, or ourselves, for the sins of our past, then who among us is truly innocent? Are we not all monsters in our hearts?

18,152 Dig This   666 Resurrections

46

Arabella
Three weeks later

Emmanuel: If it isn't my favourite dealer! I'd be absolutely chuffed to take a gander at your stash of Greek vases. If you're selling, I'm buying. And to your other question, one of my staff members does recall purchasing a cache of coins from a gentleman just last month with a long scar across his face. Unfortunately, we don't have any CCTV footage or a name, but I wish you well on your search.

"I'M CONCERNED ABOUT YOU, ARABELLA." BETH FROWNS AT ME AS she hands around a platter of mushroom cookies that no one eats. "You're not practising good self-care."

"What are you talking about? I'm a vampire. I *invented* self-care," I huff. "I've been staying inside, avoiding sunlight, sleeping all day, and biting people who annoy me for decades, and all I've got to show for it is perfect skin and immortality."

It's been three weeks since Gideon handed me the paperwork to take over ownership of Sanctus and swore not to pursue me anymore. Three weeks of blissful peace without his terrible puns, insane grand gestures, or compliments about my derrière.

I have everything I wanted. I took Sanctus from Gideon. I had my revenge.

I'm *miserable*.

I'm hiding my misery by throwing myself into my work as the new director of Sanctus – meeting the management, learning how everything works, and introducing myself to the members I haven't met, while slowly whittling down the cache Gideon has amassed and attempting to find who stole from his vault. Three of my contacts in the antiquities trade have reported a man with a scar on his face selling off treasures that might've come from the Sanctus vaults, but of course, none can provide me with a photo.

There's no one living at Sanctus who fits the description, so who is this guy and how is he getting in? Is he our killer? Could it be the same scarred man Gideon saw one hundred and fifty years ago?

That's what we're trying to figure out now. It's the Wednesday night meeting of the Nevermore Murder Club and Smutty Book Coven, but this week's novel – the latest Ana Huang – sits unread and undissected while everyone gathers around the new murder board Mina and Maisie put together. (It includes labels in Braille and string connecting suspects and clues so Mina can read it.) Well, everyone except Beth, who seems more determined to give everyone food poisoning than to catch our killer.

Beth offers me a small vial containing a faintly pink liquid. "This is a healing elixir. I think it will make you feel better. And if you like it, tell all your vampire clients. And are you sure you won't agree to run a pole dancing class? It could be in honour of Alyra—"

"Beth, could we concentrate on this murder investigation for one minute?" Mina snaps. "We now have *three* murders connected to Sanctus Estate, and our killer is going after vampires, too. I think that's a little more important."

"I'm trying to help," Beth sulks. "Arabella's not the only one who could do with a relaxing pilates class to work the tension out of their body."

"You want me to do pilates? The thing that killed Jesus." I shake my head. "Hard pass."

"What if we're looking at this all wrong?" Maisie frowns at the board. "What if the murders have nothing to do with Sanctus? There might be another connection we're not seeing."

"Like what?"

"All three victims have connections to members of the Nevermore Coven."

"That's because we're all up in everyone's business!" Isis cries.

"Isis is right." Komal chews on one of Celeste's cheese scones. "Everyone in the village knows us. And I'd hardly call Maisie threatening to have James Pond peck Danny O'Hare's codger off a 'close connection'."

I barely listen to their bickering. I want to find the killer as much as anyone, but I can't stop my mind wandering to a golden-haired terror who's done something I never expected and kept his word. I haven't seen Gideon since Alyra's funeral – no mean feat on his behalf, considering I live and work on the estate. I know he's intending to leave – I saw a moving van outside Sanctus House and workers carrying down some of his designer furniture – but there's a lot to process, especially since the phones are ringing off the hook with new inquiries after his explosive update on Sepulchrr.

Not seeing him has allowed his grief-filled eyes from our parting to haunt my dreamless sleep.

Okay, fine, not just my sleep.

I see him now on the edge of my vision, a whisper of a future I could have had.

I hear his silky voice saying the things I long to hear for the rest of my life.

We're not soulmates, Arabella. The gods didn't bring us together. I willed you back to me. I knitted the threads of fate together with the sheer force of my desire to see you again.

I thought we'd been through the foreplay. I stole from you. You tried to have me killed. Ours is a romance written in the stars.

Every time you say my name like that, I want to braid our bones together.

I wish …

I wish things had been different.

But it's better this way. I'm better off alone. And he's better off without me. In time, he'll see that.

We're vampires. All we have left is time.

My fist clenches around Beth's healing elixir. I got over Gideon once before. I can do it again.

47

Gideon

Sinead: I have a letter here from one Édouard Manet.

Avoiding Arabella is like avoiding my own dick in the mirror. It's frustrating how impossible it is to look away from the majesty.

I'm constantly diving into bushes to avoid crossing paths with her around the estate. I've avoided the village completely in case I run into her with one of her friends from the book club. I refused an invitation to hide out with Alaric and Winnie at Black Crag in case she randomly shows up to borrow a cup of sugar.

(Also, I don't particularly feel like listening to Winnie's well-meaning pleading that I should try to declare my love again, while Alaric says nothing and pointedly sharpens his swords.)

Soon I'll be gone. The pain won't be less, but at least I won't turn every corner in fear of seeing that haunted, frozen expression on her face.

I collect a stack of papers from the bottom drawer of my desk and shove them into the shredder – they're filled with ideas and sketches for the next stage of Sanctus. I could save them for Arabella, but what's the point? Sanctus is her vision now, not mine.

I've destroyed everything in my life that's good through avarice and hubris. But I'm keeping this promise to her if it kills me. And it very well might.

I've mourned her once. I don't know if I have the strength left to mourn her again.

At least I'm safe in my office, for two more days, and then it officially becomes Arabella's office and I move into my new temporary London penthouse and await the Conclave's vengeance.

I slump in my chair, staring out the window at the empire I built. Vampires move in pairs and groups through the Midnight Garden. For years, Sanctus has been my dream – high walls for broken souls. A sanctuary. I didn't want vampires to have to turn to the criminal underground if they wanted a life outside of the courts.

And I've achieved that dream, even if it is somewhat precarious.

Why do I feel so hollow?

"You shouldn't let her force you to hide away on your own estate." Sinead appears in front of me, hands on hips. "She's the one who should leave."

"I'm fine, Sinead."

"If she bosses me about, I'll make her life hell."

"Good luck with that."

She tugs on her shirt collar. "Are you sure you don't want to—"

"Go away, Sinead."

With a cry of frustration, she tosses a letter down on my desk and flounces away.

I lean back in my chair. I'm about to kick the letter into the pile of correspondence on the floor when I spy Édouard Manet's seal. I crack the seal with trembling hands.

Gideon,

This is your lucky day, my friend. I may have found your jewels. I've been contacted by a lady who seems legitimate. She described the necklace right down to the ruby eyes on the scarab beetle. She says that she'll consider selling it, but she'll only deal with you. In person. You must meet her tonight in the parking lot of the Grimdale Graveyard. That's only a short drive from the estate, correct?

I've enclosed the details. Bring absolute buckets of cash. Best of luck, my friend.

Édouard

My heart hammers.

Arabella's necklace.

I completely forgot that I asked Édouard to look for it. I didn't believe someone could have fished it out of the Seine. But here it is.

Arabella *deserves* that necklace.

I've lost her forever. But that doesn't mean I can't right the wrong I did her all those years ago.

It can't hurt to go over to Grimdale and look at it.

Or can it?

Dora's vision. What did she see?

A dim parking lot. Tombstones. A phone with a blinking message. A dark presence. A painting made of light. And blood ...

Dora also saw me holding the necklace in my hands. It's worth the risk.

"Sinead!" I call out. "Fuel up the Lambo, bring me my best negotiating-a-deal-with-a-shadowy-figure shirt, and pack ten sacks with Merovingian coins. I've got a date with an ancient magical relic."

48

Arabella

Winnie: Come up to the castle tonight. I've invited the girls around. We have brilliant plans to cheer you up with quiet reading time by the fire and mercilessly teasing Alaric about his mummy issues. Cleo VII is welcome, too – if you can keep her away from Mirabelle.

I FROWN AT MY PHONE AS I CLIMB THE STEPS AND UNLOCK MY FRONT door. My friends have been trying to help me get over Gideon. It's working a little. I feel my violent despair transforming into bitter anguish. That's an improvement, right?

I kick off my Prada boots, set my keys in the Murano glass bowl on my hall table, and move towards the kitchen to let Cleo VII out of her enclosure.

"I'm home, sweetie," I coo as I press my finger to the pad next to the enclosure door. Cleo VII slithers eagerly towards me as I swing open the interior door. "Have you been a good girl? I've got a tasty toad for you—"

A shadow moves through the enclosure with startling speed. Several of Cleo VII's impeccably-arranged sleeping rocks skid across the ground. I'm knocked back against the wall by an impossible force. The toad container flies from my hands.

"Hello, Arabella," a voice rasps as a shadow envelops me. A face emerges from the gloom of a dark hood.

The face of a ghost.

No, not a ghost. Someone *very* much alive, with his hands around my throat, not squeezing but holding tight enough that I'm aware of his obscene strength.

Someone who makes my already cool blood freeze in my veins.

Someone who is *supposed* to be dead.

The scar across his face breaks open as his charred skin twists into a mockery of a grin. Lord John Astor, my sire, speaks in a voice thick with grave dust and satisfaction. "My dear, sweet Arabella. You are mine once more."

49

Arabella

Celeste: Arabella, please come to Black Crag tonight with me, Dora and Winnie. Beth won't be there to remind you about the importance of self-care, so I will. We'll light chocolate-scented candles, do facials, and summon a demon to take vengeance on all who have wronged us while we snuggle beneath a blanket fort. That's what Beth means by self-care, right?

Astor had once been handsome – the most eligible man in the fashionable Cairo circles I ran in. As a young, naive courtesan, I thought his beauty, money and influence would be my ticket to an easy life. Instead, he took my life – and my innocence – from me.

Why do all the men who wrong me keep coming back from the dead?

Fear twists inside me – a physical, palpable weapon that blows out my chest and lodges in my throat. I try to think, but my mind is a blank sheet of white terror.

This isn't possible.

"How are you here?" I whisper.

"Do you mean, existentially, how do vampires exist?" Astor tilts his head to the side, amused by his joke. "Or do you mean, how am *I* here in your lovely home in Argleton after you cut off my head, burned my body, drank of my blood, and stole my property?"

I snap my mouth shut. Anything I say will betray my fear. I won't allow him the satisfaction.

He must have opened the outer door of Cleo VII's enclosure and climbed up the tree that twists inside it. All those blips in the Sanctus security system. The beheaded songbirds. They were from him.

But that still doesn't explain how he's alive.

Astor smirks. "I see my little songbird has gone silent. I do so love surprising you. You thought you were so clever, training yourself to endure the sunlight, hiding that blade, tempting me into bed one final time. I must admit, it was quite a shock to wake up with my head separated from my body. But one doesn't get to my age without taking precautions. A vampire is most vulnerable during his dreamless sleep, and I've seen enough persecutions to know that I could not trust my immortality to chance and good breeding. Some time ago, I had amulets sewn inside the lining of my coffin – a forbidden type of Dusk magic that would keep me alive even after a sneaky, disloyal concubine cut off my head."

My mistake blares like a trumpet inside my skull. Astor was high up within the Dusk Court – the court of magic and secrets. I never saw him use anything other than lesser magic to entertain his guests or close a drawer from across the room. It never occurred to me that he'd be capable of this sorcery.

I've never heard of a vampire bringing themselves back from death, but I guess that's because the Dusk Court hold their secrets close.

"You left me beheaded and burning," Astor continues mildly, as if we're exchanging pleasantries at a cocktail party. "My maid came home and put out the fire before it consumed me completely. I lay inside the coffin, alive but wishing I were dead, in an agony you could only dream of, while my body knitted itself together again over *months*. It was a full year before I could even rise from the coffin. By then, you'd disappeared, and the amulets and my natural vampiric healing could only do so much. I needed another magical item – one as old as I am – to return me to my full splendour. But you had stolen it."

The necklace.

That's why Astor has that hideous scar – it's from when I slashed blindly at his face. Beneath the collar of his shirt is another bulging, jagged scar from where I hacked through his neck. He's burned all over from being sealed inside the coffin I set alight.

He couldn't repair himself completely.

"You see now, don't you?" he hisses, his fingers tightening around my throat, pushing against my windpipe so I gasp for breath. "Cleopatra of the Blood Ptolemy filled her court with Dusk vampires, including yours truly. She knew her position with Rome was precarious. She craved more power, more beauty, more *immortality*. At her command, we poured our magic into that collar, creating a spell so powerful that it could return a vanquished Upyr to perfect health. But, like a foolish woman, she had to go and get herself captured before the spell was complete. She killed herself, not with a snake as the legends claim, but with the only type of poison to work on Upyr, hidden in a hollow hair comb. We were supposed to use the necklace to bring her back, but a fight broke out among us over who would present it to her, and one of my brethren threw the collar into the ocean. There it remained until the seventeenth century, when I heard it had resurfaced and spent a fortune to possess it once more. It hung around many pretty necks before yours, sweet Arabella, and now, your pretty neck belongs to me. *Give me the necklace.*"

"It's gone," I choke out. Red welts dance in front of my eyes. I rake my sharp nails across his hands, trying to relieve the pressure on my windpipe. But that only makes him grip me tighter, shoving my head back into the kitchen wall so hard that my crystal wine glasses topple from their stand and smash on the floor.

"Mmmm. I wouldn't lie if I were you." Astor flicks his wrist, jerking my head to the side with savage force. Lord Astor leans in close, his breath reeking of death, and *licks* a trail down my cheek with his cold, coarse tongue. "I can smell it. The magic calls me. The necklace is close. But never mind, I don't need you alive to take it from you. I have been hunting you for a long time, Arabella Macquart. I promised myself that when I found you, I wouldn't just kill you. I would *torment* you the way you tormented me. We're going to have such fun. We'll pick up where I left off in Paris. I was just getting started with you and your little theatre when you disappeared without a trace."

He lets go. I drop to the floor, my knees slamming against the Italian tile with such force that it cracks. Cleo VII slithers out of the way, disappearing behind the kitchen cabinet.

My whole body grows icy cold as Astor's words sink in.

He burned La Petite Mort. *He* sent the *brigade des mœurs* after me. *He* left those creepy messages and beheaded birds backstage – not for one of my ladies, but for *me*. He was toying with me back then – the beginning of a wretched game he intended to draw out for his pleasure, until Gideon stormed into my life like a cautionary tale and ruined Astor's plans.

Gideon fought Astor in Paris and *won*. And Astor died and rose again a second time, like an annoying vampiric Jesus.

But Gideon's not here, and nor are there any conveniently placed vampiric criminal overlords I can drain for strength. I carry some of Astor's power in my blood from when I drank him, but if he's brought himself back twice, if he's as ancient as he says, I don't have a hope of beating him.

Gasping, I try to get to my feet. Astor kicks me in the side. I slam against the wall, the air driven from my lungs. Plaster chunks rain down on my head. Age in a human means weakness. In a vampire, it means *danger*.

"You escaped the institution before I arrived to have my fun." Astor looms over me, flashing me that broken, charred grin. "*La dame fléau de la Salpêtrière* vanished without a trace, but I sensed the necklace was still in the city. I dug through the ruins of that wretched theatre, but found nothing. I became convinced one of the *sapeurs-pompiers* had taken it, so I had them all tortured, but that was a dead end. I lost hope of finding the necklace and I lost the chance to punish you for losing it." He unfolds something from his pocket. "Until my Thrall sent me this, and I knew I had a second chance."

He holds the paper close to my face. It takes my oxygen-starved eyes and fear-addled mind a few moments to recognise it.

The poster for Beth's studio opening.

"Imagine my surprise when a little birdie placed you and the necklace in my lap." Astor snaps his fingers.

"Tweet, tweet."

A second figure sweeps through Cleo VII's enclosure and steps into the kitchen, cheap heels clacking like typewriter keys against the tiles. She must've had a time climbing Cleo VII's tree in those.

"Hello, Arabella."

It's Gideon's assistant, Sinead.

50

Arabella

"You," I gasp.

Sinead smiles down at me as she steps forward and kicks me in the ribs. It's a pitiful human kick that barely registers after Astor's brutal blow, but I recoil from her because suddenly I know where I've seen her before.

She was Lord Astor's maid back in Cairo. The night I killed him, he'd sent her away to be played with by one of his friends. She must have returned to the mansion and found the coffin burning. She helped him become this … this *thing*.

I'd been so obsessed with my ascent through the ranks of Cairo's elite, and after Astor turned me, with my escape, that I'd barely noticed the faces of the people who worked for him.

"Of course, me." Sinead tosses her hair over her shoulder, tugging down her collar to reveal the fresh fang marks on her neck. She's impossibly old for a Thrall. But drinking the blood of such an ancient vampire must keep a human youthful for … "I've been Thralled to John for over two hundred years. The things I've had to do to keep us alive would melt your pretty little eyeballs right out of their sockets. Not the least of which was planting a body in John's grave to throw off that gormless detective you hired. This job at Sanctus was supposed to be our chance to get close to the uncourted community and establish Astor back into public life, but then I discovered something better. The ultimate gift for my master. *You*."

"Sinead is quite brilliant," Astor says proudly, as though her deceptions are his own. "She made Gideon trust her, so he gave her access to Sanctus' secrets. She siphoned off treasure from the vaults so I could rebuild my fortune. She dropped the security system to let me in and found me an unused maintenance shed to hide in during my dreamless sleep. She copied your lock code so that I could leave you my little gifts. She made sure that we silenced anyone who asked questions."

"You're the husker?" I gasp.

Astor laughs. "No. Those deaths were far too theatrical for us. Especially your vampire friend. The killer took quite a risk with her. I *was* watching through the bushes beside your home when I saw her hurry up the stairs, and when you didn't answer, I followed her through the sculpture garden, where the killer leapt out and attacked her. Although I took advantage of the situation to leave you a little note."

Mine, Arabella.

"You didn't kill her?" Even in my fear, something of the Nevermore Coven takes over. "But you saw who did?"

"Who, my love?" Sinead peers up at Astor. "If someone at Sanctus is killing, I should know."

"Now, what's the fun in telling?" Astor coos, licking another cold, wet trail down my cheek, drinking the tear that's escaped my eye. "It's more fun to know that Sanctus has a killer with a flair for the dramatic, and none of you can see the truth. You think this is a husker, but you're so *delightfully* wrong."

What?

"My darling." Sinead folds herself around his arm. "You should at least tell me—"

"You'll not speak back to me, *Thrall*. Not when you haven't done your duty and found my necklace."

His tone never changes from whimsical delight, but Sinead steps back as though he's slapped her. I remember all too well the cruelty of him – how he would pull you close with extravagant gifts and poetic promises, and make you feel like you were his most precious possession, but then he'd snatch his affection away and you'd see that you were less than nothing. I don't want to be Sinead's BFF, but I do recognise a piece of myself in her.

"I searched her whole house while she slept. It's not here." Sinead turns back to me, and her hurt is masked by sadistic glee. "It *was* my brilliant idea to turn Gideon against you, but you made him hate you all on your own, and he won't be flying in to rescue you. He's not even on the property tonight. We have you all to ourselves, don't we, John?"

"We do, my love. I have such *invigorating* plans."

I scream as Astor grabs me by the arm, bending it at an angle no arm should bend as he drags me into the living room. I know, academically, that screaming is pointless. The house is designed to be soundproof. But I'm a mess of terror and agony. Screaming is what you *do* in this situation.

Astor throws me into the corner. I hit the wall, cracking the plaster and another few ribs before knocking over a Pierre-Auguste statue sitting on a plinth beside the television. The marble shatters.

I want to be angry. I'm good at being angry, especially when a man invades my sanctuary and wrecks my shit. But I'm too busy being *afraid*.

I can't fight him. He's too strong. My body is already singing with pain, and he's barely even started. In the corner of my blurry vision, I see Sinead shoving aside my fashion magazines to unroll a leather case filled with silver blades.

I could run. The front door is only in the next room. If I can get outside and down the steps, I can scream for help.

I try to stagger to my feet, but a sharp heel in my back shoves me down again.

"Don't even think about it," Sinead growls. I squirm beneath the heel in my back. She's strong, too, much stronger than a Thrall should be. It must be all those centuries of Astor's blood. "I've given the security team the night off. The only Thrall working is on the gates, and he's so gorged on John's blood that he won't help you even if you beg."

"Mmmm. I'd like to see her beg. I think she will, once I'm done with her." Astor holds up one of his knives. "You could tell us where the necklace is now, but this way will be more fun."

"My friends were coming over tonight," I choke out. "I'm directing the variety show, and they want my help with their stupid dance."

"That doesn't sound like my Arabella."

"It's true. That's why my picture was on that pole studio poster."

"I revoked their visitor passes. They won't get through the gates," Sinead says. "And they're human – hardly worth worrying about."

"Not all are human. Do you think your Thrall on the gate is a match for a werewolf?"

Sinead pales. "John, she's right. The werewolf could be a problem."

Astor tosses my phone at my feet. "Send them a message. Tell them not to come. Sinead, watch her. Make sure she doesn't try anything clever."

With trembling hands, I pick up the phone, click on the Nevermore Coven group chat, and hit the *record* button.

"Hello, ladies." I fight to keep my voice light. "I know you were all coming over tonight to help me organise the program for the variety show. But I've decided to do it on my own. That's the only way it will be done right. I'll see you all at the next book club meeting, okay?"

Slick with my blood, my fingers slip as I click *send message*. A tick appears beneath it.

Delivered.

"Good. Don't look so terrified, sweet Arabella. It will be just like the old days." Lord Astor cracks his knuckles. "We're going to have *fun*."

51

Gideon

Manet: Just a reminder that this buyer is nervous. If you are so much as a minute late, they will disappear. You'll never get this chance again. Do not disappoint them. Or me.

MY HANDS ARE TIGHT ON THE STEERING WHEEL AS I SPEED DOWN the A40 towards Grimdale. The Lamborghini's frame judders as it hits another rough patch of road. I wince as the bottom scrapes and a cascade of coins topples from one of the sacks, scattering throughout the footwell.

Even if my precious car doesn't survive this trip, it will be worth it. I can't believe Édouard found the collar. If this turns out to be the real thing, I am giving him a finder's fee. Maybe his own unicorn. We can breed unicorns, right? I'll ask Sinead.

Arabella will be *floored*. For once in my life, I'll have done the right thing.

The magic in my blood whispers and dances.

Countryside fades into village as I enter Grimdale. My map blinks neon colours at me, directing me to the meeting place beside the old Victorian graveyard. I'm pulling into the parking lot with two minutes to spare when my phone beeps. A voice message from Winnie.

I hit the button to listen.

"Gideon, are you at Sanctus? Arabella was supposed to hang out at Black Crag with me, Celeste and Dora, but she sent this odd message saying that we were supposed to come to her house to help her with the program, but she's decided to do it herself instead. None of that's true. I wondered if she's fobbing us off to hang out with you. Are you two back together? Have you given her so many bloodsinthes that she can't concoct a decent lie? Call me back when you get this."

I listen to the message again, trying to understand. Why would Arabella tell her friends not to come over when she'd already made plans to see them?

Unless … is she sneaking off for an amorous liaison with some hot, eligible Upyr she hasn't told her friends about? Someone rich and connected who *doesn't* break her heart and steal from her and—

Wait a second.

My fingers tremble as I dial Winnie. The moment she picks up, I blurt out, "Tell me exactly what Arabella said."

"Gideon?" Winnie laughs. "Good. Maybe you can tell Alaric that he absolutely shouldn't join Celeste on one of her fossil-hunting expeditions. The last thing this castle needs is an entire wing filled with Alaric's interesting rocks—"

"Winnie, this is important. I need you to repeat exactly what Arabella said."

"Hang on, I'll play you the message."

Arabella's sultry voice plays through the phone. The sound of it clenches my heart.

"Hello, ladies. I know you were all coming over tonight to help me organise the program for the variety show. But I've decided to do it on my own. That's the only way it will be done right. I'll see you all at the next book club meeting, okay?"

Oh no.

"Winnie," I hiss. "Arabella's in trouble. Don't you see? Arabella says that she asked you all to help her. But when has Arabella *ever* asked for help? She would *never*. She has to do everything herself because it's the only way she feels safe." I close my eyes, trying to force down the panic. "She's trying to tell us that she needs help."

The Nevermore Murder Club and Smutty Book Coven Group Chat

Beth: I'm at a yoga retreat in Grimdale and I just got this odd message from Arabella.

Maisie: Me too. Apparently, we were all supposed to be helping her with the variety show tonight?

Winnie: I just spoke to Gideon. He thinks she's in trouble.

Dora: She's in trouble. I see her. She's lying on the floor, covered in her own blood. And there's a scarred monster. We have to get over there. Now.

Celeste: Me, Dora and Winnie are at Black Crag. Reginald's at his classic car club, so we're waiting for an Uber. Alaric's already left. Is anyone else closer?

Maisie: I'm working late at the Gazette offices, but it doesn't matter. We're humans. They won't let us in the gates, and Gideon is off on some ridiculous secret mission …

Komal: We have to try! Mina, get Morrie's lock-picking kit.

Mina: Morrie's away down in London at a chess championship!

Celeste: Everyone – get to Sanctus. Don't go to the front gates. Meet around the side, near the entrance to Baylor's property. I have a way in …

52

Arabella

"Do you like my pretty blade, sweet Arabella?" Lord Astor grins, that horrific scar splitting across his face as he drags the point of a knife along my cheek, opening a long, stinging wound dangerously close to my eye. "I thought it appropriate, seeing as how you used one on me. Shall I take your eyes first? But then you won't be able to see what I'm going to do to you. If you tell me where you're hiding my necklace, I could let you wear it for a few moments to heal your pretty face before I destroy it again and again. I know it's close. I can *smell* it …"

I scream as he digs his finger into the cut, prising it apart to soak his scarred digit in my blood. He pops his finger into his mouth, his tongue smacking against his ruined lips as he sucks it dry. "You are *exquisite*. I'm going to enjoy drinking every last drop of you. My revenge couldn't have been more perfect. The Sanctus vampires will think you're another victim of the husker. Meanwhile, I will introduce myself as your sire – long estranged, deeply beloved by you, and rightful heir to your fortune and the entire Sanctus Estate. Sinead has it all planned. Within a week of your body being discovered, your house and fortune and legitimacy will belong to me."

The *bastard*.

I am in such terrible pain, but I am getting angry now.

He's going to take everything I've worked so hard for? Everything I've built myself?

He's going to take *Sanctus*.

I cry out as Astor draws another scar across my cheek.

"For nearly two centuries, I've lived with the scars of your betrayal." Astor licks along the wound, pressing his lips to my skin and sucking. "Do you have any idea how cruel the world can be to someone they perceive as weak? How hard it is to exist outside of civilised society?"

I have something of an idea, yes.

"You cheated me out of what's rightfully mine, and I have suffered for it. I have waited and longed for my revenge, but now I have you, I'm going to take my time with you."

Sinead kneels down beside him. "Now that I've given her to you, you'll do it, won't you?" She tugs Astor's shoulder. "Turn me, John. You *promised*. Turn me into a vampire right now and we'll drain her together."

He shoves her away. "You'll not touch a drop of her blood. She's mine."

"She's never been yours," a voice rings out.

Gideon.

I can't see him, but I *feel* him behind me. The front door slams against the wall, which means he must have stolen my *secret* keycode.

I'm too happy to hear his voice to care.

Astor stands, straightening his lapels, wiping my blood across his starched white shirt as he regards the newcomer.

"We meet again, mouse," he rasps.

Gideon smiles, and that smile is all fangs and violence. The best kind of smile.

He turns to Sinead. "You're fired."

She laughs. "You can't fire me. I know every one of Sanctus' dark and filthy secrets. You think I haven't already copied that hard drive of yours? When I release those files, the Conclave will come for your head and every one of your members. John and I don't even have to kill you – you've already signed your own death warrant. You were so easy to manipulate, it's almost laughable."

"A bold plan, worthy of you, Sinead." If Gideon is afraid, he shows nothing, just stands there like they're all discussing the weather. I realise now that I'm seeing the man who ran the Vega empire – not a man at all, but a devil in Armani. "Brava. But you forgot one little detail. You may be Thralled to John Astor, but you're also Thralled to me, and I'm about to make his life rather unpleasant. Without his blood on your lips, you'll quickly fall back under *my* control, and I have many imaginative punishments for Thralls who cross me."

"I'm *sooo* afraid." She sidles up to Astor and wraps her arms around his waist. "Good luck trying to kill him."

"Oh, I don't want to kill him." Gideon grins. "Not yet."

He lunges.

He's *fast*. Impossibly fast. Not even my vampiric vision can keep focused on Gideon and Astor as they crash across the room. My coffee table smashes. Another Rodin statue bites the dust. I dive to catch the edge of Claude's painting before it crashes from the wall, and slide it gently behind the sofa. Sinead backs away towards the kitchen, screaming at Astor, but neither of us can see what's happening.

How did Mr "I'm a lover, not a fighter" get so good at this? Astor's ancient blood should give him an edge, but not when Gideon has Astor's blood in his veins. Gideon ducks and weaves like a dancer before diving for the silver blades scattered across the floor.

Of course. Gideon has drained *two* vampires.

Astor's magic in my blood stirs, whispers, *You have a chance.*

Gideon's fingers clasp around a knife, but Astor kicks it away. He grabs Gideon under the chin, slamming him against the wall with enough force to shatter the plasterboard and part of the internal wall. Gideon's cobalt eyes flick to me, down at the floor, then back to me again.

The magic between us hums.

Yes.

I spy the blade Astor was using on me beside the leg of the coffee table. I summon every last ounce of rage and magic I possess to push through the pain and launch my body towards it.

"Oh no, you don't." Sinead's heel slams down on my hand. She grinds her stiletto into my palm, breaking delicate bones. It hurts like giving birth to a stick of dynamite. I haven't given birth to a stick of dynamite, but I *am* currently experiencing a stiletto through my hand and can conclude, academically, that the comparison holds up.

Sinead yanks the knife from beneath my unmoving fingers. "Enough of John's games. I'll enjoy cutting you to pieces."

She raises the blade, her face twisting with triumph. And from behind her shoulder, a tiny head pokes up, hood unfurled, tongue flicking between her fangs.

Sinead barely has time to cry out in surprise before Cleo VII sinks her fangs into her neck. She drops to her knees, the knife clattering from her fingers as she grips my beautiful, brave girl, trying to tear her off her neck. But Cleo VII holds firm, and every second she clings on, more of her venom enters Sinead's veins.

Sinead may have been supping on Lord Astor's blood for two centuries. She may have a tiny fissure of his magic, but she's still human. She can't survive a cobra bite.

There's a moment – when she glares up at me, her eyes wide with pain – that she realises she's gone. Then she collapses to the floor. She doesn't move.

Cleo VII flicks her tongue in distaste, as if saying, *That's what you get for kicking my favourite rock,* then slithers back into the kitchen.

Behind me, Gideon sighs with pleasure, which tells me he's in trouble. I drag my broken body forward on my elbows, screaming as shards of glass and broken marble pierce my skin.

Not this time, Astor. You're not taking what's mine.

My fingers close around the knife. I have nothing left, my body is done. The magic in my veins has faded to a whisper. My blood streaks across the carpet. But Astor is *right there*, three feet away, holding Gideon against the wall and slurping at his throat while Gideon's head lolls back with pleasure.

Something in me *snaps*.

I remember all the nights I lay in Astor's coffin, terrified of what he might do to me. Alyra's face flashes before my eyes, and then the faces of all my friends in the Nevermore Coven – the women I've sworn to protect.

I call up the spirit of the woman who has spent the last hundred and fifty years hating the wrong man.

I listen to the whisper in my blood, and I call it closer until it's no longer a whisper, but a *roar.*

With the last of my magic coursing through my veins, I stagger to my feet and lunge at Astor. My whole body trembles from the pain of it. Bits of glass and marble fly from my wounds as I slam into him. It hurts more than giving birth to dynamite *twins.* But my hand around the blade is steady, firm, humming with magic, as I plunge it into Astor's back, over and over and over, hitting bone and organs and splitting open veins, until my sire drops his fangs from Gideon and turns to face me.

I cling to the hilt of the blade, digging it deeper, twisting it until Astor cries out. His fingers fight for the hilt, but they're too slippery with blood. My blood and his blood and Gideon's blood. I *scream* in his face. I let the magic ooze through my skin and sizzle on the surface. I let him see the monster he made.

I am, after all, of his blood. And like him, I will wait *centuries* for revenge.

Astor leans in, fangs bared. And then he sees Sinead in a heap on the floor. A growl escapes his throat as he understands that even if he kills me and Gideon now, he can't survive without her. The great Lord Astor had banked his whole plan on a human, because he was too afraid of creating another Arabella Lestrange.

Astor's hand slips from the knife.

He does what any scavenger does when he knows he might die if he stays in the fight. He turns and flees out the open front door.

I wait for a single breath, long enough to see through my blood-filled vision that he's not coming back, and then I collapse on the floor.

"Arabella."

I blink.

It hurts so much.

Gideon's cobalt eyes stare at me across the floor. He clutches the wound in his neck, but the blood is already congealing, the bite marks closing over. He gathers me into his arms. His body is smeared with blood and gore. I try not to think of how much of it should be inside my body.

"How …" I murmur, my head spinning. "How did you hold him off for so long? He should have destroyed you."

"The blood of two drained vampires, and a century of lessons from Alaric Valerian, the fiercest warrior that ever lived." Gideon strokes my hair. "He cut you."

"I've had worse nips from Cleo VII when her toad is too cold." I cough blood onto his shirt. Gideon makes a face but doesn't move to wipe it away – a courtesy that, were our roles reversed, I likely wouldn't extend to him. "You have to go after Astor—"

"Don't worry. I smelled Alaric approaching. Astor won't get away with this." Gideon uses one hand to flip his phone open. A second later, Sinead's pocket starts vibrating. "Damn it, it's going to take me some time to get used to her not sorting everything out for me."

"How …" I close my eyes. "How are you here? I never sent—"

"The Nevermore Coven."

Of course.

"I checked the security cameras and saw Astor sneak into your house." Gideon slides his arms beneath me. "I need to get you to Sanctus House. Lilac will heal you—"

He stumbles as a loud howl echoes from outside, followed by the distinct and profoundly wonderful sound of Lord Astor screaming.

Gideon gathers me against him. I bury my face in his bloody jacket, allowing the honey and red cherry scent to wash over me as he runs for the door. I rub blood from my eyes and squint at my front garden, barely able to believe what I'm seeing.

Lord John Astor stands in my fountain, his legs trapped by a strange, jaw-like contraption that's emerged from beneath the water. He flails his arms, attempting to fend off Alaric Valerian – armed with a bloody sword – and an enormous wolf that's already taken a huge bite out of his arm. The churning water beneath him is stained dark red.

Gathered around the fountain, clapping and cheering (and are those crisps?), is every member of the Nevermore Murder Club and Smutty Book Coven.

"Argh!" Astor thrashes in the pond as Morrie's booby trap tightens around his legs and Celeste takes a chunk out of his thigh.

"The cavalry has arrived," Gideon says.

"I'm terribly sorry I didn't get here sooner," Alaric says as he swipes a fresh wound across Astor's neck. "I've been in the garden for some time, but I didn't realise the door was open and the infernal Patrick Stock window glass is vampire-proof, so the only way in was through Cleo VII's enclosure, and I must confess that I'm rather afraid of snakes."

"You're afraid of snakes?" Gideon's voice rises. "That's hissssssterical."

I glance up at him, surprised that he's not smiling. A look of impossible sadness passes over his cobalt eyes. He catches me staring and looks away.

"Gideon?"

"Arabella, we're here to save you—" Isis's face falls when she sees me in Gideon's arms. "Oh, drat. Gideon got here first."

"That's not a 'drat'. It's a good thing," Dora scolds her sister.

"I mean, *obviously*. What's he doing here?" Komal thrusts her hands on her hips. "He's ruined our perfectly good rescue plan."

Astor squeals as Celeste dives in for another bite. No one makes any move to help him. Gideon sets me down and the Nevermore Coven crowd around us, laying their hands on me and all talking at once about their adventure.

"How did you get into Sanctus?" Gideon asks. "Security should have never let you past the gates."

"We didn't go through the gates."

The ladies part to reveal Celeste, back in her human form, her naked body dripping wet and covered in Astor's blood. She holds her head high with feigned dignity as she tries to cover herself with her hands.

"Could I have something to wear, please?" she asks.

Gideon grabs my burgundy coat from the rack in the foyer and tosses it to her. I try not to wince at the bloodstain she smears on the collar.

She did save my life and all, but that coat is *Versace*.

"Celeste was amazing," Dora says. "She leapt over the fence, scared the security guy out of his office, and opened the gates for us."

"She's one badass werewolf," says Mina.

"Her teeth are even scarier than yours," Maisie adds.

"Why?" I whisper to Celeste as she wraps her arms around me. "You put yourself in danger because of me. I never wanted you to reveal your secret."

She smiles back. "It's what you do for friends."

A lump forms in my throat as I stare around at these women who risked their lives for me. On nothing but a vision and a voice message, they stormed into a vampire estate armed with their wits and … is that a crucifix?

When I can breathe properly again, we're going to have a *chat* about which vampire superstitions will save their arses and which will get them laughed out of Sanctus.

Before I realise it, my arms are going around Celeste, too. I'm squeezing her so hard it hurts. Maybe it's not that hard, and I'm just broken.

The other girls pile in on the group hug, squashing me and Gideon in the middle of their circle of love.

"I'm sorry that I hid myself from you all for so long," I mumble.

"We get it, Arabella," Celeste says. "Being ourselves can be dangerous. And scary."

"Exactly. I know I can be …"

"Abrasive?" Isis supplies.

"Caustic?" Mina suggests.

"I prefer 'fiercely independent'," says Dora.

"All of those things. But I want you to know that I've never had friends like you. Real friends. And I'm grateful for you all, even if I don't always show it." I glare at Komal as she inches closer to the house. "And no, you still cannot borrow my clothes."

They pull me inside and settle me on a sofa in the second living room – the one that's not covered in blood – and someone puts the kettle on and Celeste complains about the lack of ingredients in my pantry and Dora pulls me into her shoulder and Winnie starts directing people to clean up the mess and Maisie and Komal shoo a very satisfied Cleo VII back into her enclosure and it's not until Beth places a glass of blood in my hands and they all settle in around me that I realise someone is missing.

"Where's Gideon?"

53

Gideon

Winnie: Gideon, where did you go? Arabella's looking for you. She's upset.

I drag myself back to my room and collapse on the sofa, tossing my phone beside me without checking any of the messages currently blowing it up.

I've done my job. I've taken care of everything. I recalled the security team from their "night off" to take care of Sinead's body and drag Astor down to the cells. I sent Lilac over to Arabella's house with potions to close over her wounds. And I've ordered a media blackout that absolutely no one will adhere to.

Gossip will spread through Sanctus faster than a conversation between Rory and Lorelai Gilmore – not a topical reference, I know, but Alaric was a big fan of the show for a while, and when Alaric is a fan of something, you're a fan too, *or else* – and every second that goes by without PR damage control will mean more ammunition for the Conclave to use against me. But I can't bring myself to care.

Arabella's safe.

I rub at the itchy spot on my neck where Astor's bite has already healed over. I peel off my ruined shirt and toss it in the rubbish bin.

I go to my closet, but there's nothing in there. Most of my clothing has been sent to the London penthouse, and Sinead neglected my week's laundry in favour of betraying me.

I find a shirt in the clean laundry bin and bring it out into the living room with the ironing board. I need to do *something* with my hands or I *will* sprint back to Arabella's house, snatch her from the arms of her friends, and shag her on every available surface until she begs for mercy in a fun way.

But this time, I'm keeping my promise.

I'm staying away from her.

I've already ruined her life several times over. She's made it clear she doesn't want me in it again. And with her owning a majority share in Sanctus now, there's not much point staying.

I plug in the iron and pace across the floor until it heats up, trying to force out the images of a bloody and broken Arabella by mentally running through the list of what I need to accomplish before I leave Sanctus. I'm just starting to iron when the elevator doors slide open.

I look up in surprise. No one else can get up here apart from Sinead, and—

I throw up my hands to defend myself, but I'm not fast enough. A small, hard device hits me in the face. That's followed by a pillow, and a hail of abuse so poetic that Shakespeare should be taking notes.

Arabella looms over me, brandishing the cushion from my sofa in one hand and dragging the bloody but not-quite-dead body of Astor in the other.

"How *dare* you sit there like the smug king of your domain?" she yells, drawing back her arm for another blow.

"Technically, I'm standing. How did you get up here?"

She whomps me over the head again. "The same way I got up here last time. Moriarty. And I ask the questions. Not you. What the hell do you think you're doing?"

"I'm ironing."

She drops the cushion and snatches the iron from my hands. "I'm going to strangle you with this cord and enjoy every minute of it."

"So will I. But before we get erotic, can you tell me what this is about?"

"What's this about? You *left!*"

"Of course I did." I shrug. "You were safe. You were with your friends. I wasn't needed."

"That's bullshit and you know it. You're the head of Sanctus. You have justice to dispense—"

"Technically, *you're* head of Sanctus. We signed the paperwork. You own this place outright. So that means what happens to Astor is up to you." I frown at the vampire dripping blood on my larch floor.

Her mouth twists. Even battered and bloody, she is so beautiful I can barely stand to look at her. "What if I don't want—Hey!"

I grab the iron from her and start working on the cuffs. "Do you know how impossible it is to stay here in your presence, when every corner of this estate reminds me of you? I can't walk in the Midnight Garden without remembering our night together in Paris. I can't step foot in Sanctus Club without hearing you cry my name. My private apartments reek of your ginger and myrrh scent. When I drink blood, I taste raspberries. I taste *you*." I furiously rub at the sleeve of my shirt, dimly aware of a burning smell rising from the expensive fabric. "Living here without you is *torture*. I'm tearing myself to pieces, but if this is the only way I can love you, by leaving this place, then I'll do it." My head snaps up, my eyes meeting hers. "Because I *do* love you, Arabella. I love you so much that I'm setting you free of me."

She looks stunned.

"Gideon …"

"Please leave." I turn back to my shirt. I've burned a hole near the cuff the size of a 20-pence piece. "I have the last of my things to pack."

A hand closes over mine, wrenching the iron away. "Gideon, you *fool*. Look at me."

It takes everything I have to turn my head up to hers. I'm trembling. The only thing keeping me upright is a thin strand of foolish, impossible *hope*.

A pair of dark eyes meet mine, the edges softened by a halo of golden light. Her eyebrow twitches.

"Gideon, I love you."

Did she just …

My blood *sings*.

Never have three words felt so much like magic.

"You … you're sure about this?"

"Of course I'm sure," she snaps. "I'm Arabella Lestrange. I'm always sure."

A slow grin breaks out across my face. "It's impressive how someone so beautiful and brilliant can be so humble."

"Humility *is* difficult, especially when I've never been wrong in my life, but not as difficult as it is for me to admit these words, so don't make me do it again. I love you, Gideon Blake, and I *forgive* you. I can't promise I won't occasionally want to rearrange your guts, but I'll do it in pretty shapes like flowers and hearts. Because *I love you.*"

"I—"

She kisses me.

I say this as a vampire who's had a long life filled with pleasures – you haven't *lived* until you've been kissed by Arabella Lestrange. The woman's tongue is silk, her fingers knitting in my hair, possessive and decisive. Her little moans are the only music I ever wish to hear. She keeps her eyes open, those golden haloes dancing as they draw me in until I am utterly under her spell.

She loves me.

I tug the cord from the wall. The iron hisses and smokes as it burns through my shirt, but I leave it, not caring if I burn the whole damn building down. I push Arabella back, back towards my fancy sofa, already imagining how she'll look luxuriating on the luxe fabric, surveying her kingdom through the windows, her legs spread wide while I kneel between them. I'm so busy imagining it that I almost trip over Astor's body.

"Why'd you bring him?" I say. "I'm down for a threesome, but this is a bit kinky even for me."

She raises her eyebrow at that. "I thought to make him a gift, for saving my life. Although he did almost triumph. You just *had* to do a whole supervillain 'I've got you now' speech, didn't you?"

"What happened to 'thank you for saving my beautiful neck, Gideon'?"

"Thank you for saving my beautiful neck, Gideon." She breaks away from me to haul Astor over to my sofa, leaving a long smear of blood across the floor. She sinks into the fabric like it should be grateful for her presence and pulls Astor's lolling body over her lap. With a wicked grin, she pats the seat beside her.

"We've never really been on a real date. Why don't you join me for dinner?"

I can never refuse her. I slide into the seat beside her, taking some of Astor's weight. He's in bad shape – between the injuries from the blade and the werewolf bites that won't heal over, he's barely conscious. What Arabella is suggesting is a kindness that he doesn't deserve, but I know she's not thinking about him.

I can't gift her back the necklace. Édouard has already informed me that his client spooked when I didn't show, and returned to the darkness. But Lord Astor is a much better gift.

Arabella stares down at him, her expression unreadable. She's remembering. In time, she might tell me about the things he did to her. Or they might remain her secrets forever. But the remembering is important. The remembering is her finally laying his ghost to rest.

She swipes the hair from his face with an almost gentle reverence.

And then she sinks her fangs into his neck.

Astor struggles for a moment, but then the endorphins hit and he sinks happily into her arms. A vampire is no more immune to our bite than a human, which is partly why drinking from each other is forbidden.

Arabella's eyes meet mine as she drinks deep. I'm mesmerised by the movement in her throat as she gulps and sucks. The room fills with the mingled scent of raspberries and copper – the unmistakable tang of fresh, flowing blood.

When she draws her mouth away, there's a smudge of his blood across her lip.

I wipe it with my finger. She smiles against my hand, her fang scraping across my skin. And then we're kissing and sucking and licking blood, our hands everywhere, our fangs entangled, our tongues ravenous. She tastes sharp and tangy – like raspberries and revenge, like myrrh and magic. Her ruined dress falls to pieces in my hands. Or maybe I tear it to shreds like an animal. It's all a blur of taste and magic and *her*.

Astor's blood is like nothing I've ever drunk before, and I already drank it once. It's rich and heavy with his years and his magic. Not even the memory of drinking him back in Paris compares to the hunger roaring through me as I gulp the last of him from Arabella's tongue. It is salvation and damnation at once, and I have no idea what such a quantity of an ancient vampire's blood will do to us.

There are reasons vampires don't drink from each other.

And even more reasons why we're not supposed to cheat death a second time.

But I don't care about the consequences now, not when Astor's blood flows between our lips as we share the last of his life.

It's wicked. It's wrong. But it feels right.

When he's finally drained, when Arabella's past is a dead, heavy thing between us and our veins sing with his magic, she shoves Astor's husked body from the sofa and crawls into my lap. Her body – like her clothing – is couture. That triangle of dark hair between her thighs could drive men to ruin.

And of all the men, in this eternity and the next, she's chosen me to ruin.

I do *so* enjoy being ruined by her.

Every night when I woke from dreamless sleep to find she wasn't beside me, I wished for this second chance. And now that she's in my arms, I'm not going to waste a single moment. I need to taste every inch of her.

I kiss a trail to the spot behind her ear that always used to drive her wild.

"You remember …" she whimpers.

"I remember *everything* about you."

I kiss a trail down her body, pushing her over the arms of the sofa, spreading her legs for me. She tilts her chin down towards me, and her expression is pure haughty goddess.

I lower myself to my knees, exactly where I've always wanted to be. I kiss the tiny mole on her inner thigh before I move to the real treasure.

As soon as I taste her, I know that a taste will never be enough for me. I need to devour this woman.

And I do. I feast on her clit, mingling Astor's blood with the rich, raspberry taste of her. I plunge my tongue inside her opening, tasting the juices of her arousal before pounding her clit with my tongue until she lets slip a stream of foul, delicious curses and then, just my name, over and over …

"Damn you, Gideon …"

She comes apart for me.

Before she has recovered from the orgasm, I sweep her into my arms. Arabella wraps her body around me as I carry her back to my room. Her lips twist in amusement as she takes in the large, revolving coffin-shaped bed and the floor-to-ceiling windows giving us a view across the whole of Sanctus.

"That Patrick *was* a genius." Arabella studies the glass. "These windows are an engineering marvel. I can see across to my house, and the Midnight Garden beyond."

"I thought a queen might appreciate surveying her domain."

"But this bed is absurd," she murmurs as I lay her down, flick on the LED lights, and set it to rotate slowly. "Like you."

"You're just mad I didn't have a replica of your Queen Anne mahogany monstrosity."

"It *was* awfully fun tying you to the cherubs," she admits.

I groan, kicking off my trousers. "Damn you, woman. Don't mention the cherubs again or I won't make it."

I crawl up on top of her, pressing myself into her, needing every inch where we touch. Her legs wrap around me, pulling me down. I nibble behind her ear and she laughs her low, throaty laugh, and I am utterly lost. And when I enter her, for the first time in my whole life, I know the meaning of the word *home*.

54

Arabella

Winnie: I can't wait to see you both tonight. 7 pm, don't be late. Reginald has some fine vintage blood on offer, and Alaric and I have a surprise for you. You absolutely will not believe it!

"Alaric and I are reading *The Five Love Languages*, but he thinks they aren't nearly specific enough," Winnie says.

"The book is nonsense. The true love languages are cats, villain redemption arcs, the new wheeled ladder Winnie had installed in the library, when people let me tell them exciting facts I've learned about twentieth century surrealist sculpture, slaying one's enemies, and when Winnie didn't break up with me after discovering my Egyptian room," Alaric announces.

"And hot chocolate!" Winnie adds, as Reginald presents her with one of his signature drinks.

Reginald places blood chocolates down in front of Gideon and me. I snuggle deeper into Gideon's shoulder as we lie together on the sofa in front of the roaring fire Alaric had Reginald light for Winnie's sake. Cleo VII curls up in front of the flames like a cat, while the actual castle cat, Mirabelle, stands ramrod straight on the back of Alaric's chair, hissing at the interloper.

The four of us have enjoyed a lovely evening together, drinking blood and wine and playing Catan. No one eviscerated Gideon after he made endless wood jokes. Alaric won, but his victory dance isn't nearly as hot as mine. I shall triumph in the next round.

It's been two weeks since Gideon and I drained John Astor dry and buried his body in the woods with an amulet from Lilac that should prevent him from healing himself. In that time, I've signed over co-ownership of the estate back to Gideon. It may bring the Conclave down on our heads, but Sanctus Estate needs Gideon Blake.

And so do I.

For now, things are calm. Gideon and I can get to know each other in this century. We've wasted so much time dancing around each other, plotting and scheming, when we could have been fucking and arguing and fucking some more.

So we're dating. We take walks in the sculpture garden, attend a weekly painting class, and argue endlessly over which vintage to share for dinner. And tonight, we're on a double date with Winnie and Alaric at Black Crag Castle, and it's so delightfully ordinary that I can't believe it's really happening—

"Oh, Alaric, the surprise." Winnie leans forward, her golden hair catching the firelight as she kicks her feet in anticipation.

"Of course." Alaric reaches behind his chair and removes a small stone box inlaid with precious jewels. The winged goddess Isis is carved into the lid. "I believe this belongs to you," he says stiffly, handing me the box.

"Why?" I've never seen it before in my life.

"Look *inside*, Arabella," Winnie laughs.

Frowning, I lift the lid. Inside, nestled on a bed of black velvet, is a glittering collar of jewels with a blue scarab beetle and coiled snakes in the centre.

My necklace.

The moment I touch the lapis lazuli scarab beetle at the centre, I know it's real. The Antirhodos Collar. Firelight catches the jewels so they sparkle with dappled light, like the surface of a lily pond in one of Claude's paintings.

This is impossible.

Gideon's fingers dig into my knee. He stares at his friend, his eyes bugging out of his head. "How … where …?"

"I found it in Alaric's Egyptian room." Winnie grins. "It was in a chest with jewellery and coins from the Ptolemaic era. I recognised it from the poster of you at Beth's studio."

"Then it's yours." I hold out the box towards Alaric, even as the magic in my veins hums from proximity to the necklace. *This must be what Astor meant by the necklace calling him. He felt it nearby because it was* nearby. *All this time it's been sitting in a dusty chest in Alaric's castle.*

"Don't be absurd." Alaric recoils. "The blue would clash with my eyes. It is yours, Arabella. It belongs with you."

"This certainly calls into question the integrity of Édouard's mystery seller." Gideon takes the box. "Allow me."

Gideon's fingers sizzle against my skin as he drapes the jewels around my neck, carefully fastening them. "So Dora's vision did come true."

As soon as their weight drapes across my skin, it's as if they never left. As if my neck was made for them.

I run to a mirror on the wall and study them from every angle. I can't stop running my hands over them. Mine. Mine again. Gideon comes up behind me, wrapping his arms around me and kissing my neck, trailing his lips along the place where jewels and skin meet.

"I always knew you were a goddess," he whispers. "Now the world will know it."

I touch the tip of my finger to the scarab, listening to the hum of magic in my veins. All those years I believed my luck had left me, but instead, real magic had been close. Real magic in the form of a grieving, bloodthirsty vampire willing us together again.

Looking at Gideon's cobalt eyes, I believe it. I believe even the gods bend the rules for this man.

I didn't get lucky because of magical jewels. I'm lucky because I am loved, fiercely and imperfectly, by this man.

"How do they feel?" Gideon asks, a golden curl flopping over his eye.

"Like they've come home," I say as I pull him to me, and kiss the infuriating smirk from his lips.

55

Arabella

Dora: I know it's a week early, but I've already finished packing my bag. Do you think we can go to Paris tonight? Say, just before the village variety show is due to begin?

It's standing room only in Sanctus Club. Vampires and humans mingle awkwardly. It will take more than a party in a fancy club to convince the villagers to accept Sanctus Estate, but the free-flowing cocktails (with or without blood) will go a long way to help.

I nod to Lilac, who's behind the bar mixing perfect blood cocktails for the Upyr guests. She nods back. She may come from the same court as my evil sire, but so far, all she's used her magic for is to repair my beautiful skin after the damage from Astor's blade – therefore, she is worthy of knighthood.

"Is this really what La Petite Mort was like?" Winnie asks as she spins in a slow circle, taking in the crowded booths, the twinkling lamps, the sumptuous velvet and gold everywhere. Thankfully, Sinead hadn't made much progress on redecorating Sanctus Club, and Gideon was quickly able to restore it to its original, superior design.

"The music was much better," I yell over the pounding bass. Gideon insisted that our patrons wouldn't be interested in the music I used to play, and needled me until I signed over total control of the playlist. I let him have it because men need to win sometimes.

Actually, that's a lie. I snuck on some of my favourite dancing tracks when he wasn't looking. I will make them all appreciate *decent* music, for I am correct on all matters of taste.

Make that, all matters, full stop.

"Thank you for inviting us into your world." Mina's eyes cloud over with happy tears as she hugs Celeste close to her. "Both of you."

Celeste beams at me. Our friendship has deepened since I discovered what she is. We aren't hiding our true selves from each other or our friends. It's scary, but the good kind of scary, like the first time you pat a snake and she gives you that *look*.

Speaking of snakes, Cleo VII is in her element tonight – draped over my shoulders, wearing her bling and surveying her domain. To say thank you for saving my life, Gideon gifted her with a matching scarab collar *and* added another floor to her enclosure. He's now her new favourite Upyr.

"And thank you for taking us all on a trip to Paris!" Maisie cries, squeezing James Pond so hard in her excitement that he beaks her in the face. "I can't believe we leave next weekend for four whole days. I'm so excited to see your favourite places, eat your favourite foods, go to all your favourite shops and watch you try on fabulous clothes I'd never in a million years pull off. All that art. All that cheese …"

"Dairy is awful for gut health," Beth scolds her. "I'll be packing extra mushroom smoothie sachets, and I think we should each have one every morning—"

"No!" Isis, Dora, Maisie, Mina, Celeste, Komal, and Winnie cry in unison.

I smirk. No matter what, my friends will always be a source of frustration and delight.

"Are you sure you don't want us to pay even a portion?" Winnie frowns at me. "That hotel you booked looks more like a castle. It can't be cheap—"

"Only the best for Arabella Lestrange and her friends. This is *my* treat, to say thank you for knowing me well, despite my best efforts. We should have done it years ago."

"It's wonderful to see you with a smile on your face." Dora throws her arm around me, careful to avoid touching Cleo VII, but her eyes are focused on the empty stage. She's trembling. Mike, thankfully, is nowhere in sight.

Behind Dora, Isis fiddles with the tap on an absinthe fountain and accidentally sprays herself in the eye. It's good to see the green fairy still has a sense of humour.

"I shouldn't be smiling," I tell Dora, glancing around at the faces of the Sanctus vampires. One of them killed Alyra, Danny and Patrick. "We're still no closer to finding the killer. And we don't know what Astor meant when he said we're wrong about the killer being a husker, or who this mystery person is who claimed to have my collar."

"We're the Nevermore Murder Club and Smutty Book Coven," Mina assures me. "We may have followed some false clues, but we'll crack this case. We always do."

A bell sounds over our heads, signalling for the audience to take their seats. I slip away from my friends and head backstage to herd performers and glare at people until they stand where they're told. Once the show starts, I stand in the wings, giving the performers my infamous last-minute pep talk: "You will not throw up on my Manolo Blahniks. Or you will lick them clean. You will be wonderful out there. You have no choice. Now, get on stage and woe them with your brilliance."

"Don't you mean 'wow' them?" Isis asks.

"I do not."

Every act gives it their all. Dora is amazing. I honestly thought she *was* going to be cleaning puke off my shoes. But then she struts out there and opens her mouth, and it's as if the spirit of La Petite Mort takes over her and she becomes a cabaret singer. When Dora sings, the whole audience falls into one of those rare silences that feels like a prayer. Even Lilac stops wiping down the bar and stares gape-mouthed at the stage.

Then their song finishes. Dora runs straight offstage and throws up in the bathroom. At least my shoes are safe.

The audience claps, cheers, and hoots for each performance – the sublime and the surreal alike. Finally, there's only one act left.

"Are you ready?" I ask Gideon. He flashes me that delicious smile that makes me believe I'm invincible.

I hand Cleo VII off to one of the stagehands, pull the hood of Gideon's costume down over his golden hair, kiss him on the nose, and send him out with a smack on his derrière.

The lights dim, and The Stooges' "I Wanna Be Your Dog" starts up. Gideon picked the song, and he even came up with the concept for our act. I guess he figured anything was better than being a meerkat.

With one self-satisfied smirk, Gideon drops to all fours and galumphs out on stage, his shaggy dog costume bright beneath the lights.

Gideon yips and chases his tail around the base of the pole. Everyone cracks up laughing.

And then he lifts his back leg, wiggling his butt at the audience. He's a natural on stage. Or maybe he's just a natural puppy. Komal falls out of her chair with laughter as Gideon makes a face like he's about to pee all over the front row while gritty punk music blasts through the darkened club.

He's everything La Petite Mort stood for – subversion, eroticism, outlandishness and joy – and I *love* it.

I hear my cue and enter stage left, dressed to kill with my collar at my throat, and waving a leash like a doggy dominatrix. It's the first time I've danced on a stage for an audience of more than one since La Petite Mort burned. And it feels good to be back.

The stage lights shine bright in my eyes. I can barely see the crowd, but I hear their whoops of awe as I swing myself around the pole into a Russian split.

Gideon's eyes widen in mock-terror. He scrambles to get away, his legs going in all directions, eliciting another round of laughter from the audience.

I use the pole to twist and dip and flare my legs as I pretend to "search" for Gideon, who hides in the audience and begs for treats. An Upyr tips a glass of blood into his mouth, and Isis kisses him on the forehead while I hang upside down in a variety of complex, skin-pinchy poses.

At the end of our act, he slinks back to me and lies down at my feet. I clip on his leash and he rolls over, accepting belly scratches for being a good boy. The song finishes with a clash of drums, and I knit my fingers in Gideon's and drag him downstage. We bow together, deeply.

I never should have stopped dancing. My body hums with electricity. My heart smiles. I know that I'll be a frequent performer on the Sanctus Club stage. Maybe I'll even let Beth talk me into running that vampire pole dancing class once she gets her new studio built.

Maybe.

The Nevermore Coven throws flower petals, which pleases me more than I'll ever admit.

We bow a few more times, and then I turn to exit stage left, because it is *definitely* time to hit the bar. Gideon and I have agreed to become equal partners in Sanctus, and he wants to hear my ideas for improvements. Which is good, because I made an extensive list.

But Gideon tugs on my hand. "Just a moment. We have a final act."

The audience, sensing something happening, falls silent.

"What's this? This isn't part of my *very detailed* stage directions." I try to yank my hand from Gideon's, but he holds tight. The smirk on his face is a little lopsided, nervous.

Intriguing.

"Arabella," his voice cracks on my name, and I know to stop trying to free my hand and to *listen*. Because while Gideon Blake has said many infuriating things to me over the centuries, when he says my name like that, he's speaking something precious and true. "I can't believe I'm here, under these lights, with you. I can't believe I got a second chance to make things right between us. I feel like the heroine from a romance novel who realises she gets to have everything in the world she wants, and while I partly have to thank some well-meaning romance novel enthusiasts—"

"Go us!" Isis yells from the crowd.

"—for getting us to this point, I also know that I owe a debt to the magic that brought you back to me, and an even larger debt to the woman with the body that should come with an FBI warning and the heart big enough to forgive me. I can't promise you everything you deserve, but I promise you this: if you'll have me, I will love you fiercely and imperfectly until the end of our days."

From the recesses of his shaggy dog costume, he pulls a small black box.

Only good things come in small black boxes.

Gideon flips it open, revealing a golden ring. In the centre, surrounded by glittering emeralds, is a beautiful, gleaming lapis lazuli shaped like a scarab. My heart squeezes like it's trying to fit through my ribs to get to him.

His smile is pure wicked surrender.

"I thought maybe this could be your new good luck charm. What do you say?" That smile of his twists into a full-blown boyish grin. "Will you marry me?"

I take the box from his hand. "I suppose."

"You *suppose?*" he laughs, wrapping me in his shaggy embrace. "I'll take it. I'll take it and I'll take you, my soon-to-be wife, straight back to my apartment to shag you into submission. Or should I say *our* apartment now?"

"Don't be absurd. My house is superior to your apartment. I'm not sleeping in a revolving coffin bed. It makes me feel like I'm a cinnamon bun on display in Celeste's bakery. We will be getting a *proper* bed."

"Fine. But no cherubs—"

"There will be no discourse. I am correct in all matters—"

"Stop arguing and kiss already!" Celeste yells.

So I do. I stop arguing, second-guessing, and living in the past. And I give myself up to the mysteries of the universe and the concept that maybe, sometimes, it's not terrible to trust other people. And I kiss Gideon Blake, my *fiancé,* beneath the stage lights until my lips are raw and Isis is demanding another round of cocktails for emotional trauma.

56

The (Real) Killer

I fold my copy of the *Argleton Gazette* and place it on the table beside me as I watch Gideon and Arabella on stage, being swarmed by their friends and admirers. I raise my glass to my lips and take a long drink, relishing the taste.

I took too big a risk with Alyra, but Maisie Collins has come through for me once again. Alyra Maythorn's death is officially reported as accidental. A fall. The Nevermore Coven will investigate, but they'll never find out the truth. I'm just too good. That's how I can stand in this room with them, right under their noses, and they have no clue.

And the only person who knew I was the one pretending to sell the necklace was Sinead, and she won't be blabbing my secrets anytime soon. I'm only sorry our plan didn't work. I'd been looking forward to the surprise on Gideon Blake's face when I slid my fangs into his skin.

I've killed two bad men. They deserved to die, and their blood has given me so much. They're more valuable dead than they ever were in their wretched lives.

But Alyra has changed everything.

Now I have a new purpose. I think about the wine bottles stored in my home, each one carefully labelled after I drew them from the vampire's dying body. A vampire's blood. Each bottle holds magic that

I can't yet comprehend. I can't believe no one else has ever discovered these properties before.

I take another sip.

Yes. It's *perfect*.

But I'll need more. Fresh, from the source.

The darker and more depraved the monster, the more they deserve the fate I have decreed for them.

Gideon Blake may be safe from me now, under Arabella's watchful eye. Luckily for me, in Argleton, there are almost too many vampires behaving badly to choose from.

Soon, the night will belong to me.

A Note from the Author

THANK YOU FOR ALLOWING ME TO INDULGE MY LOVE FOR THIS ERA of history and incorporate some real characters and settings into this kooky vampire story. Allow me to correct some of my more egregious historical inaccuracies.

La Petite Mort is a mashup of various Paris cabarets like Moulin Rouge and the infamous Grand Guignol – the horror theatre with shows so notoriously graphic that the theatre employed doctors to be on hand during each performance to tend to audience members who swooned.

Sarah Bernhardt's infamous balloon ride over Paris took place in 1870, not 1879, as I have it here. She did have a pet alligator named Ali-Gaga and a beloved snake who died from swallowing a cushion.

Manet, Monet, Renoir, Morisot, Rodin, Hugo and Zola did hang out together and travel in the same circles, although they tended to frequent coffee houses, not vampire horror cabarets. *Dawn of the Belle Epoque: The Paris of Monet, Zola, Bernhardt, Eiffel, Debussy, Clemenceau, and Their Friends* by Mary McAuliffe, PhD furnished many of the anecdotes (like the one about eating zoo animals) and some of the artists' quotes. As far as I'm aware, Édouard Manet is not a vampire. The only way to find out for yourself is to ask him.

I'm grateful to Catherine Hewitt for her book *The Mistress of Paris: The 19th-Century Courtesan Who Built an Empire on a Secret*, which provided information on the life of a courtesan in nineteenth-century Paris, and to Cleo Quinn from Fired Up Stilettos and Lo Morales for helping me with aspects of Arabella's character as a Black sex worker.

The story of Arabella's invention of the pole is pure imagination on my part. As a pole dancer myself, I've been dying to write a book with a pole dancing heroine. In the modern pole dance community, you sometimes see dancers citing the history of pole as originating with Chinese acrobats or Indian *mallakhamb* practitioners as a way of distancing themselves from pole's real roots – sexy dancing and strip clubs.

Pole dancing as we know it today originated with eighteenth-century hootchy-kootchy dancers in the United States – these travelling circus acts would involve Romani or Egyptian performers of titillating belly dances who used the pole holding up the circus tent to entertain their audiences. Pole started being incorporated into burlesque acts, and during Prohibition poles became commonplace in speak-easies to give dancers something to hold onto in the tiny spaces. When Prohibition ended, poles started being incorporated more openly in bars and clubs, and during the 1980s and 1990s in LA and other centres, strippers innovated the style, incorporating acrobatic moves into stripteases, naming specific moves, and teaching pole dance as an art all of its own.

It was important to me that if I depicted an apocryphal story of "inventing" pole, it included elements of this history and was told by a sex worker.

Acknowledgements

ONE OF THE JOYS OF WRITING ABOUT VAMPIRES IS BEING ABLE TO indulge my love of history by giving them backstories resplendent with details from my favourite time periods.

Another joy is something called the "tax-deductible research trip", in which my assistant Amy and I spent a week in Paris eating all the macarons, hurling ourselves into terrifying traffic, and wandering the same streets of Montmartre where Arabella and Gideon once trod.

This book would not exist without that trip. My writing was fuelled almost entirely by macarons. I fear I may now be part macaron.

Some of you might not know this, but I'm legally blind. My eyes have no cone cells, which means I see no colour. All my life, I've dabbled with painting and art, and I'm relatively knowledgeable about art history. For most of my favourite artists, like Leonardo da Vinci and Caravaggio, I still find much to enjoy in their composition, technique, and use of contrast. But with the impressionists, and Monet in particular, I always feel like I'm standing on the edge of his lily pond, grasping for something I'll never quite reach.

In Paris, we went first to Monet's gardens at Giverny, then to see the Water Lilies cycle at the Musée de l'Orangerie. I wept. To see these paintings in person is a lifelong dream for me, but it also makes me sad, because truly understanding Monet will forever be out of reach.

Writing Arabella and Gideon's romance against the backdrop of Belle Époque Paris gave me a chance, through words instead of pigment, to step into the lily pond and grasp a little closer. I hope you enjoyed my alternative world of vampire cabaret and sumptuous art.

A Grave Mistake wouldn't exist without Anthea, Jarred, and the amazing team at Atria Australia. Becca Mysoor, my husband and Celia each took up a testicle-severing sword and slayed my beloved adjectives. Thank you to all the booksellers who have enthusiastically championed this kooky, spooky romance about eternal grudges, second chances, and increasingly absurd grand gestures of love.

Many people support me and believe in me, even when I struggle to believe in myself. My family – Mum, Dad and my sister Belinda. The writers with whom I've celebrated and commiserated – Erin, Danielle, Kelly, Selena, Angel, Vic, Rachel, Kim, Isa, Amber, Mel, Marie, Devyn, Elisabeth, Ali, Sarra, and all the others I've missed. To Amy, my girl Friday, for all the adventures and always agreeing that it is macaron o'clock. To the bogans, my brothers and sisters of metal, for keeping me grounded. I apologise for the volume of our shenanigans that end up in my books. (That's a lie. I'm not sorry.)

Always, to my cantankerous drummer husband, who is everything. Every hero I write is a piece of you and what you mean to me. Except for Gideon's smart fashion sense – that is but a wistful dream.

Now, if you'll excuse me, it's macaron o'clock …

Steff

About the Author

STEFFANIE HOLMES IS THE *USA TODAY* BESTSELLING AUTHOR OF kooky, spooky romance. Her books feature clever, witty heroines, secret societies, quirky villages where nothing is as it seems, creepy old mansions, and mysterious antiheroes with dark eyes and even darker secrets.

Legally blind since birth, Steffanie received the 2017 Attitude Award for Artistic Achievement. Steffanie lives in New Zealand with her husband, a horde of cantankerous cats, and their medieval sword collection. Learn more about her on her website, www.nevermorebookshop.co.nz.